William Falconer

Bloom and Brier

Or, as I saw it, long ago. A southern romance

William Falconer

Bloom and Brier
Or, as I saw it, long ago. A southern romance

ISBN/EAN: 9783337064846

Printed in Europe, USA, Canada, Australia, Japan

Cover: Foto ©Andreas Hilbeck / pixelio.de

More available books at **www.hansebooks.com**

OR,

AS I SAW IT, LONG AGO.

A Southern Romance.

BY

WILLIAM FALCONER.

PHILADELPHIA:
CLAXTON, REMSEN & HAFFELFINGER.
MONTGOMERY, ALA.: JOEL WHITE.
1870.

THIS flashing effort at the portrayal of Southern life may be drawn with a feeble hand, but it is as I saw it, and as I understood it; and however much it may fail in artistic finish, it, at least, possesses the virtue of truth in its spirit, and points to a prouder, and a more magisterial period than was ever held by any other modern people of the earth; and, alas! prouder, too, than we, ourselves, will ever hold again.

The quiet and conscious grandeur of the South, during the Slave *régime*, swept as far beyond that of any other order of society, as one planet sweeps beyond another in the splendor of its light, and the radius of its orbit. Royalty, itself, could not claim, through the authority of the throne, that nameless homage and social power which the Southron was born to, and receiving the one so unostentatiously, and wielding the other so gracefully and so kindly.

Nature herself, as if careful of the history and position held by the South, did not permit her to drag through a long, dreary story of decay, but let her fall from the highest point of culmination, amid the wrecks of her splendid fortunes, and the lances of her peerless chivalry; and even now, in her prostrated condition, she lies like the Spartan upon her shield, with the flames of an eternal fame ascending from the crumbled altars of her past glory; her ancient prowess, and her honor, blazing so dazzlingly too, as to sear the very eyeballs of those who would now look upon her nakedness, or dare to jeer it. The nameless numbers of her conquerors are even forbidden all honor in the fall of the victim, and all participation in the rites of the sacrifice, but the rather, are condemned to feel their hearts to wither with a silent hate, as they see the lonely cortege passing on to history and to immortality.

To Southern excellency and eminence in letters, and in statesmanship in the time that is gone, you, sir — permit me to say it — contributed your full share, in the brilliancy of a classic oratory, and in the beauty and strength of a flowing pen; and let the mutations of fortune have been what they may, or for the future be what they will, you can now, in the evening of your life, rest satisfied with what you accomplished in its morning, and that nothing can destroy your relationship to the unfading glory of your own great people, and of your own lovely South.

Believing that, outside of all consideration for the literary merit of this light romance, you will properly appreciate the feeling which prompts me to take this liberty with your name, I remain,

Very truly yours,

THE AUTHOR.

SNOWDOUN,
Montgomery Co., Ala.,
March, 1870.

PREFACE.

THE following story — if by grace it may be called a story — is only intended to represent Southern life, in certain coteries, as it existed under the old *régime*, and to represent the same by contrast, under the present. In doing this, I probably have made some remarks upon Northern society, which under ordinary circumstances might seem to deserve apology; but as these are not only, not ordinary, but anomalous, I shall quietly wait to have them pointed out, when I will take pleasure in making the *amende honorable*, as I would not willingly wrong any part of my country, or any class of my countrymen.

In the meanwhile, the author will suggest the idea, that no people who persistently strive in the cause of their own degradation, and loudly boast through their lawmakers and representative men at large, of their successes in that direction, can expect many bright touches of either pen or pencil, from outside sources. A people, no less than an individual, must respect their own dignity before they can secure the respect of others. No outside attributes, of whatever excellence, can secure them against merited contempt, for a violation of this vital law. Much less will they do this, where political science is biased by every possible obliquity, where religion tinctured with infidelity, is made attractive by the license which it gives, and where social organization is vitiated by breeding and countenancing every abnormal interpolation.

No, my friends, you must not expect us to respect you while such vices of omission and commission stream pendent from every limb of your moral, social, and political, organization.

If you wish our regard, purify the fountains of your social, political, and religious life, of its deadly heresies; cease to paint your literature in the meretricious colors of the bawd, the blasphemer, the reviler, the hypocrite, and the slanderer! and forbid your chief men longer to boast of the low level to which they have reduced your society.

Some things have been said of *negroes* in these pages, and said by one who knows them perfectly, and is willing to credit them with every good quality they possess; and yet, he could not, if he would, concede either their intellectual, moral, or social equality, with his own race, let that race sink to what it may; and, therefore, is not willing to so degrade himself, as to assert the African's capacity for holding the high places of enlightened society, and *joyfully* inviting him to occupy them — nor so to stultify himself, as to assert the peculiar glutinous mucilage of negro intellect, as spilled out in the legislative hall and the lecture-room, to be the finest lubricator of the philosophic frame and jointwork of society.

These may all be the media through which are to come those organic changes, so certainly, positively, indicated in American sociology. They may indeed be the significant agencies, and yet they are vessels of dishonor, and the penalties attending their use will be terrible indeed. At least, we shall be our own judges of these matters, and of a people to whom they relate. In connection with this, it may not be improper to remark, that second to this in significance of *sectional* degeneracy, is the occupancy of the lecture-room by females of questionable fame and character, in advocacy of a class of subjects ill-omened at best, in theory, and certainly degrading and unchaste in practice. Drive these female nuisances out! drive them home! if they have any, ye men of the North! If they have none, drive them to the house of correction! and by that much, your society will be purified and elevated.

Though, as we have said, these things may be the media, through which American society will pass on to its GREAT REVOLUTION — they themselves are not to be revered, however desirable the change may be which they foreshadow.

Changes, great ORGANIC changes! are certainly ahead. Your own men will overthrow you; their apparent wealth is not *legitimate*, it is the price of blood, the representative of civil strife — fratricidal blood — and is the price of *our property*, wrongfully carried to their credit on their own ledgers. Planted in corruption, it has sprouted up in dragon's teeth, and will yet tear your flesh.

The question is — What next? When? and WHO? There is ONE among ye who *might* if he WOULD. We shall see.

THE AUTHOR.

BLOOM AND BRIER;

OR,

AS I SAW IT, LONG AGO.

PART I.

CHAPTER I.

INTRODUCTORY.

THE author of this story of Southern life has heretofore always been a reader of romances, and not a writer of them; as he knows nothing, therefore, of authorcraft, beyond a mere appreciation of it in those who do, he deprecates in timely advance the censure of the reader. Now quoth the reader, "Why, sir, do you attempt that of which you are ignorant?"

Ah! that's the mystery, and quite as great a one to him as to any one — but it is too late now to retrace the step; the story is already named, and this much of the first chapter already writ; too late now, dear friend, to give advice, good or bad: 't is fate — the story shall be told.

"As I saw it." Saw what? Why, the incidents in the life of some young people who were my friends, perhaps, "long ago;" and could they be written out as beautifully as my memory pictures them to my sad, old heart, they would make a pretty story indeed.

"It must be memory, then, at work," quoth again the astute reader,

> ". . . watching o'er the sad review
> Of joys that faded like the morning dew."

Yes, perhaps it is; and if feeling was poetry, there would be many poets; and if memory could be transferred to paper, there would be many a tenderer, sweeter romance than ever yet was written. All the feeling, sentiment, and inspiration of a story is thus upon me; but whether I shall ever convey it, or even a part, to the reader, is the thing I have now undertaken.

"Ah! happy years! Once more, who would not be a boy?"

The gurgling of an old man's memories hath often fallen upon my ear as the softest music; and if it be to others as it hath been to me, my story will not be all a failure. For, as I have already intimated, it is but to be a little *love story*, compounded of things familiar to me in the happier days of a bright, young life, long, long ago; and I have undertaken to write it, wellnigh as much for the pleasure of those of my own age as for that of the younger people — for the simple reason that the former, from destroyed hopes, have but little to look forward to in the future, while the latter, from destroyed fortunes, have but little to enjoy in the present; and all that I aspire to, is to beguile a few sad hours of their gloom, by leading them back on the track of life to some greener, more joyous spots. If the times were *now* as they have *been*, we should observe the rules of hospitality, and ask at least the younger portion of our *Northern* friends to participate in the *symposium* we propose; but a wide and deep river of feeling now flows a current of bitter waters between us, and we yield to the necessities of the situation.

It may be but a melancholy enjoyment we shall furnish,

but there is often a certain sweet and peaceful pleasure in the memory of our sorrows, which, at least we hope, will come to the relief of its romance.

Now, before we set out, we wish it well understood that we have only undertaken to write a *love story* — not a philosophy, a history, nor yet a belles-lettres treatise — in which we will relate many things in our own way, that may or may not have actually happened; not intending to give vouchers for either, nor to be bound down by any foreign rules in the manner of our telling them. In short, the manner is to be personal, and the story to be local; and most that we intend is to write something devoted to "useful mirth and salutary woe," regarding the olden times as we saw and remember them — ay! and of the *present* too, mayhap, as we see them.

In doing this, according to the plan which we have in our mind, it will be necessary to speak of the style of life led by that better class of planters, who early emigrated from older States to those of the extreme South, and gave the true ring to their character as since developed in the political arena and on the battle-field. We, of course, do not refer to those adventurous, roving nomads who followed the path of the wild deer as he retreated from the sight of the human eye and the whistle of the rifle-ball; but to those who came with their families, their servants, their herds, their books, their genius, their enterprise, and their love of adventure and freshness, for the purpose of building homes and casting their fortunes here.

In this, no portion of the South was more distinguished than Alabama. Attracted thither by the great fertility of the soil, and the surpassing loveliness of the scenery everywhere to be met with, were representatives of the wealthiest and best-bred families of the old Slave States of America. It was not indeed in many instances that the older members of these families had joined in, and followed the "course of empire." Of consequence, those to whom we allude, while generally the heads of families, were yet young in years, free and dashing in their thoughts, gay and daring in their amusements, gallant and chivalric in their conduct and bearing; and being, as we have just intimated, the representatives and off-shoots of the old colonial aristocracy, bore themselves as such in all the lighter walks, as well as in the more serious relations of life. These, and it is only to these that we refer, were all slave-holders to a greater or less extent. This fact, in connection with the extraordinary productiveness of the soil, afforded them the amplest time and means for those indulgences, pastimes, pleasures, and entertainments which previous habit and education inclined them to. The sporting field and the race-course were their chief out-door amusement, and many kept both their hunters and racers; while their in-door life was marked by that refined and airy abandon and cultivated intellectuality so peculiarly characteristic of the old colonial *régime*. Many of them had been led to some one of the learned professions, without reference to practising it; and all of them were familiar with the leading principles of either law, medicine, or state-craft. Discussions, therefore, of a political and legal character, were as striking a feature of the intercourse between themselves, as literature, music, the song, and dance characterized the social relations of the sexes.

With all such features as were peculiar to aristocratic life, there was yet an almost perfect absence of those frigid and dull formalities which older communities so generally establish for their regulation; which, though they may not detract from their elegance, certainly contribute nothing to that heartiness and sincerity of enjoyment and graceful ease always felt when not surrounded by embarrassing conventionalities.

Indeed, it was English rural life of the olden time, modified, elevated, and ventilated by the circumstances of a new country and freshness of organization, and still intensified at some points by the natural influences of *slave labor*.

In view of these facts, it may safely be asserted that there was never a people who possessed in greater profusion all the surroundings and sources of joy, brightness, and hope than the early settlers of the Southern States. A climate of rare mildness, yet sufficiently tempered to meet all the demands and ends of health, energy, and intellectual development; a soil that brought harvests of wealth, almost without labor, to the granaries of the planter; game of a wellnigh fabulous variety and abundance; and a landscape whose alternate lines of grandeur and beauty, mountain and valley, stream and wide-spread prairie, can now be described by neither pen nor pencil, but only cherished as among the trembling beauties of an old and happy memory — all of these united in giving a swell and rapture of emotion that lingers still about the ruined altars of our Southern hearts.

These sadly glimmering recollections are the soft and distant echoes of a day that's gone forever, and belong to a once lovely land, and to a proud and noble people now fallen from their high estate; but whose former glories make up the history of the South. What the future will be, God only knows.

Suffice it, that no people of modern days have ever held, and none will ever hold again that conspicuously eminent position which the SOUTH once did, and fell so gloriously in defending. Her deed was the last red lightning-flash of the world's *dying chivalry!* call it by what other name we may — rebellion, if need be.

2 *

CHAPTER II.

"An elegant sufficiency, content,
Retirement, rural quiet, friendship, books."

AS we have described the South at large, such was Alabama in especial degree, and such the people who early came to it.

Of that class of gentlemen whom we have just spoken were two brothers from the State of Virginia, St. George and Robert Brandon—each the head of a small and interesting family. They were patrician in birth, and handsomely illustrated all the generous traits of a long line of ancestry distinguished in colonial history. Possessing ample fortunes, and highly accomplished in education, they were a pair of as honorable, gallant, gay, liberal, and intellectual gentlemen as had ever emigrated from the proud "Old Dominion."

With large plantations in the middle portion of Alabama, near the present town of ——, their homes presented those scenes of hearty hospitality, munificent elegance, and genuine taste which may be easily supposed to proceed from, or to be the result of the feelings, training, and customs of the Virginia gentleman, revelling in unlimited abundance, and feasting his eyes and soul upon the beauty of this wild, romantic country.

The Brandon neighborhood was known far and wide to be one of the very best in the State, which had the effect of drawing to it all who could get homes in or near it; and, at the time we write of, presented all the enchantments of a fresh and lovely country, standing boldly out from a background of order, peacefulness, and dignity that would have done honor to any of the older States. The very first evidence of which—situated as centrally as possible, for the convenience of all! — was the neat little church, with its spire and cross and gothic windows, embowered and half concealed by, yet looking out from a grove of majestic oaks that clustered upon the gentle eminence upon which it stood; and next, the neatly built academy standing near by; — both of which were well supported by the wealthier classes, but in the benefits and pleasures of which every one participated. The privileges of the church were open to all, and enjoyed by all, white and black, rich and poor, while the facilities of education were generously flung open to those who saw fit to embrace them for their children; for though the particular limits of society were well drawn and equally respected, there was no *dead-line* between its circles, and a happier few than they who first enjoyed the intercourse and advantages of this little country academy have never met nor parted. They who live till now, and, mayhap, have grown old since then, and weary too, may despairingly turn back upon the story of life to find one day of equal joyance with their school-time gladness. Its memory grows fresher and greener with its age; and now, when years have cooled the warm currents of the blood that of erst did flow so softly and so swift, and dimmed the young vision of the eye, ever and anon there come back again the joys, the beauties, and the little loves of the merry boyhood time. Ah! 't is easy now to see the lovely little girl with the jet-black curls and the coquettish smile, and that little pair with the soft blue eyes and the sylph-like forms, and ay, that other, too, with the nut-brown hair and the mellow hazel eye. We do remember still the noble-hearted play-fellows that went there too, all comrades then. Yet, yet these morning memories must not, cannot last; for even now the lights of the olden time darken into shadows, and these fresh and dewy visions of the soul bring unbidden tears, and die away into an evening grief. Some low, soft breathings, as from the grave and the slab, now sadly whisper to the heart that they with the soft blue eyes, and she with the dark ones too, have long since passed away.

Of that little band of brother comrades, many long have slept the "sleep that knows no waking," while others may-hap there are, who still are wandering on in life's long, dreary paths, and to them I now send these greeting lines.

But let us return to the Brandons, who, we have said, had settled in Middle Alabama, and had surrounded themselves with every comfort and elegance to be obtained in this new country. Being men of handsome fortunes and of a high order of intelligence, they exerted great influence in the public affairs of their new home and State, but were never aspirants to office, seeming always to be satisfied with the superior private position which they enjoyed, and with dispensing a munificent hospitality. In private fortune, they went along for years, prospering and to prosper; when the death of the younger brother, St. George Brandon, cast a gloom over the neighborhood, and threw heavily increased family responsibilities upon his brother Robert. The management of his brother's estate, and the care of his young family, together with his own, seemed to engross both his mind and time, while the blow to his feelings appeared to change the entire current of his character. The gay and joyous life which had for years been led by the two brothers, appeared no longer to furnish the survivor its wonted zest, and becoming a more serious man, he gradually fell into other channels of thought and pleasure.

CHAPTER III.

"This bud of love, by summer's ripening breath,
  May prove a beauteous flower, when next we meet."

MRS. ST. GEORGE BRANDON, at the time of her husband's death, had scarcely passed the bounds of youthful life and joyous womanhood, and was the mother of only two children, a son and a daughter — but, while possessing every prerequisite for again entering the gay world, she yet chose to devote herself to their pleasure and welfare — watching with most scrupulous attention their education, their moral and social culture, and imbuing their minds with the proper ideas of honor, duty, truth, propriety, generosity, and affection, which only a mother can successfully do; but which too many, alas! neglect.

There was every arrangement for her remaining at her plantation, which she made as attractive as possible to her children and friends; and amply was she repaid for these home influences and exertions, in the appreciation in which she was held by them.

The neighborhood had already grown sufficiently populous to call for a male and female "high school," and the little boys and girls who had long been educated under one roof, by the same solemn and good old pedagogue, were now separated. Henry Brandon, the elder of the two children, was continued at the male academy until thoroughly prepared to enter college, while Violet, his sister, continued at the female department until she had completed quite a thorough and an accomplished education.

Mr. Robert Brandon also had but two children, both of whom were daughters, and about the same age with their cousins; and the families still continued in the same unbroken intimacy which had always existed between them.

In his sixteenth year, Henry Brandon, a tall, handsome youth, free with his purse, gay and mercurial in his disposition, and pleasing in his manners, was preparing to leave for college, and was now spending a week or two in visiting his young friends of both sexes, with all of whom he had ever been a very decided favorite; but with none more than his cousin Laura, the older daughter of Mr. Robert Brandon, who in turn, it is but gallant to say, was as great a favorite with her cousin Henry. This preference was a pretty well established fact among the young people of the neighborhood, and rather suspected by Henry Brandon's mother, who had often very gently cautioned him against it; but had almost entirely escaped the observation of Laura's parents, with whom he was even a greater favorite than with any other of his friends, though known to them to be wild, reckless, and greatly disposed to fun and frolic.

The afternoon before his departure for college, his horse was brought to the gate, and in a few minutes he came from his room dressed in the handsomest style, when he was met by his mother and sister.

"Ah! whither now, my handsome brother?" asked Violet, with a cunning smile playing about her mouth, and a look of mischief in her eye.

Hesitating but for a moment, he replied, with only the slightest shade of petulance passing over his handsome face, at his scheme of going alone being discovered:

"I am going to pay my farewell visit to Uncle Robert and his family: any objection, sister?"

"Why, brother, did n't you know that I had expected to ride over with you?"

"Yes, something was said about it this morning; but

then I did not suppose you cared to do so particularly," smiling as he made the reply.

"Ah! well, I will not embarrass you with my presence, as I fancy you have prepared something very pretty to say to cousin Laura, which you do not wish me to have the chance of hearing."

"No, you little vixen; I believe I would be willing for you to hear all that I have to say. But Thomas Hunter told me that he would come by this evening, and as I thought you would like to see *him alone*, I would not propose to deprive you of that pleasure."

"Ah! brother, that's but a lame excuse; you know he will scarcely come by this evening, when he is coming by to leave with you in the morning."

"Indeed, he said it was quite probable, when we parted yesterday."

"Probable — yes, that is a little different. But tell the girls why I did not go over."

"Certainly," said he, evidently pleased with Violet's resigning her trip so easily.

Mrs. Brandon had as yet said nothing; but as her light-hearted, happy boy was about leaving the house, she remarked to him, "Come, my son; your cousin Laura is one of the sweetest girls I ever knew; but you must remember that you are soon to enter upon a very arduous course of study, and it will require your undivided attention; and a little boyish love-scrape would distract your mind more than you might suppose; and beside, it would be very displeasing to your aunt."

"Pshaw, mother, that is some of Violet's nonsense: no danger of my getting into a *love-scrape* with cousin Laura, more than I have always been in; and as to displeasing aunt, I can please and displease her sixty times in an hour."

In a few moments more, the joyous, laughing youth was

in his saddle, and at half speed was on the way to Mr. Robert Brandon's. A few minutes more, and he was at the gate of "STARLIGHT," the name of his uncle's residence.

The family were expecting him, and were glad to see him. Spending an hour or so in general conversation, and in receiving some particular injunctions as to his deportment at college from his uncle, he proposed to his cousins to walk in the flower-yard, and for each of them to gather him a bouquet as a keepsake. The proposition was immediately accepted; and the three were soon busy in strolling over the grounds in search of the choicest flowers.

Henry succeeded very soon in separating the sisters and getting Laura off to himself. A conversation quickly sprang up, by a sort of electric understanding, conducted in an undertone, as though in regard to the flowers, but really of a very different nature; and as she was offering him a half-blown bud, he slipped a little gold ring upon her finger, with the request that she would wear it and remember him. This she tremulously promised to do, as he kissed her blushing cheek; and the three very soon returned to the house *together*.

CHAPTER IV.

"Light winged hopes, that come when bid,
And rainbow joys, that end in weeping."

THE ecstasy of Henry Brandon at the success of his first real love-making with Laura, although they had been *sweethearts* from mere children, produced a kind of restless joy in his young heart, that wanted room, as it were, for expansion. He grew more and more nervous, even in the presence of the smiling girl who had just responded so

prettily to his professions of love, and in a short while rose
to take his leave of the family. Bidding his uncle and
aunt farewell, he next proceeded to his cousins; but in addition to his *good-by*, gave each a kiss. A tear fell from
the eyes of Laura, to which her young lover responded
by another shake of the hand, but choked in his second
"good-by." He then left the house, and was not long in
reaching his own home.

Laura's mother observed the feeling which she showed,
and laughed at her; but the young girl not seeming to
recover from it, a gentle reproof had the desired effect of
appearing to soothe her.

Mrs. Brandon, though a very accomplished woman,
and possessing many high qualities that were ever in full
play as wife, mother, and friend, yet had her strong prejudices, tinged with a certain unyielding haughtiness, which
made persons of a milder character shrink from opposition
to her views and opinions. In the instance of Laura showing such feeling for the departure of her cousin, an apprehension was at once excited. The fear of a *love affair*
between the cousins seemed in a moment to rouse an an-
tipathy which she never after surrendered.

The morning after this, all arrangements having been
made, Thomas Hunter, a youth of about the same age with
Henry Brandon, and the son of Colonel Hunter, a wealthy
planter of the same neighborhood, came by in his father's
carriage, according to appointment, and the two candidates for collegiate life left the residence of Henry's
mother, together, for the town of ——, where they were
to take the stage coach. The separation between Henry
Brandon and his mother and sister was tender and affecting in the extreme—the more so from the consciousness on
the part of both that the loneliness of their home would now
almost amount to desolation. Mrs. Brandon felt, too, that
she was casting upon the temptations of life, a youth who,

3

though honorable in feeling, and gifted in intellect, was yet strongly disposed to gayeties, and not knowing how far he might be allured to go, felt very great solicitude. In spite of all these affections and anxieties, Henry Brandon left for college on the first day of September, 18—, where he remained four years without returning, even on a visit to his mother. In this there was something of the vanity of young collegians, in having to tell how long they have been absent from home, and of laying up an increased interest for themselves in the hearts of their friends.

This little romantic sort of conceit, together with a desire to visit the various points of interest in the Northern States, and to observe the — to a Southerner — idiosyncrasies of that people, was the excuse of his not returning South during his vacations.

His general course at college was somewhat eccentric, and he was often held accountable for his youthful irregularities, though always managing to be " excused." Having been thoroughly " prepared " before leaving home, he found no difficulty in maintaining a good " average " in his class, while it left him time for indulging in many reckless amusements, such as college-life affords all opportunities for, to those who are inclined to indulge in them. In this wise he was not distinguished for his accurate scholarship, though universally recognized as possessing a high order of talents, and even genius, both by professors and students, and was so much a favorite with the former, that, as we have already intimated, neither his delinquencies nor offences were ever visited but with the lightest penalties, or excused. By his long, unbroken residence, his profuse liberality, his rich and graceful style of dress, his spirited and pleasing manners, he was as well known to the citizens of —— as one of their own young men, and there were but few social entertainments given to which the gay, dashing, and handsome young Southerner was not an invited and a welcome guest. Such were the salient points in the youthful and educational history of the hero of our story. Those of his manhood we will permit to develop themselves as we proceed.

Thomas Hunter, his classmate at home and at college, and room-mate there too, was more sedate, more reserved, and far more scholarly in his course and attainments, yet neither so well known nor so popular. During the nearly four years of his absence, he had regularly returned to Alabama during every summer vacation, and from the old family intimacy, and the intimacy at college between himself and Henry Brandon, always made it a point to spend much of his time at Mrs. Brandon's — while Violet, who was growing up to be a very beautiful and an accomplished girl, may naturally be supposed to have been not the least attraction there.

Though a young fellow of fine common sense and great good-nature, he was thoughtful, poetical, musical, and slightly disposed to sensitiveness; and, when conceiving himself trespassed upon, had all the spirit of the lion.

Only a few months before his graduating "commencement," he had reason to believe that an insult had been intended him, by a classmate, who was much his superior in physical strength, but this fact was no preventive, and illustrated this feature in his character, by immediately making an attack upon him; and in the course of the rencontre, freely used his knife, and perhaps might have done so to a mortal extent, had he not been prevented by young Brandon. The latter, immediately seeing the probable result of such an act in a *Puritanic* old community, who were accustomed to hearing the lie given, and a retort of the accusation as the settlement of the difficulty, advised him to leave for the South without an hour's delay. Adopting the advice, he thus preceded the return of Henry Brandon by several months.

CHAPTER V.

"The proper means of increasing the love we bear our Native Country, is to reside some time in a foreign one." — SHENSTONE.

HENRY BRANDON was now in his twenty-first year, and was once again at the home of his wild, uncontrolled, merry boyhood. The morning after his arrival at the town of ——, he left the hotel in search of a conveyance to his mother's, and, while walking along the street, casually met with his old friend Thomas Hunter, accompanied by a young gentleman, named Campbell, of whom he had heard, through letters from his cousin Laura, as an admirer of Lucy Brandon, Laura's younger sister; but had never seen him, as he had become a citizen since his absence, as a young lawyer from Virginia, and by invitation of Mr. Robert Brandon, who was an early friend of Campbell's father.

The joy of the two young college-mates can easily be imagined, while it would be difficult to describe, which young Campbell appeared equally to enjoy from sympathy.

The latter directly excused himself, and left them to themselves, who, after an hour or two of running conversation, separated, with the understanding that Hunter should spend the following day with Brandon at his mother's.

"Yes," responded Hunter to the proposition, "and ride over to your uncle Robert's in the afternoon, as a surprise to him; ay! boy, what say you to *that?*"

"Excellent idea, Tom; and let me add — to my fair cousin Laura, too."

"Of course — that's understood, for what in the name of Satan would you wish to *surprise* an old *gentleman* for?"

"All right; I see you are beginning to learn the nature

of such things better than I once feared you would. Suppose, too, you bring your friend — Lucy's friend, Campbell, with you."

"Well, I shall propose to him to go out, and I presume he will accept."

The friends now parted with these understandings.

Brandon very soon procured a conveyance, and was on his way home.

After an hour's drive, he was at the gate of "Buckhorns," a name given to it by his father. The meeting between himself and mother and sister was joyous, tender, and affecting.

The intelligence of his return soon went from the house to the "Quarter," and from the Quarter rapidly spread through the plantation; when all the negroes, both old and young, left their employments and almost flew to the house to meet their long-absent young master. No authority could have restrained them, even had it been attempted; but so far from it, drivers, foremen, men, women, and children all hurried in promiscuous flight to the house, and there the scene was at once ludicrous, affectionate, and touching. The young master, who had been a great favorite with all classes in his boyhood, but with none so much so as with his father's negroes, discovering that they were coming *en masse* to see him, met them in the yard, and but a short time elapsed before he was surrounded by largely over a hundred negroes of all ages and sexes, striving to get to him. Last among those who had heard the intelligence of his return, was one who had acted as his first *body-servant* in the time of their youthful boyhood, and his *chief-of-staff* in general, now grown though to be a tall, sinewy, fine-looking fellow — black as jet, but with an eye, face, and figure that denoted intelligence, cunning, courage, and quickness.

"Sam Brandon," the name that he was universally called by, as a distinction from other *Sams* on the place, and from

3 *

his former association with his young master, now came pushing his way through the crowd, regardless of whom he ran over, and reaching Henry, embraced him, and with tears of joy in his eyes, screamed out, "Oh! my dear young master, is I got you agin in my own arms, safe an' soun' as when you lef me?"

"Yes, Sam, back once more, and all right," replied Henry, sympathizing in the gladness and emotion of his boyhood servant.

"I is glad of it, Lord knows I is, and all the devils an' ole Satan hisself can't git me way from you no mo', Mass Henry."

This meeting between the returned young master and the family slaves, in the shaking of hands, congratulations, and other demonstrations of pleasure, were truthful and sincere — as such always were, in the olden time, before that mixture of New England *jealousy* and prurient fanaticism had intervened to throw its sombre shadows of distrust and dislike between the happiest laborers and the kindest employers of the modern world. They finely illustrated, too, the patriarchal character of African slavery as existing in the South, at the base of which there was a strong feeling of protection, defence, and safety on the one part, and a determination to meet the whole obligation on the other, and a burning, hissing refutation of the wholesale slanders published and circulated by feeble writers and hypocritical religionists against the welfare of the South and its domestic peace.

We will take the liberty of here remarking that while a blind, jealous, and relentless feeling may succeed in mangling and destroying the laws and established institutions of a country under the alleged sanctions of *religion*, yet that same religion will never hold it *guiltless*. No ideal standard of right is permissible of being brought up in extenuation of a palpably evil result. Religious efforts, as all others, are judged of by their *fruits*, to which reward and retribution are accordingly measured out.

A few years since the laboring population of the South was exclusively composed of a strong, but helpless, affectionate, confiding, and a *heathen* race of people, transplanted from one of the remotest quarters of the earth: in this the hand of the Almighty was plainly discernible, as they had been under the ban of Heaven in their own land, from the beginning of time; and only in this beautiful, genial land had they been relieved from it, and had here received the first and only spiritual light they had ever received, or — now — likely to receive, let the extent of it have been what it may.   There was affection, reliance, and a complete capacity for obedience on the one side — interest, good feeling, and authority on the other; and these constituted the entire base of his feeble civilization.   Now, that these persuasives, relations, and obligations have been removed, it is but fair to infer that he will again relapse into his native barbarism, or soon become extinct.

This position requires no argument in its support; the statistics of the West Indies, Liberia, and his already relapsed condition among ourselves, point with a terrible significance to the probable path of the negro; and with a scoffing derision of the pseudo-philanthropy of men, when directed against the laws of nature and the manifest appointments of Heaven.

The negro, by the unauthorized scratch of a pen, on the part of one who, in the fleeting time of his glory and conceit, reckoned upon his right so to use it, has been turned loose upon society, in all his necessary ignorance and native licentiousness, and *legislated* into being an EQUAL, when every possible circumstance has placed upon him the indelible sign of inferiority and degradation.

As a *pet* of the Government, he will, by the necessary operation of all human law, become a disturbing element, an aggressor.   Neglected, he falls.   This is the *dilemma* of those who wish to use him as a political influence — a tool.

If there was any evidence necessary to establish the loathsome falsehood of those who professed to be guided by philanthropy and *religious* duty, it would be in the well-known fact that every possible *bitterness* and *hatred* has been infused into his heart toward his old master, and his only real friend, by the teachings of these same men since his emancipation.   With his changed relations has passed away nearly all the good feeling of which he was the cause and the object: his slavery to us, and our care of and obligations to him, developed some of the finest traits in Southern character.

The caducity of a people — a country — a government, may be very correctly measured by the legislation which lessens the aggregate of the generous sentiments.   For, as lightly as the assertion may be estimated, it is nevertheless a truth, susceptible of demonstration, that *good feeling* enters largely into the intellectuality of a people, and their capacity for permanent endurance in history.   As matters now are, it will approach the inspiration of a miracle to save the *republic,* and bear it up through this sea of calamitous legislation.   The lightnings of tremulous rage already glimmer upon the skies, and foretell the gathering storm, which, when full grown, may at any moment leap from the clouds, and sweep from the earth the last vestige of the old *régime* forever.

Nature, so we will call it, MAY so respect her own good work ; and so mysteriously direct her laws, as to check a people and a government from following to the bitter end the path that so clearly leads to national destruction ; and prevent them from becoming an accursed blot upon the records of the earth.   But we fear.   *Nous verrons.*

CHAPTER VI.

"Youth on the prow, and pleasure at the helm." — GRAY.

THOMAS HUNTER and Mr. Campbell, in accordance with the appointment made the day before, had come to pass the day with Henry Brandon, expecting to accompany the latter on a visit to his uncle that evening; and having insisted upon Violet accompanying them, she had consented. The horses had already been ordered, and were now standing at the gate in charge of "Essex," the pompous negro-servant who was to accompany them; and all of them were ready at least half an hour before Henry Brandon, upon whose movements they were now waiting. Hunter and Campbell were leisurely sauntering up and down the long gallery enjoying a fresh cigar, as Violet, also ready, joined them; but stopping occasionally and looking impatiently toward her brother's room, she nervously switched her skirt with her whip. The time had quite arrived when it was proper that they should be on their horses, and again casting one of her impatient glances toward her brother's room, she turned to Hunter, and said :

"I congratulate you, Mr. Thomas Hunter, and you, Mr. Campbell, too, upon being better representatives of your sex than my exquisite brother, who I suppose. is engaged in selecting a neck-scarf of suitable color to his complexion."

" You are disposed to be severe upon your brother, Miss Violet Brandon," replied Hunter, "and I feel in duty bound to defend him against your causticity, by refreshing your memory with the fact that my young friend is to meet with a fair cousin this evening, and the necessity for his attire being faultless."

"There might be something in what you say, sir, were she *not* a cousin."

"Methinks I've heard of that frail barrier being over-leaped, young lady."

"Come, Mr. Hunter, you must not hint such dangerous things to my brother, or he would endeavor to put them in practice on the very first occasion. I know his old love of adventure, and I have heard it has been said by some very wise person — though I do not profess to know — that the boy is father to the man. Not only that, I expect to have a personal use for his services for the next ten years myself."

"Ah! pitiless maiden, why wring our hearts by such cruel threats?" replied Hunter, his eye laughing with fun.

"Had I known, sir, that my words would carry pain to the heart of any one, I might, perhaps, have been less plain in their use, even while equally resolute in my purpose."

"I thank you for even that — "

At this moment Henry Brandon joined them, when Hunter said to him that he was greatly pleased with his presence, as he had just been engaged in a most desperate game of cut and thrust in his behalf.

"Yes, brother, I have been performing one of Shakspeare's tableaus, Patience on a monument."

"Ah! well, I hope you smiled at your grief."

"No, I did not."

"Then I suppose you told your love?"

"Told my love? No, sir! I have none to tell!"

"You only acted the simple part of looking silly on your monument, then?"

"Yes, that is about the idea I have of my conduct, if it will please you for me to say so."

"Far from it," replied Hunter; "she has been playing —"

"Never mind, Mr. Hunter, I will excuse any further accusations of myself, or defences of my delinquent brother." Then turning to the latter, she said:

"Well, brother, you must really permit me to admire the justice you have done your toilette—or that your toilette has done you: you are really quite a handsome young fellow, and I shall take great pleasure in exhibiting you to the kinsfolk of "Starlight"—indeed, gentlemen, as I shall the three of you; since no Eastern princess did ever have a more handsome escort. Not even Lalla Rookh."

"Nor did the vale of Cashmere afford one Violet Brandon," added Mr. Campbell.

"Thank you, and bravo! Mr. Campbell. I shall recommend you to Miss Lucy Brandon as a most proper Ferramorze."

"You place me under too great obligations, unless you will signify to me wherein I can perform some knightly service in your behalf."

"Rest satisfied, Mr. Campbell, with what I shall do for *you*. I should fear the personal consequences to myself, of taking you in my service in any capacity, while another has a better claim to it. But, brother," said she, again turning to him, "Mr. Hunter had but insinuated, as you came out of your room—or from your toilette, I should say—that you were preparing to captivate cousin Laura. What think you of that idea? Absurd, is it not?"

"No, not so terribly absurd as some things I have heard of; that is, if Laura is as nice a girl as she promised to be the evening I saw her last. Do you remember the time, Violet? ha! ha! ha! I robbed you of *that* ride, but you may go *this* time."

"Yes, and I think it quite probable that you had better have let me go with you then."

"Why so, my mysterious and lovely little sister?"

"Oh, never mind for the reasons now—may tell you

some other time. But as to cousin Laura being as nice a girl as formerly, I can say to you that she is, and improves in something every day she lives. She is the prettiest girl of us all, and is even sweeter in her character and her mind than in her person. So, my dear brother, if you are to be governed by her looks and her qualities, I shall look for a certain vain young collegian to fall into trouble very soon."

"Trouble! pshaw! I want a great deal of just such trouble."

"Very well; but let me suggest that we ride, as I am anxious to see my handsome cavalcade under way."

"I believe we are all ready now, and fully prepared for exhibition, as we are certainly as handsome by reciprocal compliments as the two Yankees were wealthy by swapping knives."

"*Allons,*" said Henry Brandon.

At this proposition they left the house, and went to their horses, where Essex, with "Sam Brandon," who had been taken immediately into service, stood holding them. As Hunter came up to him for the purpose of getting that one which Violet was to ride, he quickly and in an undertone said: "Mass Tom, I wishes you to ride with Miss Violet." Without appearing to hear the words, Hunter's heart responded to the spirit of them, but felt bound to give the place to Mr. Campbell, and, as they rode off, fell back with Henry Brandon, Essex and "Sam Brandon" bringing up the rear. The arrangement did not altogether please Essex, but he had too great politeness to give any evidence of his displeasure.

As we have undertaken to give an outline of Southern life in several of its coteries, we must be allowed frequent allusions to the negro servants belonging to them; and just here we will say that not the least injury which their (so-called) freedom has inflicted upon them, is the destruction of that pride — aristocratic feeling — which they entertained for the superiority of their own master's family over all others. This identification of themselves with the dignity and standing of their owners was a very decided elevation to them, the elements of which they did not have within themselves, and which their own *race* can never furnish.

Offensive as the aristocratic *planter* of the South was to the democratic *farmer* of the North, he was yet not to be compared in aristocratic feeling to his *body-servant* or his carriage-driver; nor to him, either, in his dislike of "Yankees" — the latter term being ever used as one of contempt, and is so to this day — growing out of the fact universally asserted that they knew nothing about negroes, and made the *stingiest*, hardest masters.

In the present instance, Essex was proud of his young mistress; and desired that Hunter should ride with her, as he thought him the handsomest, wealthiest, and most liberal young gentleman that visited her: of Campbell he knew nothing, and was therefore disposed to ignore his attentions.

From a feeling of identity of welfare, all the better and more intelligent classes of negroes, throughout the whole slave period, were the most inveterate *match-makers* for their young mistresses; and discussed with the utmost freedom and sharpness the pretensions of any gentleman to their hands, and as far as possible imitated them in their own courtships. But woe be unto the young fellow who had the hardihood to ride up, who was not known to possess his full share of DARKIES!

A certain female writer of Northern notoriety, by selecting some exceptional characters, both black and white, and by adding to the extravagance of her pictures all the *sentimental* malignity of ignorance and fanaticism, did more to slander the domestic life of the South than all the crazy-headed Garrisons *et al.* together. Theirs were but

4

the mad ravings of the bull at the baiting, and most men laughed while uttering the unceasing cry of "pan y toras;" but *hers* was the shriek and wail of distress from a woman, and all men rushed to the scene of pain.

This same woman has since had the disgusting effrontery to make some sort of home in the *orange groves* of a land which she assisted to destroy, and as we suppose, aspires to drink in fresh inspiration for a slanderous page; but orange groves can furnish no inspiration to such a mind. When no slander can be uttered her pen cannot move: the gigantic malignancy of her first falsehood has fortunately paralyzed all future efforts of her wretched brain. She should now devote the remainder of her life to penance for the wrong she has done; and even one life is insufficient for an adequate repentance! With these remarks, we leave her disgusting pen to English Reviews.

CHAPTER VII.

"And both were young, and one was beautiful." — BYRON.

THE gay cavalcade was now sweeping swiftly and gallantly across the beautiful country which lay in the direction of Mr. Robert Brandon's. Essex had been thoroughly studying the æsthetics of the expedition, from the moment he had first received the order in regard to it; and, thinking it proper, in consideration of the arrival of his young master, to invest it with all the augustness possible, had ordered even a third subaltern into his service, in order that each gentleman should have his particular groom. This third party, who, in some patronymical significance, responded to the name of "JACKO," was a full-blooded negro; and rejoiced in nothing more than his love of laughter, in which he now frequently indulged with a rather loud "yah, ha!" to the great annoyance of Essex, who was desirous of conducting his end of the party with the utmost gravity and decorum. Henry Brandon had not discovered the extent of Essex's retinue, until, upon the occasion of an extra loud "yah, ha!" from the unrestrained risibles of JACKO, when, turning to him, he said, "Why, Essex, you have all the boys from the *quarter* with you."

"Oh, no, sah! JACKO, he b'longs to me anyhow, and I jest brung 'long 'Sam Brandon' on you' account."

"That's all well; but Uncle Robert will think we are coming to storm his house."

"I speck not, sah; he 'most always does see me have Jacko, and 'Sam Brandon' is you' servant: oh, no, sah! thar ain't too many of us."

"Very well; the more the merrier on a frolic."

Violet and Campbell were riding together, and carrying on a lively conversation, the latter appearing more pleasant and more at his ease than she had ever seen him; while Hunter and Henry Brandon were but a short distance behind, feeling all the joyousness of youth again, as they galloped over the broad prairies through which they had so often rambled together in boyhood.

It was in the early autumn of the year; and as the golden sunlight rested on the broad landscape, it seemed to soothe its exhausted summer life to a soft repose, while the gentle breeze fanned the brow even more lightly than a young maiden's hand, and gave the scene a mystic sadness, which was yet a joy to the heart, and swelled it with sweetest emotions.

The merry little party had now reached the outer demesnes of "Starlight;" and as Essex opened the large double gate, the two daughters of Mr. Brandon — LAURA and LUCY — were seen off at some distance to the right, as if taking an evening walk among the great oaks of the enclosure, which even partly concealed from view the stately mansion that stood in their midst.

The first impulse of the young ladies upon seeing the party, and not recognizing the persons, was to return to the house; but as they appeared to have inclined a little in the direction of themselves, they at once turned and came meeting them, still unable, however, to comprehend the nature of so uncommon a cortege, though recognizing Violet as one of them.

Henry Brandon now rode in advance, when Laura, in spite of the change in appearance that had taken place, at once recognized him; and clapping her hands in expression of her joyous astonishment, exclaimed, even before speaking to others, or appearing to observe their approach: "Oh, cousin, cousin! is this Henry Brandon?"

Henry, feeling the same pleasure, addressed her in return — in imitation, too, of her own gladness:

"Cousin, cousin! is this Laura Brandon?"

Lucy, in this while, had received her friends — Laura, as we have said, not appearing to be conscious of their presence.

Henry Brandon had dismounted from his horse before these words were clearly out of his mouth, and, holding his cap in one hand, had seized hers with the other, and with a half-comic, half-serious expression, knelt before her, and pledged his *knighthood* and eternal fealty. While in this pretendedly imploring position, he discovered the little gold ring still upon her finger, which he had placed there, four years before, in the flower-yard, on the eve of his leaving for college; then immediately, kissing her hand and rising, said:

"Fair lady, as I have pledged my knighthood to thy noble service, wilt thou now, as *cousin*, permit me to place the seal of my affection upon thy ruby lips?"

Laura, in this while, had recovered from the surprise of this eccentric salutation, and laughingly addressing her young friends, asked them to pardon her not speaking to them before; then smilingly turning again to her cousin, who still held her hand, replied:

"Ah! no, sir knight! I will reserve that favor as future guerdon of thy truth, and some noble deed of valor."

But no notion had he to thus be foiled by the mock gravity of her refusal, but instantly placing his arm around her chiselled neck, gave her smiling lips a gentle kiss. Oh! that fatal kiss! 't was then there went from earth to heaven a soft, low tone of music; and still it lingers on the harp-strings there, in echo to the pledge of a heart's *first love.*

After going through these mock heroics, Henry Brandon turned to Lucy, whom he had not yet spoken to, and addressed her in the fullest terms of natural affection and pleasure. In the mean time Campbell had found his way to her side, and was enjoying the odd mixture of extravagance and antique gallantry which young Brandon had so unexpectedly seen proper to indulge in.

In reply to his hearty and good-natured salutation, Lucy said to him, as she received his hand:

"Cousin, I am of course delighted to see you, after so long an absence; but this wicked humanity of mine demands an apology for so decided an expression of preference as you have just exhibited for Laura."

"Ah! my lovely cousin, this is not a moment for rhetoric, speeches, expletives, or explanations, but one for affectionate inquiry after health and welfare, loves and hopes, and for asking you, too, to never again use so cold and earthly a word as *humanity* when speaking of so perfect an ideality of all beauty as *yourself*—say *celestiality.* Yes, as you are really more beautiful, cousin, than I even remembered you to be —"

4 *

"Come, cousin," she said, interrupting him, and at the same time laughing; "stop, I pray you, or I shall think flattery the chief fruition of your college life. Was the mastery of that art embraced in your curriculum?"

"Indeed it was not, but truth was highly enjoined; and that being my inheritance and vernacular too, I have only had to cultivate a native virtue; yet, even now my tongue can only lisp, in feeble numbers, nature's rich profusions in yourself. Never mind all of this, however," he added, as he saw her about to interrupt him; "but let me ask why thy anger at the supposed preference for thy sister? Is she unworthy?"

"Indeed, no, not by any means; she is worthy any manner of homage; but yours was so unexpectedly peculiar, as to make it quite remarkable: you seemed to think these old oaks surrounding some old enchanted castle, and Laura, a noble damsel held in vile captivity."

"Ah! coz, thou mayest charge thy jaundice to the green-eyed monster. Didst thou suppose that I, Henry Brandon, gent., after years of absence, could renew the fealty of my youthful heart after the humdrum style of your man of clay? Moreover, coz, wilt thee permit me to say that thou seemest amenable unto that particular law of thy gender whereof the poets have so often sung, and concerning which Shakspeare was moved unto saying:

> "'Trifles light as air
> Are, to the jealous, confirmation strong
> As proofs of Holy Writ.'"

At this unlooked-for imputation, Lucy's eyes flashed with a merry fire; but the flighty accuser gave no time for a reply, by moving quickly again to Laura, who was conversing gayly with Campbell, and said:

"Pardon me, fair lady; but, on meeting thee in this ancient grove, some mystic shadow did flit athwart my vision; and thy sister's ready wit or instinct supplied the phantom with a name — perhaps a prophecy — "captivity." Now let the future tell who the captive or the captor is," and, with affected reverence, cap in hand, bowed gallantly; then laughingly turned to the amusing scene transpiring at his side, in which Hunter, somewhat at a loss as to what he should say or do during the extravagances of Brandon, had pretended to have somehow caught the gallant infection, and, kneeling at Violet's feet, was repeating the words of Virgil, "Omnia, vincet amor, et nos, cedamus, amori," while she, with an affected assumption of dignity and doubt, replied: " Men have died, and worms have eaten them, but not for love."

Hunter then rose, and, swearing by St. George and the Dragon that he was ready to perform her least or greatest pleasure, announced himself prepared to put his protestations to the proof, and was willing to undertake all the labors of Hercules — bring her the golden fleece, or to fling a girdle round the earth in forty minutes — if these heroic feats could extort one smile from her coral lips, or one beam of love from her lustrous eyes.

"Glorious! Hunter; most glorious! You have neither forgotten your early college lore, nor your youthful warmth of heart, and must certainly have been recently engaged in reviewing your classics, and begun with Ovid's 'Art of Love.' But see thee, mine ancient friend — I most solemnly protest against thy victimizing mine unsophisticated country sister; for even now, while assuming such indifference, she is half disposed to yield to thy siren words."

All parties then joined in the merry laugh, when Hunter, speaking to Campbell, said:

"Now, Mr. Campbell, comes your turn. We two have declared our knightly devotion to our ladies, and called the weird spirits of this ancient wood to witness our truth and noble purpose; and yet there is another damsel, all

forlorn, whose charms are still without a suitable defender."

Campbell, pleased with this timely impudence of Hunter,
gladly accepted the banter, and bowed low and gracefully
to Lucy, when she, in return, pronounced him *knighted*,
and accepted his championship, as she touched his shoulder with the little wild-flower she held in her hand; then
screaming with uncontrolled laughter, said:

"Well, if father has witnessed any portion of this very
unique and eccentric meeting, he will certainly take out a
commission of lunacy against us, and we richly deserve it."

They now walked in the direction of the house, paired
off, as may be easily conjectured. The horses being in
charge of the servants; Essex, with his corps of assistants,
had witnessed the whole scene, with their senses ravished
with delight; but he, too proud to confess his want of comprehension, waited, with a most knowing look of silence,
until some one else should speak.

"Essex," at length spoke Sam Brandon, "ole feller, did
you see into all dat talk?"

"To-be-sho I did, nigga; it means when dey is all gwine
to marry."

"Ah, ha! dat's so, I speck. Well, it looked mity fine;
an' Mass Henry, he's gwine to git Miss Laura. He always
did had her for a sweetheart when he war a boy; an' he
beat em all to-day, for he got de kiss, if dat's any sign.
Mass Tom Hunter, he seem to git along purty well, too,
wid Miss Violet. Mr. Camell, he seem to fight behine.
Who is he, anyhow, Essex? Whar is his niggas?"

"Well, I jes don't know. Dey say he is a big lawyer,
and makes a heap o' money. If he do, he's dog-gone
stingy wid it, for I never sees him spen' any. He ain't got
no niggas 'bout here, dat's certain, I knows. But yes, sah,
Mass Tom, he is certain to be some of we darkies' master,
and dat very soon: he been comin' to our house a long

time; and did n't you see how Miss Violet looked at him dis evenin'? An' it 's jist what I wants. Miss Violet will den be de riches' lady in all dis neck. Mass Tom hisself is got close on to a hunderd niggas, and dey is mos'ly young; an' everything else accordin'. An' if old mistiss will gin me up, I wishes to be dey carriage-driver."

"Ah, ha! Well, dat 's all good enuff; but I myself specks to foller Mass Henry, from dis out, to the eend of the wurld, ef he wishes to go dar. I 's dun wid de cotton-patch arter dis. But, Essex, I likes de way de young gentlemen done dis evenin'; an' ef they kin make de young ladies marry 'em, les us try to do de same wid de house-gals; for nigger gals ain't as good as white ladies, and ain't as hard to be kotch, no how."

"Dat 's so, Sam Brandon. Agreed den: we 'll try em dis night."

With conversation of this sort, the negroes entertained themselves while in charge of the horses — thus demonstrating their natural love and reverence for white people, and particularly their masters, during their slavery, and their strong proclivities to *imitation*, which, together, were the source of their original civilization, and of which they are now prevented from availing themselves, by being *forced* into an antagonistic position.

Mr. Brandon had caught a glimpse of the last scenes of the meeting in the grove, and not exactly recognizing the parties, was almost disposed to think his daughters beside themselves; and, taking up his hat and cane, came meeting them as they were on their way to the house. On his nearer approach, he was much surprised, as well as pleased, at finding one of the parties to the uncommon proceedings his own handsome young nephew: after greeting him most kindly and cordially, he very naturally inquired as to the nature of the apparent confusion which he had seen from the house; but when explained to him, appeared to enjoy the sport of it equally with the young people themselves.

On reaching the house, they were met by Mrs. Brandon, a matronly looking, but very elegant lady, who, after a most gracious welcome to the nephew of her husband and his friends, conducted them into one of her large and elegant parlors. The conversation soon became general and animated, as there was no gentleman more happily capa-ble of putting a company at its ease than Mr. Brandon, or who more highly appreciated the mirth, joyousness, and humor of young persons, or entered with greater zest into the spirit of their intercourse. Mrs. Brandon possessed an almost equal felicity in her own deportment, with only a slight touch too much of stateliness — a very great draw-back to true politeness.

"Why did you not come over this morning, and spend the day with me, my young friends — and you particu-larly, Henry?" asked Mr. Robert Brandon.

"Well, sir, I was scarcely more than through with grat-ifying the curiosity of mother and Violet, before Hunter and Mr. Campbell came: we then concluded that we would ride over and make you a short visit, with the understanding that it would not relieve me of the respon-sibility of spending a day with you on private account, very soon."

"Yes, uncle, that is a correct account, so far as stated," said Violet; "but the visit, though not intended to be a regular, or a long one, would yet have been much longer, had brother not consumed more than a proper share of the time in the extra preparation of his *toilette*. I must tell on him, as he shall not appear here so much more hand-somely dressed than any of us, without letting you know that he took a part of *your visit* to prepare himself, and an unfair advantage of us."

"Ah, Violet, none of your tale-telling."

"No, I was only giving uncle the cause of the necessarily short visit which we pay him."

"That's all right. Now go to the piano with the others, while uncle and I have a few words on personal account."

Violet now left them, and the uncle and nephew spent most of the hour that they remained in private conversation. Some one or other of the girls alternately played, while all of them joined in the singing. Very soon Laura played a waltz, by arrangement, when Hunter and Violet, Campbell and Lucy, went through the mazes of that elegant but voluptuous dance.

It was now drawing nigh time for them to leave, and Violet made the proposition. Mr. Brandon then pleasantly insisted upon their staying until he could have a bottle of wine, saying that "a spur in the head is worth two in the heel," and that they therefore could more than make up the lost time. "What say you, Violet?"

"Oh, certainly, uncle, as these young gentlemen would never forgive me if I refused *that* proposition."

"Nor forgive *yourself*, Miss Violet," said Hunter.

A very choice old bottle was soon brought in, when Mr. Brandon remarked: "My young friends, you may esteem yourselves especially favored by the opening of this bottle: it is of a very old vintage, and I have only a few left — and only introduce it upon what I esteem *great occasions.* I have not brought one out since the visit to me of Washington Irving."

"Ah!" said Campbell, "I did not know that he had ever been this far South."

"Yes, several years since he made a flying sort of trip through this country, and he made Henry's father and myself an afternoon visit, in company with a party of gentlemen from ——, just to look at the scenery, which was then far more beautiful to the eye than now."

"It must indeed, then, have been very beautiful."

"It most truly was as lovely as human eye ever beheld."

The wine was now opened, and Mr. Brandon proposed the health of his returned nephew.

The party soon left the house and mounted their horses, Henry Brandon promising to return in a few days and make a full visit.

After they were all on their horses, Mr. Brandon put in a claim for the company of young Campbell, saying that, as they had paid him so short a visit, they should at least be willing to make a fair division. The proposition was so natural, and so perfectly accorded with the young gentleman's own feelings, that he could not conceal his inclinations to accept — when Violet spoke, saying:

"Mr. Campbell, I *sympathize* with you, sir, and give you my permission to remain, although we had promised ourselves the pleasure of your company at our house this evening."

Campbell thanked her, and accepted.

CHAPTER VIII.

"Odds life! must one swear to the truth of a song?"

AS it will not be a difficult thing to suppose that Henry Brandon allowed but a very few days to intervene between his first and second visit to STARLIGHT, we will pretermit all circumlocution, and state, in few words, that on the third day from that of the first, he did truly make this second visit; and, further, that it will not be a violent presumption to suppose that this promptness was, to a very great extent, attributable to the attractiveness of the beautiful daughters, rather than the — certainly — many excellences of the uncle.

He had been a little expected even the day before; but the very slight disappointment — if such it was — had only appeared to increase the cordial interest with which he was now met by his uncle. His aunt too received him with a very affectionate graciousness — all of which was very especially agreeable to the young gentleman, as there was a certain little secret hope in his breast which this reception seemed to flatter. But to Laura his visit was a *perfect delight;* and the feeling conveyed itself to *his* heart, without the help of words; while to Lucy it was all that he desired it. There may be some breach of confidence on our part — who may be supposed to know these things — in exposing them; yet we hope to be forgiven, promising to tell no more secrets out of season.

However, that our readers may have a better comprehension of matters as they shadow themselves out — but not intending to betray any facts reposed to our keeping — we must let it be known that, during Henry Brandon's absence at college, he had regularly corresponded with Laura; but from fear of detection, probably, he had not been more than ordinarily tender, except upon a few occasions, which Laura had always guarded him against, telling him that her letters from him were always of so much interest to the family generally, they had to pass round to every member of it — never omitting to say, at the same time, that his pretty speeches were very pleasing to *her.* In this way, each of them had kept up the interest in the other which we have seen was felt by them at the time of his leaving for college.

This fact, together with the eccentric, but amusing greetings of their first meeting, destroyed all the stiffness or formality which might otherwise have marked their intercourse after so long an absence. No feeling of estrange-

5

ment impressed itself on their passage from youth to maturity, and they were as easy as when children together. But while their conversation was replete with wit, repartee, and innocent pleasantry, there was a certain concealed gallantry in his attentions to her, which was unobservable to others, but perfectly understood by the sweet and loving-hearted girl. And what young girl, indeed, did ever fail to detect an intended gallantry, however well disguised from the common gaze?

For the first two hours after his arrival in the morning, Mr. and Mrs. Brandon remained with him, and, quite as much as their daughters, appeared to enjoy his sparkling conversation. Mr. Brandon then left the room, and was very soon followed by Mrs. Brandon, leaving the young people to themselves.

"Ah! now, girls, we are all alone, and I want you to tell me everything you have done, said, or thought for the last four years — in particular, all that you have done, said, or thought concerning *myself.*"

"Your demands are heavy, cousin," said Laura.

"Yes, and very conceited, too," said Lucy. "You certainly think we have been pining over your absence."

"Well, certainly; and I expect you have pined over many worse matters."

"That we *may* have; but then we have had the pleasing novelty of *fresh* sorrows occasionally."

"Then my conceit is in advance on that point: so let me inquire what else has engaged your thought — love, music, French, or cooking? in other words, has aunt prepared you for the kitchen or the parlor? What are you — fine ladies, or useful ones?"

"I," said Lucy, laughing, "have been educated for the parlor, while Laura's taste has led her into the culinary department. You know there had to be one fine lady of us. But why the question, cousin?"

"Well, first, because, since eating in College Commons for four years, I am thoroughly of the opinion that proficiency in the noble art of cooking is of far more importance, and a far higher accomplishment, than music, French, or painting — unless the French be used to learn the number of dishes that can be made of four eggs, and how elegant a dinner can be got up with six."

"I comprehend you now, and think yourself and Laura will grow to be admirable friends — your 'Admiration;' as I think she has not read a word of French for a year past but with reference to some 'new dish.'"

"I am delighted with cousin Laura, in advance."

"Lucy has left out one *practical* accomplishment of hers, and as they are so few, I must give her all the advantage of it — she is the stocking-darner for the whole family, cousin Henry, and some weeks has a small mountain of work around her," replied Laura.

"That is very well, so far as it goes, Lucy; but still I have to regret your inaptitude to kitchen duties; for if I read the stars aright, as they conformed last night, thou 'lt have some early occasion so to employ thyself, even ere thy sister will."

"Indeed! then tell me, thou ancient Magus, what signs you have been reading, or what the signs you profess to be governed by."

"The stars, Lucy; the stars! for by what less than them would I, or any one, dare to read the fortunes of so fair a girl?"

"I cannot say; but see that, in addition to being one of the most accomplished flatterers, you also profess to be an astrologer, and when failing to reach your object by the cunning insinuations of the one, like the first great tempter of our sex, you change your form, and make approaches through the weird problems of the other."

"Even so, fair lady; and your own insight and solutions seem themselves to pass the bounds of human reason, and by them almost break the charm of my skill. Yes, you are right — I do profess to a knowledge of that sacred lore, the arcana of which are only intrusted to a chosen few; and most truly, wherein my human faculties fail to inform me of future events, the spirits teach me — the stars of heaven."

"Wonderful, indeed, but rather difficult of belief."

"Ah! had you seen that which last night I did see, as the planets met upon the dividing line, you would surely select more cautious terms of expression."

Laura, who had not joined in the conversation, but sat listening to the ludicrous jumble, at length said:

"Most learned cousin, you must either tell us of what you saw in this starry realm of yours, or permit us to doubt the truth of your mystical inspiration."

"Ah, sweet lady, it is one of the sternest laws of our solemn brotherhood, that we shall bear with our truth being impugned, before we may expose the workings of our holy league. *Silence* is the spell under which we live. I may not, cannot tell thee that which thou wouldst know."

Laura, evidently desirous of some sort of answer, banteringly said to him:

"Then, Sir Astrologer, we will pronounce your secret league and mystic lore both apocryphal; but, somewhat to redeem your order from so vile a charge, suppose thou tellest us of those whose fortunes were last night appointed in this assemblage of royal arch-spirits."

"I may not even tell thee that, fair lady; yet again I may: that, in our last festal hour, each star did fling a gentle beam to that which with it had revolved in the magic ring. More methinks it forbidden to reveal."

"Cousin, thy doubts and chopped expressions rather dub thee necromancer than wise astrologer, and such we will surely call thee, too, unless thou revealest more of thy charmed assemblages and their strange incantations. Canst thou not even tell the number that made up this magic circle?"

"Lady, in refutation of so base a charge, I *will* say that we work with no *odd* numbers; and will even further tell thee, even with the certainty of bringing down upon me the wrath of those who have been my friends, that we hold our meetings when eclipses are, and send down to mortal hearts the aspects and conjunctions by the shooting stars; and these are all made manifest at the proper hour. But let it now be told, by mortal tongue, that thy own lovely form did, last night, highest float in the shadowy throng, where all were paired, and all did hail thee queen of happy fortune."

"Indeed?"

"Indeed."

"Now, since thou hast forfeited all thy favor, pray tell me, thou fallen spirit, what bright star did welcome mine."

"Ah! mine earthly tempter, let me break, forever, the sacred charm that would have borne the enchanted two, together, through the span of time, and tell thee that *mine* did float with *thine*. But now we are as others are. Our fortunes fell, and fate itself did fail, when I told thee of these sacred cabalisms!"

Lucy, catching the glimmering meaning of what Henry Brandon had been so artfully aiming at, clapped her hands, and, breaking out in a hearty laugh, said: "Oh, cousin! read the enchantment backward: that will restore the charm. There is an old couplet which runs as follows:

"'The incantation backward she repeats,
   Inverts her rod, and what she did, defeats.'"

But, before young Brandon could reply, his uncle and aunt entered the room, and found the young people in ecstasies of laughter.

5 *

"Ah," said Mr. Brandon, "you young people appear to be very joyous. Suppose you give us old ones the benefit of your mirth?"

"Oh, father," said Lucy, "cousin Henry has returned among us a wiser person than any of his old-fogy ancestors; and, if he progresses through all his life as he appears thus far to have done, will deserve canonization."

"Come, my daughter, I think you endeavoring to exhibit your wit. You know I always protest against what young women are pleased to call *sarcasm:* they are dangerous qualities at the best, and young women only succeed in making a failure in its use, and themselves more or less ridiculous, and always avoided."

"Oh, father, you are too severe; I did not —"

"No, Uncle Robert, cousin Lucy was only jesting," said Henry.

"Yes, I only meant a jest, in regard to our college cousin discovering to us his proficiency in the long obsolete science of astrology, and that he had even calculated our nativity since his return."

"You are wrong, my daughter, in the choice of your words — a nativity is only cast at the hour of birth."

"Well, I dare say; but as he had such a jargon of phrases, I thought it about as well to use one word as another."

"I am glad of your explanation, Lucy; but your manner appeared a little brusque, as well as your words a little rough. But, Henry, we are not yet all so old as to be insensible to the warmth of *Promethean* fire: suppose you repeat to us the results of your communion with the stars."

"Excuse me, sir; the nonsense will not bear repeating: I only indulged in it for the amusement of the girls — of myself, rather, by rousing their curiosity, which, if they are like their *Yankee cousins*, they will go a great way to gratify."

"Thank you, sir; no Yankee cousin for me, if you please; and, besides, cousin, that is an unhandsome opinion of yours. But one thing I do thank you for, and father will also, I think, as he very often says that Laura is the finest girl in the whole country, and the most admired, but has never yet broken a single heart, nor even had one certain, acknowledged beau; and tells her the prospect is that she will always remain a spinster. Is it not so, father?" said she, addressing him.

"I believe I have jokingly used such words."

"Your fears may now be at an end, sir, for cousin Henry has promised her one, by the conjunctions of the planets, as he calls it — certainly they cannot make mistakes — and was so generous, too, as to — "

"Come, Lucy," suddenly interrupted both Laura and Henry, the latter reddening with the deepest rose-flush, "don't repeat our mischievous nonsense!"

"Oh, well, certainly not, if it occasions a mutual blush; but I really did not look upon it as such nonsense; that part of the affair seemed very fine to me."

It is but just to Lucy to say that she had begun to tell of the prophecy in regard to Laura and Henry in all good feeling, having, in the winding up of her cousin's strange jargon, conceived the idea that he was insinuating a future *union* between himself and her, and at once approving it, was about to disclose the *fanciful* prophecy, just to see how the *real* proposition would be received by her father, if it should ever be made.

"Ah, Henry," said Mrs. Brandon, who had not before spoken, and at once catching at the idea which he and Laura had unitedly interrupted Lucy in disclosing, "I had little thought to see so wild a boy turn sentimentalist in his manhood; and none but the purest romancist ever dreams of admiring a cousin. I am so matter-of-fact as to render all such arrangements very distasteful to me."

Lucy saw, by this reply of her mother, that her suppressed remarks had been perfectly comprehended, and was quite astonished at its evident significance and sharpness.

Laura, seeing it also, saw proper to say, while she blushed very deeply, " You need feel in no danger of having your opinions disturbed, mother, for our astral cousin did himself break his own magical conjurations, by revealing (as he says) the story of our confluent fortunes, and thus I am still left to pursue the solitary pleasures of spinsterhood."

Mr. Brandon now turning to his nephew, said, " Come, Henry, walk with me into the library. I presume you have had enough of this ' woman-kind' for an hour or so."

And the two left the parlor together for the place appointed.

CHAPTER IX.

" Let us consider the reason of the case; for nothing is law, that is not reason."

WE have elsewhere said that the two brothers, Robert and St. George Brandon, were educated men, and gentlemen of high culture in the arts of polite society. Even when participating in the sports peculiar to the country at the time of its first settlement, the chase, the infant race-course, and the gay meetings of the social circle, they still were students, and each had his select law, political, and literary library, which occupied much of his time.

After the death of his brother, Mr. Robert Brandon suddenly and entirely gave up all sporting of whatever kind, and divided his time between his books and attention to his increased business responsibilities; and at the time of which we are writing, he had already been pressed into the service of the State, by having had conferred on him several positions of honor, and was at the immediate time one of the "electors at large" on the Whig ticket, Mr. Clay and Mr. Polk being candidates for the Presidency of the Republic, and was especially preparing to meet Colonel Haywood, a speaker of very great ability on the Democratic ticket, for Mr. Polk. The canvass had been already opened, and very soon Mr. Brandon was to visit a distant part of the State, which would occasion him to be absent for several weeks. This was his reason for wishing to have all the private conversation possible with his nephew, as the latter was already within a few months of his majority, and thought it proper to give him some general account of his property.

After explaining these matters to him in general terms, he cursorily advised with him as to his future personal course, saying to him that "the law, apart from its being a profession, was the highest finish to the education of a gentleman, and in all countries the chief high-road to distinction — particularly is this the truth in a republican country. It may be a little sophomorean, perhaps, to bring up the instance of Rome; but the history of its leading men, during its most eminent period, is so aptly in point, and so frequently referred to, that you must pardon me for directing your attention to it. There were but two roads to fortune and fame in that republic — one of which led through the army, the other through the law. If I mistake not, in the time of Cicero — and certainly the most brilliant period of her history, and the culminating point of her glory — all men of prominence, whether engaged or not in the law at the time, yet had been, at some previous time, distinguished as advocates: Cæsar had been, Mark Antony had been, Pompey also, I think, and indeed all who figured at the time of the Triumvirate.

These facts are almost literally true in English, and in our own short history. As I have said, this is particularly the truth in representative governments, where all questions of importance come before the people for discussion and judgment, in some manner or other, either as to their practical bearings or constitutional features. The correctness of these assertions is generally undeniable, and, for peculiar reasons, applies with especial force in the South, rendering it important that every man of intelligence, whether his fortune and taste invite him to the study or not, should thoroughly inform himself in all matters of political economy and constitutional law, even should he see proper to go no farther."

Young Brandon replied to his uncle, that he had always intended directing his attention to the law, but had never attributed to it that importance in the affairs of the South with which he seemed to invest it; but, in the face of this intention, he had to confess to some disrelish, on the score of what had been represented to him as its pettifoggery.

"Yes," replied his uncle, "that objection can be easily urged against it by young men of fortune; yet you must remember that the abuses which attend upon any profession are not legitimate objections to it — they are as barnacles upon the bottoms of great men-of-war."

"Then, uncle, as you look upon the profession in that light, would it not be better to lay a scientific foundation by attending some one of the law-schools?"

"Your general idea is correct, but subject to a specific qualification, which is, that the law-schools of this country do not sufficiently confine themselves to the common law, but involve and complicate their instructions with *local* constructions of constitutional law; and these sectional idiosyncrasies of interpretation are already exerting a prejudicial influence on the peaceful relations of the Northern States with the Southern."

"Perhaps I do not clearly comprehend you. Will you give me a more definite idea of your meaning?"

"I can give you a clearer general idea of it, but have not the time to pursue the subject in its ramifications: for instance, I mean that the HAMILTONIAN, or high Federal style of opinion, prevails in the Northern schools, while the JEFFERSONIAN, or ultra State-sovereignty doctrine, rules in the Southern. These theories differ widely in practical results, and will assuredly lead to sectional collisions before the lapse of many years; indeed, they have nearly done so already, in the case of South Carolina and the Government."

"It has never occurred to me that the sections would ever come in serious sectional collision on the score of constitutional law; but I have thought that this fanatical excitement they are beginning to get up at the North, in regard to African slavery, might lead to some trouble."

"Yes, even that movement is remotely based upon the teachings of their schools. But the case of South Carolina is a substantial premonition of what is to come. Mr. Calhoun still pushes the doctrines of Mr. Jefferson to the farthest extent, while Adams, Webster, and others as strenuously advocate the Hamiltonian-federal doctrine. Mr. Calhoun's centrifugal doctrines, carried out to their legitimate results, are destructive of all government; while Mr. Webster's idea of the centripetal forces of government are equally destructive of our federative system. Where to go, and how far to go, with each of these doctrines, so as to preserve the republic, and save the only institution upon which the prosperity of the extreme South entirely depends — at this time, at least — is the great obligation resting upon Southern intellect. We have some certain mental and social features, in the South, of which it is difficult to trace the lineage, but which we know are well-nigh as dangerous and destructive, from *resentment*, as we

know the correlatives to be in the North, from *fanaticism.*
The Northern people, even in their very best intellect, furnish nothing that can be called *statesmanship.* The leaders,
equally with the people, are ever crossing their own paths.
We know not what to expect from them, but have every
thing to apprehend.   But, to return to the subject directly,
I would advise you, from this antagonistic condition of
the law-schools, to enter the office of some one of our own
best lawyers, so that, if you are to imbibe *any* prejudice,
it may be a *home* prejudice ; but be as guarded as possible
against all of them.   We shall not want *provincial* prejudices in the terrible day that is coming, but sentiments,
ventilated by a thorough *national* spirit, and having for its
object the preservation of popular liberty untinctured of
personal license, and the welfare of all the sections without
bias in the distribution of favors."

Continuing this style of conversation for some time
longer, with a gradual return to matters of a more personal
character, they ended their interview at the library, and
returned to the drawing-room.

Mrs. Brandon was still sitting there, seemingly engaged
with her needle, and as young Brandon thought, with her
face wearing something like an expression of *ungraciousness,*
while Lucy was sitting near a distant window with a book
before her, but scarcely to be said had been reading.   An
evident uneasiness had grown up from some quarter.   Laura
was not present, and as he did not ask, her absence remained unaccounted for.   But Henry, while sensitive and
in some respects timid, had a certain sort of boldness which
vivacity of intellect always furnishes, and, though young,
was too well skilled in a knowledge of the human heart
to allow himself to be trampled down so soon.   Seating
himself near his aunt, as he entered the room, in some
measure he renewed the conversation which had been interrupted by going to the library with his uncle.

"Aunt," said he, "a very interesting subject had somehow most inadvertently suggested itself just as I left the room, and I do not feel willing to leave it in the rather *bedrabbled* condition we had placed it in." Lucy immediately drew nearer to her mother, with a shy sort of fun twinkling in her eye, as the conversation was again introduced, which she had come out of rather more *shabbily* than any of the party. "I think you remarked that no one but the purest romancist ever admired a cousin. I think, madam, you have forgotten the fact that the subject, so far from being looked upon from a sentimental point, has long engaged the attention of the astutest ministers in the Cabinets of Europe. The heaviest matters of state are made to turn on the marriages of cousins; even the balances of power between their governments often turn on these alliances. Indeed, the nobility of Europe marry no one else *but* cousins. Now, aunt, I dare not say that this romantic question, as you call it, possesses any especial interest for myself; but then, just stepping on the threshold of joyous manhood as I am, I have some few twitchings of the nerves, if not of the heart, at seeing the broad and beautiful field of my observations lessened in any of its boundaries. I may yield you the specific question of matrimony with *my cousins*, but cannot give up the general one — by no means, madam."

Mrs. Brandon, not able to suppress a smile at the evident ingeniousness of the young gentleman, and being very clearly pleased with his dashing but respectful elegance of manner, said to him, in an agreeable tone of voice:

"Henry, I think you must aspire to a foreign embassy, you seem so well skilled, or informed, in the diplomacy of foreign courts, in regard to matrimony at least."

"No, madam; as yet I have looked no higher than the diplomacy of *domestic courts*."

The ambiguity of this remark again brought the slightest

6

appearance of a shadow over her handsome face, and she made no reply. Lucy then made the remark, that "though it was the general practice of royal and noble families, it was always between cousins who were strangers to each other; and therefore there was but slight *social* resemblance, and a perfect obliviousness to the few or many faults of each other; and consequently but little more harm of any sort could grow out of the custom there than from marriages between strangers. On the other hand, she did not think that any considerable harm could grow out of the system in this country, even if the question was left open, and recognized without prejudice; from the fact that so very few would ever take place, for here, families generally lived near each other, and their young members were familiar with each other's *foibles, failings, faults,* and *infirmities,* of all kinds, and presented to each other but few inducements to *love-making.*"

"Most grandly delivered, my pretty cousin; but methinks a little involved in its meaning — something of the blow hot and blow cold about it."

"Ah, you need not be so spicy in your remarks, cousin," said she, laughing. "I was not *personal.*"

"Of course not, as I am vain enough to believe that, if you had desired to be, you *could* not have *so* expressed yourself."

Laura entered the room at this moment; and, as if by some strange common consent, the subject was dropped, and conversation assumed a general tone, until the servant entered and invited her mistress to the dining-room.

At the table, conversation still kept up its gay and lively character, not a moment being allowed to flag. After several courses had passed, Henry spoke to Laura, and asked if they were indebted to her skill for any part of the sumptuous repast they were enjoying.

"Yes, everything of this kind at STARLIGHT is in some-wise connected or associated with me, as I have for more than a year now, held the high office of chief butler. Mother gives general directions, and I have the details executed. I begin to think that she has made a lifetime appointment of it, *nolens volens* on my part. I have sometimes been a little remiss, just to see if it would affect my involuntary tenure; but it did not, and it still clings to me as the old man of the sea did to Sinbad."

"I can congratulate you upon the honorable post, and for the very handsome manner in which you perform its duties; and by way of encouragement will promise to make you happy with my frequent presence. Four years at college has just put me that much behind in matters of the table; and I expect to devote a good deal of time to catching up. What say you to my dividing time between yourself and Violet?"

"Oh, I think the arrangement would be delightful indeed. I could please such a boarder to the ninth part of a hair."

"Perhaps I do not understand your figure, Miss. You do not certainly mean to leave that —"

"Certainly not, sir," she replied, laughing; "I meant to express perfection."

"Pardon the misapprehension; but perhaps, as I hear no echo to your welcome, I may be letting my gustatory enthusiasm bear me ahead of an invitation. Would it not be better that I get one from some higher authority than that of the *chief cook*, to attend the *cuisine* of STARLIGHT? What says Lady Brandon?" archly turning to his aunt as he referred to her.

"Certainly, Henry, make the table of 'Starlight' your own, just as you did in your boyhood; but with the understanding that you never forget that I am *Aunt*, and not *Lady* Brandon, or anything else — that you are to be my *nephew*, and not a ceremonious visitor. Now, sir, is not

that a sufficiently welcome invitation?" saying this, as
Henry thought, with rather a *forced* smile.

He was something at a loss to comprehend the meaning
of his aunt's various postulates; but choosing not to observe any probable peculiarity in them, merely replied:

"Most assuredly, madam; nothing shall be otherwise
than as you say, unless you yourself shall see proper to
make a change."

In spite of his assumed indifference to the meaning of his
aunt, his face flushed as he made this reply. Lucy, observing it, said to her mother, that cousin Henry would be
qualified off from them, even before he became fully domesticated again.

" I cannot see why," she answered; "as my requests are
very simple, and my invitation very cordial; they are, at
least, so intended," smiling very pleasantly both at Henry
and her daughters, as she said this.

The shadowy apprehensions of a possible love - affair
were certainly indicated by the words of Mrs. Brandon,
which Mr. Robert Brandon perceiving, said to her that
she and the young people were clearly getting into a tangle
which might result in a Gordian knot.

This remark, instead of making matters easier, only increased the little embarrassment that was brewing. He had
more than half intended it, and was now enjoying his pretended mistake in the laughing eye and blushing cheek of
Laura; but asked pardon for his unseasonable interference
in their *imbroglio*, and begged to withdraw.

Henry Brandon laughed heartily, and, resolving not to
become embarrassed, said in an undertone to Laura, while
his uncle was speaking:

"Cousin, there is something here suggestive of an unde-
fined event, wherein you and I are to act a part. Shall we
attempt to name it now, or leave it to the wiser fates?"

At this bold question, a look of innocent confusion came

over the beautiful face of the happy girl, as she quickly replied, in the same undertone, "To the fates."

Henry, now addressing his aunt, asked if he might propose a sentiment to the girls, to which she of course assented. He then raised his glass, first to Laura, and then to Lucy, and said, "Every heart to its earliest hope." All treated it as a jest, and drank to the sentiment.

But oh! the terrible truth of many a jest! and there was a strange truth in all their jests that day, that threw their long shadows into many a distant year, which only faded all away in the still twilight of eternity, with the sad, sweet life of one who sank beneath the sorrow of a broken heart.

In spite of the many little glimmerings of a *coming tempest* that had showed themselves that day, Henry Brandon was delighted with his visit; and as he rode over the beautiful prairies, on his return home, at half-speed, and with a merry heart, there constantly rose before him the half-sad face of Laura, as she said, "To the fates." He was happy at the vision, but wondered why it came. It was the first star of evening; and the light was soft and lovely, as it danced away off on the distant sky; and the first, too, of a long and gloomy night, which was to darken his own sad way through many troubled years.

CHAPTER X.

"The dog, to gain some private ends,
Went mad, and bit the man.
The man recovered of the bite,
The dog it was that died."

A MILD Indian-summer sun was shedding its mellow evening light upon the landscape, and gave to nature that look of sad and sweet repose which ever drapes the

6*

dying year in this Southern land. The soft October breeze, while floating along, seemed as gently to breathe its life away, as doth despairing love when whispering the low music of a last farewell. Oh! who hath never felt the charmed influence of its strange romance! and not felt, too, that even human life itself was an angel's happy dream wandering off from heaven!

As the careless young rider dashed wildly over the wide prairie, with the swiftly moving wind sweeping out his long black hair, and fanning his high, broad brow, there came a beauty and a freshness to his thoughts and feelings such as he had never known before. There was no method in their passing, nor was there any action of the mind, but rather the unfettered communings of the soul with the spirit of nature, as it lay nestled in the chambers of his noble heart; these commingling their lights and shadows into one, threw out a bow of promise to his gaze that told of love, of hope, of joy, and ambition, and shed the bright, but fleeting light through which his life would pass. There were colors there, that told of death and sorrow too, but *these* he did not *see*, and knew not of. Ah! who doth not, in later years, remember the blindness of a boy's eye, and the boldness of a boy's heart, and loveth not the sweet memory too?

Such were the visions, the hopes, the feelings, and confused emotions of Henry Brandon, in his wild, half-speed ride from STARLIGHT.

The sun had just sunk down, and the first gray twilight had swung its mystic mantle over the lawn that lay spread out before the gate at "Buckhorns," as Henry rode up. His arrival there was seen by a gang of little negroes at the "quarter," all of whom, according to the old custom, had assembled to sing their parting evening song, and came at full speed to open it. As soon as they discovered it to be "Mass Henry"—of whom they had just heard for the first time in their lives — they raised a yell of the wildest delight, and each increased his speed as far as possible, with the great ambition of being first to meet him.

In the times long ago, when these gates were in sight of the "quarter," they were most closely watched by the little negroes, who were trained to do so by the old ones having them in charge, and no one could approach without finding a little fellow there ready to open it and welcome him, who, in turn, seldom went without his recompense in the shape of a sevenpence, or a piece of tobacco for "granny." But this is all over with: who the loser will be, let the future tell.

As the gate was opened for Henry, the whole gang of little fellows crowded round his horse, to tell him "*howdy:*" some were fortunate enough to get his hand, while others got him by the feet, and others still had to content themselves by calling from the outside of the crowd: " Here I is, Mass Henry; howdy do, sah?" and gratuitously informing him: "I is well, sah; how is you?" Henry Brandon, the master, the protector, the friend, the *servant* of a hundred slaves, appeared quite as delighted with this meeting together of himself and little dependants as they did themselves, and answered every question it was possible for him to reply to, in the style of their own garrulous speech.

As they followed him to the house, closely packed about his horse's head, sides, and heels, each one was relating, in the highest key-note of his voice, some wonderful performance and qualities of his own, which were, of course, disputed by his nighest friend whenever he could get time, in the periods of his own narrative, to do so; but all united in promising to do some considerable service for "Mass Henry" before he went away again. Happy little creatures, many of whose lives were destined to end in the most squalid misery, through the mistaken philanthropy of those who came and proclaimed themselves good *friends*, and sang them siren songs of LIBERTY!

The old of the people, as they wander along in *friend-less freedom*, will sigh and weep again for the old master's care, and for the old quarter home, and in blind despair will oft reach out their long, thin hands for the string of the cabin latch. But alas! the door no longer swings upon the rustic hinge, and the old cabin has gone to decay, while they who called thee *free*, have early come to claim the guerdon of their work in thy *wretched suffrage*. Thy little ones are already taught to think the little masters of their early day, who joined them in their joyous evening songs and revelries, to be their only enemies. But time sets all things even, and then — and then — no matter now, 't is over.

Thou wert our household once — we knew thee, and we loved thee, too, but now, thou art estranged and gone away. Peace be unto thee! For the past, we thank thee; for the future, farewell!

As Henry Brandon entered the house, he was met by Violet and Thomas Hunter, who had come to the door for the purpose of learning the cause of the rather extra-ordinary discussion and clamor. Comprehending the nature of it in a moment, as they saw the retiring group, Hunter said to him, jocularly:

"A small imitation of Sir Roger de Coverley, Henry."

"Yes, an involuntary one, however; but a very noisy one. It was a scene for a painter. Do you recollect the painting, Hunter, that hangs in the rotunda at Washington, 'Saturday Evening in Old Virginia,' by Trumbull, I believe?"

"Very well; and it never failed to bring up a thousand home feelings."

"So it did with me; it was national in its character, as well as local in association, and I used to notice that it pleased even Yankees, who knew nothing of the South. That scene a while ago, would make a good picture to hang beside it: 'The return of the young master.' But I am glad to see you, Tom. I expected you this evening. That Friar Tuck sort of establishment of yours, over which you went into such ecstasies when first placed in proprietorship, I knew would soon stale, and lose all its charms. Do you remember those sylvan idyls you carolled of it, in your letters, when you first came home?"

"Very well; but then, my vain friend, do you forget that 'Buckhorns' hath other inmates than yourself, who may well divide the *honor* of my visit with you?"

"Well, Tom, I hurried away from the presence of my pretty cousins, to meet you here; and I think I shall be tempted to return, if you will confess that this visit was not to me, and that I am not under any obligation to entertain you."

"Just as you please, young man; but I shall make no *confessions*," said he, laughing.

"Young gentlemen, your salutations at the least have the recommendation of perfect ease: is such the college *à-la-mode?*" said Violet.

"Yes," said Henry, jocularly; "if no particular mode at all is *à la mode.*"

"No, Miss Violet, this is some new style which my hopeful friend has picked up in the last few months. During my stay there, we were the very pinks of etiquette; the knightly rules of the Round Table prevailed among us in all the noble punctilio of the court of King Arthur."

"I had half supposed as much; and that is just why, my brother, that Mr. Hunter has done this violence to his feelings, and created the impression that his visit is to mother and myself, when we are bound to believe that it was to yourself, as by the teachings of Sir Launcelot, Sir

Tristram, and other noble knights, females were given the preference and precedence in all things."

"Ah, Tom! behold what a defender you have in my learned sister — previous training, I suspect; and those heroics over at uncle Robert Brandon's, the other day, have had their full influence. 'All's well that ends well,' and has my sanction, too, always provided there is no fainting or 'sighing like a furnace' in my presence."

Hunter had been a familiar visitor at Mrs. Brandon's house since his boyhood, and had ever been an intimate friend of Henry Brandon in all the years of their youth and manhood, and consequently was not at all abashed by the insinuation that his visit was to Violet.

"Well, and what effect, Sir Knight, may we suppose your own assertion of love and fealty had upon the beautiful Lady Laura?" retorted Hunter.

"A very happy one," said Violet, "if any inference is to be drawn from the very pleasant humor in which he has returned from her presence. He must at least have intensified his relationship."

The three young people would no longer have restrained their rising laughter, had not Mrs. Brandon, who had just joined them, prevented it by saying, "Come, my daughter, you should not make a jest in that direction; you know that your brother feels almost as nigh to Laura as to yourself; and such jests get afloat so easily, that they assume all the proportions of a reality, which would certainly embarrass Laura, without serving Henry."

"Thank you, mother, for your reproof of these young folks. I feel that they deserve it, from a sort of bashfulness which had already begun to creep over me. But really, if the truth must be told, cousin Laura does begin to feel very *nigh* to me, more than I thought it possible for a cousin to become."

"Perhaps mother is right then; so, for the future, my

imprudent brother, I shall watch you, and take my revenge in some other quarter. Cousin Laura is not the only nice girl who has grown up within a day's ride of this, since you left for college;" and then looking at her brother, with a sly mischief lurking in her eye, said, "Henceforth pretty Laura Brandon shall only be COUSIN LAURA."

"Ah, sister, why not let me have a small love-pass or two with our lovely cousin before you enforce the Mosaic law. I can't say that I know anything of these matters actually, but it occurs to me that a gentle little affair of the heart with a sweet young cousin is the most natural thing on earth, and the very prettiest branch of love-making. One could just glide into it without ever knowing when or how, and only wake up to a consciousness of the truth by finding his whole soul filled with happiness. I become more charmed with the idea the longer I contemplate it. Rather think I must obtain some experience in that direction. But, in good truth, Violet, what maiden fair would you suggest in the place of our lovely cousin? provided I should consent only to call her *cousin.*"

"There are several."

"Well, out of your several, name some particular one."

"Yes, I will. Let me see. Suppose I say Miss Mary Gray, daughter of old Mr. Gray, in the lower prairies. She has just returned from Le Fabre's, in Richmond, and is said to be one of the finest-looking and best educated girls in the whole country. Old Mr. Gray, too, is said to be a most intelligent gentleman, and very wealthy, if these facts are of any importance to you."

"Certainly, very great. Are you acquainted with this fine-looking, well-educated Miss Gray, just from Le Fabre's school, and the daughter of old Mr. Gray, a gentleman of greatly reputed intelligence and wealth?"

"Yes — no; not exactly. I mean that I have *seen* her; but, brother, you appear so annoyed at the suggestion, that

I shall be more wary of bestowing my kind offices upon you."

"Oh, no, you are mistaken; far from it. The idea strikes me; it has some ring to it, and you make a very decidedly strong case of it. Fine-looking, highly educated, and of course young, and charming as a siren. Such rare combinations seldom meet in one person. How far is it over to the mansion of this old Mr. Gray and his beautiful daughter? I have forgotten all about that country."

"About eight or ten miles; probably not so far."

"Phew! sister, you certainly would not be reconciled to seeing me skylarking over eight or ten miles of prairies every few days, engaged in the doubtful labor of securing a sweetheart, merely to keep me from falling in love with one of the sweetest cousins any young gentleman ever boasted of — would you? On reflection, I don't think I can make the sacrifice; too great a draw on my humanity. Indeed, it would be placing myself in antagonism with Leander for posthumous fame. These prairies would be my Hellespont, and I should certainly come to grief in their passage — my horse certainly would. Never mention it again. It would be worse than any of the twelve labors of Hercules. No, I can't do that, not if she were as beautiful as Hebe. The only manner that suggests itself to me of solving the difficulty is for her to follow the example of the Queen of Sheba in her designs upon Solomon, and come to *see me*, or at least, as the Methodist preachers do, alternate visits with me. Ha! ha! ha! Do you think you could negotiate that point?"

"You misapprehend me, brother. I am not opposing you in having a little sentimental affair, as you call it, with cousin Laura, if you both desire it; but then you have forgotten aunt's peculiar disposition, her prejudices, in event of her not relishing the idea. You know she never yields a point, when she has once made up her mind, and cousin Laura never disobeyed her in her life."

Catching at the last idea, he said, "Then she would make me a most dutiful and loving *wife* — ay, I got the word out."

"No, not if she refused to marry you," said she, laughing.

"Oh, hush, Violet! you treat the matter as if already begun, and wish to nip my young passion in the bud. You compel me to take down all my castles in the air."

"You confess, then, to have been engaged in castle-building, with cousin Laura for your lady-love?"

"Certainly; who could resist it — who *would?* She has the chastest, loveliest face, says the brightest things, sings the prettiest love-songs; and to all of this, the very spirit of love itself seems to swim in her eyes. But, never mind, you have frightened me away. Eight miles — ten, did you say, over to old jockey Gray's, and only *three* to Mr. Robert Brandon's — two and a half by the near way? Terrible difference! But, ho for the maiden ten miles away! How old did you say?"

"About nineteen, I think."

"What the color of her eyes?"

"Deep blue."

"Fine, again! Hair black, of course? Don't like your pale-haired girls — too namby-pamby and weakly, like pale sorrel horses — rather have blood-red. Tall, or short?"

"Quite tall, with a superb figure and walk."

"Most excellent — grand! I can't bear your short, shambling, scuffling little women — generally conceited and petulant; but the devil of it is, I believe the *tall* ones are too. You do not know whether she sings and dances?"

"No; but I suppose she does, as she was educated at a very fashionable school. Old Mr. Gray, however, is an

7

enthusiastic Methodist, endows their colleges, builds their churches, and supports their preachers, and all that sort of thing."

" What? That's a bad feature in the affair: I fear the old man has n't 'much ready cash wherewithal to endow this lovely daughter. Wonder if she knows how to *cook?* That's the chief excellence in a girl. Yes, give me one that understands making apple-dumplings — 'them's the jockeys for me,' as the cockney English traveller in Venice said to poor Shelley."

" I can't say as to her cooking capacity," said she, laughing; " but I think Mr. Gray must have a great deal of money, as I have heard he makes good crops and good bargains; and perhaps Miss Gray does know how to *cook.*"

" Yes — well — the idea you give me of the old gentleman's character is, that he drives his negroes, as if the devil was after him, all the week, and pinches and screws his friends and neighbors, to obtain the wherewithal to purchase an interest in heaven on the next *meeting*-day."

" No; that is not the character I have of him: I have always heard that he was an enthusiastic Methodist, a strong Whig, a very energetic, thrifty man, but a very liberal and a very hospitable one."

" The last sounds very well; but the Methodist part — oh, heavens! Do you suppose the divine demoiselle belongs to that unhappy, self-torturing denomination?"

" She probably does, but, I fancy, without any of their old-fashioned peculiarities. She might follow you, brother," said she, smiling.

" Perhaps she might; I should certainly not follow her. Now, I don't so dislike the Methodist people — they are as good, perhaps, as others; but then they have talked so much about free will, free grace, hell-fire, and such-like matters, until their leaders always look to be in agony, lest, by some misstep, they fall flat into the *bottomless* pit;

and I have heard them pray with as much imploring unction as if already partially into it."

"Come, brother, you should be more particular in what
you say: we have some friends who belong to that church."

"I can't help it, if all my friends belonged to it; but I
will remember your caution. Mary Gray—a very pretty
name—handsome, young, accomplished, wealthy; father
builds churches, etc. On the other hand, Laura Brandon
—a majestic name! But, never mind, I'll think the
matter over. In the mean while it is growing dark. Suppose we go into the house."

At this suggestion, they walked into the drawing-room,
which had already been lighted up, Violet and Hunter
going directly to the piano, while Henry flung himself
upon the sofa, as worried with his own thoughts, and
indifferent to the promised music.

After selecting some favorite pieces of music, Hunter
turned to Henry, who had not spoken a word, and said:

"Henry, Miss Violet and I have brought the science
of music to its highest *provincial* proficiency. Of course,
we do not pretend to come in comparison with the metro-
politan masters of either this country or Germany; but
we will allow *you* to call for whatever you admire most,
whether march, waltz, or song."

"You can make the challenge with impunity, Hunter,
since you know, of old, that my musical tastes and attainments reach no higher than singing, out of tune, some
half-dozen old songs, beginning with the 'Rose of Allan-
dale,' and ending with 'Twilight Dews.' However, since
you left college, I branched off into sacred music a short
distance, and can now go through a stave or two of 'Old
Hundred' with a very commendably solemn fervor."

"*That* accomplishment may be of some assistance to you,
my son," said Mrs. Brandon, pleasantly, who had just seated
herself on the sofa by him. "Should you see proper to

embrace the suggestion which I think I overheard your sister make to you."

"Ah, I fear, mother, that Violet and you are in some universal conspiracy against any connubial hope that I may entertain. I had but just begun to think formally of the 'Mary Gray' idea, when forthwith you make a sly fling at the family of my contemplated lady-love."

"You misapprehend me, Henry," she again good-humoredly replied. "I only made the remark in the same vein of pleasantry in which you yourself indulged."

"I accept the explanation, mother; but then I see that the lovely Miss Gray is associated in your mind with psalm tunes, long agonizing prayers, and the whole framework of Methodism; but that shall make no difference with me now. I have taken the matter under consideration, at least —Methodism; plantation, money, and all. Hunter, you and Violet to the music."

Hunter performed handsomely on the flute, and had one which he kept at Mrs. Brandon's, for the purpose of joining Violet on the piano, when visiting there.

They had already begun, and, like all real lovers of music, became absorbed in their own sweet sounds, and paid but little attention to what was going on around them —while Henry Brandon, seated on the sofa with his mother, gradually fell into an undertone conversation with her, in the course of which, he asked if there was not some sort of engagement between Hunter and his sister.

"Yes, he has addressed her, and there is some understanding between them, which I have not thought proper to interfere with."

"I have thought, from several little moves in his conversation, that he wished to broach the subject, but seemed to retire from it again, as if a little too sensitive; and my reason for speaking to him so jocularly this evening, was for the purpose of opening the way for his doing so: he understood it, and will speak to me now. He used to show me the letters he received from her; and though there was no more apparent feeling in them than warm friendship, I could see, in some allusions she made to his, that there was a little sly love-making in them; and then he always spoke of her in a very different strain from that in which he spoke of other girls."

The two young performers concluding a piece at this moment, Henry asked if they played a new song, called the "Carrier Dove."

"Oh, yes! it is one of our favorite songs."

"I am happy to be so highly endorsed; then, as Hamlet might say —*play on.*"

CHAPTER XI.

"For just experience tells, in ev'ry soil,
   That those who think must govern those that toil."
                                            GOLDSMITH.

THIS sort of animated and desultory intercourse, such as we have described, had been going on for several weeks between the Brandon families and their young friends; and Henry had learned to be more cautious in his style of conversation before his aunt, from the frequent hints to that effect from both Lucy and Laura, and was getting along with her rather pleasantly; although he was now well assured that she was suspicious of his intentions, and would be bitterly opposed to any alliance between him and Laura, on the score of their relationship — a not uncommon prejudice in most families.

The two daughters of Mr. Brandon had just concluded a very pleasant visit of two days to Violet, which it may be supposed Henry Brandon had enjoyed after his own

7 *

fashion, and, with his sister, had accompanied them home. Henry was met by his uncle with a most cordial pleasure; and invited by him to come the next morning and accompany him to ——, where he had an appointment with Colonel Haywood; to which he very readily consented, promising to be over early next morning. They remained but a short time; and while riding along on their return, the conversation turned on Laura, when Violet said:

"Brother, I think cousin Laura certainly the sweetest girl I ever saw. I love her more and more every time I see her; and I don't blame you for loving her a *little*, which I know you do; but then I would advise you to be particular, and go no farther with it, as aunt will certainly oppose you."

"Yes, I see the good lady has her eye on me; but she need have no fears. I do admire Laura greatly, and always did love her a little, as you say, outside cousin bounds; but aunt need not make herself disagreeable about it now, any more than she might have done ten years ago, as she really is beginning to be to me; and which I dislike on Laura's account: were it not for her, it would afford me some pleasure just now to hate aunt a good deal."

"Yes, and you show it just about as much as she shows her suspicion—and the girls see it; and, therefore, I really think it best for you to make the acquaintance of some other girls, just to divert her attention from you. You have scarcely visited any others since your return."

"Why, have you forgotten that I have been several times to call on Julia Hunter and Miss Sally Morton?"

"But then they were mere formal calls."

"Yes, I know; but I do not wish to get in the way of this young Dr. Wilton, who is said to be an accepted admirer of Julia's, and of our Rev. pastor, Mr. Irwin, Miss Sally's beau."

"Oh! you would not be in their way. I do not mean

that you shall go there in an old-fashioned courting way; but as an easy, friendly visitor, which would be very agreeable to you, as there are few girls more accomplished than they are, and no family more pleasant to visit; all of which you know. It would, too, divert aunt's attention from your visits to Laura, the exclusiveness of which evidently annoys her."

"That is very sensible sort of advice, and I must pay some attention to it, my most sagacious sister."

"Day after to-morrow, uncle Robert and Colonel Haywood are to speak at Gregory's Spring: the only two appointments they have in this county are at ——, to-morrow, and at Gregory's the next day. At Gregory's, I think, every one that can, will be present, when you can see all the finest girls of this portion of the country; and I will suggest that we all go."

"A very nice trip, and we must get it up."

Conversing quietly in this manner upon various matters, their ride was pleasantly passed off.

The morning after this, Henry Brandon left home quite early, designing to take breakfast at his uncle's, and to go with him to ——, according to the appointment of the evening before.

The uncle and nephew left the residence of the former in time to reach —— at ten o'clock, at which time the speaking was to commence.

In the course of conversation, while riding along, Henry asked who this Colonel Haywood was, as it was a new name to him.

"Yes, it is; he has not resided but a few years in the State."

"Is he a man of mind?"

"He is, indeed, a man of genius, education, and temper, and a complete representative of the extremest ultraism of the South Carolina State-rights doctrine."

"I should judge him then to be an unpleasant competitor in debate."

"Yes, he is not as agreeable as I have seen. He is disposed, if permitted, to be imperious in his manners, and presumes quite as much on the timidity of his opponent, as he does on his own courage. He is insinuating in his innuendoes, bold in his assertions, plausible in his arguments, quick to take advantage of the weak points of his adversary, very fluent, at least can command in a moment every word that he knows the meaning of, and at times impassioned, though not a very eloquent speaker."

"He is rather a dangerous opponent, I should take it."

"Yes, very truly, a dangerous opponent, not only to me, but, in his daring character, will some day prove more so to the country."

"I shall begin to believe that you think yourself full matched, uncle," said Henry, smiling.

"I know I am. Colonel Haywood is a full match for any one in popular debate, though not a statesman, and his fallacies are easily detected. But he has that faculty which Mr. Calhoun possesses most eminently, of impressing his audience with the idea that he is particularly their *friend*, and then being the advocate of a sort of mixed agrarianism and aggression, he carries the *populace* even farther than his *party* can do it. His manner, however, is very different from Mr. Calhoun's. Mr. Calhoun is really a very sincere man, and infuses the sentiment of his truth into everything he says — always calm, generally logical in his deductions, whether his premises be correct or not, and truly believes that he is ever battling for the South, as he resists her hypothetical wrongs. Colonel Haywood, as I have said, has a very different manner, yet comes out pretty much at the same point. He is very courageous, impassioned, ambitious, and some call him eloquent, but he is not: he is only an orator, and by a sort of electric influence, which passion only can exert, he inflames the feelings of the multitude with the fire of his own heart. While he does not inspire that perfect personal confidence which Mr. Calhoun does, he yet moves his audience pretty much at his will."

At this point in their conversation they had arrived in sight of the town of ——, where a very large number of citizens from that part of the country had already assembled.

At the appointed hour, Colonel Haywood ascended the stand, and delivered one of his best efforts. He was at this time a practising lawyer of high reputation in the State, and master of all the arts of fiery declamation, and considered one of the very finest speakers of his party. About forty years old, he exactly occupied that line of demarcation between youth and age, when a speaker of ability comes before an audience with all the advantages of both, being at liberty to enter the fields of fact and of close argument, supposed to be the peculiar forte of experience and cool judgment, and not only excused, but encouraged, by applause, to wander off in the brighter realms of declamation and daring oratory. This advantage Colonel Haywood used with surprising art and a terrible power. On the present occasion he began with a high-wrought eulogy on the *stern virtue* and *Roman integrity* of the MASSES! This cajoling of the thoughtless, ignorant multitude into a belief of its great excellence and superior intelligence, had from early times been steadily growing into a systematic demagoguism; and, while feeling the very least of it himself, he used it with wonderful effect. This wretched flattery had, at length, become almost the necessary political sustenance of the masses, and placed them perfectly in the power of the ambitious leaders, who, through them, precipitated the South on her ruin in 1860 — destroying almost the least resemblance to a republican government.

If all of the which shall have the effect of deterring any and all other peoples from endeavoring to establish such a political absurdity as a democratic republic, demagoguism will still be entitled to the thanks of the world.

On this occasion, Colonel Haywood eulogized, in the very highest terms of laudation, the doctrine of *State-sovereignty*, as recognized by the Constitution, and elaborated in the celebrated resolutions of '98–'99. He then apostrophized the shade of Jefferson, as the first and chief apostle of those sublime truths, and as the author of that almost inspired scroll, the Declaration of Independence, whose blazing light had sent a knowledge of human rights into all the dark despotisms of the earth, and told all the nations of the great truth, that men were born *free* and *equal,* and endowed by nature with the right of self-government.

He next condemned the Tariff, United States Bank, as measures growing out of the "monarchical, Federal, Whig party," of which Mr. Clay was the founder and defender, and concluded his masterpiece of sophistry and declamation with a second high-wrought eulogy of the masses, ending by crying out, "Vox populi, vox Dei."

Colonel Haywood subsequently acquired a leading reputation in the South, and was, indeed, a very remarkable man — such an one as society seldom develops or nature produces — and to the day of his death retained that strange power of holding his friends under fire long after all *hope* was *lost*, and still held the confidence of his party, however unpopular as a man, to the very end.

When the darkest hour that ever threw its gloom over the civilization of a people, and hung as a funeral pall over the high mountains, the sweet valleys, the broad plains, and lovely homes of the South, and when the "bonny blue flag" floated over the battle-field — representative of his long-cherished hope — he fearlessly sat upon the wing of the storm and cheered the havoc of the fray.

There were those whose souls knew no mortal fear — whose minds, in most part, were equal to his own — who foresaw the terrible results of his desperate counsels — and yet a glance from his fiery eye, and a menacing gesture from his hand, hushed their voices as with the stillness of the tomb.

Wellnigh at his bidding alone, a handful of his countrymen went out to the tented field, and measured arms with the hosts of the tributary world; and for four dreary, bloody years, with a valor unequalled for its chivalry and its deeds, not only held that host at defiant bay, but swept the best-appointed armies of the world out of existence, and tearing the laurels from the brows of their greatest captains, dashed them to the earth with a laughing, but a bitter scorn.

Such was Colonel Haywood, and such the armies *he* enrolled. We know their fate. The future will do them justice — the present cannot.

CHAPTER XII.

"No opinions so fatally mislead us as those not totally wrong, as no watches so effectually deceive us as those that are sometimes right."

COLTON.

SO soon as Colonel Haywood had concluded his speech, Mr. Brandon was enthusiastically called for by his friends, and ascended the stand amid their deafening applauses. He was the senior of Colonel Haywood by a few years, but far more *distingué* in his person, above the ordinary height, easy and elegant in his motion, with not a particle of affectation of any kind, and considered one of the handsomest men of his day.

Socially, no man was more highly regarded by all classes,

and known to be, too, one of the most chaste, classical, and eloquent speakers in the State. As has somewhere been said of another, he " wreathed the club of Hercules with the garlands of the Muses," and had, on these accounts, been selected as elector, with especial reference to meeting Colonel Haywood in the canvass, which had early promised to be a heated and a bitter one.

The speeches of Democratic candidates, up to the very moment of the dissolution of the party — albeit, as a universal fact — were made up of unmeaning generalities, which had gradually become incorporated into their *platforms*, and which its orators were expected to reiterate to the ignorant masses: these, together with such eulogies as we have already mentioned upon the superior intelligence of " *the people*," made up the warp and woof of their addresses.

In this manner, but little argument was necessary in reply to them — as argument will not be listened to by the man whose immaculate intelligence may be disproven, when the endorsement of the assertion is the criterion of its truth, and the sweetest aliment to his ignorance and his vanity.

In replying to Colonel Haywood, Mr. Brandon said, when coming to speak of Mr. Jefferson, that he looked upon him neither as a myth nor anything sacred, but a mere man, mortal, finite, and erring, from whom nothing more extraordinary had issued than his errors — or, at best, but the ideas of a strong and peculiar, but warped mind, which, even in its great ability, had committed mistakes of the first magnitude. As the author of that terrible absurdity that "all men are born free and equal," he was certainly, as has been claimed for him, the founder of the Democratic party.

That the prominent idea in that " burning scroll," so magniloquently alluded to, was a social, moral, and intellectual heresy of the first water, which, from indications already given out, was bound to result, at some future time, in shedding the most baleful rays, social and political. That all men were not born free and equal; and the absurdity of the assertion was too manifest to justify even an attempt at refutation; and for the utterance of this sublime hallucination, Mr. Jefferson did not merit canonization.

In regard to the Tariff, he said it was more of a Southern measure than a Northern one, if the South could only be induced to look at it calmly, with the fact before her of an unsurpassed adaptability for manufacturing to advantage — in climate, production, and water-power. That the South was comparatively poor, just from the want of an internal commerce. That negro slavery was not wealth — rather the absorption of it; and as an investment of capital, was bad, because of its producing but little more than its own support, producing nothing new, but only *reproducing itself*. That Yankee *moralists* had found it out at an early day of the experiment, and had long ago *fobbed* their interest in the *wicked traffic*, and could well afford to *pray* for emancipation. "When slavery," said he, "in some way shall become modified, and loosed in its grasp upon our purse-strings — as the philosophy of its manifest · introduction teaches us it will be when the original causes for it shall cease — then the South will cease to be that 'purely agricultural country' so foolishly boasted of, and, entering on a system of manufacturing labor in connection with its production, become the leading country of the earth."

In conclusion, he made a very handsome defence of Mr. Clay and the Whig party, and retired amid the thundering cheers of his friends.

During the canvass between Mr. Clay and Mr. Polk, political excitement ran very high in the South. The partisans of either appearing to identify themselves with their

8

political champion, was often the cause of much violence. The truth was, that the friends of Mr. Clay — than whom no political leader in this country was ever more personally loved — had become exasperated at the causeless slanders of him by Democratic leaders, and were ready now to make his cause an individual one.   It was from some reason like this, that, very soon after the speaking was over, a difficulty took place, of a most tragic character, between an old man and his son on the Whig side, and two brothers on the other, in which one on each side, immediately killed, fell a sacrifice to their parties, and each of the others, very severely wounded.

The old man Miller and his son were planters, and very respectable citizens; but, while peaceable, were known to be quick-tempered and resolute.   Conceiving insult, from the use of some bantering language on the part of the two Democrats, they at once made an attack upon them, which resulted in one of the most sanguinary rencontres of even that day of bowie-knives and broils.   Young Miller, who was one of those who escaped with his life, was yet badly wounded, and was removed to an hotel, where he was compelled to remain for several weeks before even being able to appear before the proper officer on preliminary trial. At length there was a day appointed for this purpose, and the case was decided to be a bailable one, when his political as well as personal friends united in making a bond for his appearance at the next court.

After his recovery, his whole character seemed to undergo a change — from the gay and frolicsome young planter, he became the most perfect outlaw, and seemed implacably exasperated against the Democratic party.

On the first day of the next court, he appeared within the bar, accompanied by his bondsmen, and surrendered himself formally to the sheriff.   This operated as a release to those who had gone security for his presence; but after sitting, seemingly with indifference, for some time, he carelessly picked up his hat, and walked out, apparently with the intention of returning; but, by arrangement, his horse was near by, and mounting him, never appeared there again.

Scenes of violence had been of such common occurrence up to about this period, that we should scarcely have taken occasion to give the details we have, were it not this one afterward became slightly complicated with the fortunes of our young friend, Mr. Henry Brandon.

It was near the middle of the afternoon before the excitement in regard to the difficulty had in the least subsided, and there being continually recurring probabilities of fresh difficulties growing out of the Miller affair, Mr. Brandon remained, for the purpose of allaying them, which his well-known courage, and good feeling, and good sense, enabled him to do with more success, probably, than any other man in the county. The political features of the difficulty gradually died away, as the time approached for men to leave for their homes; and Mr. Brandon, seeing that all probability of further troubles had passed off, began looking around for his nephew, and also for Mr. Campbell and young Hunter, who had promised to return with him. The two last were soon found, but Henry was nowhere to be seen — when it occurred to Hunter that as he was an old boy-friend of young Miller, he might have gone to see him. Immediately going to the hotel, he there, indeed, found him in Miller's room, assisting to make him comfortable.

When he saw Thomas Hunter enter the room, he immediately knew the purpose, and turning to Miller, told him that he would have to leave him, but would return in a few days to see him.

Miller had not before seen young Brandon since his return, and appeared greatly pleased with the attention, and begged him to come again as soon and as often as he could.

In company with Hunter, he now went to the appointed place of meeting with Mr. Brandon, and very soon after the party were on the road to the country.

CHAPTER XIII.

"Where be your gibes now? your gambols? your songs? your flashes of merriment, that were wont to set the table on a roar?"—SHAKSPEARE.

CONVERSING over the various incidents of the day, as they rode along, the time passed off very pleasantly until they reached the point whereat the roads divided — one going to Mr. Robert Brandon's, the other to Henry's own home. Here they seemed to come to an involuntary halt, when Mr. Brandon said :

"Here — why do you stop, young gentlemen? I believe you are all under contract to go home with me to-night, and to accompany me to-morrow to Gregory's Spring."

"Yes, uncle, we are under promise to go with you to-morrow; but my understanding of it was," said Henry, laughing, "that the young gentlemen were to accompany me home to-night, and go by for you in the morning."

"I think, Henry, they are my guests, as they certainly came out at my request."

"Yes, that was so ; but I think there was an after arrangement, to the effect that I speak of."

"Well, I will leave it to the young gentlemen themselves to say," said Mr. Brandon, who saw that his nephew was jesting.

"Oh, no," he replied, breaking out in a laugh ; "but I

will make a fair division of spoils, and give you first choice
of the three of us."

Although Henry knew his own selection would make
Hunter and Campbell feel a little awkward in going to his
mother's without him, he slyly hoped that his uncle would
choose him. But Mr. Brandon, pleasantly accepting the
compromise, invited young Campbell. They now separated, and Henry and his friend rode off at a merry pace,
and were not long in reaching home. On getting there,
however, he was a little surprised at finding his mother and
sister absent; but a note from Violet was handed to him,
saying, that "her mother and herself had concluded to
make a visit to 'Starlight,' in the morning after he left, and
that since that time they had determined on remaining
till the next day; that he must come over, and bring Mr.
Hunter, if he was with him."

Henry then asked Hunter to his room, where the two
young gentlemen readjusted their dress for that evening,
and even prepared for the next day, at the expense of the
former's wardrobe.

While dressing and making their preparations, Henry
appeared even so unusually animated and happy, that
Hunter was induced to ask him the cause of it.

"You appear very uncommonly delighted, my good fellow, with the prospect of getting to your uncle's. Shall I
pass it to the credit of that excellent gentleman himself,
to your equally excellent aunt, to the beautiful Lucy, or,
indeed, to the sweet face of our lovely cousin, Laura?
Come, out with it, Henry, and tell me, in a good old-fashioned way, the especial name of that little secret emotion
which plays with such pleasure on your face, and imparts
such unusual animation?"

"Hunter, you astonish me. For one who has always
prided himself on his power to read the heart by the face,
to even approach such a misapprehension, all but surpasses

8 *

credulity. Now, sir, if you had only a tenth part of the keen perception which you claim, you would discover at a glance that my face only expressed an *intellectual* emotion — a very sharp desire, with the prospect of gratification, of becoming better informed of, or more fully initiated into, the mysteries of Whiggery. You would have seen, also, that the lovely face of my cousin Laura had no claim whatever in these aforesaid emotions. You can believe me, Hunter, as you know that I would not deceive you," saying this with a manifest jocularity.

Hunter replied, "No, no, never! I must give you credit for that, both in the past and in the *present,* as your jesting words of denial, your manner, emphasis, look, and emotion, all speak for themselves. And my opinion is, that our sweet cousin, Laura Brandon, has touched some deep - hidden, delicate chord of your frolicsome heart, which no other damsel has ever done in any of your rollicking flirtations. Though I cannot say that you are 'in love,' yet it occurs to me that you are nigher falling into the gossamer web of the 'rosy god' than ever before."

"Hunter, you frighten me, man — yea, you agitate me to my deepest foundations — you knock the devil's conceit out of me. I have never thought of falling 'in love' since I was sixteen."

"And who was that with, but Laura Brandon?" said Hunter, interrupting him.

"I have only thought of girls falling in love with me," said he, not appearing to hear him; "nor am I willing to acknowledge anything else till yet. Though I am really afraid for you to make any of your *d—d* prophecies, for you know I always looked upon you as half wizard, guilty of holding communion with evil spirits;" and then adding, "Tom, do you talk in your sleep as much as ever?"

"Yes, I expect so, as I never did it: that was a scandal

of your own. I sleep very silently and innocently, as I always did."

"Pity your innocence did not come sooner, before cracking that fellow's skull; you might have remained at college a few months longer. A fig for your innocence! Tom, have you never been mad with yourself for that thoughtless difficulty?"

"Yes, a thousand times; but innocent or not, I was never in half the difficulties that you were — no, not a tenth."

"Oh, me — difficulties! I was born to difficulties, and I expect to die in one. They come naturally, not even involving the question of guilt or innocence. They are my *natural element*, as Miss Gibbons said to me the last time I called upon her, while speaking of her poetical tastes and feelings, and reciting a very touching effusion of her own."

Both breaking out in a laugh at this, Hunter asked him how he deported himself during the recital.

"I grasped the back of the sofa convulsively, and most rigidly clenched my teeth, while I rolled my eyes up like an ox in the agonies of death, and ever and anon grunted out, '*Charming.*' What the devil else could I do?"

"What has become of her?" asked Hunter, when sufficiently recovered from his convulsive laughter.

"She is there yet, I suppose, waiting to marry Potter, that Congregational beneficiary who was in our class, and will do so, as soon as he receives the preliminaries of ordination, and procures some village pulpit from which to *fumigate* the gospel. You know these fellows do not have any trouble in regard to the sanctity of the priesthood. All they require is some sort of plebiscit to preach, which they get after learning something of the Synod of Dort, Martin Luther, Calvin, and old John Knox, predestination and election, hell-fire, etc."

"You are disposed to be severe on our old Yankee friends."

"No, you know what I say is the truth."

"But you have not told me all about Miss Gibbons."

"Oh, no. Well, I called upon her, just out of a sort of old habit, the day before I left, as I told you, when this affair of the poetry took place. I had often heard that she was engaged to Potter, and therefore thought it would be safe to make a little harmless love to her, particularly as she would always remember it as quite a distinguished honor to have been made love to by a young Southerner. So I began by very seriously alluding to the many happy hours I had spent in her society, and the regret which my departure would occasion me. After a few other silly remarks of this sort, I thought I would go a little farther, and added, that having heard of her engagement with Mr. Potter, I should leave with *less* regret, however, than I otherwise should; and a good deal more of such stuff; when, without my in the least looking for such a scene, she put her handkerchief to her face, and extended me her hand!"

"What?"

"Extended me her hand!"

"The old scratch! What did you do then, my gay Lothario? Ha! ha!! ha!!! Tell me, or I die."

"Well, I took it, placed it to my lips very gently, but slightly *bit* her *finger*."

"What?"

"Bit her finger very gently."

Hunter crying out, "Oh, heavens!" both roared out in laughter, and Henry Brandon continued:

"What in the name of common sense was I to do? The thing was becoming too *tender*."

"Pshaw, boy! Tell me what you really did do."

"Well, to tell the truth, I kissed her extended hand,

and heaving a deep-drawn sigh, just sufficiently audible for her to hear, left the house while the scene was at its culmination — but precipitately, I assure you — for I found that she was not all clay in Potter's hands, and having no need of such myself, thought it best to escape in the dust of our *grief*."

At this there was another peal of laughter. Brandon then again added:

"This scene happened, Tom, just as I have told it, and you know I do not tell it in any *vanity*, but as a good joke, and a good illustration of the sort of estimation in which Southern young men are held by Northern girls. Seven in ten of them would turn off a good, clever Yankee for an indifferent Southerner, and I am almost at a loss to account for it. There is Potter, for instance, who in a few months will obtain 'orders' to preach. Some village will *call* him, and, of course, he will accept. Some few mechanics, laborers, servant-girls, or *helps*, with a small sprinkling of those who call themselves the *better classes*, will be his congregation. For his salary he will get a pittance of money, some contributions of apples, potatoes, with now and then a cutlet of veal, a few butternuts, and an occasional present of maple sugar. In addition to this, he may get charge of the village free-school, and be chosen president of the Female Beneficent Society, or of an Abolition Society. Altogether, he will pick up a very good sort of living, and become a man of some note among his particular class of people. Now all of this *brilliant* prospect she was willing to throw away, just to get a Southerner, of whom she knew nothing, and who, it is quite probable, will never reach such *heights* in his own country."

They were now ready to ride, and going out to the gate, found "Sam Brandon" holding their horses, and one for himself, saying:

"Mass Henry, I could'n bar the thoughts of seein' you

go by you'self in the night so. You might want some 'sistance : so I cotch a hoss for myself."

"All right, Sam ; I am obliged to you." Mounting, they rode off rapidly.

Hunter continued the conversation, by saying, "Yes, you are right, Henry, in your ideas of Northern character, and there is some deep-laid ethnological reason for it. Women are all creatures of emotion, and have much higher instincts than men. The latter protects them, to some extent, against the influences of the former. In most all instances, these attributes give them a keen insight into the leading points of character of the opposite sex, and Northern women discover in the character of the Southerner something that better pleases them than in their own men."

"Hunter, your remarks broach a doctrine which I was laughed at, just before leaving college, for advancing — a *difference* of *race* between the Northern and Southern people. The Yanks can't bear it ; but the differences so often spoken of are not accidental, but fundamental — organic."

"Come, come," said Hunter, interrupting him, "the subject of Yankee idiosyncrasies is not a fit one for young Southerners on a night ride to see their sweethearts."

"Well, no ; perhaps you are right ; but I object to your classification, Tom. You can keep it for yourself, if you wish."

The suddenness of this sort of retort, or correction rather, confused Hunter, who replied :

"Well, Henry, just as you please ; but, my dear fellow, I very unwarily gave you that advantage ; but my idea was to please *you*, and you should have been more generous than to have used it so unkindly, as to drive me either into a confession or a denial."

"Ah, as you appeal to my generosity, I will excuse you

from a reply, but will reserve the right to construe your silence into a confession of the general truth."

"Your generosity takes a very singular direction, and forces me into a dilemma. I had better get the credit of an open avowal at once."

"So be it, and let me play Father-Confessor. Now, my erring, mortal son, I hear there be three maidens fair, not many miles away, one of whom you have impliedly asserted to be my lady-love, and there be two others yet, who rejoice in the pretty names of Lucy and Violet; now choose ye, before which of these fair damsels ye shall bow in your devotions."

"As thou dost give me choice, most Holy Father, I will select the lady Violet."

"So be it, then, thou unhappy son of man, and victim of a maiden's toils : yet thou hast my blessing."

The dashing eccentricity which Henry Brandon had thus given to the conversation, at once relieved Hunter of an embarrassment which, he said, had "been weighing upon him for several weeks," and in the next moment he spoke to Brandon, in modest terms, of the long-felt preference for his sister, and said he hoped it would not be unpleasing to him.

Henry replied, "That he so well knew his feelings towards him, that it was unnecessary to assure him of his approbation." Then, laughing, asked his pardon for forcing him into a confession of attachment for his own sister.

"I am obliged to you, Henry, for doing so, as I knew that you had been told of it, and I was only waiting to overcome my bashfulness sufficiently to speak to you respecting it."

"'All's well that ends well,' you know, is one of my favorite old maxims; so for the present let's ride faster — ride to our ladies' bowers on the wings of love," and gave his horse the rein.

"I thank thee, most Reverent Father."

"Agreed as to that; but now answer the question I first put to you — Is the anxiety to meet with your cousin or your sweetheart?"

Young Brandon, laughing, as if the subject were not a disagreeable one to him, said:

"'Still harping on my daughter.' Well, Hunter, I will tell you all I know, and leave you to decide on it. To begin at the beginning, you remember the ludicrous meeting in the grove?"

"Yes, of course."

"Well, when I first met her, I cannot say that I was 'in love' with her, though we were acknowledged sweethearts when we were young, and you know we corresponded quite regularly while I was at college."

"Yes."

"In my letters, I frequently alluded to the fact of a certain promise she was under to me, to which she always assented; but I had been away from her four years, and cannot be supposed to have been very deeply enamored when I returned, and when I knelt before her, it was as pure a piece of impromptu extravagance as ever entered an idle head to perpetrate. But while going on with the nonsense, I saw the same little gold ring on her finger that I had placed there the last time we met; straightway the ardent love of boyhood came back upon me, I do believe, and when I rose, I could not resist the inclination to kiss her pretty, pouting, laughing lips; and I should have done it, if every uncle and watching aunt, from Noah's time till now, had been present. When I placed my arm around her neck, she gave such a look of innocent surprise out of her soft blue eyes, that I had to stop for a moment to gaze into the mystic depths of their almost angelic beauty. And now, may my dear aunt forgive me, but I really believe myself hopelessly in love with her daughter, and to-night

I intend to call her sweetheart, out and out, even if it brings upon me the bitter hate of my most *affectionate* relative, Mrs. R. Brandon, which I believe it will do."

They had now reached the gate of "Starlight," where a servant stood waiting to take charge of their horses, and still another to take them to a private room, to prepare, before entering the drawing-room. They were then informed that other visitors were there for the evening.

CHAPTER XIV.

"She was a form of life and light,
That, seen, became a part of sight."

AFTER Henry had left in the morning, Violet proposed to her mother to go over and spend the day at "Starlight," which, after a little persuasion, was consented to, Mrs. Brandon having no idea that her daughter had any ulterior purpose in view, further than the pleasure of Laura's and Lucy's company for the day.

The family at "Starlight" were delighted at seeing the carriage drive up, and met Violet and her mother with that usual pleasure which the presence of either family ever gave the other.

It was not a great while before the two elderly ladies were left alone by their daughters, who, by some understood sign from Violet, withdrew to another room, where their whole plan was discussed and determined upon, which was nothing more nor less than an extemporized dancing party that evening, made up of such of their young friends in the neighborhood as could be notified in time. So far as *they* were concerned, the whole enterprise was very soon matured; and the only thing left to be done, was getting the consent of their mothers, which they now left the scene of their conclave for the purpose of obtaining. The request was granted without hesitation, further than by Violet's mother asking, if that had been her purpose in wishing to visit her cousins that morning? Violet laughingly admitted that it was, and would have told her of it; but fearing it possible, at least, that it might not be thought practicable, concluded it was as well to say nothing of it.

Mrs. Brandon laughed at the cunning; but told her she must write to her brother, so that he would know the cause of their absence.

"Oh, certainly; we could have no party without brother, Thomas Hunter, and Mr. Campbell; both of the latter, I am satisfied, will come home with either brother or uncle."

It was then decided to whom each one of the girls was to write. Laura, by general consent, being considered the favorite of Mr. Parson Jerome, was to write to him, and to invite Dr. Wilton also, a young physician who lived with him and practised medicine from his house; while Lucy was to write to Miss Julia Hunter, and Miss Sally Morton; the latter being an orphan relation of Judge Hunter, and a member of his family.

As we have grouped all of our young friends without previous introduction, it may be expected, perhaps, that we shall say something of them *seriatim*. Henry Brandon, Thomas Hunter, and Mr. Campbell, we have already had before us. Mr. Jerome, the young parson who had recently been called to the charge of the parish, was a gentleman who had grown up in the neighborhood; and was at this time living on the plantation which he had inherited from parents, who were long since dead, about five miles distant from Mr. Brandon's. Dr. Wilton was his very early college friend, before he had united himself to the Church; and while playing the role, in common parlance, of a "very wild young man." After the return of Mr. Jerome to the old paternal estate, he had been invited by him to make his house his home, it being an excellent point from which to practise his profession.

Miss Julia Hunter was the sister of Thomas Hunter, and the daughter of Judge Hunter, a very accomplished gentleman and wealthy planter, who resided but a few miles away. Miss Hunter was a pretty sensible girl, about nineteen, and quite well-known to be admired by Dr Wilton, who, however, had never visited her at her father's house, having only met her, up to this time, at church, or at one or the other of the Brandon families. And now last, but not the least of this little circle of young friends, let me say a few words of Sally Morton, for she was a friend of ours, in that long-gone day which we call our youth; and gallantry forbids that we should pass her over without more than a mere cold, passing introduction to our readers.

Surrounded even by the pleasantest circumstances, age hath but little to cheer it in its twilight walk, outside the recollection of its early friends and its early joys. Nature, however, seems kindly to rekindle these morning memories, as the casualties of time add to our sorrows. And now, as we stand amid the wrecks of fortune, and well-nigh upon the grave of hope, surrounded, too, by the most wretched revolutionary and anarchical elements, we live over again with a sweeter zest, the bright and happy scenes of our better days.

But humanity will still be frail humanity; and as we turn back to the loveliness, prosperity, peace, order, and joyfulness that once did mark our Southern homes, and then turn forward to the bruised poverty, dilapidation, haggardness, and the almost universal woe of the present hour, we curse, in all the bitterness of a human heart, and with an unseen force and fire, that no earthly power can yet avert or quench, the rude hands that wrought this misery. Ay!

> ". . . Time sets all things even;
> And if we do but watch the hour,
> There never yet was human power,
> Which could evade, if unforgiven,
> The patient search and vigil long
> Of him who treasures up a wrong."

But never mind. There'll be an arbitrament of our wrongs before the century expires, when, perhaps, the odds will not be so great as now.

We had just begun to speak of our old friend Sally Morton, we believe; yes, we had — well, Sally at this time was about twenty-two years old, we remember it well, for we had long been no ordinary friends, Sally and I; and even now, upon the dull ear of age, as in the wild gladsomeness of youth, her joyous laugh still rings so sweetly and so merrily; and verily too, doth startle some slumbering feeling well-nigh forgot, but still mayhap too tender to be told. But of these we will not speak again — they were long, too long ago, before the silver-grey had thatched these brown old locks.

Sally, we say, was about twenty-two, and a very remarkable combination of intellect and beauty. She was rather more than medium in height, delicately formed, but well-developed; her features were exquisitely moulded, and the dimples that rested on her blooming cheek, with the defiant but coquettish smile that ever played in wanton beauty about her mouth, told of the bright and festive spirit that ever revelled in its own mirth and wit, and which no early sorrows long could cloud.

She was an orphan, and the only daughter of a gentleman of fine estate, whose embarrassed condition, at the time of his death, had left her not penniless, but without fortune.

Such was Sally Morton, and such the young friends, whose youthful story we have undertaken partially to relate; and to give a clearer insight into their style of social intercourse with each other, and their intimacy, we take the liberty of transcribing the notes of invitation sent out for their extemporized dancing party:

"STARLIGHT, Oct. 10, 18—.

"DEAR JULIA—Every arrangement has been made for the assurance of a very happy time to-night at 'Starlight,' in the programme whereof, your name stands conspicuous. Although these arrangements are *extremely impromptu*, they yet admit no refusal to *shine*, on the part of objects coming within their disc; on your part particularly is this thought to be the case, as there would be no enjoyment without it. This much, by way of preliminary, which I will follow up by a greater elaboration of details. Violet and aunt are with us, and will remain till morning. Father will be at home, and somehow we have learned or think that Mr. Campbell will accompany him — and look upon the information or thought, as reliable. Your brother Thomas, and our *meteoric* cousin, Henry Brandon, have been commanded to be present by those who are thought to possess great influence in that direction; and as a matter of course, will recognize the obligation of obedience. Laura too, is widening the range of these extemporized hospitalities; and at this very instant is deeply engaged at my side, in the preparation of a correspondence for the parsonage, mandatory to the recluses thereof, to emerge from their seclusion and *ghostly* meditations, and to report to us at 'Starlight' this evening. With the very benevolent view that yourself and Miss Sally shall not be each without a revolving satellite; rumor having already assigned the orbits of these two modest pseudo-anchorites, no farther designation is required even to prevent collision. Now, was there ever anything to exceed the true beauty and artistic skill of this diagram, for a fantastic evening? perfect in all its diplomatic and social aspects!

"Say to Miss Sally, that she will doubtless be called on to play a double part in the proposed enjoyments, and must prepare herself, Ajax-like, (I hope I commit no classical solecism,) to excel herself. Our cousin Henry, already delighted with her, will be greatly attracted by her wit; and we wish her to rise in the very highest flight, and sweeping down upon him, deplete him, of a part at least, of

9 *

his college conceit, of which he has far more than his
honest share; and is quite disposed to put on airs to everything that labors under the disability of wearing *petticoats*:
indeed, even goes so far as to use the word *namby-pamby*, in
connection thereof.   Now, of this 'vain delusion,' we believe it in the power of Miss Sally to disenchant him. The
other, of the double part to which I have alluded, is that
of playing *prioress* to the *prior* — in that, however, she already has had some experience.

"Now all of these details of arrangement, dear Julia,
are subject to emendation by the circumstances of the evening; and it may even be so, that this eccentric cousin may
wander off into *your* periphery, provided anything shall
check him in his bold and open *love-making* to Laura; defiant as he is of the presence of father, mother, or any one,
will look upon me, I believe, as his *Fidus Achates*, in the
enterprise of winning her heart, which, indeed, I believe he
has more than half accomplished. I laugh and tell her
that she is inveigling her rollicking cousin into the meshes
of her heart. She laughs too, and merely says he is her brag
cousin for genius, craziness, and impudence.

"He was here yesterday, and I heard him say he intended
very soon to enlarge the radius of his social enjoyments, and
threatened to tread down the flowers between 'Buck-horns'
and 'Oak Hill.' It will, therefore, be an excellent idea to
meet him this evening on an open field, where you can, by
observation rather than contact, break the spell of conster-
nation — as I am very sure that, otherwise, his flights will
frighten you. But I *must* stop writing, as I am consuming
time which the messenger should be using, in flying to
'Oak Hill.' But, 'bless me!' my dear Julia, I had forgotten to tell you that it was a *dance* we had extemporized.
Now, I know you will come.   Your friend,   LUCY B.

"P. S. It is said that the point of a woman's letter is to
be found in the postscript; nor shall I urge this to be an
exception, but leave the question to be judged of by yourself, or whomsoever it may concern. Whether it be the
point or not, my postscript purpose is to ask you to bring
your brother Robert with you, who I learn has not yet consumed all of his college vacation. Tell him it is *my own*
especial invitation; and though no *particular* provision has
been made for him, it is yet not too late to say that, if he

will accept Lucy Brandon as his partner, chaperone, or what-not, she hereby covenants not even to look at any other young gentleman during the evening — if he demands it. ·   Yours,   L. B."

As Lucy had said to her friend, Julia Hunter, Laura, at the same time, was busily preparing a letter to be sent to the parsonage, which she had now concluded, and ran as follows:

"STARLIGHT, 10*th October.*

" HONORED PARSON: A goodly number of your parishioners, having met at our house this morning, and not wishing, under all the circumstances, to be deprived of your presence until the next Sunday, through me send greeting this *epistle* — and, though not such as you are more particularly familiar with, we yet hope that its tidings will bring a thrill of earthly joyance, if not of spirituality — the particular import whereof is, that you make your appearance this evening at the ingle-side of 'Starlight' by seven o'clock, or at an earlier hour if more convenient to you, as some matters of moment to the history of your parish will certainly be agitated.

" We have just heard with much pleasure of your return from the 'General Convention'; but, during your absence of several weeks, there has made his appearance among us a long-absent young citizen, whom you knew in his youth, I believe. . The said young gentleman, according to common report, was ever slightly disposed to something of social outlawry; but has returned almost confirmed in this disposition, much to the chagrin of all his staid and well-deporting relations, of whom I am one; so much so is this the truth, that it is manifest to every one that he is ready for any desperate enterprise, from the breaking of a young girl's heart up through all the catalogue of such wicked deeds. At a *family* meeting, therefore, between Violet, Lucy, and myself, it has been decided to hand over to your pastoral care this peculiar case of deviation from the solemn dignity of his ancestors, with the request that even this night you come and begin your vigils of him, lest delay may put it beyond your power to effect any salutary change. Thus far, the occasion for your presence may be considered professional; further, it may be personal to yourself.

"Wherefore the latter, you eagerly ask; — the answer, though rather more than monosyllabic, is yet not quite *poly-syllabic*—Sally Sumpter (did you discover my effort at wit?) will be with us this evening. So, for this reason and for that, we think it advisable that you come — yea, that you absolutely *do come;* and I, as your best lady friend, do demand it of you. Can you resist that logic? I think that may be termed *argumentum ad hominem.*

·"In plain words, Reverend Sir, our cousin, Henry Brandon, whom you may remember something of as a boy, is returned; he will be with us this evening, and we wish you to see him. Violet, Julia, and Miss Sally, Thomas and Robert Hunter, and Mr. Campbell, have all been asked, and we of course expect them. Music and dancing may be expected: I need scarcely say, that you will not require your *surplice.*

"Every word of this letter, in its spirit, is equally with yourself intended for *Dr. Wilton,* whose presence cannot be dispensed with on any plea, not even that of 'professional engagements,' as his name has entered largely into the arrangements we have made for the evening entertainments, and has been especially set apart as the accompaniment to Miss Hunter's. Now let me close this idle style of writing, before you think me either jesting or a fit subject for the asylum; assuring you that I am neither, but as ever,

"Your friend,   LAURA BRANDON.

"P. S. I had not forgotten Mr. Thaxton, but found no suitable place in my letter to ask after his health. Say to him that we all frequently speak of him; and if he would come over with you, any and all of us would see to it, that he was entertained and enjoyed himself.   L. B."

CHAPTER XV.

"There is not a string attuned to mirth,
But hath its chord in melancholy."

DR. WILTON reached home from a professional visit but a few minutes after the invitation came.

Mr. Jerome hearing that he had come, called him and Mr. Thaxton to the sitting-room, when he read the letter he had just received. Dr. Wilton was so highly pleased with the prospect of enjoyment, that he immediately proposed that all of them should ride over.

"You and the parson can go, doctor," said Mr. Thaxton; "but I am a little too old now to enter into such pleasures, though I should like to see them all, particularly Laura and Henry Brandon. Laura is an old favorite of mine from a child, and used to come to my 'bench,' when working at her father's, nearly every day; and always had some little job for me to do for her, making a new stool, or a bedstead for a doll, or a pleasure-carriage to be made out of spools; yes, she was a sweet child, and has grown up a very lovely woman. Lucy was a nice child, but was shyer, and rather fiercer — took more after the mother, who was and is yet, I reckon, as proud as Lucifer, and as self-willed, though a very nice woman."

"What kind of boy was this young Henry Brandon," asked Dr. Wilton.

"One of the finest boys I ever knew. I was more about Mrs. St. George Brandon, both before and after her husband's death, than any family over there; and this boy Henry I saw a great deal of, clear up to the time of his leaving for college — a very fine boy; but very wild, careless, reckless, and loved his fun. He had a negro boy that was called 'Sam Brandon,' that always went with him, and a great rascal Sam was; except when Henry was at school,

he was always to be found near him. Henry was a sort of
boy sweetheart to Laura Brandon, and judging from that
letter, I think it is about to be revived."

"You appear to know all about them, Mr. Thaxton,"
said Dr. Wilton.

"Yes; almost as much about them as I do about myself.
I worked among them for numbers of years."

Mr. Thaxton was an old man — a mechanic by trade — and
had made the house of the elder Mr. Jerome his head-
quarters since his first coming to the country, and had been
asked to do so by his executors, after his death; and since
the young parson had returned, had been invited to remain.
He had already acquired a competency, and was leading a
life of quiet ease.   Having always been a great reader, he
now passed most of his time in the library; he was a man
of fine sense, and greatly respected by all who knew him.

"You say you can't go, Mr. Thaxton," said Mr. Jerome.

"No, I can't go; but tell Laura I'll get over there before
long, and stay a day or two among them, just to see what
manner of grown people my little favorites of old now
make."

Mr. Jerome and Dr. Wilton made preparations for going,
and about the hour which had been designated, reached
Mr. Robert Brandon's, just after that gentleman and Mr.
Campbell had arrived; and not a great while after them,
Henry Brandon with Thomas Hunter rode up.

"Hallo!" said Henry; "what can be the matter here
to-night?" as he saw the house very unusually lighted up.

"I can't say, Henry, unless your aunt is illuminating on
account of your coming."

"Yes, possibly so; but I think it far more probable, if
that was the cause of her doing anything, for her to blow
out every light for a mile around."

"Humph! you don't rate your popularity very high
with the good lady."

"Yes, about as high as Haman! if the comparison is not a solecism."

"Sam Brandon," who was with them, took charge of their horses, while they proceeded to the house. They were met, however, at the gate by a servant, who had been stationed there to receive them, and by him were told who was present, and what the occasion; they were then invited to the gentlemen's apartment, where they could prepare themselves. Having but little preparation to make, they were soon ready, and were conducted to the drawing-room. Mr. Brandon met them very cordially, and congratulated them on becoming his guests so soon, under so unexpectedly pleasant circumstances. Mrs. Brandon, too, came up and gave them both a very friendly salutation, with but little formality, and much real zest.

"More gracious than I had expected," whispered Henry to Hunter, as Mrs. Brandon turned away from them.

It can easily be seen that in so small a company, where each one, too, was so well-known to the other, that intercourse very soon became easy and pleasing. Henry Brandon renewed the slight acquaintance of his boyhood with Mr. Jerome, and Dr. Wilton he had already met several times previously.

Henry Brandon was speaking to Mr. Jerome, and asking about his old friend, Mr. Thaxton, when Laura approached them, and said:

"I congratulate you, cousin, in so soon falling into the hands that I intended you should. I particularly enjoined Mr. Jerome to be here to-night, just for your benefit. I informed him of the peculiarities of your case: he is aware of your reckless character, and all other idiosyncrasies."

"You scarcely gave the whole condition of your patient, cousin. Why did you not describe it as reckless *love?*"

"Well, sir," she replied, blushing very prettily, "it is about the same."

"Yes, as I think, it might be classed with 'vaulting ambition,' which we have good authority for believing sometimes 'overleaps itself.'"

"Ah! that is a confession of the whole charge, and very good evidence of some mental derangement."

"No, I think not," said Mr. Jerome, pleasantly; "at least not such as the law takes cognizance of; but certainly it is amenable to the charge of great ambitiousness, since he aspires, in a day as it were, to an honor which some I might speak of would be too happy to acquire after a seven-years' service." Bowing, as he said this, with an affected reference to himself, he turned his eye inquiringly to theirs, as if in the act of saying something further, but suppressed it. "What would you say, parson?"

"Oh, nothing — an idea flashed over my mind, but I believe I have forgotten it — at least it ·is too unfinished to be expressed intelligibly." He might have said, "Your merry jests may bring a sad reflex to the flowing current of your fun."

Laura then spoke, saying that her conquests were so easily and so rapidly made, as to deprive her of all the pleasure of an effort. Seeing Sally Morton, at the instant, off at a little distance, in conversation with Mrs. Brandon, she spoke to her, and requested her presence for a short while. As Sally came up, she begged her to accept a portion of her *spoils*, as she really had more than she could bear off from the field of her victories.

"Will you receive Mr. Jerome? He is perfectly at my disposal, I assure you — the right of *conquest* conferring that power upon me."

"Yes, with pleasure, when so freely bestowed; but you should remember that the vanquished have rights which all the laws of civilization require the victors to respect," said Miss Morton.

"I will waive all such rights," said Mr. Jerome, "and

willingly transfer my allegiance, since it is valued so lightly."

"Ah! I see I have conferred a pleasure, instead of inflicting a punishment. You owe me at least a debt of gratitude for managing matters so happily for you, even if inadvertently done, and now leave you to your good fortune," at the same time taking Henry Brandon's arm, and walking off.

Mr. Jerome laughingly replied to her, as she left: "And to my admiration, too, for the skill with which you manage *your own*."

Laura did not choose to reply to the last insinuation, but went directly to the piano, where, instead of playing, as her first motion indicated, she still held carelessly to his arm, as if unconscious of her position. Henry Brandon then said:

"I thought you were going to play, Laura?"

"Oh! do you wish me to play?" she said, starting a little as he spoke.

"No; not if you do not wish." Looking at her then, with what feeling he scarcely knew, he continued: "If this be a right of the vanquished, defeat is worth ten thousand victories."

She only replied to this remark by a pleasant smile, and seeming, for the first time, conscious of her familiar sort of position, quietly withdrew her arm, saying: "You must not be any way exclusive in your attentions to me, cousin, but to some extent must play the host."

"Play *host* so soon!" said he, laughing. "Should I not get aunt's permission?"

Laura, seeing that she was not likely to foil his jests, said:

"I will leave you, my young humorist, till you cool the temper of your waggish tongue," and, with a coquettish menace of her finger, left him standing at the piano, and joined Dr. Wilton and Lucy, who were near by, talking very gayly.

"Doctor," said she, as she came up, "this is not the part of the entertainment which you are under obligation to sustain: your duties are specific, and were clearly designated. This my sister knows, yet she assists you in their violation. Which shall I hold responsible?"

"My unworthy self, Miss Brandon, if there is any penalty attached; as I assure you none can be too great for the sweet enjoyment of conversing with Miss Lucy Brandon."

"Very handsomely spoken; but you might have added, 'unless it be for a sweeter;' therefore, sister, as a matter of magnanimity, you must let me introduce the doctor to this sweeter joy, and better fortune."

Lucy replied that she very reluctantly yielded, after so gallant a speech; but rather insisting on Dr. Wilton accepting her sister's proposition, left him with Laura. The doctor offering her his arm, the two walked to where Mr. Robert Brandon was sitting, by the side of Julia Hunter.

"Father," said Laura, "pardon me for interrupting your pleasant little talk with Julia, but you are unconsciously infringing on a right which had previously been conferred on another. Dr. Wilton had been assigned to the post of honor, at the side of Miss Hunter, even before he came."

"Certainly, my daughter; I willingly yield my position to the doctor's fresher years. The evening sun may be as bright, but not so warm as morning's," at the same time rising, offered the doctor his seat.

Dr. Wilton had already met with Miss Hunter; but the occasion being wanting in those easy features which Laura's familiar words to her father at once imparted, he had got separated from her. The conversation soon growing unembarrassed and pleasing, Laura left them to themselves, playfully enjoining the doctor to make himself exceedingly agreeable to Miss Hunter, saying, she would be back very soon for a report.

Dr. Wilton gracefully bowing to her, and regretting her absence, very easily and naturally assumed the assigned obligation of acting as the "gay cavalier" to Miss Hunter.

CHAPTER XVI.

" And all went merry as a marriage bell."

WHEN Lucy Brandon had left Dr. Wilton with her sister, she immediately joined Mr. Jerome and Miss Morton; but had not been with them but a few minutes, when young Robert Hunter also came up. Lucy immediately addressed him, as if with reproach, for not observing the understanding between them, of being her attendant during the evening.

The youth rather bashfully but boldly replied, that if he had looked upon it as a right on his part, he certainly should have attended to it, as he had more than once seen it endangered.

"Come, Robert, come! soothe that look of blushing indignation, I pray you, as I do most honestly assure you that your rights have not been damaged by any act of mine; so let me take your arm and leave Mr. Jerome and Miss Sally alone. There is an old saying to the purport, that over two often spoils company, and this may be one of tho occasions, both to them and to us."

While these little ingeniously artistic changes and conversations were going on, Henry Brandon still remained at the piano, apparently listless, but really in a sort of speculative revery. A strange desire was in his heart to follow

Laura in person, even as he was following her with his eye; but he could not, dared not. He wished to take her by the hand, and to look into the calm depths of her soft, beautiful eyes, and to laugh and be happy as he did so. "And must I call this, love?" said he to himself. As yet he dared not; and yet it was his first — his maiden love.

"Ah! what is love?" 'Tis that which, even after years have scattered their tinsel-grey through the once glossy locks, and the vicissitudes of life have brought the chill movement of age to the heart, still thrills the bended frame at the mention of its name, and brings back to memory the wild and bounding impulses of the early day.

Oh! what is love? It is that manly, generous, genial feeling that breathes into the youthful soul such thoughts and promptings to glorious actions, as may be favorably brought to the feet of beauty, wherewith to claim the guerdon of its smiles.

'Tis an emotion that reaches beyond the bounds of human life, and seeks in the bright realm of the spirit-land the realization of its gorgeous dreams! It is that which comes to the heart again, in the gloom of the olden time, and lights up the evening hour of its sadness with the sweet recollection of its morning hopes! It is that which, in after years, doth bring back the maiden form that floated so gently along the unclouded skies, and gave its brightness to the early paths of life. Ay! and it may be a holy memory, linking the living and the dead! A lovely thing, perhaps now folded in the cold still purity of the shroud — a lost but remembered joy — an angel now, that comes alone, from the silver courts in the hushed hours of the night, and with unseen hand soothes the throbbing brow, and gives to age and sorrow the happy dream and smile of youth once more. A star! in the eternal azure dome, which from its far-off home still points our way through time!

But heigho! Our readers must pardon us for this garrulous, sentimental sort of episode: it is the privilege of age, and now let us forward to our story.

The conversation of our little party had now become so gay and animated, that the *dance* which they had met for, appeared well-nigh forgot. But there was *one* just making his appearance, whose whole soul was absorbed in the responsible duties to which he had been invited. This was the old black fiddler. SANCHO was now an old negro, very black, slightly cross-eyed, tall and sinewy; and, in his own language, had been "much of a man in his young days." He had come to Alabama with his master, and had long remained his chief driver; but was now too old for active business, and had for several years done but little else than wait upon himself. Between his tobacco patch, basket-making, chair-bottoming, and fiddling, his life was gliding smoothly on to its close. His family had belonged to that of his present master's family since the arrival of Sancho's first *African ancestor* on the coast of America, a fact upon which he, in common with all negroes, under the same circumstances, ever prided themselves; but particularly did he pride himself upon it, as he thought there was no family whose standing equalled the Brandons; and looked upon his young mistresses as very queens of perfection and beauty, with whom he, and his old wife also, were very great favorites.

The proudest hours, now, of old Sancho's life, were those when notified that his services on the violin were required by "Miss Lucy and Miss Laura."

It is rather a singular fact — in which there is a deep philosophy — that the most reliable and intelligent negroes were those who felt the greatest reverence for white people generally, and their owners particularly.

In addition to these common predilections, Sancho had an especial respect for all Virginians, but a more especial respect for those who were raised on the tide-water of

10*

"James River," and any recollections of the habits and customs of that particular locality were always sufficient with him to settle any disputed point of either conscience or fact.

Sancho had walked in at a side door, and seated himself in the corner, near the piano, with an ostentatious but very polite dignity. His arrival not occasioning that cessation of mirth and general conversation as quickly as he thought so important an event deserved, he spoke out, very audibly and commandingly: "Ladies and gentlemen, whilst I plays a *chune* solus by myself, selec' yo' partners. Dat which I is gwine to play you bein' once de favorite wid de great folks on the tide-water, and are knowed by the name of 'Ole Virginny Break-down,'" and, without further ceremony, led off in fine style, with the tune known in negro minstrelsy by that name. Concluding it, after so long a time, with a grand flourish upon all his strings at once, as nigh as he could do so, again sang out: "Gentlemen, has you chose your ladies? If you has, lead em out, and I will play you what ar' called 'De Lady on de River,' sposed to be Miss Marthy Dandidge, afterwards the lady of Gineral Washington, bof of which I ar' ofin sede when I war a boy, and bowed to em too." After these commands and this sublime piece of information, he said to Laura, in an undertone: "Miss Laura, will you sist me in dis, young Missus, on de pianer?" and then leading off in grand style, was directly followed by Laura, who was not in the dance.

Henry Brandon had not joined the set, and now came up to the piano, and stood near Laura as she accompanied old Sancho.

As the lovely girl was rattling along with her music, there was an expression of disinterested joy in every feature of her innocent face, which seemed to him scarcely belonging to earth. There was in it no taint of self, but purely a desire of giving pleasure to others. She caught his eye beaming abstractedly into her own, as these thoughts were passing through his mind, and rather confusedly said to him:

"Why so quiet, cousin? A penny for your thoughts."

"They were of thee; but if 'music be the food of love,' play on."

"Ah! I feel honored in being the subject of so poetic an abstraction. But tell me of the thoughts."

"I was just thinking why it was the fates had made us *cousins*.

"'Earth holds no other like to thee,
Or, if it doth, in vain for me.'"

This was his first approach to calling her sweetheart, as he had threatened.

"Why so, cousin?" she asked, blushing deeply in her confusion. "Do you so regret the relationship that you wish to repudiate it?"

"No — unless I could improve it," said he, with an effort at a laugh.

"It's improvement then you desire, is it? What would you substitute, my noble kinsman?"

She was innocent in this open question, but immediately saw the force of it, and, her cheek again suffused with blushes, was tremulously awaiting Henry Brandon's reply, which was fortunately interrupted by old Sancho saying:

"Excuse me, young Misses; but you is raly playin' outen chune;" then turning his cross-eyes to Henry, and striking his instrument with an extra force, said: "You was de occasion of dat, Mass Henry;" and fearing that the dancers might notice the confusion, quickly gave out, "Promenade!" Then speaking to Thomas Hunter — who had not appeared to hear him — said: "Promenade, Mass Tom!"

The set was soon over, and the old fellow again sang out:

"Seat your partners!"

CHAPTER XVII.

"Our revels now are ended; these our actors, as I foretold you, were all spirits, and are melted into air, into thin air."

OLD SANCHO, after a few minutes rest, resumed the sweet discourses of his violin, which gave a bright animation to the conversation between the young people.

Some little incident of the dance being mentioned, Dr. Wilton — who pretended to be a Presbyterian — appealed to know if it was allowable for the Episcopal clergy to participate in so unspiritual a pastime as dancing.

The question had been suggested to the doctor by Sally Morton, who immediately declared that, even if permissible, it certainly indicated great looseness in the rules of the church.

Mr. Jerome was not prepared for the suddenness of this attack, and particularly for the coinciding with it of Miss Morton, who had danced with him; but quickly discovering the pre-arranged jest, joined in with the spirit of it, and replied:

"Miss Sally, neophytes are always zealous, if not sincere: I shall therefore have to excuse you for following up the prejudices of the *Baptists*, to whom you belong. I believe they say that dancing was the cause of JOHN THE BAPTIST losing his head, whom they very boldly but erroneously declare to be the author of their church. Yet *you* have no right to a use of this singular prejudice, since you, on this occasion, played the part of *Siloam*."

"Yes, I agree with you, parson, that Miss Morton well represented the part of Siloam, if beautiful dancing is all that is necessary; but we cannot let you escape, even to pay her a just compliment."

In this while they had nearly all gathered about Mr. Jerome, as if to charge him with an unclerical example —

even the rather retiring Mr. Campbell, while professing to be a liberal Methodist, joined in the general attack.

"Wrong, as I may be, my most exemplary parishioners, I yet occupy a better position than any of you, since I discover that I am a victim to a conspiracy, and ought to put in a plea to the jurisdiction, and not make any defence whatever before this inquisition, particularly as I discover so strong an element of heresy in its composition. I will say, though, to Dr. Wilton, that as there is nothing in the Scriptures against dancing, there is nothing against it in our rubrics; it therefore can only be condemned where there is some reprehensible feeling. Sterne, in his 'Sentimental Journey,' speaks of a very pious class of people, whom he met somewhere in Switzerland, that *danced* as a part of their religious ceremonies. I will dismiss the doctor, however, with the remark, that *his* denomination is not a proper tribunal before which matters of *church* can be arraigned. It is but a Puritan association or institution, given over to all manner of heresies, from *witchcraft* down, and possesses no more apostolic consecration, and no more usefulness, than a Yankee free-school."

There being no other, even nominal Presbyterian present, they all enjoyed the manner in which he dispatched the doctor's church.

"But, Mr. Jerome," said the doctor, "I hardly think it fair that you let the Methodists off. Mr. Campbell here united in the charge against your church."

"No, you are right, doctor; I think I must tell the truth on Mr. Campbell's denomination also, since he has made it an accuser of my church. Mr. Wesley was a good man, and had always been a good Churchman; but becoming possessed, I suppose, of something like worldly ambition, after he came to America — where the field was open — thought to get up a church of his own, which he supposed himself privileged to do, so long as he did not pretend to invest it with an apostolic character. In few words, Methodism is a root, of lower order, of the Church, and a higher one of Puritanism. As a practical system of preaching to meet the religious requirements of this country at that time, it was an improvement; and the error of it was, that he detached his improvement from the Church, and endeavored to get a *patent* for it. Their 'Discipline,' as they call it, in regard to worldly matters, had its foundation, first, in the spirit which arrogated superior grace, and next, in the peculiar circumstances of the people — they were in a sort of quasi exile from the mother country, poor and sorrowful. Their ordinances reflect these facts — their music, even, tells of social dejection, while their songs were the outpourings of human despair, and clearly express a *brighter hope* in *death* than in life. Their happiness seemed to date itself from the hour of dissolution. Poor, moaning, and resigned in its submissions, it was yet bitter in its expressions, and even happy in its grief. This is Methodism as it was: what it is, it is difficult for any one to say."

All laughed heartily at Campbell and his Church; but he, in reply, said:

"To show you, Mr. Jerome, that I am not amenable to any of these grave charges, I not only forgive you, but invite you to join us in our next dance."

Old Sancho was now called on by Henry Brandon for music. The old man responded promptly, and cried out to them to get their partners. Every one insisted on Mr. Jerome joining them again, but he pleasantly refused, assigning as his reason that he had not danced before for several years, and it had fatigued him.

As the company went out on the floor, old Sancho very pompously announced that the "chune" he would play them was called "Ronoke," and said to be the favorite of the great PATRICK HENRY, who was "hisself a great fiddler."

Sally Morton, by agreement, was this time left out, and had consented to assist old Sancho, who had requested it, in his music. When the dancers had got fully under way, and she in full accord with the old black fiddler, but apparently unconscious of the elegance of her execution, Mr. Jerome walked to the piano and seated himself near her. Observing her seeming indifference, he remarked that she certainly did not appreciate the beauties of " Ronoke."

" Yes, sir; I think it has a very decided melody, and I really admire it."

" I thought not, as I have never heard you play such music."

" No, I do not very often ; but for no other reason than that the world is governed in music, as it is in other things — by fashion — even certain styles of opinion get to be fashionable, and few are found bold enough to differ. Fashion too, always, I believe, relates to that which is new — indeed, is almost synonymous with newness. In music, certain songs, pieces, and styles, get to be called *old ;* and, therefore, ceasing to be fashionable, are never called for."

" The reason then of you playing *scientific* music, is simply because it happens now to be fashionable ? "

" To a great extent, yes ; and because no one has the courage to ask for any other kind. Music, up to a certain point, represents feeling ; beyond that it becomes a science. My tastes and feelings run entirely with the simpler styles, and I confess that, at heart, I am old-fashioned enough to love that most to which our old love-songs are set."

The expression of this sentiment particularly pleased Mr. Jerome, for two reasons — first, because it coincided with his own ; and again, because it was significant of some sympathies between them, which he was anxious to believe did exist. It struck a chord in his own heart, and he replied with much apparent interest :

" There is nothing that more decidedly reflects the character of a people, and illustrates their social life, than music. You will seldom see an individual who loves simple, natural melody, who has not more or less refined feeling that can always be appealed to. Nature seems to meet its own laws; and so far as this country is concerned, I have remarked that artistic music has only succeeded to the age of great mind, and to truthful and just thought and action. I mean that as one has appeared to recede, the other has seemed to approach. Of course, I do not say that one is the cause of the other, I only speak of a fact; and the fact is first observable in those quarters where the natural nobleness of society, with its generous feelings and gentle sympathies, have first given way to heartless artificialities, and cold, senseless abstractions. I would instance the large cities."

"Your observations are quite sweeping, Mr. Jerome, and unless you modify them, I shall be compelled to take up the foils in defence of my new friends — the Operas — come, sir; can't you?"

These words while banteringly, were so pleasantly spoken, that he was half disposed to yield from complaisance; but true to the expression of his opinions, he replied:

"No, I cannot; what I have said, I am satisfied, is even less than true. From observation and from reflection, I have concluded that most of the great thought and correct feeling, which permanently direct good government and healthful society, proceed from the *natural* and simpler circles, where there is but little artificiality of any sort. Nature produces the one, while what is called society forces up the other."

"There are two cities, Mr. Jerome, which you might except from the sweeping tones of your anathemas. One is Charleston, my own paternal city, and the other is Boston."

"The claim you put in for Charleston is certainly a very good one with *me*, Miss Sally, yet the truth of what I have said, is especially illustrated by those very two instances. There are idiosyncrasies peculiar to each of them, which gives them a seeming antipodal appearance. Yet there is a sympathy and similarity in results between their life and style of thought that make the cases quite remarkable. Neither of these, however, are at all remarkable for their musical tastes."

"I did not request you to make an exception of Boston because of any sympathy or admiration, but because of its acknowledged literary tastes; but you astonish me when you place these two cities in parallel lines, and will still ask for the exclusion of Charleston from the severity of your sentence."

"Where you are concerned, Miss Morton," said the young parson, smilingly, "my emotions are all of the most gallant character, and I now have every desire to grant your request; but as I cannot identify you with Charleston, you must allow me to leave her beside her Puritan sister. Sociological heresies are the chief fruitage of *Bostonism*, while political heresies is that of *Charlestonism*. And on the principle that extremes meet, there is a baleful sort of sympathy in their individual results; and I have an idea that, unitedly, they will exert a malign influence on our national fortunes, at no very distant day. Puritanism and Huguenotism have the same ethnology *remotely;* the only difference is in the grafting — one has an English stock, the other French."

"Pardon me for interrupting you, Mr. Jerome; but have you read Captain Maryat's book on America?"

"No, I have not."

"There is a very laughable burlesque in the article on Boston, in regard to the money-loving character and literary qualifications of the pretentious Bostonians. He says, being in conversation with one of the leading *literary characters* of the city, the gentleman, in speaking

11

of certain speculations, regretted not having gone into them, as he "would not only have *doubled* and *thribbled* his money, but *fourbled* and *fibbled* it."

Both of them laughed heartily at the characteristic jest, and rose from the piano, as the set was over.

Mr. Robert Brandon at this time saw a good opportunity, as the little company sat grouped together, to make the proposition for them all to accompany him to Gregory's Spring, on the next day. The proposal was readily agreed to — as it had already been spoken of before — and every arrangement was quickly made.

As soon as they were a little rested, dancing was again resumed, and kept up at a merry pace until twelve o'clock, when Mr. Brandon, announcing the hour, proposed that the evening be closed with an old-fashioned Scotch reel — every one to join it. This suggestion was at once adopted, and a reel soon formed, with Mr. Robert Brandon and his sister-in-law, Mrs. St. George Brandon, at the head, with Mr. Jerome and Mrs. Robert Brandon, at the foot.

The fun now ran high and furious, so much so, that many of the negroes, who were dancing on the galleries, stopped their own amusement to witness that going on in the parlor.

We have not, as yet, mentioned a feature of the evening's entertainments, but will now do so, as one so illustrative of the relationships, in the olden time, between the whites and negroes, masters and slaves, and so refutatory of the falsehoods since uttered in regard to them.

Individual falsehood is certainly very disgraceful to the guilty party, whether published or spoken; but for a whole people to unite in a chain of wretched slanders upon an innocent party, surpasses all history except that of our own Northern people.

Though the South is to be blamed for her ill-advised manner of retaliation — *secession* — it was yet but a law of nature that she should have felt a thorough contempt and a bitter hatred for such a people. And now that their undoubted malignity has been gratified by a destruction of our fortunes, they might at least acknowledge the slander —and even more, since they have grown *rich* by their philanthropy. They might at least propose some method of honorable compensation.

As soon as it had become known on "the quarter" that there was to be a dance up at the "yard," every young negro on the plantation assembled there, and, during the entire evening, were dancing on the galleries, and in the yard, to the same music, and with the same well-marked pleasure of their young masters and mistresses within. Just after the dancing stopped, Mrs. Brandon had sent out the remainder of the abundant and elegant supper — which had been standing in the dining-room — to be divided among them. After eating, they all united in one of their simple, but highly musical walking-songs, and marched in order back to their cabins — never dreaming or desiring that this happy and patriarchal sort of relationship to their masters would be destroyed by *Boston fanaticism forcing* them upon an effort at equality, which the God of nature has designed never to be consummated. But so goes the world — the wheel of fortune is everything, and *we* may be up next, and possibly will behave as *meanly. Retali-ation* seems to be the highest law of human morals; but retribution is God's own law. We had slaves — they have the bonds for which they were sold. We bide our time.

CHAPTER XVIII.

"And there is e'en a happiness,
That makes the heart afraid."

THE eleventh of October, 18—, was one of the blandest, gentlest days of the year — it was clear, calm, softly beautiful, and had that mystic ring peculiar to the requiem which nature ever sings in the South to the departing glory of summer. The landscape mingles in this sighing lamentation, this gentle melancholy, and adds its share to the sweet sadness of the season. The leaves of the trees have faded away their heavy green, and the shadows they cast are not so deep and dense. The flowers, too, that in their hour of gorgeous beauty reflected proudly back the blazing rays of the summer sun, now droop their heads, and tint their petals with the mellowed hues of the surrounding scene. These make up the epithalamium of our Southern winter, ere the harsh hours of its boreal reign begins.

Human life owes much to the autumn of the year — the boiling blood of summer flows cooler to the heart, and its swift emotions are soothed to a gentler speed. It is a season of generous forgiveness — a type of death itself, before it flings upon the human form the stark shadows of the tomb.

We have said the day was clear and calm, and lovely, and so it was; yet there was that peculiar sadness in it which some days have, that none can feel or see, save those whose fortunes are to be effected.

Henry Brandon felt this strange influence, but could not trace it to its source; the conformities in the far off, unseen diagram of life, and the combinations in the crucible of events which make up each one's destiny, had not yet developed themselves; but only glimmering their slanting rays upon his heart, were already lightning him on to the point of its solution. He was only waiting for its coming.

Carriages, horses, and servants were already at the gate, in readiness for the trip to *Gregory's Spring*. Neither of the Mrs. Brandons were going, but had united in arranging every possible thing for the comfort of their daughters and their company. Mrs. Robert Brandon had attended to a most sumptuous lunch being prepared, while the girls had taken the extra precaution to store away a few bottles of wine, "for the pleasure of father and *his* friends," as they *said;* but quite likely with an eye to their own friends.

After a delightful drive they reached the SPRING in good time. We might have said delightful drive and *ride;* for be it known that in those days it was the style for young gentlemen to accompany the carriages of ladies on *horseback*, and we have to regret the subsequent change — *buggies* being far less knightly in appearance, and very decidedly *Yankeeish.*

Though reaching there quite early, there had already met a very large concourse of people from the surrounding country, for the various purposes of seeing each other, enjoying a good dinner, and hearing two speakers, considered by their respective parties as the most eloquent of the State, and not inferior to any in the South.

These semi-social, semi-political gatherings, with a public dinner gotten up by subscription, for hearing the discussion of topics which subsequently lent their influence to bringing on the late civil war, were at that time, and long continued to be a marked feature in the political life of the South; and had much to do with the cultivation of that peculiar eloquence, by which the multitude was lashed into rage at the overdrawn pictures of its *wrongs.* The perfect equality of all who met on such occasions, the general abandon of the surroundings, and the political rivalries, amounting to personal identification with speakers, were the sources of great encouragement to aspirants for the honors of "stump

11 *

oratory." It became a perfect system of action and reaction, of people upon the speaker, and speaker upon the people, in which both became terribly damaged at a later day. This style of political debate propagated quite as much error in statistics, opinions, and theories, as it did of truth as a sentiment, (to say the very best of it.)   Contributing very greatly, not only to the prejudices between the sections, but to bitter antagonisms between our own people, it had much to do with the defeat of the South in the subsequent war, by creating party resentment. What one party desired the other invariably opposed.   Without that deep-set party division of sentiment, the South *would not have been defeated*.   However, right or wrong, her NERVE, with all the odds against her, was *sufficient* for *victory*.

At the usual hour the speaking began.   Mr. Brandon and Colonel Haywood, each occupying an hour, were each in turn pronounced to be unanswerable.

The "Barbecue" was very soon announced, and the vast concourse began to move in the direction of the tables.

Just at this time, Mr. Brandon was approached by old Mr. Gray, and cordially congratulated for his able and eloquent defence of the Whig party.   This was very pleasing to Mr. Brandon, as Mr. Gray was one of the leading Whig citizens of the county, a gentleman of excellent sense, and fine general information; and one of the really wealthy men of the South.   After some general conversation between the two, as to the prospects of Mr. Clay's success, Mr. Gray said:

"Well, sir, I have, at the particular request of my wife and daughter, come to ask you to lunch with us privately, at our carriage."

"I would do so with pleasure," replied Mr. Brandon; "but my own daughters are here, and have a good deal of young company with them."

"Oh!" said the old gentleman, rubbing his hands with

delight at the prospect of an increase to his company; "the more the merrier. I expect we have enough for all, and to spare. I will be very happy to be introduced to your daughters and their company."

Mr. Brandon saw that he *had* to lunch with his old friend, and proposed to walk to his carriage, where he said he should find them. On reaching there, all Mr. Brandon's young friends were present, except Henry Brandon, who had not yet come up.

Mr. Brandon introduced Mr. Gray to his daughters, when the old gentleman told them he had a special commission from his wife and daughter, to ask Mr. Brandon and friends to lunch with them at their carriage.

"And not being present themselves, I can't well return without him; indeed, I almost fear to do so, as you know the welcome of a bearer of bad news."

The girls seeing that the invitation looked to no refusal, consented to go without further hesitation.

"But, Mr. Gray," said Laura, "you probably are not aware of the extent of our dining retinue. Mrs. Gray will certainly not expect such a train as we bear."

"Ah! the length of it will only give us the greater credit for hospitality; and then, too, if we should possibly fall short, we will send and *borrow* your dinner. Oh, no, my dear daughter, the train you carry can be no objection, not at all; so far from it, a very decided recommendation."

"Another objection to our swooping down upon Mrs. Gray in such unexpected numbers is, that we shall never get through the introductions intelligibly."

"Yes, yes, that is a great difficulty; so we will not attempt it, but all get acquainted as they can. Come, let us go; we are already expected, and every possible difficulty is removed."

They found Mrs. Gray and her daughter standing near their carriage. A general introduction of Mr. Brandon and his friends was given by the old gentleman, and particular ones by the young people to each other, as well as they could manage it; at all events, they were not long in getting very well acquainted, and very easy.

They had quite half finished their repast before Henry Brandon came up. His uncle immediately introduced him to Mr. Gray and his wife; and as he turned from them, LAURA introduced him to MARY GRAY.

CHAPTER XIX.

"Care to our coffin adds a nail no doubt,
And every grin so merry draws one out."

QUIZZICAL glances shot from the eyes of Violet and Henry Brandon, as Laura introduced him to Miss Gray. But she was all that Violet had represented her. She was tall in stature, but very handsomely developed, and moved with an ease of action not often equalled. Altogether, her appearance was distinguished, and well calculated to attract attention and admiration. Her eye was a full dark-blue, with just enough of fire in it to give its expression a high intellectuality, while her exquisitely chiselled mouth and chin at once conveyed the impression of great mirthfulness, good feeling, and fearlessness.

For some mysterious reason, Henry Brandon found himself irresistibly drawn to her, and was not long in engaging in a free and pleasing conversation. Old Mr. Gray, with his quick eye, soon observed the friendship which had been so suddenly extemporized between them, and with evident pleasure took frequent occasion, while talking to Mr. Brandon, to look that way.

Among many high, stern, and manly qualities, the old

gentleman had many little eccentricities, among which was an unsurpassed delight in the *love affairs* of young people, and with all his industry and energy, always found time to direct attention to them. Nothing was to him of more importance than *helping* such matters along.

Observing, from time to time, the cozy, mirthful sort of intimacy which we have just spoken of between his daughter and Henry Brandon, he could no longer restrain his inclination to join them, and, suddenly leaving Mr. Brandon in company with Mrs. Gray and some mutual friends who had come up, he turned his attention to the young people, as if to inquire whether they had been properly attended to by his daughter, and became engaged in a general conversation with them, seeming to enjoy it, too, with great zest. After conversing with them for several minutes, and making himself very agreeable, he managed to cut Henry Brandon off to himself, but as if by accident, saying to him, as he did so:

"I knew your father, Mr. Brandon, rather intimately, in his lifetime. He was much younger than I was; but as we had both come to the country when it was new, and both strangers, we became quite friends. He was very fond of hunting; and as I lived in a very fine deer range, he frequently called in to see me; and I remember, too, having seen you with him occasionally. You were a little fellow then, but rode your pony very finely. I should not have known you, however, to-day, as you have grown to manhood since. Why is it I have never seen you?"

"I suppose it is because I have been absent for several years at college, and have only returned within the last four weeks."

"Ah, ha! yes, so I suppose. At a Northern college?"

"Yes, sir."

"Well, I must confess to some prejudice against the North, of late, particularly though on account of her pragmatical conduct toward the South in regard to African slavery. I have travelled among them a great deal; and though I knew them, in a general way, to be a very small-minded, inquisitive, conceited sort of people, I was willing to forgive them for their littleness; but I am not disposed to excuse their hypocritical interference in matters that do not concern them. The whole movement is entirely one of meanness; for even supposing that slavery is wrong, *their* ships brought them over as long as the *trade* was legitimate, and after it ceased to be, *their* ships it was that long ran the 'middle passage.' But soon finding that slave labor was not profitable in their cold climate, they sold them to us; and scarcely had they got the *cash* in their pockets, before they began crying out against it as a great *sin* and a national disgrace."

"Yes," said Henry Brandon, "you are correct in your remarks upon their character as a people; and though I met with but few abolitionists, they were yet organizing very resolutely, and will before long become formidable. They are essentially a democratic people, and giving every question a political complexion, they soon have them before the public, and make political success turn upon them. In short, they make *every* subject a political one, just as they have free-masonry, temperance, religion, etc. I was struck with a remark which Mr. John Randolph made to me, on meeting with him at Philadelphia. He had known my father, and took the liberty to advise me to go back to the South — 'to William and Mary, sir; to William and Mary, the only gentlemen's college on this continent. These people will not do, sir; not reliable, sir, in anything — you can forgive a crime, but not a *meanness*.' "

The old gentleman, after laughing heartily at the ferocious humor of Mr. Randolph, said:

"Yes, there is too much truth in the remark; and unless the course of the abolitionists, which is, as you say, from the peculiar character of that people, bound to identify itself with political questions — and, unless the course of the Democratic party in the South can be arrested in some manner, our government is sure to fail."

"I have never paid a great deal of attention to political matters, but am disposed to think with you; so far as I know, I am a Whig, from instinct and from reason."

This announcement was so pleasing and so satisfactory to the old gentleman that, after a few other commonplace remarks, he turned from the young people back to Mr. Brandon, who was now surrounded by other friends who had come up to see him.

Miss Gray, by an apparently careless movement, came to the side of Henry Brandon, and relieved the awkward sort of silence in which he had been left by her father, by saying:

"Has my father been examining you, Mr. Brandon, as to your classical attainments or political affinities? for next to his Church, he believes in the Whig party, and next to that, in education."

"In neither *directly*," said Henry Brandon, laughingly; "but indirectly in both."

"You are a Whig, of course."

"Oh, yes; and I went into a regular confession to him, and I think we are now most wonderful friends."

"I am glad to hear that you impressed each other so favorably; there can be but one drawback to his taking you into fellowship with him, and I am astonished that he omitted bringing you out on that point. I mean your *Church* relationships."

"No, he did not even refer to that subject; but I am easy on that head, and am ready to subscribe to any that he prefers, provided it will perfect the bond of amity between us."

"Will you let me ask you, Mr. Brandon, what Church

rejoices in the pleasure of your preference and patronage, outside of such influences?"

"The Episcopal, of course."

"Then there is some excuse for the plasticity of your conscience."

"Well, Miss, I will only retort the sarcasm, by asking if no consideration can be offered, sufficient to induce you to come to that church."

"No; I cannot think of any just now."

"Then," said he, bursting out in a laugh, "shall I have to go to yours — your father's, I mean. Will you now be kind enough to inform me which that is, so that I may take the required steps of admission?"

"Methodist, of course; which other could it be?"

"Methodist! Oh! spirits of the just made perfect! Right bad, most truly; but then I will stand to it, if need be: so when we meet again, you may expect me to have acquired many of its grim accomplishments, and to be an adept in many of its sombre ceremonies. I believe Mr. *Watts* is your *psalmist*, and with a rueful face I will sing you a song most dolefully; in short, I shall be prepared to perform any part, necessary to securing your favor — no, excuse me again — your father's favor."

"Except to pray without a book," she added, in his own vein of fun.

"Well, yes; I may have to use a book for a short time, but think I shall soon be able to make up as long, rambling, and tangled an orison, as your most gifted gospeller."

"Mr. Brandon," she said, laughing outright, "I fear you are either witty at our expense, or too willing a convert; if either, and I should communicate the belief to my father, the charm which you have thrown around him would at once be dissolved forever."

"For mercy's sake, then, never breathe so sacrilegious a suspicion against my new-born zeal, or make a suggestion that would so cruelly affect my spiritual fortunes; as I have fully made up my mind to ally myself with him in some manner."

"Have you any preference?" said Laura, who had just come up.

"Perhaps I might have, but then any will do, cousin Laura."

With a mischievous twinkle in her eye, she then said:

"How would you like to get the appointment of *sexton* to the church in Mr. Gray's neighborhood?"

"I had not *exactly* thought of *that* degree. But, hush! cousin Laura; you break the chain of my speculations, and make but a ghostly jest."

"Pardon me, Miss Gray, for my interference in your conversation: I only wished to put his professions to some test."

"Oh, certainly! I am glad that you came to my assistance and suggested that idea, as I think that office is now vacant, which will allow of his opening negotiations with my father immediately for promotion to it," and laughed heartily at catching him so amusingly.

"Young ladies, I shall have to become offended with you, if further derision of my new-born zeal is indulged in."

Both of them protesting against having any such feeling, he said:

"Well, to be in earnest—as this matter properly requires me to be—I can say that I have one advantage, which will gainsay any evil report which you may make of me, and that is that I am a *converted* man. I believe what is called 'CONVERSION' is an article in the Methodist faith, is it not?"

"Yes, I will suppose it, just to let you develop your plan. Let me hear you, Mr. Brandon."

"We will suppose, then, that penitent persons are *converted* in one thing at a time."

12

"Yes, we will consider it so for the present."

"Then I come in under the saving ordinance, for I came here in the undivided idolatry of my lovely cousin Laura; but now I find myself—shall I say it?"

"Certainly!"

"A worshipper not only of that bright morning star of my life, but of that beautiful dawning *gray* that follows upon its setting."

All three laughed heartily at the conceit, and assured him that his effort at being facetious was very decidedly meritorious, on the ground that perfect and unexpected absurdity was a nigh approach to humor.

"My cousin," said Laura, "your infatuation even surpasses your impudence. Allow me, Miss Gray, to intervene in his behalf, by informing you that we had a bottle of wine or so in our carriage."

"Now, dear Laura, do not, I beseech you, destroy my budding reputation with Miss Gray! You insinuate that my asseverations are *intoxication*, instead of that heaving of the heart in an effort at unweaving its destiny—yea, the very inspiration of love itself for Miss Gray's Church and its *members*."

At this both girls literally screamed with laughter, Henry Brandon joining them. Miss Gray then said to Laura, that no apologies were necessary, as she felt too greatly flattered to be offended—"He has invested me with almost magical powers of infatuation," then turning to Henry Brandon, remarked:

"Yes, sir, I invite you to the bosom of our Church, where you will always find the brothers ready to receive young wanderers into the fold of safety and love."

"And love! did you say, Miss Gray? Are the sisters, too, as kind?"

"Oh, yes, sometimes," laughing at his cunning humor.

"Say but always; and I go without standing on the order

of my going. Yes, Miss Gray, our meeting has had a good deal of magic in it, and let me explain. Some six or eight weeks since, I returned home after a four years' absence; since then I have seen nothing after the fashion of your lovely sex, save these two beautiful cousins of mine, and as you may easily imagine, my fate was fast being sealed." Then pointing to Laura, said — "What could I do, but yield this young heart of mine to her love and worship. Even knowing too, that it would bring upon me all the woes of Troy; since I would have to steal this lovely Helen, did I succeed at all."

"Cousin," said Laura, "your figure, or comparison, is an unfortunate one, as well as a solecism. Moreover, neither Miss Gray nor myself will consent to hold this alternate sort of position, particularly when so boldly avowed."

"Oh! Miss Brandon, I scarce know how to refuse an interest in so fine a gem, and am even quite willing to accept a secondary one to your own."

"His value is full sufficient for division, I acknowledge; but as his kinswoman, with some show of right, permit me to be generous and confer upon you a perfect title."

"Laura," interrupted Henry Brandon, rather more hurriedly than he was aware of, or was consistent with the careless, dashing part he had been playing, "will you not consent to retain an interest in your forlorn kinsman. Methinks the security which two such proprietors would afford, is not to be yielded up without some trepidation at the possible results."

"Do, Miss Brandon, retain an interest. I will only ask a reversionary claim, in event of your becoming weary of the original possession."

At this moment, Mr. Gray, attracted by the merriment, returned to them, when Henry Brandon became quite reticently grave and dignified. The two young girls, with whom he had been indulging in his mad jests, could scarcely restrain an outburst of laughter; and stepping a little back, shook their fingers banteringly at him, as much as to say, Now, my gay Lothario, let us see you behave yourself.

CHAPTER XX.

"But I am constant as the northern star,
Of whose true-fixed and resting quality
There is no fellow in the firmament."

IT was near the middle of the afternoon, and many persons were leaving, when Mr. Brandon remarked to his daughters that he disliked breaking up their pleasant enjoyment, but as they had several miles to go, it was time to leave.

Mr. Gray remarked that as it was nearer to *his* house, they had better stay a while longer, and then spend the night with him; but the girls gave their reasons for refusing, and thanked him. Miss Gray had joined her father in the invitation, but, understanding the nature of such things, only insisted on their coming over to church on next Sunday, and to come prepared to spend some time with her. These invitations were reciprocal, but not definitely appointed, by either.

Old Mr. Gray gave a particular invitation to Henry Brandon to visit him at any time, as the young people would see to it that his time should be spent agreeably.

Carriages and vehicles of all kinds, and horses, were moving around as in preparation for going, and our company of gay young people had already begun to take leave of each other, when Henry Brandon, lingering a little in the rear, said to Miss Gray, in his original vein of humor, that if there was no likelihood of her coming over to *the church*, he thought it quite probable that he would go over to her *meeting-house*.

In his own strain, she replied that since first making her negative assertion, she had felt some faltering of resolution, and by the time he came to "Walnut Hill," she would give him a more definite answer.

"In the mean while," she added coquettishly, "I will refer you, by way of hope in your evangelizing effort, to the answer of Ruth to Naomi."

At this, they shook hands very cordially, and separated to meet no more for many years.

Mr. Brandon, after getting his company well on the way home, came along in the rear, that day riding in his sulky; but finding them disposed to loiter, drove on to the front, and before very long had left them entirely.

Thomas Hunter, being compelled to go to his own home that evening, had made the suggestion to the gentlemen of the party to spend the night with him, at his "Bachelor's Hall," just by way, as he said, of giving them an idea of how "housekeeping" should be done. The proposition was accepted, and when they reached the road that turned off to his plantation, he informed the young ladies of this intention, and also that they would accompany them no farther. The young gentlemen now strung along among the carriages, and, as Henry Brandon said, had "quite a parting talk with their lady-loves."

Mr. Jerome and Dr. Wilton were at the carriage of Miss Hunter, in conversation with Miss Julia and with Miss Morton.

Thomas Hunter was at the carriage of Violet Brandon, talking in an undertone to her about their own private affairs — while Henry Brandon and Mr. Campbell were at the carriage of Laura and Lucy, each of the girls with their heads a little out of the carriage on their respective sides, talking to their separate admirers, and so intent, as not to pay the least attention to the other.

In reply to some excuse which Henry Brandon had just

12 *

made to Laura; for something he had said to Miss Gray, Laura said to him:

"Ah! cousin, I shall find it difficult to forgive you. You openly asserted that you had always been an admirer of mine, but had become divided in your feelings."

"Pshaw, Laura! you know I had to say something pleasant to the daughter, after her very respectable old father had put himself to the trouble of talking to me in that *family*-like sort of way, and I thought a little love-making just the thing to meet the case; did n't you see how well it was received?"

"Oh, yes, I saw it all, and don't think it was all *fun* on either side — rather think you will be going over to 'Methodist meetin',' as you call it, before very long. Will you allow me to go with you?"

"Yes, certainly I will; but Laura, you don't know the masculine gender very thoroughly, if you don't know that I could not help loving as handsome a girl as she is, *some*. And then that dash of wit and deviltry, when out of sight of the old man Methodist, should be encouraged. I think we might proselyte her: what think you of that?"

"Yes, that would all be very well, if you had not expressed such a willingness to *be* proselyted yourself."

"Ah! these were mere idle words. I could very well afford to fall a little in love with so pretty a *heretic*, but you know I could never go back to her idolatry. But my dear Laura, I have a charge to bring against you too, which is, that unasked, yea, even begged by the young lady herself not to do so, you really did, with evident bad temper, *give me away* — remember that, fair lady!"

"Ah! two bites at a cherry is an obsolete idea, nor do I know how to divide a hair 'twixt south and southwest side."

"Truly, Laura, your literary references are absolutely odious — desist, I pray you, unless you wish to see me dwindle to the size of passing through the eye of a needle with safety — just perish away under their influence."

"They suit the subject most opportunely," said she, laughing, "and I have more of just such at my tongue's end, when occasion shall occur again for their use."

"Then you will forget them, for by all the gods of Olympus I declare unto you, that there shall never be the same fault found with me again, in jest or otherwise."

"Very well, we shall see."

"Why, Laura, after that penitent speech, I expected you to receive me, with open arms, into your favor again, or as the Baptists say, into full fellowship; but your reluctance rather shows that you have fairly turned the tables on Othello."

"Who — what?"

"Nobody — nothing."

"I am glad you made that retraction to your last speech."

"So am I, since I see the personal danger I was about to incur."

While this conversation was going on, Laura had rested her hand on the window-sill of the carriage, and Henry Brandon taking it up, just as he finished his last remark, said: "A truce to that; now tell me, my lady, who gave thee this ring?"

"I will, most noble sir; it was the gift in girlhood's merry years of a generous, rattling, but I fear me, now, a truant boy."

"Hast thou never displaced it since that generous, rattling boy did place it there?"

"Never."

"Then it seemeth unto me that this generous, wandering boy did *love* thee, in thy young girlhood, and that the merry girl did somewhat love that boy."

Blushing deeply for an answer, she replied: "Perhaps thou didst know, fair sir, the little boy?"

"Yes, I do remember a little lad who once did tell me the little story of his heart. It is many years ago, and if I now can tell the story as it was told to me, it was that he did deeply love his cousin, and something tells me that if the noble girl is true to the little maid — the man still loves as loved the boy." Then raising her beautiful hand to his lips, said: "Let that wanderer wander whither he will, his heart untravelled still fondly turns to thee —" and. laughing a joyous, happy sort of laugh, said: "Now you understand me, good-by."

Blushing and trembling, with her soft blue eyes swimming in unbidden tears, she sweetly said: "Good-by."

In a few minutes they were all on their separate ways.

CHAPTER XXI.

"Devotion wafts the mind above,
But heaven itself descends in love."
BYRON.

THEY had driven but a short distance after parting with their young beaux, when Lucy, who had caught a glimpse of the "good-by" scene between Laura and Henry Brandon, said to her sister:

"Laura, what new extravagance was that of cousin Henry's, as he bid you good-by?"

"I scarcely know, Lucy: he says and does so many odd things."

Lucy now discovered that her sister had been shedding tears, and said:

"Why, Laura, I really believe you have been crying."

At this Laura began afresh a sort of mixed hysterical laugh and cry, without making a reply. Lucy again laughed, and asked what was the matter, but her sister still remained silent; and now, with her hand to her face, continued the same hysteric sobbing. At length, Lucy still urging her to tell the cause of her excitement, she said: "Lucy, I have never before kept a secret from you, or from mother; but *this* I have never told to either, for my heart shrinks from its exposure."

"Now, that I know that you have something at your heart that gives you trouble, I cannot bear you to keep it from me: does it relate to cousin Henry?"

"Yes, Lucy, it does."

"Have you become displeased with him in any way?"

"No, far from it—how could you think that?"

"I really think nothing Laura, as I know nothing, and only asked the question because your tears were so unexpected."

"I have desired to tell you, Lucy, before this, something of my feelings; but my cheek would so burn with woman's delicacy, that my heart would fail; but now I will tell you, cost me what it will to do so. I must tell you, or my poor heart will break—first, promise never to reveal it."

"I certainly promise you, sister, never to do so without your leave."

Laura then, hesitatingly, began the first sad story of her life, by asking Lucy if she remembered, when they were children, that she would often attempt to tease her by calling their cousin Henry her sweetheart, and with what resentment she would tell her, that she did not care if he was."

"Yes, very well," and at once catching at Laura's story, said—"I believed so then, and I believe so now;" saying this with a certain tone of voice, which at once secured not only Laura's confidence, but gave her assurance of good feeling and sympathy.

"Little girl as I was, I was really not conscious of it being that feeling which I afterward knew it to be—love—yes,

love, Lucy; I have spoken it now, the first time in my life.
You will remember too, that he gave me this ring on the
evening before he left for college; and at the time he gave
it, he asked me to remember him, which I promised to do.
This you did not know, as I did not tell you; but you do
know that we corresponded somewhat irregularly all the
while during his absence.   This correspondence was based
on that mutual obligation, and at our first meeting after his
return, though it assumed so ludicrous a form, I somehow
felt that I would be called on, either to fulfil the purpose
of the promise, or to forever give it up.   This evening he
referred to both directly, and told me that his feelings toward me now, were still as they then were.   He said no more,
but—"

"What?"

Shrinking for a moment from the confession, she at length
said :

"But my heart is his, has always been — can never be
another's.   There Lucy," she continued, "you have the
cherished secret of my life, from girlhood till now; and the
beginning, too, of my life-trouble; but the pleasure has been
mine, let the sorrow be too."

"But, Laura, he did not tell you that he *loved* you, did
he?"

"Only as I have told you, Lucy."

"Are you not *afraid* to let your feelings bear you along
so recklessly?   Cousin Henry is a noble young fellow — in
mind, in character, and in person; but you must remember,
even when a boy, and while at college, he was known to be
wild and eccentric, and as we all see, is quite so disposed
even yet; and may not settle himself, but wander off, and
forget you."

"Yes, Lucy, I am aware of all you say, yet am not
afraid; nor can I, if I would, break the chain which has
bound my whole life.   I have no fear of his truth, his honor,

or his eccentricities : nature never lavishes such gifts as his
on unworthy objects, and as seldom, I fancy, bestows them
without some commensurate design. With his mind and
heart, there is nothing human to fear; and he will be a
man of mark when the proper time arrives—and come it
will—when the cautious, plodding, censorious characters,
who in their very littleness may condemn him, shall have
faded from mortal memory." Seeming to acquire confidence
from her own words, she raised her head and said — "That
which the world calls eccentricity in men of mind, and of
known probity of heart, is but little else than a species of
the mind's own recreation, before the appointed time and
occasion have come for its normal action. You see I fear
nothing so far as *he* is concerned ; but what I do fear, is the
very probable course of our mother. Whether it is imagination or not, I have always thought she suspected some sort
of feeling between Henry Brandon and myself; and, as you
have often heard her, has ever expressed herself in very
strong terms against the marriage of cousins. Of late she
has been more pointed than ever—so much so, that he as
well as myself must know her feelings."

"But Laura," said Lucy, attempting to laugh, "suppose
he should say nothing more to you about this ? "

" Oh ! my sister, do not torture me, do not speak thus. I
am not afraid, I know him better than you all ; my *heart*
it is that guides me;" then passionately clasping her
hands, she continued, "my soul — the very essence of my
being, leads me to trust him, and I do ; there is no power
within myself, or in any other, which can shake this confidence —'t is fate ! 't is my life, or 't is death, and all, perhaps ! "

With these impassioned words she caught her sister round
the neck, and in tears of real grief gave her swelling heart
relief.

"Oh, Laura, Laura ! you must not give way to your feelings in this manner; there may be fewer difficulties than you apprehend."

"No, Lucy, the difficulties are greater even than I have expressed. My heart could not ache as it does, unless its very life was at stake; and I tell you that Henry Brandon is as near to me now as he will ever be, and yet the *hope* is dearer to me than life itself."

"Come, sister, you grieve me by this wildness, this frenzy!"

"Yes, Lucy, I must, and I almost frighten myself."

At this, they both ceased talking; but Laura continued to rest her head upon her sister's shoulder, and to sob. This violent expression of grief soon brought its own relief. Then raising her head, and looking her sister timidly in the face, she said — "Forgive me for this, Lucy."

"Certainly," said Lucy, smiling; "but you must learn to restrain your feelings more, and work the harder for them."

The remainder of the road was passed over in silence. They all reached Mr. Robert Brandon's in good time, and separated with mutual congratulations for the pleasant time they had enjoyed.

CHAPTER XXII.

"When I said I would die a bachelor, I did not think I should live till I were married."

ON the return of Thomas Hunter from college, his father had placed him in possession of a very superb plantation which had already been assigned to him, with an ample number of able negroes, and every facility for conducting a large planting business with ease and success. Few young planters had ever begun life with more flattering assurances of success, pleasantness, and usefulness. With aristocratic opinions tempered into good sense and feeling, by the generous and chivalric instincts of the Southern gentleman, his tastes, habits, and circumstances refuted every charge which it afterwards became popular to make in slanderous newspapers, pseudo romances, and tracts, falsely pretending to morality and philanthropy, against Southern planters, as a *class*. We no more pretend to say, however, that every man who made cotton was of this stamp, than we would assert every man in the NORTH to have been a Southern slanderer or abolitionist. We write of Southern *society* and not of individuals, selecting only such of the latter as represented the former.

As Hunter rode up to his gate, he was met by his house servants, who had been anxious in regard to his continued absence, and a man-servant with a retinue of stable-boys received "Sam Brandon," and the horses. The house was flung open immediately, and presented a most inviting appearance of pleasantness and comfort. The house itself was of the cottage order, with verandas extending on all sides, with transverse passages running through, and intersecting at the centre of the building, thus arranged for the benefit of shade and breeze during the long Southern summer. It was elegantly furnished, but furnished with especial reference to comfort and abandon. Hammocks, rocking-chairs, and lounges were scattered through all the rooms.

Fresh water, a bottle of good wine, and a box of cigars were soon placed on the side-board for general use. When Hunter saw his young friends distributed according to their own inclinations, and at perfect ease, he asked to be excused for a short while, as he wished to see his "driver" before night, and asked Henry Brandon to act as *major domo*, during his absence."

"Yes, go along, Tom, I'll see that matters are administered *secundum artem*; for instance, I will take charge of

13

the wine and cigars, while Mr. Jerome will see that the water is not left all unhonored."

Hunter in leaving the house passed by the kitchen, and seeing old "Aunt Jinny," his chief of cuisine ordnance, told her to have one of her *very best* suppers, but not to let it come in before nine o'clock.

"Yes, Mass Tom, I understans zactly what you wants — you wants a supper for young gentlemen — need'n' trouble youself 'bout it no mo'." It was not long before the old woman could be seen stirring round most industriously, gathering up a suitable corps of assistants, and ordering them up to proper quarters, with an authority which showed the importance with which she invested the occasion, and a determination to meet it as became an official of her reputation.

This was the last of Hunter's attention in that direction. In passing about, the old woman at one time passed in full view of Henry Brandon, who remarked:

"Gentlemen, as Hunter is not here, I will discuss his cook. 'Old Aunt Jinny' is famous among us all, as one of the best cooks on the globe. If you get a full view of her face, you could almost fancy yourselves eating broiled chicken, broiled ham, mutton chops, hot rolls, and wafers; and drinking as fine a cup of tea or coffee as was ever drawn in Pekin, or sipped by the Sultan."

"Stop, Mr. Brandon," said Dr. Wilton, "or you will excite both my hunger and thirst."

"Very well, we will let supper elaborate the remainder of her virtues."

At nine o'clock, old Aunt Jinny's virtues spoke for themselves, in such a supper as only a Southern planter can set, and only an old slave cook could prepare. The whole negro race have a *genius* for the *cook-pot*. But alas! for Northern philanthropy, and Northern statesmanship! Together they have destroyed the best *cooks* of the *world*, and the most benevolent system of cooking, on the earth; and what is more, destroyed the kindly ties between the negro and the only *true* friend the negro race has *ever* had — the Southern white man. And now, in September, 1869, we inquire in all earnestness, what is to be the result? Leaving out all considerations of interest, we ask with the liveliest apprehension what good effect on the course of society the extension to him of suffrage can possibly produce? While all well-ordered governments strive to restrain suffrage to a proper representation of the material interests of society, ours has sought out the most ignorant and impecunious class upon which to confer that dangerous privilege. Suffrage is no *natural* right — it is a privilege growing out of property, and property grows out of civilization. All civil wars very soon result in its extension — it is an effort of each leader to secure the masses; and there is no surer indication of a people being in the high road of revolution, than to see them extending this power to the lower classes, who can possibly have no rights of the sort; and none have ever secured peace, until it was wrenched back from them in some manner.

This fact is universal history, and at this age of enlightenment should have prevented a recourse to it. In our own especial case, the man upon whom it has been conferred belongs directly to a *heathen race.* This fact, together with his former condition of slave, and his *universal* ignorance with his natural imbecility, even without the power of suffrage, is calculated to engender an alienation between him and the white man; but with it, to make him an *aggressor* upon the society which is superior to him, and upon the property of which he has none, and cannot have. He knows not how else to use this dangerous weapon: ignorance, idleness, and poverty drive him into this position. Instead of being told the real cause of his freedom, whether a good one or not, and that it was a *penalty* to the

white master for some great violation of law, he is told
that it was a special interposition of Providence in his behalf, through the *intercession* of the North.   This at once
gives him a most bloated idea of his importance, and he
immediately falls into the most superstitious worship on
account of it.   He next looks upon himself as one of the
children of Israel, as he understands it, and upon the whole
South as his Canaan, of which he wants immediate possession ; and through *theft* and suffrage strives to get it. He is
led to believe by his *present friends* that his past slavery
has been a great wrong ; never once seeing that if he is as
improved as he thinks himself, that it is *altogether owing*
to the *only man* whom he is taught to hate, and to injure if
possible.   He is never told that but few years since, as it
were, he was brought to our homes, through all the horrors
of the "middle passage," by the humanitarians of Old
and of New England, and wreaked upon us in his bestial
heathenism ; and that his *race* is still besotted in the lowest
form of paganism and cannibalism in its own land.   No,
these facts are most *tenderly* kept from him, while he is
being taught to believe his *superiority* to us, and urged to
every species of aggression.   The upper classes of the North
may plead — or wish to — ignorance of these wretched facts,
but they cannot.   There are paid hirelings — paid by the
Government, in the shape of preachers, teachers, Congress-
men, etc. — of both sexes, from their midst, who associate
with negroes of the lowest character, assemble with them
at their Congo celebrations, join with them in their miserable worship, on terms of perfect equality, and urge them
on.   What, we ask, is to be the result of this on American
society?   Thousands upon tens of thousands of men and
women, who were once orderly, well-behaved, and engaged
in the useful pursuits of life, are now wandering thieves,
keepers of dirty shops, peddlers of stolen goods, hucksters
of filthy fruit, street-walkers, idlers, and vagabonds ; while

their children are growing up around us in idleness, vaga-
bondism, and lewdness. And yet these are the chosen suf-
fragans of a *party* which aspires to the control of American
nationality. Men and women of the North, can you blame
the South for despising you? You have intelligence, and
know better. Why do you persist? "Quousque tandem
abutere nostra patientia."

Property is the basis of all civilization, even as it is the
creature of civilization. It is, therefore, the legitimate
object of legislation; and there should be no legislation
except by a legislator who bases his right to that position
upon his relation to property: all other is spurious—and
by that much will, must, and does exert a harmful, dangerous influence.

There is a natural antagonism between property and
labor — it is the very law of labor and property; but still
there is that natural relation between them which *compels*
property to sustain labor well up to a working point. Any
effort, therefore, whatever, to interfere or to set up new
theories against this law, but by that much disturbs society. This law, blind, strong, muscular labor does not see,
but, consulting its own instincts of force, seeks to aggress,
and, whenever and by whatever accident it secures political power, never fails to use it in that direction. Give
universal labor universal suffrage, and it at once organizes
a universal attack on property and position. The largest
liberty and the greatest ease is the first law of *all animal
life;* but under the laws of civilization it cannot be
granted, and we but give way to a miserable, maudlin
sentimentality when we do so.

When the masses acquire suffrage, there is but *one power*
that can recover it from them, and that is the ONE-MAN
POWER. Let us wait.

We have already had to ask pardon for so many digres-
sions, that it would seem a mocking to do so again; we

13 *

shall therefore return to our story, without apology, by
telling the reader that our young gentlemen continued to
enjoy themselves as we have seen they had begun.

At the appointed hour, the supper was announced, which
they passed at least an hour in the enjoyment of.   After
this, cigars were lit, and each one fixed himself for his own
personal ease.

"Tom," said Henry Brandon, while looking around the
brilliantly lighted room (it was Hunter's library) from
the lounge upon which he was reclining, and puffing at
intervals his long-drawn Havana, "you really live in as
great comfort and elegance as *we* did at college; indeed I
believe you have imitated the style " — meaning this as a
burlesque allusion to college-life — and, without waiting
for a reply, said: "Oh, Tom, I have always forgotten to
tell you that I am your banker for the sum of twenty-five
dollars — the half of the whole amount for which I sold
our four-years' furniture.   What do you think of the sale?"

" Oh, excellent! "

"There came a couple of very nice chaps, to be ex-
amined at commencement, for the purpose of getting
choice rooms, I suppose, and said that they had been
informed that I had a very good set of furniture for sale,
as I was going out.   I told them yes; and, showing them
every article, proposed to take fifty dollars for it, rather
than peddle it off, which old *Grimes* had already proposed
to do for me.   They took me up at a word, and rather
apologized for buying second-hand furniture by modestly
saying that they 'were not very flush of means, as the
apple and *onion crops* had both failed the year before; but
as ours seemed to be the furniture of *gentlemen*, they did
not regard it much.'   I was so well pleased with the boys,
I had a damned — excuse me, Parson — good notion to
give it to them, and would, but feared it might hurt their
feelings; while I knew fifty dollars would neither hurt

their feelings nor their purses. Shall I pay it to you now? I shall never think of it again."

"No, never mind; just add it to what you have owed me all along for four years. You must have improved in your financial memory. You owe me about five hundred beside, I think."

"The devil I do! Then what did I do with mine?"

"Spent it, loaned it, and gave it away together."

"Ah! 'scandalum magnatum' — from first to last, Tom. But excuse us, gentlemen, for intruding our college business upon you."

"Oh, we have been quite amused," said Mr. Jerome, "and would like to have you proceed with your reminiscences — it reminds me of my own glad old days."

CHAPTER XXIII.

" I 'll talk a word with this same learned Theban."

"MR. CAMPBELL," asked Henry Brandon, "were you educated at a Southern college?"

"Yes; at William and Mary, first, and afterward at the University."

"Did you attend the Law School at the latter?"

"Yes; I graduated there."

"Ah! then — according to Uncle Robert Brandon — I can account for the stringent *State sovereignty* doctrine I heard you express this evening. He says that all Southern schools inculcate that, while the Northern schools inculcate the Federal doctrine."

"I can't say that that is my reason for entertaining it; but State sovereignty is certainly taught there. And with all deference to Mr. Brandon, I can't see how he can avoid believing in it, if he acknowledges this to be a *confederate republic.*"

"Well, I don't think he goes very far with that doctrine. *I* have not studied such questions with any great attention, but confess my instincts do not go very far in that direction either."

Campbell replied that he had been educated in its belief, and very sincerely entertained it.

Campbell belonged to that style of young men who observe all the polite forms of social intercourse, leaving but little to speculation, doubt, or accident, but act in accordance with all established prescriptions. He was generally grave and dignified in his deportment, and very respectful in his manners — especially to those from whom he expected advancement. Though finely educated, he was not brilliant, and ventured but little out on the unreckoned seas of original thought. In political matters, therefore, he adopted the opinions which had already been raised up to a system under the lead of men whom he had already chosen to follow, and who had already been *successful.* The Democratic party furnished these, as he thought, and he had thoroughly identified himself with it — in this, following the lead of most of the second-class intellect of that day.

Henry Brandon, on the other hand — as may be judged from the shadowy indications of character which he had only, till now, thrown out — was, as near as it was possible to be, the opposite of this — considering that he strictly observed the status of the *gentleman* in all his antitheses. He saw through and ridiculed the Korhassan veil which ignorant but cunning old prigs throw around the altars of public affairs, and looked at them just as they were, and spoke as he thought, with nothing more than common regard for that almost fiction of society, yclept " public opinion." In short, he was just such a young man as seldom rises, let his mind be what it will; attracting, as they do, the combined attack of all inferior grades, and too often falling before their united charge.

For many long years the Democratic party, almost without interruption, maintained control of the Government, and had at length become strong enough to shut out all the first-class talent of the country; and the Government finally fell between the manipulations of jacobinical, fanatical charlatans on the one side, and a class of second and third rate politicians on the other.

The histories of Mr. Clay and Mr. Webster are illustrations of this assertion.

"Then you are in favor of a consolidated government?" said Campbell, in reply to the remarks of Brandon.

"No, not one entirely so; but even such an one is preferable to this slack-twisted affair, with an everlasting tendency to revolution, civil wars, and all manner of State deviltries."

"In what manner would you propose to avoid such?"

"Well, I propose to avoid nothing; but if I had the power, I would very materially lengthen the Executive term, from four years to twenty, or life; limit State legislation to matters *strictly* local, and, first and last of all, I should confine suffrage to native citizens, with a *good property qualification.* Those are my present ideas."

Campbell replied that he had been taught to believe the people should all have suffrage, and that they were capable of self-government.

"The people! I am very much afraid of *the people.* The American people are no better than other people; and the people, whenever they get hold, never let go until everything goes to the devil. It has ever been so, and I expect will ever be." After some further running conversation of this sort, Brandon said: "But come, Mr. Campbell, I am no politician, and perhaps am in error about these matters — let us listen to these gentlemen, who appear to have up a pleasanter subject."

At this moment, Mr. Jerome said to Hunter that he might urge his suit on Miss Morton; but whenever he mentioned the subject — rather alluded to it — she always raised the *Church subject,* and rather accused him of *heresy,* which looked a little like a disinclination to listen to his lackadaisicals, and forced him to maintain the *pastor* at the expense of the sighing *lover.*

"Ah! she is just trying your earnestness," said Hunter, laughing. "I know all about Sally's church feeling; and she cares about as much for the Baptists as I do for Mohammedanism. She joined the Church from some old family association, just after her father's death. But Baptist or not, she would make an elegant Church woman. There is scarcely such another girl to be found. I rather promised to be her chevalier, when we were young folks; but when I came back from college, a few months ago, she laughed at the idea. But then *you* had been visiting her, Parson, and I always thought you had something to do with that laugh."

"Oh, no! Let me assure you that I have never been encouraged to get in any one's way. It was only your native modesty. She is certainly a very superior girl, and I admire her greatly."

"Yes, I will vouch for the Parson's admiration," said Dr. Wilton. "Miss Morton is his constant theme. We can seldom converse on any subject, however foreign, longer than twenty minutes, before he makes a quotation from Miss Morton. I tell him it is fast getting to be a Hamlet case."

"Ah! the matter is indeed getting to be a melancholy one. Quotations are a sure indication that the virus has taken," said Hunter.

At this moment, Henry Brandon rose to get a fresh cigar, when he remarked to Hunter that he had not yet played his *Goldsmith* rôle, and he was getting anxious to have it over with.

Hunter comprehended the allusion, and replied: "Yes, you always badger me into playing for you, by scandalizing me."

Henry Brandon explained to the company that Hunter's friends used to say that *fluting* would some day be his *profession;* "but," added he, "I believe Judge Hunter has provided against this extremity, for a few days, at least, judging from the present *surroundings.* But, never mind, play for us, Hunter, and let us go to bed under the influence of some of your sweetest old airs."

Hunter gratified him by doing as requested, in his very best style, when the proposition was made to retire.

CHAPTER XXIV.

"But earthly hope, how bright soe'er,
Still fluctuates o'er this changing scene,
As false and fleeting as 't is fair."

AFTER their friends had left, on the evening of their return from the spring, Laura and Lucy went to their own chamber to rearrange their dresses; and while there, Laura said:

"Lucy, sister, I fear you will think I transcended the bounds of — I may say — delicacy, in giving way to my feelings as I did this evening; and perhaps I did; but I could not restrain them. Something came over me, and I had to let you know my feelings, my secret, and my trouble. That is all the explanation I can give."

"Do you regret having done so, Laura?"

"No, I do not; though it may seem premature to you."

"It does not appear as premature as it would otherwise have done, had not Cousin Henry made the same committal to me last night."

"Oh, why did you not tell me, Lucy?"

"I did intend doing so at the earliest possible opportunity."

"What did he say to you?"

"Only that he could not get over his boy-feeling for you, and that he intended to tell you, not caring whom he offended. He did it in his usual light sort of way, and I would not encourage it until I knew how *you* felt; but asked him if I might tell you. I know, however, that you always had some sort of preference for him, even from a boy, and of late I have been satisfied that your *feelings* were really involved."

"Yes, Lucy, they are — my very *life* is involved; and yet I would have sacrificed it before I would have expressed it in words, had it not been for what he said to me this evening. And yet I knew he *loved* me."

Their maid now announced that tea was waiting, and the two girls tripped to the supper-room with as much apparent lightness as though nothing unusual had taken place. Mrs. Brandon entered into the conversation, that immediately began, by asking her daughters how they were pleased with the speaking, saying, "You know, girls, I am compelled to feel some interest, as Colonel Haywood is one of the most accomplished orators in the South."

"Yes, we felt all the apprehension that you did; but we very soon felt every confidence, after father began; and by the time he had concluded, I think we felt very proud."

"I am obliged to you, my daughter," said Mr. Brandon, laughing very pleasantly. "How did *you* think I sustained myself, Laura?"

"Most admirably. You know I am not a great politician, and could not judge of your arguments; but in chaste eloquence I thought you *excelled* Colonel Haywood, and so Miss Gray expressed herself."

"But do you think your opinions impartial?"

"I do," said Laura; "and yet I think Colonel Haywood deserves his reputation. He is confident, bold, impassioned, and quite eloquent at times, I thought."

"Oh, that is quite a compliment to us both; and I am obliged, too, to your beautiful new friend, Miss Gray. But what did Mr. Campbell say, Lucy? You know he is a Democrat?"

"He came up and congratulated me, most handsomely, on your effort, and I think was *quite* proud to be seen with me afterward," said she, laughing.

"Well, how did Henry Brandon speak of the affair? I suppose I must ask *you* that, Laura."

"Ah, he is such a Whig, and such an admirer of yours any way, that he was willing to make his *affidavy*, as he called it, that every word you spoke was *Promethean*."

"Really, I must like the wild, rattling lad even better than ever."

At this remark from her father, coupled with his reference to her for the answer, a ray of hope and gladness lighted up the innocent and beautiful face of Laura; and in a few minutes she ventured to ask him when her cousin Henry intended leaving the country for his law studies.

"I cannot say; but as soon, I suppose, as he gets over his home-romp with you girls. I had almost thought to ask *you* that, my daughter, as you and he appear quite confidential."

Laura's face reddened at this, but with an effort at calmness she replied that she thought he had made a very fair division of his time and confidence between all his friends.

"Up to last night, I believe he had; but, since then, I think you have had decided advantage of us all."

14

"Are you not laboring under a misapprehension, sir?"

"No, I think not. Time passes without note between young people so well pleased as you have appeared to be to-day."

"Pleased! Yes, you yourself appear pleased with the company of the 'rattling young lad.' Any one would be who had any relish for wit, humor, fancy, and fine sense; but then I did not intend to engross his time. I did not appear desirous of doing so, did I, father?"

"No, no; at least not more than he did of yours. But then there was clearly a very high zest on both sides, and you managed to be together nearly all the while at Mr. Gray's carriage."

"Oh, father, you should not say that, as it was mere accident that placed him near Miss Gray and myself; and you could not have expected me to be rude enough to leave them; and if you noticed us, you certainly saw that it was to her that he directed his attentions. By the way, how did you like her appearance?" displaying some nervousness at the question she asked.

"I thought she was a girl of fine style, and very fine face. Did she seem pleased with Henry?"

"Very decidedly; and I thought old Mr. Gray quite as much so."

"It would be an excellent family for Henry to get into. The old man has a way of making people fear him; and that is all that Henry requires to make him a first-class man. I think I must encourage the idea."

Laura had watched the face of her father, through all this jesting sort of conversation, and had begun to think that he comprehended her feelings, and was disposed to favor them — as it was only in *him* she looked for a friend; — but the last remark led her to fear that he was entirely ignorant; and the pleasure that had suffused itself over her happy face, now instantly faded away, and she listlessly replied:

"Yes, I made Miss Gray a present of him, in jest."

Lucy, seeing the change, and resolving to sustain her, said, quickly, "But I thought I overheard him object to your doing so."

"Yes, he jestingly said that he wished me to retain an interest in him."

At this remark, Mrs. Brandon, who had not spoken for some time, nor had seemed so well pleased, asked why he had wished her to retain an interest in him. "Had you any in him, Laura?"

"None, more than of cousin, mother," she softly replied to the rather sharp question.

"I should not suppose that your doing that, then, would have deprived him of such an interest."

Laura saw the direction of her mother's words, and very prudently made no further answer. She knew that, whatever there was of antagonism in her present position to her mother's wishes, it had not been wantonly entered into, but was the growth of years and circumstances — a flow of feeling that had come unbidden as the wind, and swept the strings of her maiden heart even from its girlhood-time. Mrs. Brandon was an unexceptional woman in all those kind, generous, and self-sacrificing qualities that made her the best of mothers; and she loved her daughters as her life. Her relations too with Henry's mother had ever been of the most pleasant and confidential nature. No cloud, from first to last, had ever passed over their intercourse to darken its peacefulness. Henry himself, from earliest boyhood, had been as one of her own children. She had known him as a wild, bold, generous, rambling, uncontrollable sort of a boy; yet she loved him, as in all this she knew there was no *taint* — that these qualities belonged more to his mind than his heart, more to his genius than his disposition, and more to his temperament than to his character. She knew that with all this there was no aggressiveness, such as too often accompanies these characteristics. His daring and recklessness was that of innocence, intending no wrong, and fearing no danger. Knowing these things, she had loved him — could but love him; yet *now*, she feared him, as a husband for her daughter; but above all, her prejudice against the intermarriage of relations could not be overcome. It proved to be ingrained with her very life.

This last Laura had found out, and it was the source of her greatest anxiety. Without having intended it, she found herself running counter to one of the strongest sentiments of her mother, and saw that she must either meet it, or prepare to sacrifice herself.

Here was to be the great conflict of her life, and here rose a cloud upon the early morning sky that was to drape in darkness and sorrow, the bright sunlight, the summer-joy, of one whose purity of soul and gentleness of heart, were as flowers of love and truth flinging around frail humanity the freshness of their fragrance and the softness of their beauty. The conflict came.

CHAPTER XXV.

"For virtue's self may too much zeal be had;
The worst of madmen is a Saint run mad."

HUNTER'S guests left next morning, after enjoying an excellent breakfast, fresh and hot, from the department of old Aunt Jinny. Brandon asked Hunter to go over home with him; but the latter had to decline, as he had already sent a wagon to the city, for the purpose of bringing out fall supplies of clothing, etc., for his negroes, and must meet it.

Ah, ha! Now speak, ye tender friends of the "nation's wards," and tell us who of ye, on this 15th October, 1869, have sent your wagon for supplies of clothing for these poor creatures! Answer, ye wrong-headed, fanatical philanthropists, who have spent your lives in seeking objects of *charity* beyond your own bailiwicks, while numberless thousands were suffering with poverty and disease, in abodes of wretchedness, guilt, and shame, within your own limits! Answer, ye tender-hearted female sentimentalists, who, in your lecture and society rooms, have writhed and shrieked in vicarious agonies for the *wrongs* of the Southern negro, thousands of miles away, while the daughters and sons of your own wombs were rioting in assignation and rolling in brothels on the thoroughfares of your own great cities! Answer, ye forked-tongued, libellous priesthood, from whose loins have too often issued the spawn of depravity, bastardy and woe, and shame and poverty! Yes, answer! Then come and see the ruin your lying has wrought in this fair land of the South! BAYONETS stand ready to protect your reply and your shame. Come, and see, and answer! Yes, and you too come, oh, immaculate statesmen — there is no gallows now for the incendiary, the robber, or the murderer — and behold your wisdom and your prophecy reflected from this Southern mirror!

The negro is *free*. Let him be free forever. We would not have him back. The charm is broken. But why were *we slandered* and *reviled*, to free him? Tell us that. Was it to work upon our feelings, or to get up a *crusade against us* among your own people? What is it that so pointed to his freedom, that we should still be persecuted for his slavery? Was it his color, his beauty, his morality, or his intelligence?

Now, remember, ye tender-souled old women, ye pious preachers, ye weeping congregations, ye lying tractarians,

14 *

ye slandering romancists — and, ay, ye jolly fine statesmen — that society, life, every form of human association calls for *labor* and the laborer — that in these Southern States, by a peculiar divinity, were the best provided, the least worked, the most contented, and the most orderly *laborers* of the world, and *from* THESE VERY FACTS had proceeded the great advances which universal society had made within the last century. Yes, learn that the structure of *modern civilization* was based upon African labor — *slavery* — and with its fall must fall many *parts* of the noble old edifice, though new ones may rise. Yes, now come and see the beginning of your mighty work — see that same laborer in his lawlessness, his aggressiveness, his debauchery, his filth, his poverty, his already departure from the religious ministrations of those who led him out of his total, besotted darkness, to his late modest but practical excellence, and view *your evangelization!* Yes, we invite ye, in the name of the slandered, the wronged, the down-trodden, and pauperized South, to come and view the *beginning* of your millennial work. Come and see the delicate mothers and daughters filling the most menial and laborious places, quietly trudging on, through poverty and weariness, to death — and then ask us to LOVE ye! to love ye!! to love ye!!! Ha! ha! ha! To love ye! and to love the *Union!!* Ha! gloat in your *blood* bonds, and your thieveries! Your days are numbered! ay, NUMBERED!!

Yes, the slaves are freed, and may they ever remain so — and so they will, unless some yet undiscovered country should require their services; and then Puritan *enterprise* and hypocritical casuistry would soon discover some "middle passage" to transport them thither; but for the present, the final overthrow of your own power, the wrongs you have inflicted, and the hate you have engendered, is all that you may claim of this great event: the rest belongs to destiny — to the future; and these, neither regard

him who precipitated, nor him that approved its decree.
We can only view the wrong and silently await the end.
In the meanwhile, let us hear no more of the "*Rebellion*."

Henry Brandon was now on his way home, with no one
in his company save his boy, "Sam Brandon," who
accompanied his young master whenever he could get a
possible excuse to do so, and was as happy as it was ever
intended a negro should be.

After riding nearly a mile in silence, Henry suddenly
turned and asked him why he did not talk.

"You look so serious, Mass Henry, this morning, I jis
thought to let you had yo' own way for a while."

"Why do you say that I look serious, Sam?"

"I sees it in yo' eye, Mass Henry, and you don't sing nor
whistle none yo' old chunes, nor yo' don't ride fass."

Sam had stood near the carriage of Laura Brandon, the
evening before, and with the usual instinct of the negro in
such matters, had come to the conclusion that his young
master was about to get into a *love scrape* with his cousin,
and was now drawing on what he had seen.

"What do you suppose has made me serious, Sam?"

"Don't know, Mass Henry, 'ceptin' it war that kiss you
gin Miss Laura, sorter strikin' in on yer," he replied, with
a hearty chuckle.

"The devil you say, Sam; did you see anything of that
kind, you dog?"

"Yah! ha! Mass Henry, I sede it every bit; but nobody
else did, for I looked all about."

"Ah, you are a great rascal, Sam; what were you watching for?"

"I wan't watchin' ov you, I was watchin' *for* you, Mass
Henry."

"Ah! that will do better; but Sam, why have you never
got a wife — you are old enough?"

"Yes, sah, and I is ben kinder engaged and sorter married

two or three times; but I always flewed the track, 'case I
knewed that you would want me soon as you come back,
and den a wife would jist be in my way, and a never-een-
din' trouble."

"Well, do you think of getting one when I do?"

"Oh! yes, sah, I'll get a gal then in yernest."

"Have you seen any one yet that you would like me to
have?"

"Well, yes, sah; but I ain't exac'ly made up my mine
yet. De young lady at ol' Mr. Gray's carriage was a mity
fine-looking young lady. She's his daughter, ain't she, Mass
Henry?"

"Yes."

"I thought so. Well, she looked mity pleasin' at you, an
I was jist making up my mine 'bout de case when, de good
Lord! I sede you kiss Miss Laura; den I thought to myself,
dat is a case itself."

"What would you think of that, Sam—would she do?"

"Do? I speck she would. Miss Laura is the fines' young
lady in dis neck; but den you is cousins—what you gwine
do 'bout dat?"

"I don't know, I'll see about it; why do you object to
cousins getting married?"

"Oh! no sah, I dus not, but I hear it whispered 'bout by
de house gals, dat dere has been some sort of tork 'bout it
over at Miss Laura's."

"You have, eh! well I don't know; but now while I
think of it, let me tell you that you must learn to talk
better. You 've gone backward, Sam, since you were a boy."

"Yes, sah, I knows I has, but who could help dat, 'sociatin'
fer four years with the ding-feel niggers; but I'll larn
again to speak proper 'fore long, Mass Henry."

"You must notice how I talk, and try to talk as I do."

"Yes, sah, I is watchin' you."

The remainder of the road was passed over in silence,

Henry Brandon in thinking over what Sam had said about the "house girls" over at Mr. Brandon's, and Sam, over what Henry had said to him about talking better.

When he reached home, he found his mother and Violet looking for him, and rather expecting Hunter to be with him. Henry explained the reasons why Hunter had not come, and said to Violet that he had not brought his welcome with him, and that she appeared to be disappointed. Violet replied that she could not have had hers yesterday, or she supposed he would have come home with her last night.

" Whom do you mean, my sharp little sister ? "

" Whom do you prefer, Laura or Miss Gray ? "

" Mother," said Henry, " have sufficient authority to suppress such malignant insinuations."

" I don't know, my son, that Violet intends to be malignant, but I would prefer her ceasing to use Laura's name in that connection."

The latter part of this reply was a little chilling to Henry; but he at once resolved that it should not be discovered, though really exposing it by his impatient answer, in saying that he was happy to have the tender considerations of his friends — but really believed that he was not yet a full subject for their sympathy, in this particular matter.

" I hope not, and only said what I did, my son, to guard you against becoming such."

After some further conversation in regard to the incidents of the day before, Violet asked him how he liked the *Methodist girl.*

" Elegantly, she is a great female, I like her."

Subjects of a more sober, matter-of-fact character were gradually brought up by Mrs. Brandon saying:

" Have you forgotten, Henry, that you will be twenty-one years old in a few days?"

" No, no mother ; so important an event in the prospective

history of the world has not, could not escape my memory. On the contrary, I have it constantly in my mind, and reflect upon it with all the solemn gravity due to its possible happening."

"I am not jesting with you, Henry, as —"

"Nor I with you, mother," said he, interrupting her.

"As there are matters in connection with it, of some importance to others as well as yourself."

Henry, still following the bent of his humor, replied:

"You almost alarm me, mother; is it so unparalleled an event, that a young gentleman of twenty years old, and eleven months, and twenty days, should reach the next anniversary, that himself and all the world beside should grow serious at the prospect?"

"No, it is not, nor do I intend to alarm you," said his mother, smiling; "but truly there are some matters for serious consideration in connection with it, which will have to be provided for."

"Ah! very good; proceed, mother, I am all attention."

"Brother," said Violet, a little impatient at his continued levity; if there was not the best evidence that you are nearly twenty-one, I should think you only sixteen. Will you never grow serious?"

"Not one hour sooner than I shall be compelled to, as I can reach perfection in that direction, when I have exhausted myself in all others; indeed, seriousness only follows exhaustion or age, unless in born fools — they come serious; but, Violet, why do you wish me to grow melancholy — will it do you any good to see me miserable?"

At this she rose to leave the room, saying, with a laugh, "I said serious, brother, not melancholy or miserable."

When Violet left, Henry turned to his mother, saying, "Forgive me mother for my levity. I am aware of the matters you alluded to, and have been thinking very soberly over them all the morning."

"I supposed you had of course; but as they related to Violet's marriage, I wished to speak of them before her. I suspect she left for that reason."

They now conversed of family matters for some time, when Henry remarked that he had talked over the whole affair with Hunter the night before. "It appears to have been a very quiet sort of thing, and seems to be progressing very quietly still."

"Yes, their long acquaintance and friendship precluded anything very novel."

Mrs. Brandon next approached him on the subject of such continued attention to Laura, telling him there was danger in it to them both, that she had long known Laura's girlish preference for him, and it would be very easy for him to change it into real affection; and assured him that, from her knowledge of his aunt's character and mind, she would make it very disagreeable for him and Laura to meet at all, should she once discover that Laura's feelings were becoming involved. She then spoke of Laura's habits of implicit obedience to her mother, "which indeed is very commendable; but that she carries it into a sort of morbid romance, and is the only real weakness of her character, and for that reason would not sustain herself."

Henry answered affirmatively to all this, but felt anything else, for two very good reasons — first, because it was an entirely different channel from that in which his feelings flowed, and again, because he had already committed himself to Laura, in different ways, and intended to follow the fortune of his position to whatsoever end it would lead.

CHAPTER XXVI.

"I have set my life upon a cast,
And will stand the hazard of the die."

VIOLET had now returned to the sitting-room, and Henry said to her, by way of changing the direction and style of conversation —

"I have to regret your absence, sister, for the last hour, as for the whole length of that time I have proven, in a most eminent manner, my extraordinary capacity for serious reflection and for entertaining the most solemn propositions. I have not only been serious; but been sitting in grave judgment on *your* affairs, and arranged them on the purest and most formal rules of equity, however unpleasant it was to me to do so. Yes, I have displayed a *Roman* firmness, in deciding against the prospect of some pleasures which I had promised myself."

"I rejoice, brother," she replied, while blushing deeply; "that you have had an opportunity of refuting my assertion of your never-ending *juvenility*, and that my own affairs were the cause of it."

"Quite a handsome speech, my pretty sister. But I will re-open the subject, if your ladyship's nerves can bear the shock."

"Give me two minutes to prepare, and I will be at your service;" then, as if adjusting herself for the rehearsal, she said to him with a blushing consciousness of what was coming, "I am ready, most noble judge."

Henry then began addressing her with great mock gravity, in the following words:

"Sister, I have been correctly informed, that without a proper regard or consideration for the enjoyment of the sentimental portion of the world, and for my own future fame as a *novelist*—you did, yes, actually did, previous to my coming home, destroy the materials wherewithal I had for many years intended to weave a most tender and beautiful romance. I, of course, refer to the events of your *first love-affair*, having determined that these events should well conform to the historic rules of all 'true love,' in never 'running smooth.' But now, I find the entire prospective fabric of my fame destroyed, by your having launched your fortunes on the smoothest, calmest, summer sea that ever bore upon its bosom *first love's* frail bark, and now float as

> 'Idle as a painted ship
> Upon a painted ocean.'"

"Even with humility, do I something bow to the soft impeachment, and most sincerely, brother, do I regret the loss which the world will sustain from the destruction of your romance; but as the only compensation in my power to make, I have this instant resolved to devote much time to the collection of even better material than my own affairs could furnish, and may even draw *some such incidents* as you speak of from *your own* personal history, judging from the evidences now gathering along your path."

Here was a covert allusion to the probable difficulties of a "love scrape" with his cousin; made in that prophetic style so unwelcome to young persons, who already half see their coming trouble through the surrounding haze.

"Yes, I thank you; and whether it be a promise or a prophecy, if fulfilled, the result will be the same, and quite uncommon — the chronicle and the chronicler united."

"No, not so very; we at least have one noble instance of an author making merchandise of his own sorrow — Lord Byron."

"Your instance clears up the doubt. Suppose we next name the style of the effort — whether autobiography, epic, chronicle, or romance; for I promise you my pen shall be

15

equally facile in either composition, though it sound presumptuous for me to say it. I have an equal admiration for Froisart and for Sir Walter — one undertakes a chronicle and ends with a romance, the other begins a romance and ends with a chronicle ; both, however, succeed in giving the most charming stories of love and chivalry."

"I am glad, brother, that our nonsense has really suggested an idea to me — a good one too — that you do indeed set to work at writing a novel." Then smiling, she continued, "it will suit the character of your mind. That love of the *marvellous* — that *inventive* faculty for which you were so distinguished when a youth, in both of which I think you have *wonderfully* improved — will have a fine field to revel in ; one in which, as Sheridan once said, you can 'draw on your memory for your jests, and your imagination for your facts.' But then I must stipulate that you do not indulge too far in that direction, as I cannot bear your *stilted* romances, where all the heroes are larger, finer-looking, braver, and wealthier than ever men get to be, so far as I have seen ; and the heroines, nobler bred, more accomplished, more deeply *in love*, and more perfect, than we poor girls ever get to be ; and having the two making grand speeches on subjects that never come up in real life."

"Yes — well, I thank you most graciously for your compliments to my 'marvellousness,' my 'inventive faculty,' and my 'imagination ;' but I see that you are anxious to clip my wings immediately in the beginning. I fear your own easy love-life has made you so matter-of-fact, so plebeianized your ideas, that you think every heroine should be named Polly, and every hero Peter."

"No, no, brother," she replied, laughing heartily ; "I do not think that, nor do I think that every hero should be a Colonel *Mortimer*, nor every heroine a Lady *Fitzgerald ;* the one wrapped in a splendid military cloak, but allowing the hilt of his sword to peep out, and the heroine in a splendid velvet riding-robe, with a white plume sweeping from her hat; both superbly mounted on Arabians, and accidentally meeting at a dark wood on the highway, just as the lady's bridle is seized by a robber, etc., etc. No, none of that, I charge you. Such perhaps never happened, and certainly never will again."

" Yes, I understand you, I think, and shall endeavor to benefit by your suggestions. Palinurus-like, I shall endeavor to avoid the Scylla and the Charybdis of the too common, and the too uncommon. Indeed, the thing shall be perfect. What else could it be, since my noble self is to be the hero, and lovely cousin Laura the heroine?"

" Even so; but as I see you either intend to act or write a romance, I will give you my general idea of such things, as perhaps suggestive of something new."

" Exactly so, my learned sister."

" Well, a romance is indeed a history — the history of ideal events; and therefore the mirror should be held up to nature, that it may reflect life as it actually passes before us: that is, if the narrative refers to the present period."

" Yes, confine yourself to the present, sister; the story must of necessity be one of to-day."

"Then, I will further premise, by saying that you of course intend a presentation of patrician life; if so, there should be no *plot*, (plots are old - fashioned,) involving strange and unnatural *contretemps* — that grade of life furnishes no plots; every event has a natural relation to the succeeding one; and though they cannot be foreseen, there is no mystery. All the events of life in that stratum of society are plainly connected, and develop themselves in a simple manner, showing the paternity of one event to the other; and so far from exciting the mind, we are astonished afterward that we had not foreseen them. Indeed, there is very little plot or mystery in *any* grade of life.

There are general laws of universal application, and all the ends of life are worked out within those limits. Purposes fail or succeed, according to rational laws ; all other representations are but ridiculous absurdities. The variously distorted *plots* of our romance writers is the chief basis of the arguments used against romance reading, and — "

"Stop, sister; I think you should allow me the privilege of some slight plot in this novel of mine ; for you tell me that I will never be able to persuade my cousin to become Mrs. Henry Brandon ; and what sort of novel would it be to break down right in the middle?"

"Oh! that must often happen according to your own theory, by adoption, of 'true love never running smooth ;' and better break down at the natural termination of the story, than to uphold it with an absurdity."

"Ah! well, well — write a *short* one — yes, I will consider your suggestions ; but just for the present, let us leave the future romance, and come back to those actualities of the present that make up romance."

"Very well," said Violet, who had been playing shy of the subject, "let me hear you."

"Mother informs me that you have given your consent to become Mrs. Tom Hunter, at no very distant period ahead.   True or not?"

Affecting great self-possession, while the crimson rose to her very temples, she replied : "Yes, brother; have you any objection?"

"Very far from it — I approve your choice; but you should have made some show of *consulting* me — your elder, and your only brother."

"Well, brother, I have met your views, by asking if you had any objection."

"Very well, all right; but allow me to submit a few catechetics to your maidenly consideration."

"Certainly."

"Has it ever occurred to you, in these young hours of roseate love, whether you would be as willing to be a '*help-mate*' to said Thomas in the hours of adversity, as you are to be his lady of ease, elegance, and luxury, in the gay time of his prosperity?"

"No; I had not thought directly about it; but now that you point my attention to it, I can answer that I would."

"Very fine; well, has it ever occurred to you that your united fortunes would be such as seldom falls to the share of young people in beginning life, and that you would occupy a pre-eminent position over your past associates in that respect?"

Violet, thinking that he insinuated mercenary motives, quickly replied, "No, brother, no; the idea of property, fortune, wealth, has never once entered my mind. I have never thought of wealth. In all the walks of life I shall ever aim to be true to the peace and honor of my — husband; and above all, be true to my own heart and character; to these ends I would meet adversity with an unflinching, fearless heart, and with a stronger, readier hand, than you may think I possess; health is all that I ask — my heart is right, and ready, and willing, to meet every demand of life."

The last words were spoken with an energy, and a brightness flashing from her eye, and with a glowing bloom suffusing her cheek, that told of their noble source.

Both of them rose at once, as if by some common sentiment; the brother placing his arm affectionately around her, kissed her blushing cheek, saying, with a laugh:

"Glorious! transcendent! you play the heroine, sister, even in our mother's chamber."

"Oh! brother, you should be ashamed to have so excited me, merely for your amusement."

"I had a purpose in it, Violet. I am looking out for a heroine for my forthcoming *romance*."

15 *

In the course of further conversation, Mrs. Brandon asked her son when he thought of beginning his law studies?

"In a few days; why, mother, are you all getting tired of seeing my idleness?"

"Oh, no; only I had heard you speak frequently of late of going into the office of Judge Royal."

"Yes, I had spoken to him in regard to it; but he is away so much of his time, and is away now, that I think I shall read with some one else."

"Brother," said Violet, "why not read with Mr. Campbell?"

"For several good and sufficient reasons; the first of which is, that it comes up to the parable of the blind leading the blind; and next, and last, and all, I do not think *my style* suits *his style*, and his suits mine as little. He is clearly a well-bred gentleman, but belongs to that class of deferential mannerists, who were never agreeable to me. I would not, for instance, be as seriously reverential to Uncle Robert as he is, for *both* of his girls."

"That is the surest method of winning," said his mother.

"It may be; but somehow I prefer losing with a contest, than to win by servility."

"Yes, and with such notions you will always have contests, whether you win or not."

"Perhaps I may; but let me follow the law of my life. I would lay a small wager that at college, Campbell always behaved with the most scrupulous regard for every silly by-law, and in every little difficulty in his text-books, he bolted off to a tutor's room, for a grave and reverential consultation. But in the world he will follow precedent strictly, and by a most deferential respect for his superiors in place, will very soon reach those small positions which they keep in reserve for the faithful. In political life, the system of securing office has been reduced to such completeness, that those who hold them, frown down anything like an original idea, by combined censure; and thus, the whole pack live in mediocrity by prescription, and commit the gravest errors, from pure ignorance and original timidity. While they are the best-behaved, sleekest-looking men you will meet in a summer's day, they are the most dangerous men to society, simply because they do not know when they enunciate error or commit faults. Indeed, from the front to the rear one, they think they can do no wrong, while following precedent. I speak evenly of those only who *intend* to do *right*, and I often fear that we have more to apprehend from our *good* men than our *bad.* Yes, I think Campbell will succeed in life, by just such gradations, policy, and his extremely obsequious manners. I want no such success. He will marry Lucy Brandon, and she will do what the world calls well, while I — but never mind."

"Oh! brother, you are just a little envious of his smooth-sailing before aunt. You should follow his example," said Violet, banteringly.

CHAPTER XXVII.

"But then her face,
So lovely, yet so arch, so full of mirth,
The overflowings of an innocent heart."

AS Mr. Jerome and Dr. Wilton were riding along on their way home from Hunter's, with nothing to disturb the silence save the occasional humming of some *love-song* by the Doctor, the latter suddenly turned to Mr. Jerome, and asked him how he had liked the "round trip."

"Oh, finely, elegantly," said Mr. Jerome. "I think the little extemporized dancing-party the very nicest affair of the kind I have seen for many days — really artistic. The conception of it, the manner of getting it up, the handsome and unique style of the notes, the hospitable reception, the gay, social, and intellectual abandon, the music, old Sancho, and the joyous assembly of negroes, and the splendid supper, all presented one of the best miniature pictures that could have been drawn of social life, happiness, joyousness, and abundance of Southern plantation homes."

"Yes," said Dr. Wilton; "but you have left out of your very just enumeration of features, the most striking and chiefest of all."

"What do you refer to, Doctor?"

"Why surely, the *beautiful daughters* of these plantation homes," replied the Doctor, with a hearty laugh.

"Yes, I beg pardon; it is indeed seldom, either in plantation homes or elsewhere, that so many very beautiful girls, for the number, can be found; by the way, Doctor, which did you think the handsomest?"

"It is a difficult question to decide; but there was one that I thought approached *perfection*, nigher than the rest."

"Pray, which one was that?" asked Mr. Jerome, smiling at the Doctor's extravagance; "Miss Morton?"

"No; I will not say it was Miss Morton, unless you demand it."

"Miss Hunter, then? if I should make no demand."

"Yes, Miss Hunter; if you allow me full scope of expression. Though possibly her sweeping beauty is more in my own eye, perhaps, than in any one else's — in yours at least."

"I discovered that you construed Laura Brandon's temporary bestowal of her into a real *fee-simple* title."

"Why, was I very pertinacious in my attentions to her?"

"Oh, no; not beyond a very decided expression of preference."

"Did she appear wearied with it?"

"Not at all; rather to the contrary — that's the style to win, *l'amour*, always with a girl — in the teeth of jaundiced speculation, to the contrary."

"Well, I am glad you tell me so, since I even more than hinted that I should do myself the pleasure of calling very soon at Judge Hunter's. By the way, the old Judge did the handsome thing yesterday. He came up to me, and after conversing a little, remarked that he had wished to see me for some week or two, for the purpose of getting me to practise on his lower plantation, if within my circuit. I thanked him, and accepted. There is one objection to it, however."

"What is that? it pays six or seven hundred dollars a year."

"Yes; but then I do not go by his *house* in going there — ha! ha! ha!"

"Oh! you will frequently meet him, and he will of course ask you to come over to see him when you can, which invitation you will, of course, very modestly accept, though professing to have but little time at your disposal."

"Yes, I am obliged to you, Parson, for the idea and the *modus*. I wish the Judge and his negroes all possible good health; but what sickness there *is to be*, I wish would begin right away. I'll do my best on it. But I am making all the confessions — let me hear from you, Parson."

"I can't say that I have any great confessions to make, Doctor. I suppose you expect me to say something of Miss Morton."

"Yes; as I fancy you would select her as your preferred subject."

"I scarcely know what to say. I certainly do admire her; more, doubtless, than she admires me. There is more of the subtle essence of intellect indicated in her physique, than in that of any young woman of my acquaintance."

"Make an exception, Parson, in favor of Miss Hunter, if you please."

"No, I cannot; Sally Morton has more intellect than any girl I know — too much for her happiness, unless she had more means of using it. She has too much mind for a female, unless it runs in the channel of *book-making*, or something of the kind; but, even that is a sort of capacity to itself, requiring more mechanical art than genius or learning. With a small share of learning, the mechanic who builds an old woman's hand-loom, can write an average book. Miss Morton has ten times more capacity for writing than nine in ten have, who succeed at it, yet I think she would fail. A book written by persons of high genius, is too great a draft on common intellect. She could not adapt her thoughts to that lower level, which the critical and the every-day reading world demands — her mind does not move in the direction of every-day practicality. She will perform every-day obligations if called on, as she appears to have a high sense of her duty; but not *con amore*. She is, peculiarly, a type of the highest Southern female character, in which there is a want of adaptability to the lower grades of duty. This style of woman seems more, than for any other purpose, intended to *reproduce* their character in *men*. The sons of such women, it is, that give the true tone to Southern life and character. Her intellect is of the highest female character; her attainments are handsome, and very accomplishing; her wit is keen and elegant; her mirth is as pure and joyous as a child's; her love of genuine sentiment, and her appreciation of true romance, give her character that charm which few can resist who come in association with her. I had nighly said, compels them to love her; and to love her — is infatuation."

"Then you confess yourself *to be in love* with the young lady?"

"I confess that I have that feeling, which, if left to itself, would soon lead me to love her; and all that keeps me from it, is a sort of conservatism which my feelings exercise over themselves, while not encouraged to give loose rein to their inclinations by herself."

After this, both gentlemen again relapsed into silence, and spurred their horses to quicker gait. The remainder of the road was travelled over, with scarcely a word from either.

Reaching home they each went to their own rooms. Dr. Wilton, finding two or three notes from patients, was very soon on the road again. Mr. Jerome, after making some inquiries about home affairs, put on his studying gown and went to the library.

Mr. Jerome, as we have already said, had been left an orphan at an early age, and the heir to a handsome estate. After the completion of his education he had, as too many young men of genius and wealth do, passed several years of high frolicsome life; but in the height of his mad career, some private circumstance had directed his thoughts to the subject of religion; and he very soon, not only united himself to the Church, but resolved upon entering the ministry. On finishing his divinity course, he returned to his old home, and was immediately called to the parish of which he now had charge; but still resided at his own home, where, as we have already said, Dr. Wilton lived with him, and practised his profession. He and old Mr. Thaxton were his only home companions. The latter we have also spoken of, but it may not be amiss to say of him in this connection, that he had always been remarkable for his scrupulous honesty, his quiet gentlemanly manners, a keen insight into character, and a fine natural mind, which had been well cultivated by reading, and by constant association with the best society of the surrounding country. No one ever thought of Mr. Thaxton but as an equal, and a welcome visitor at any time that his employment permitted the recreation, simply, because he never *pushed* himself upon any one out of his sphere. In this manner, he was highly esteemed by the older members of the families, and a universal favorite with the younger ones.

Mr. Thaxton was in the library looking over some books when Mr. Jerome entered.

"Ah, James," said he, "back again. I am glad to see you — had almost begun to think something serious had happened to you; and had begun to think a little of taking a neighborhood search for you, or getting out letters testamentary on your — library, at least."

"Oh, no; nothing out of the way, but the overstaying of my appointed time a little."

"Yes, I think so; where is the Doctor?"

"Come — and gone again."

"All right; several have sent for him. You must have spent your time very agreeably. How are they all over there?"

"Very well; and asked why you had not been to see them of late. Miss Laura Brandon asked particularly about you."

"I am obliged to them; and particularly to my sweet young friend Laura."

"And your old boy-friend, Henry Brandon, seemed never tired talking and asking about you."

"I am obliged to him, too; and have really wished to go over there, ever since I heard he had returned, just to see how he looks and to hear him talk."

"He says he has appointed several times to come to see you, but something prevented."

"Yes; he was a great favorite of mine when a lad, some five or six years since. I worked near a year at his mother's, if you remember? No, you do not; you were off at college about that time. Well, I was there when he was preparing for college himself, at the academy, and a wild chap he was.

I always noticed though, that there was no taste for low dissipation in him, nor anything smacking of meanness. His uncle did not entirely comprehend him, and used to say that he did not know how to manage him. I told him to let the boy *alone*, that he was all right, and that his wildness was little else than love of action and joyousness of heart; but he did not altogether take in the idea, and he and his wife both, rather got it down that Henry was a *very* wild youth, though they appeared very fond of him, and he was a great deal at their house."

" He is at home now, and about as gay a lark as you have seen for many a day."

" I expect so; he used to go to every country dance he could hear of, particularly down in the *Hills*, without letting it be known to any one except his boy ' *Sam*,' who made all the arrangements for him, and went with him too. I have not seen Sam for several years; he was a sharp imp, with as great a genius for deviltry as his master. Henry loved him better than any white boy on earth, and Sam would have fought to his death for Henry. Yes, Sam would have the horses ready at the right time and place; and I'll wager, that not a man or woman down there but remembers Henry Brandon and his boy Sam."

" How did his mother like all that ? "

" Oh, not much, of course; but she seldom found it out for some time, as he was always back by day, before she had risen ; and you say he appears wild and gay yet? "

"Yes; all life, animation, and fun, and one of the finest dancers I ever saw."

" Yes; he was a fine dancer, and one of the handsomest boys I ever saw. Laura was a very fine dancer also. I have seen them dance together often, at their little neighborhood parties. Henry used to claim her for his sweetheart when a boy, and is quite likely to do so as a man.

16

But the old people will object to it *now* — it was a little sly fun for them then."

"I rather think you have a correct estimate of him. I remarked in his conversation, the other night, with the young people, a rich vein of wit, humor, and thought, and last night, in conversation with Campbell, he appeared to handle him with all ease; and you know, Campbell is viewed as a young man of fine mind."

"Ah, just from the *style* of them, without knowing anything of them as *men*, I would lay my wager on Henry every time. Henry will be longer in maturing; he will be a man just coming in, when Campbell has culminated. Campbell will come on the carpet first, because he will court favor, which Henry will never do; he has too much mind — he is gay, and will always be gay, and for years will pass for less than his real worth; but he has the true ring, and the world will eventually call for him. But tell me, who else did you see?"

"Oh, a great number, of whom I have often heard you speak, some old, and some young — among others, Miss Gray."

"Did you, indeed? She is a game-looking girl, isn't she? How did you like her?"

"She is a *game*-looking girl, as you say. I felt a little shy of her; but young Brandon and she seemed to get along admirably. She is very handsome, and very gay."

"Ah, he would get along with the *devil* — begging your pardon — if he would go at all. By the way, that would be a superb match, if old Gray should take a notion to it."

"He and the young lady both took quite a fancy to him yesterday, I assure you."

"Good! Henry will win, if he starts; and old Gray couldn't stop him, if he would. I would bet my wig on that. The only objection to that family is its disposition to religious fanaticism. They all belong to a little piece of the Methodist denomination lately shivered off, called *Reformers*, I believe. But did you see any girl that you liked better than yourself, James?—as I am getting tired of a household where masters play mistress."

Before Mr. Jerome had time to reply, a message came to him that one of those little difficulties had taken place which were of frequent occurrence, on large plantations, between a driver and the overseer, which only the master could arrange. He was not long engaged in the settlement, and, making things satisfactory to both parties, he returned to the library, where Mr. Thaxton still remained.

CHAPTER XXVIII.

"Genius is supposed to be a power of producing excellencies which are out of the reach of the rules of art; a power which no precepts can teach, and which no industry can acquire."

YES," answered Mr. Jerome to Mr. Thaxton's last question, "I saw several that I would be willing to *swap* myself off for, and that I could love, too; but whether that will avail me anything, is the point. I saw Miss Morton, and absolutely danced with her."

"Ah! an Episcopal clergyman dancing with a Baptist sister! *That* is something *new* under the sun. Well, she is truly a *great* girl. But then it appears to me that you have had that affair, as knuck boys say, in the nine hole, and can't get it out; but, now that you have *danced* with her, perhaps the matrimonial skies will brighten. I am rejoiced that you have made a move. Any direction, in such matters, is better than standing still. If a love-affair ever stagnates, ten to one if it survives."

"You will discourage me, Mr. Thaxton, with your hard philosophy."

"I do not wish to do so; for Sally Morton possesses very rare qualities, and is another of the young people for whom I have prophesied well. I knew her father, and a most excellent gentleman he was; and I have seen a good deal of Sally since she has resided at Judge Hunter's; but with all of her very high attributes, she will never be *generally* admired by young men — she has too much wit, too much mirth, too much gayety, too much sense — *genius;* all of which are very grave offences to the dull plodders of this every-day world. *All people make war upon genius,* whether it is rich or poor, but particularly if poor. Make a note of that! I, however, have a philosophy of my own to meet that fact, which is, that every one's own life is a law unto itself, and the beginning, when clearly and unmistakably given out, always foreshadows the end. In her case, every-thing calls for an influential position, at some time of life. Nature must be true to itself — cannot waste its own wealth; and, by all the laws and affinities of life, she is bound to get back her lost place. There is everything in BLOOD."

"You have just developed that idea, Mr. Thaxton. I have never heard you broach it before," said Mr. Jerome, smiling.

"I can't say; but whether I have or not, I have long believed it, and believe more than I say. I have had no occasion to express it to you before."

"According to that idea, there would never happen any-thing permanently adverse in life. Nature, as you *call* it, ultimately restoring all we may have lost."

"Ah, I don't mean what I say to have so literal and matter-of-fact a construction; nor do I mean to say that the human mind is *always* able to control the direction of affairs. I only say that the gifts of nature always become recognized at some time or other during life — that life never ends till they are — both go together, and that this recognition is by that much what the mind covets, demands, and will have. For instance, a man may have intellect and parts, and yet be very little able to control the course of events; yet, the ultimate recognition of the fact that he is a man of intellect carries with it a certain influence, and that influence, however modified, is personal eminence, and a restoration of the rights which, to that time, had been obscured. I don't mean that, in the course of time, a man will receive some *office* equal to the quality of his mind — for they are generally received by the *least worthy* of all; nor do I mean that a man will receive back any certain amount of *coin* which he may have previously lost; but that his mind and character will be estimated according to their true worth; and estimation is influence, with or without position."

" You think, then, that real worth is generally obscured for the time, and that *error* is the law of life."

"Yes, to a very large extent, I do. How else could we account for the periodical derangement of society? Yet they have their periods of correction. The derangements come through the *lesser capacities* — who, as I said, generally hold position — and their correction through the greater. These lesser capacities are largely in the ascendant — as nine to one. For instance, I mean that about nine in ten of our public men are absolutely unfit for the place, and would be far more respectable if they were — where I have always been — at the jack-plane. They are nothing more nor less than moral and political maggots, breeding rottenness and stench; and were it not for the *influence* of the *tenth man* — who is, nine times in ten, out of power — the whole machinery of life would go to the devil in ten generations. This is what Nature calls for — influence, and it is bound to be recognized at some time or other."

" Why, Mr. Thaxton, you have elaborated quite a system of philosophy since I left home; but I am afraid it is a little *cranky*. What has happened to you?"

16*

"Nothing has happened to me. 'Cranky,' your great grandmother! What I say is just as true as your preaching — not saying anything against that, either. But I suppose you think me 'cranky' because I happened to get a little out of sight of Sally Morton."

"Perhaps that *is* the reason," said Mr. Jerome, laughing.

"But I was *talking* of her."

"Yes, I know; but be more direct, and not so *abstract*," he said, laughingly.

"I thought so. Just the way with you preachers — get love into your heads. But, never mind, if you can get her, do so; she will adorn any gentleman's house. I only fear you can't do it."

"Why do you fear it?" asked Mr. Jerome, with an evident interest in the answer.

"I will answer you, James, provided you will not get hurt if I bear heavy upon you."

"Oh, speak your mind freely, Mr. Thaxton. You know you always have that privilege."

"Well, then, Sally Morton is, by the law of her nature, supremely ambitious. She does not show it now, because she does not feel any identity with the situation, which precludes her mind from its normal action. When she marries, or comes to marry — as all girls expect — the sense of responsibility for the future will come back, and this ambitious nature of hers will suggest the selection of such a man as will secure the success which the law of her life spreads out in gorgeous beauty before her. In this selection, that which we may call *instinct* — for the want of a better word to express that subtle feature of the mind which penetrates the shadowy future — would lead her to *fear* you — to fear that you would not meet the demand — unless you could clear up the apprehension."

"Mr. Thaxton, you are quite transcendental in your reasoning. You say that marriage is not directed by reason, but by some unseen power that influences our lives, over which we exert no control."

"Yes, but not so emphatically as you interpret me. Nor do I mean it to be of universal application — only to special instances. Nor do I exactly mean as you say. I mean that there is a certain aspiration, which more controls *some* hearts, in the matter of marriage, than those faculties of the mind which we are in the common habit of exercising; and these faculties are subservient to that aspiration, even when we least know of it. But let me be more specific — less *abstract,* as you say — and you will comprehend me better."

"Very good, proceed; I am ready for an excoriation."

"If you think I intend to excoriate you, I shall say nothing more."

"I was merely jesting, Mr. Thaxton. I am really anxious to hear your opinions."

"First, then, I will give them in familiar language. You are an *indolent* man — rather so. I mean that, having never been under the *necessity,* you have never trained yourself to putting out all your strength; and no man can put out his whole mental force, unless he knows how to put out his whole physical power. They are indissolubly connected."

"Are you going to argue that inertia is the law of my life?"

"No; but it certainly modifies its momentum. It is a sort of negative quantity — *vis inertiæ* I may call it — and no man who has it can work his mind to high achievement, no matter how complete in its parts, unless he forces himself above it. In as far as he fails to do this, he fails to bring his mind up to its capacitated standard of action; and the qualities left unexercised are, of necessity, the higher qualities, because of being the most difficult to move. Now, for instance, in the construction of any complete mind, there enters, to greater or less extent, that capacity for glowing imagination which we call poetry — eloquence — when evolved in proper language. To possess this power of language, is a thing of first necessity, and can only be acquired by patient, laborious industry. Byron did not write Childe Harold without a great deal of patient thought and persistent effort. Language comes by study, is the child of thought and emotion, and they act and re-act on each other. Thought begets a word, and another word another thought; therefore, in organizing thought for expression, you go to the deep intricacies and machinery of language; and from this laboratory of language you return, newly armed, to conquer in the realms of thought. Eloquence, poetry, etc., are but little else than the expression, by one man, through patient, laborious industry, of what every other feels, without the power of expression. That is why they are so esteemed and applauded. 'Poeta nascitur, non fit,' is not altogether true —they are made as well as born. Now, you being deficient in thorough training of your strength, you are deficient in this noble capacity of organizing thought into language. Being deficient in language, you also are, in tracing delicate emotions to their subtle sources, and 'wreaking them upon expression.' Byron, by the use of that very word *wreak*, gives out the idea of *labor*. Nothing without labor."

"Do you think then," asked Mr. Jerome, "that poetry and eloquence rank higher in the scale of intellect, than strong reasoning power?"

"No matter what *I* think; a woman does, nor shall I go into an analysis."

"But, Mr. Thaxton," said Mr. Jerome, rather apologetically; "I am not in a profession that admits of this ambitious display which you speak of."

"You are mistaken; the ministry presents the very highest field of oratory. It is the *subject*, that to a large extent lends Paradise Lost its splendid eloquence. You content yourself with too little. You content yourself with a simple presentation of the truths of the Bible, which is very well, but that is not *all* that is necessary; the Bible points to *eloquence*, but without a great deal of true persistent labor, you will never be an eloquent divine. You will, therefore, but *half develop* your profession, while you do not elaborate — dive deep."

Mr. Jerome somehow thought, that from these opinions of Mr. Thaxton he had obtained a key to many things Miss Morton had said to him, and almost unconsciously rose to his library. The old man broke out in a laugh, and said that he had not intended to drive him to his books so soon, as the old bachelor was in "Bracebridge Hall."

"I am not ready to leave you yet, James. I have not asked you all that I wished to know. How is my very favorite from childhood, Laura Brandon, getting along? You have scarcely mentioned her name."

"She is as pretty as ever, even grows sweeter-looking; and really more easily graceful and agreeable, than any of the girls over there, I think, which is saying a great deal for me; and just as you said, I should be much astonished, if she and young Brandon did not get up some few love-passages yet; they were much together, and seemed highly delighted with each other. But you don't think the mother would consent to anything of the kind?"

"No; I know she would not. Campbell will suit them both better; from what I have heard of Campbell, he is a fine young fellow, but then Henry Brandon is worth a battalion of him. But let me ask after our young friend the Doctor, how is he doing over there? I hear him frequently speak of Julia Hunter: is she the bright particular star of his devotion?"

"Yes; I think the Doctor supposed himself sent for, to attend to her particular case, and he did his full duty."

" Well, the Doctor is a nice, deserving young man, and she is a very nice girl, and the two would make a nice match. But how about Thomas Hunter and Violet Brandon ? "

" That seems to be a well-settled matter. I suppose they will marry very soon, from all reports."

" Every one appears to be doing rather better than my old favorites, Henry and Laura."

" I don't know, they seemed very happy together."

" Ah ! they will have trouble, if ever they call each other anything but cousin. You say though, he was with Mary Gray; that rather complicates matters a little. But I will leave you now, James, to your books and your next sermon," said the old man as he left.

CHAPTER XXIX.

" He was her own, her ocean treasure, cast
Like a rich wreck — her first love, and her last."

HENRY BRANDON had appeared to have forgotten his purpose of reading law; and between cousins, home, and Thomas Hunter, his time seemed speeding along most joyously. The cloud gradually thickened around the brow of Mrs. Robert Brandon, as his easy intercourse with Laura had appeared to increase; but as he purposely abstained from the commission of any *ouvert act*, he disregarded as yet the threatenings of the coming storm.

Both of the young people seemed satisfied with the existing relationship, and both feared any positive change. Laura played a little shy of receiving any direct declaration from him, as he would sometimes approach the subject, in a manner though, that perfectly satisfied him of his place in her heart.

The contemplated marriage of Hunter and Violet was now an acknowledged thing, and preliminary arrangements had actually begun for the wedding.

Young Brandon saw Mr. Campbell more frequently, and was beginning to have a higher appreciation of him.

In connection with Violet's preparations, Laura and Lucy had appointed when they would come over and spend a day or two with her. This Henry was informed of, which he took advantage of, and despatched a note by Essex to Hunter, requesting him to come over next morning as he wished to see him. He then wrote to Campbell, by his *friend* "Sam Brandon," informing him of all the facts, and to be sure and come out and spend the day with him. Next day, not long after Laura and Lucy had arrived, Hunter rode up, and not a great while after, Mr. Campbell came. Violet and her mother, not knowing that it was through Henry's agency that they had come, treated their visits as a very agreeable *contretemps.* A suspicion to the contrary, however, soon obtained among the girls, from some remark of Henry's, but required no apology.

It was the last day of October, and a happier one was never to be passed by that joyous little company. One there was of the number, whose wit, mirth, and gladsomeness that day, glittered with the flashing, sparkling freshness of morning dew on the tinted rose. It was "Love's young dream," that flung a soft effulgence on a flushing heart, which drooped and paled in its beauty and joy, ere time had cast its shadows there. The day had been genial and lovely, and its evening gentleness was only too commemorative of the sad stillness of its closing hour. As the sun went sinking down the sky, it shed upon the wide lawn in front of "Buckhorns" a sea of golden light, as soft as the hopeless languor of dying love. The appearance of it, all in an instant, appeared to attract the attention of Henry Brandon, who at once proposed they should take a walk in due honor to the last October sun, saying, "there had never been so sweet a one, since great Cæsar had set the calendar to its present measure, or so pretty a one for making love, since the gay old Roman had walked the streets of Tarsus with its bewitching queen."

"Your ecstasy deserves success, Henry, whether it meets with it or not," said Hunter; "with one or two more such efforts you will gain your point."

"Here goes then — since Cupid in his small cloth nestled in his nurse's arms, or love-lorn Leander dared the swelling waves of Hellespont."

"That will do — we will not *crack* your capacity, but take the walk." The proposition was then accepted, and all proceeded to leave the house. It was not long before they separated in pairs — Henry, of course, with Laura — and had not gone far before each party had established considerable distance between itself and another.

Henry and Laura had not more than half-way reached the extremity of the lawn, when he said to her:

"Laura, I purposely proposed this walk, just to get a suitable opportunity to make a most eloquent speech to your ladyship, which I have been nearly bursting with, for more than a month; so much so, indeed, that I am at length threatened with — combustion, if I do not get relief in expression." Then, half turning in a sort of tragico-comico attitude, said — "Now, hear me, lady, for my cause."

"Certainly, cousin," she replied, laughing, "if it will prevent such a dire catastrophe — not only so, but should I return without an attendant, I should necessarily be accused of complicity in your mysterious disappearance — proceed."

"Good, my lady; and you promise to lend a willing ear?"

"I do, my lord."

"But even with that consent, I have resolved to fly into invisible atoms, unless you also allow me to *oratorize* on my own stipulations; do you accede to that proposition also?"

"I do, unless too severely exacting."

"It is merely that you do not interrupt me."

"*That* is truly a very hard exaction to make of a woman; but then to prevent so unfortunate an event as you threaten, and too, for the pleasure of the eloquence, I consent to that too. You will at least allow me the privilege of *looking* assent or dissent?"

"No; not even that to any intensified extent. I only desire an *audience* of the simplest form. Now, which do you choose — the speech, or eternal silence? Under which king — speak or — not?"

"Oh! under such dreadful alternatives — the speech, of course. I should never otherwise hope for forgiveness," said she laughing.

With a mock reverential air he began — "Oh, Cupid! oh, Venus! and all ye little viewless spirits that have small offices in the gorgeous court of Love! Now, hear ye my prayer, and prosper me my suit! Oh! plume my wing for the loftiest flight into your highest happiest realms; and let me there record, in letters of eternal light and truth, the sacred secret of my heart and life! 'T is that I — love my —COUSIN!" Then suddenly turning, said: "Now, by the shade of Apollo, I must have reward for that splendid dash of eloquent love," and placing his arm around her waist, he kissed the glowing cheek of the blushing, happy girl.

With eyes beaming with light, and truth, and love, and mirth, she refusing to consent — consented — gave the kiss, and yielded up her heart forever!

Choking for utterance, she at length found words to say, "Cousin, cousin! why, oh, why, did you tell me this?

17

Why not have left my life to pass smoothly along in its nameless bliss? Why not have left my girlhood's joyous dream to slumber still in my woman's breast?"

With his arm still around her, and her hand in his, he pressed her gently to his side, as she spoke these passionate, hopeless words. Both seemed to comprehend the relation in which they were to stand for the future, and for some seconds remained silent. She presently continued:

"Cousin, you will forgive me, I know, for giving way to my feelings; but your singular manner of approach to so serious a subject — and one that I have long known was so near to us both — betrayed me into a response which probably I should not have made so madly."

"Ah, ha!" said he — and at once destroying the formality of the occasion — "you intended to keep the advantage of position, my lady-love!"

"No, cousin, I wished no advantage, any more than I know you wish it of me; but then, perhaps, a girl owes something to *delicacy*, even when she has perfect confidence."

"Probably she does; but you have not violated it, that I can see; for I certainly would not have betrayed you into doing so."

"I am glad you say that, as I feared you might think differently. But I know you would not deceive me."

"Laura, your caution shows apprehension; and now that we perfectly know each other's feelings, tell me fully the nature of it."

"I certainly have very great apprehension, and thought you knew the source of it."

"Is it that an engagement between us will not meet the approval of your parents?"

"Yes, that is it, particularly that of mother."

"What course have you then thought of pursuing, Laura?"

"I cannot answer you now — the question is too new."

"Have your feelings, then, any qualification?"

"Your question does me injustice, cousin; but as I have expressed some hesitation in answering your first one, it is perhaps due to us both that I should now tell you that your image, and *only* yours, has ever, gently, but indelibly, trembled on my heart. If it knows, or has ever known, the sacred feeling of *love*, you are its source and its possessor; and if you do not doubt me now, you never will."

"Thank you, Laura, for these confiding words. And now let me speak boldly and sincerely for myself, that for the future there may be no doubts between us. It is no secret to you, that all my life I have been called *wild, fickle,* inconstant, and a young person of great levity. In all these things the charge has been superficially correct; yet, intrinsically, I knew it to be incorrect. I have often permitted myself to pass for what I knew I was not — partially through indifference, and in something, to a concealment of facts which I thought no one had a right to know, which I did not see proper to express. As, for instance, since my return home, there has scarcely been a moment of seriousness in my manner to *you;* and yet the instant almost that I first saw you, after our long separation, the feeling of the boy rushed upon the man, and I loved you with all the tenderness and earnestness of both; and though I have all along known your feelings, habit and whim made me keep up the partial disguise to others, but not to you."

Laura here interrupted him by asking if Lucy had never told him anything in regard to her.

"Yes, she has; but not before I was assured myself of your feelings toward me."

"Then, cousin, I must have been incautious — too much so."

"Oh, no," he pleasantly replied, as he playfully patted her on the cheek; "it was a fair game between us, and

why not *you* receive the arrow of the rosy god as soon as
I? But let me say on. With all this levity, my feelings
have been undivided in their devotion, and my purpose
resolute; and there is nothing now can make me yield.
It therefore appears to me, that if yours are as unqualified,
there is no opposition on earth that will prevent you from
promising to be MINE."

These last words brought a chill to Laura's heart, as,
in the whole course of her life, she had never contemplated
an act of wilful disobedience to her parents; on the contrary, both as a matter of religious duty and of social habit
and training, she thought it even wrong to consider its pos-
sibility.

Looking him calmly in the face, as he concluded his
words, she said to him:

"Cousin, you should not make such an insinuation, after
what I have said to you. The *promises*, too, are to honor
and obedience; and if you will allow me to claim a proper
delicacy, I will say that I have given you every evidence
of no ordinary feeling; and as you have been so plain in
the expression of your own, I will do the same, and re-
assure you, that neither as girl or woman has any other
name than yours cast the faintest shadow on my life;
and now, whether right or wrong, for grief or gladness, I
tell you, if ever one heart was entirely another's, Laura
Brandon's belongs to you — how, or why, or when, I scarce
can tell, yet it is as I have said;" then, stepping a little
to his front, with an expression of truth and purity and
innocence in her eye, never to be forgotten any more than
heaven's own bright stars shall cease to float in beauty
upon the azure sky, she continued: "And, cousin, having gone so far as I have, let me all unveil to you the
workings of my bosom. You may treat the treasure as
you will; but this heart which I have this day given to
you, can never be another's. Yet, my hand may never be

yours more than as I give it now. Will you receive it as I give it?"

Henry took the proffered hand, and affectionately sealed it with a kiss of love and truth that time never cancelled from his memory.

During this conversation, they had been entirely out of view from those who had left the house with them, and as Laura made her last remark, she proposed returning. Henry offered her his arm, and they began slowly to retrace their steps, talking more calmly of the subject which now engrossed their thoughts.

"Laura, this evening's scenes can never be erased from the history of our lives, and yet they scarcely bring that joy which they should."

"That they may not now, cousin, yet we will hope for more brightness in the future."

"What course must I adopt — speak to uncle Robert?"

"No; I prefer not at present: just let the matter go along for a while, and perhaps the prospect will grow more promising. I have not the courage to let it be mentioned just now."

"Why? it can only still be opposed."

"I know; but even that seems, if openly done, to be more than I can bear, as mother and father have yet to oppose me in the first wish of my heart, so far as I can remember."

"Why do you think, then, they will oppose you now?"

"For several reasons — first, I have often heard mother express her disapproval of the marriage of cousins; and then, they will be apt to think you too young and unsettled in your notions; again, that our attachment is *too recent* to be lasting; and quite as much as all, cousin, they, in common with many others, think you wild, reckless, and high-tempered."

"But you do not regard these things?"

17*

"No; else why should I have said what I have, and received your caresses?"

"Well, well, Laura; we can at least be old-fashioned sweethearts for a while longer; so let me fancy that I have turned back on our young school-days, and do, as I used often to do, as we parted in the evening," and suiting the action to the word, kissed her smiling rosy lips; and the woman yielded with the confidence and sweet innocence of the girl.

They had now recovered from all excitement, and appeared as happy and guileless as, indeed, they ever had in their school-days. About to come again in sight of the house, Henry observed that Laura's hair was a little displaced, and said, "Stop, stop, Laura; this beautiful hair of yours has fallen down; let me act as *coiffeur de cheveux.*"

"Cousin, your French is abominable; but I will let you adjust my hair, as that is what I suppose you mean."

Henry laughed heartily at his French, and said: "Yes, yes, that is what I mean; for whether my French is good or bad, those impudent girls would, as soon as not, accuse you of having had my arm around you, which you know is not so — is it?"

The happy girl looked him innocently in the face as he replaced her hair, and said:

"I can scarcely say, cousin, what has happened within the last half-hour; it looks like a dream of joy, that I almost fear to ask, lest in asking, I may find it fled."

"Oh, no, Laura; we will have it more than a dream."

They now walked on to the house, where Hunter and Campbell, with the two other girls, stood waiting for them.

"Where have you two been, and what have you found to talk about?" said Violet, as they came up.

"Our beaux gave out half an hour since, both in strength and conversation, and we were forced to return in pure self-defence," added Lucy.

"Oh, pshaw! you, nor your beaux either, have any of the divine afflatus."

"But do tell us, Laura, what this bright genius of a brother of mine has found to entertain you with," her eye twinkling with fun as she spoke. "Has he been telling you of some of his glowing visions of future glory and greatness, which are to begin on the first day that he opens 'Blackstone,' I believe he calls it — if that ever comes — which I begin to doubt. Or has he been enlarging on the beauties of Miss Gray; or has he been indulging in a little sentiment, with your own sweet self for the subject? Come, tell us, for I know there is a tale to unfold, or has been unfolded."

Laura reddened up at the last words of Violet, but before she could reply, Henry came to her assistance:

"Ah! most cruel sister, since we have found you out in your sentimentalities, you wish to avenge it after the fashion of the fox who was caught in the steel-trap; nevertheless, I'll answer for Laura. Yes, I have been making up a small love-story for some time past, and this evening rehearsed a few of the chapters — any objection?"

At this bold stroke to ward off suspicion, Laura colored so deeply as to occasion Henry to add, "Come, Laura, if you blush so, these impudent people will think, indeed, that I have been making love to you, and that you accepted me." He then quickly added, by way of changing the subject — "Come, it is quite cool for thinly dressed young ladies — let us go in the house and finish the examination."

There was a small fire burning. The lamps were soon brought in, and the remainder of the evening was passed most delightfully to them all, in music, dancing, etc., and perhaps, a little more love-making.

CHAPTER XXX.

"Lay not that flattering unction to your soul."

IN November of this year the Presidential election was over, and the great quadrennial excitement of the American Republic had again subsided into quiet. The people were once more pursuing, with their usual peacefulness and energy, the various occupations of life, while all parties had equally submitted to the decision of the ballot-box. There was but a grim resignation on the part of the WHIGS. Their great leader had again been defeated, and with his fall fell the last remnant of political decency and intelligence that had remained to the republican United States. Every intelligent Whig felt and knew that final oblivion was to overtake many long-cherished principles and the general conservative policy of their party, which had ever exerted its strength in the effort to influence the administration of the Government. It was now universally conceded by its friends that its power and tone was forever gone, and that the destinies of the Government were completely in the hands of the wild, reckless multitude, which was led by men as wild, reckless, and wellnigh as poorly informed as themselves, and far more corrupt. To hold power, however unworthily, and however unworthily obtained, appeared to be the leading idea with the best of them. The canvass against Mr. Clay thoroughly represented the character of the Democratic party of that day, marked as it was by all manner of reckless and unscrupulous assertions touching every act of his public life, and in many matters, of his private life.

Discussions of measures with which he was identified were not conducted with a view to developing truth, but with a predetermined purpose of suppressing it, and of exciting the prejudices of the masses against him.

Their favorite charge against the Whig party, and a very effective one, too, before the masses, was that of its Federalism. The charge itself was not discussed as a question, but advanced as a loathsome stigma; and while it answered every purpose of exciting the prejudices of the people, was as little comprehended by them as by the wild Bedouins of the desert.

The charge itself was true, in contradistinction to the absurd, double-back-action theories of the State-Rights school, which had naturally grown out of that idea common to all republican governments, that central authority is necessarily despotic; and from that other, too, which had taken such strong root in this country, of the *people* being capable of *self*-government. These social and political fallacies, dangerous to the order and peace of society even with a limited application, had been first suggested by Mr. Jefferson, afterward assuming shape in the Resolutions '98 – '99, and then carried to the extremest abuse by the statesmen (?) of South Carolina. They were, however, very flattering to the vanity of the people, who responded by keeping those in power who advocated them.

Now, in 1869, behold the wisdom of the idea! Come and look in upon us, all ye outside world, and, in the wretchedness, poverty, humiliations and degradations of the brave-hearted but misguided South, see the capacity of men for self-government! Look at the almost open corruption in high places, and view for yourselves this tremendous capacity!

Every government should have the unqualified power to rule all its parts, but running parallel with it should be the obligation to protect them. Every other is only an absurdity, and a premium to revolution.

The theory of self-government does very well for the

majority; but woe be unto the minority! In the case of the United States, the North was largely the majority section; and while it had committed every conceivable political excess, and every possible trespass upon the social sentiments and domestic and political rights of the South, under the cover of State rights and the right of self-government, there was no power adequate to its punishment. But when the feeble South, with every equity on its side, attempted to redress itself by a sort of negative movement only, this same imperious horde, from brothel to sanctuary, rolled up the whites of its eyes in *patriotic horror* for the violence done the *"flag."*

Right for the nonce, say we, was this self-governing majority, if only by accident, or from *hate;* and had its character been equal to the *cause*, the South would indeed have been crushed back to its place "in ninety days," and having done that, might have corrected all the complained-of evils. But, out upon ye, ye great self-governing majority! Shame upon the chivalry that required a world of numbers four years to assert itself against a handful!

Henry Brandon had previously resolved not to begin his law reading until after the great election was over with, and all its excitement had died away. His appointed time for doing so had now come, and he was on his way to ——, for the purpose of seeing Judge Lorn, with a view to reading in his office. Judge Lorn was an old family friend, and a gentleman almost as greatly distinguished for his eccentricities as for his classical, literary, and legal attainments, and was at this time in full practice.

As Henry entered his office, the Judge, rather more than was usual for him to do, rose and met him cordially. After some general conversation, young Brandon spoke to him in regard to his purpose in calling. The excellent old gentleman told him that his uncle had already spoken to him in regard to it, "and I have told him that I would take much pleasure in having you for a student, and was ready to receive you whenever you saw proper to come."

Henry said to him that he would be ready the next morning.

"The sooner the better, in such cases, Brandon."

Young Brandon made his arrangements during the day for coming to the city, and returned to his mother's that night with a view to a final departure — which he did the next morning, never to return again as a regular member of her family.

Going back again to the city, he completed his arrangements, and reported at Judge Lorn's office. The Judge asked him in a few moments, if he desired to go through only a short course of reading preparatory to entering the practice, or did he wish to pursue the study as a science, from which all principles for the regulation of society and the direction of government emanated.

Brandon replied, that he did not desire to enter upon the practice very soon, and would therefore prefer a more liberal course.

"I am glad," said the Judge, "to hear you say that, as it is the first time in years I have heard of any such wish. Most young men that have been with me for several years past, seemed anxious for the *small practice.*" He continued his conversation by saying that "most students begin the study with the commentaries of Blackstone, which, though the very best compendium of the English law, are yet *but* a compendium, and argue quite an advanced intimacy with the history of England and of Europe, which very few young men have in this country; an uninformed student, therefore, loses much of their real value. For that reason I would advise the laying of a good historical foundation, before entering upon Blackstone, or any of the short-cut text-books."

Beginning to rather regret his temerity in saying to the

Judge that he preferred a liberal course, he rather cautiously asked him —

" What work would you recommend, Judge, that I should begin with ?"

" I would propose Robertson's Charles the Fifth, as one of the chastest and most elegant of English authors; and his history of Charles embraces one of the most important periods in European history."

" Yes, sir; but I have read that, partly in connection with the historical course at college."

" So much the better; you will now read it the more intelligently, and with greater pleasure, as I dare say you were not very critical in your reading of it, at that time."

" Yes, sir; I gave it a very thorough reading, and still appreciate it as one of the finest works in the whole roll of history. The language is clear, elegant, and strong, without any affectation whatever; and presents among other things the most intelligible view of the feudal law, and the progress of society from the period of the Roman power, up to the time of Charles — that I know."

Henry Brandon said all this to convince the Judge that he had read the work, as he was trembling at the probable length of the course which he would suggest; acknowledging to himself that he did not entertain those lofty views of the profession which the Judge had given him credit for.

" Yes; I see that you appear to have read it with some care, which very few have. Excuse me for asking you a little historical question, Mr. Brandon."

" Certainly, sir."

" Will you tell me what occasion, or events, gave rise to the original theory of a ' balance of power,' as it is yet called in European diplomacy ? "

" You will find it spoken of in Robertson's dissertation on the progress of society; and the immediate occasion of the idea was the invasion of the Italian States by Charles VIII.

of France, when the Italian princes confederated for the purpose of expelling him from their territories. Afterward, in the course of the wars of Charles V., the plan of the Italian kings grew into a system."

"I am glad, indeed, to find that you have read this great writer so carefully — he is a favorite author with me. I have found few young men, in an experience of forty years, who knew anything of him, and I remember none who could have answered the question I asked you. I will, therefore, suggest, that you begin with 'Malthus on Population.' "

"What, Judge?" said Henry, both astonished and trepidated to the ends of his toes, at the extent and antediluvian course which the Judge was prescribing for him — " 'Malthus on Population?' "

"Yes; 'Malthus on Population,' " said the Judge, very exultingly, as he supposed that young Brandon knew about as much of Malthus as he did of the Koran, or the Talmud. "Have you ever read him?"

"No, I can't say that I have; yet, I have a very good idea of his theory, which is now treated as entirely obsolete — is it not?"

"Obsolete, indeed! No; it is as true as any mathematical demonstration, or axiom in philosophy."

"Then, Judge, you must think the Creator made a mistake, when fashioning man and the earth."

The Judge, a little nettled at the remark, replied:

"No, I do not; does n't the Bible speak of the end of the earth?"

"Yes, I believe it does; though I must confess to have read that too little; but I suppose, by that, and by Malthus, the end can be calculated?"

"No, I can't see the exact rationale of your words."

"Why, Malthus argues and demonstrates in his way, that the natural tendency of population is to too great

18

redundancy for the capacity of the earth in its support; and the necessary conclusion is, that at a certain point the human race, or the earth, or both, must or will give way, and this period we can easily arrive at by arithmetical calculation, taking the present population and its increase for a given time, and the arable area of the earth for data."

"Ah, but you make no allowance for 'wars, pestilence, and famine,' and the tides of emigration, etc."

Henry Brandon came nigh bursting out in laughter, as he now saw an instance of that eccentricity of the Judge for which he was so noted. But the Judge himself preserved the most dignified gravity, while Henry Brandon replied:

" Why, sir, the modern theory is all but the reverse of Malthus's, and rather borders on the idea that the denser the population the better the human family is supported, provided industry and intelligence keep pace with the increase."

"Mistake," dryly said the Judge. "My observation and experience are just to the contrary."

The sun was now setting, and Henry rose as if to leave, when the Judge said:

" Well, Brandon, if I don't get you along faster than I have this evening, the earth will be likely to collapse before you get to the Bar, even beginning with Blackstone; and as it is too late to begin this evening, suppose we commence with Blackstone in the morning, according to the custom of these degenerate days."

The following morning, according to appointment, Henry met the Judge at his office, and not many minutes transpired before he was installed as a law student of Judge Lorn.

He fell very easily into the old harness of study, and all his levity at once left him. Indeed, levity was but the feather to the arrow—more an assumption than an organic feature of character. Levity, in persons of intellect, is often but an exaggeration of health and animal spirits. Such persons, too, almost universally possess more of the finer sympathies and higher attributes than those· who frown upon them.

CHAPTER XXXI.

"All wanton as a child, skipping and vain."

YOUNG Brandon had now been in the office of Judge Lorn nearly two weeks, and had found his time so agreeably taken up in conversing with him, and in his new study, that he appeared to have but little time or desire to visit the country, and was very constantly to be found in his place. His mother and sister had been to the city, and he had promised them to go out, but had not yet done so. His cousins he had not seen; but Mr. Robert Brandon had that morning been to the city, and calling upon him, found him at his books. Expressing much pleasure at seeing him so studious, Henry replied:

"Why, uncle, that is nothing new for me, as you certainly know; but I believe many of my old friends are quite astonished that I am not found spending all my time in the gambling and drinking saloons."

"Oh, no, Henry; you are quite mistaken in regard to your friends: they are only pleased to find you so different from most young men of the day who have fortunes."

"Well, uncle, that is some better than I have had reason to suspect. I fear, though, I have but an indifferent reputation for steadiness, even with my·nighest friends."

"I hope you labor under an entire misapprehension, Henry. I at least do not injure you by such a thought."

"I really thank you for what you say; though I must

tell you in advance that I cannot say what the reason is. I hope you will excuse me for speaking as I have." And then, by way of changing the subject rather than in any particular relevance, he said: "Oh, uncle, though I have been quite busy at my law-reading, I have found the time to read Bulwer's novel, 'The Last of the Barons;' one that I like quite as well, if not better, than any I have ever read of his, which I will send out to the girls. After they read it, they can send it over to mother and Violet."

"Yes, I have seen some notices of it, and should think it very fine. The period and the events possess great charms even in the dull narration of history. Hume, however, throws around them all the brightness of romance."

"Yes, it is quite as interesting as you may suppose. Will you call for it this evening?"

"Yes, if you have n't it here."

"No; it is at my room. I will have it here against the time you are ready to leave."

Mr. Brandon called that evening, as he was in his carriage to go home, and Henry handed him the book, neatly wrapped up and tied. While riding, Mr. Brandon, supposing it not improper, thought to secure the only opportunity he was likely to have of looking over it; opened the wrapper, and was hastily perusing it, when a neatly folded and well-filled letter, directed to Laura, dropped from its leaves. Picking it up, and looking at it in silence for a minute or two, he slowly replaced it, and, wrapping up the book, sat as if in deep thought the remainder of the way home. He was now satisfied in his own mind that the suspicions of his wife, in regard to an attachment between Henry and Laura, really existed. What course to pursue, knowing her unrelenting opposition to such a marriage, was *now* a new source of anxiety.

The carriage at length driving up to his own gate, and the meeting with his daughters, who had come out for that purpose, wearing joyous and welcoming faces, at once seemed to dispel all previous and further thought.

After answering such general inquiries about friends and affairs in the city as may easily be conjectured, he handed Laura the book which Henry had sent her, but telling her it was for them both, he believed, and afterward for Violet.

"How is our young lawyer? I begin to wish to see the gay fellow," asked Lucy.

"He is well, and studying very closely; and told me to say to you that he would not be out to the country for a week or two longer. I did not ask him to come earlier, as I dislike to disturb any one in well-doing."

These simple remarks were the source of much pleasure to Laura, who now watched both every favorable and un-favorable word that was spoken in connection with Henry, by either of her parents.

"Father," said Laura, "since Lucy appears over-bash-ful to ask after Mr. Campbell, let me do so; did you see the young gentleman?"

"Oh, yes; I saw him — was in his office — he is well, and sends his regards."

"We are obliged to him," she replied; and left for her own room, for the purpose of opening the package, confi-dently expecting to find a note from Henry enclosed. Shutting the door as she entered, and seating herself near the window, she proceeded to open it — glancing only a moment at the title of the book — at once held it up and shook the leaves, when out dropped the expected note. A second scarcely elapsed before she had it open, and was all insensible to everything else but its contents.

She had read and re-read it, and was still straining her eyes by the twilight in again reading it, when Lucy entered.

"Why on earth have you not lighted your lamp, Laura?"

18 *

"I could not take the time Lucy; here is the most beautiful note you ever read."

"I should think so, from its so engrossing your attention as to prevent your thinking of a light."

"Oh! there is as much light in this, as in a world of lamps."

"Indeed! Well, suppose you let me have the advantage of it, to assist me through this darkness."

"Yes, I will; after sufficiently feasting my own eyes."

"Why, Laura, I believe you will lose your senses over cousin Henry yet."

"No, not if they will let me have my way."

"I suppose you will though, if you do not get it, just out of spite?"

"I fear so, most truly; but not out of spite. Now, just read it, Lucy, and say if I am not right," at the same time handing Lucy the note, who by this time had set a lamp upon the table. It ran as follows:

Room No. 37, *December 1st.*

"DEAR LAURA,—I have forced the great 'king-maker' of Edward's reign, from his high estate of arbiter between royal lines, into the more beautiful, if not more magnificent service of Love; and from being the bearer of England's crown from one royal head to another, I make him the bearer of a missive from one heart to another, as big with the fate of individuals as ever was his lordly will with the fate of kingdoms. And if he cannot help me win a woman's *hand*, and place a *Laural* (what an effort) wreath upon my brow, I will endeavor to tear that one from his own brow, which history has so honorably placed there, and in its stead hang a cypress wreath. With the threat of so dire a calamity, I am satisfied that the 'last of the barons' will execute his present trust most faithfully, and bear in most diplomatic style this missive to the bower of Love— to my sweet Laura Brandon. Enough of exordium, say you, and so say I; and for your pleasure as well as my own, let me 'wreak upon expression' something of my heart's deep love, and joy, and hope.

"When I left the beautiful prairies, it was really a source of apprehension, that I should be found retracing my steps thitherward, at least as early as the third day; if not in my waking-hours, at least in some somnambulic excursion, to the presence of my lady-love, where I might soothe the throbbings of my breast in the pure Dianic fountains that rise in hers. During the passing of the said three days, the trial to my nervous system was terrible indeed; but thanks to a finely supplied '*table d'hôte*,' and perhaps, too, to the presence of a very pretty girl who has sat opposite to me for several days—between whom and myself there have been some sly glances thrown—I have been able to survive not only the three days', but near three weeks' absence, from the light of your eyes. In regard to the said young lady, and the sly glances cast, I will say, that her striking resemblance to yourself was the secret of my pleasure; so let me beg you to be *calm*. Nonsense. Well, by this, or by that, or by nothing, finding that my amorial fortitude has enabled me to stand up against all temptation for this near three weeks, I have resolved to put it to the test, for another like period of self-torture.

"But, really, let me come down from this sort of love-scraping, to this real world of ours, in which you wonder why it is that I have not allowed myself the pleasure of basking in the sunny light of your lovely smiles. There it is again! I meant, allowed myself the pleasure of visiting the country, and why it is that I have resolved on a further penance of absence. Of course, I must answer the supposed question, even before I ask why it is that *you* have remained away so long from this *great* metropolis, whose presence here I have been as anxiously expecting as you have mine in the ruralities of 'Starlight.' Well, first, I have been right down at my books—book, rather—in despite of all the temptations of the Evil One and *Cupid* too. All of which, both study and temptation, come quite natural—often dreaming, however, that I am thus preparing a higher worthiness for the sweetest girl I ever knew.

"But in real good earnest, my dear Laura, I have even been more than anxious to see you. Thousands of things a day suggest themselves which I wish to say to you, and sometimes can scarce resist the inclination to order 'Sam' to bring me my horse, and fly to your presence; but then I haven't, ha! ha! But, truly, I have sometimes feared that my absence would make you sing, in your *pensive* hours, that 'Absence conquers love;' but right away my heart would answer with the refrain, 'But oh, believe it not!' and at once check the apprehension that had tried to rise, and in a moment more would feel that the heart of Laura Brandon could cherish no fear of him who had loved her from his youth, and now loves her in every hour of his manhood.

"Yes, Laura, the little clouds that throw their shadows on our hopes, only make you more lovely to my eye, and dearer, too, to my heart, than if the heavens were all blue, and the stars all bright, and every meteor, that speeds its trackless flight on the bosom of the night, were a sparkling promise and a spangling joy. Bravo! How do you like my love asseveration? Every word true, I do assure you; but not half the truth. In full accordance with which, I am on my very best behavior; indeed, I am quite sentimental in the performance of this rôle — and all to please the good master and mistress of 'Starlight,' with a slight credit to *your* claim. Oh, that these aforesaid good people could only see the workings and good intentions that move and burn in my anxious breast! They would clasp me to their bosoms forever. At least let me clasp my own sweet girl to mine. Yes, my heart is this moment filled with good intentions—not such as they say hell is paved with, but with the real *New Jerusalem* sort, and verily believe that I would almost do anything for this desired result, except turn 'Methodist circuit-rider.' *That* would be too much for my frail humanity, unless their people would *pay* them *better.* How does Lucy act her part of friend? Tell her that, if she does n't give you all the benefit of her sense, courage, persuasiveness, and beauty, I will haunt Campbell and her after I am dead, and bring bad luck on them forever — that there is enough of the true wizard about me to do this, if not enough to bring good fortune to myself.

"But you are too good, and true, and sweet a girl to write such nonsense to, so I shall inflict no more of it upon you, but promise to be very serious the next letter I write to you. Write to me by some chance or other. In the meanwhile I shall watch every breeze and every bird that floats this way, and expect the one to breathe to my listening ear some low, soft note of hope, or the warbling music of the other — some song of joy and love as it was sung from the coral lips of my lady-love. Will this do for my first real *love*-letter? I might do better, if I could further proceed; but uncle is to call, and I write in a hurry, if I *have* written long. Let me hear from you, in some way, very soon.

   " Very affectionately,   HENRY B."

Lucy appeared quite as much pleased and amused at the odd mixture of fun and sentiment in the letter, and handed it back, laughingly, to Laura. It was, indeed, her first " real love-letter " from Henry, and she looked it over and thought of it with the transport of delight. At length, overcome by her feelings, she fell upon her sister's neck, and sobbing, said :

" Oh ! Lucy, Lucy ! my heart will break at this ! Is it not better that I should tell it all, at once, to mother, and be over with this terrible anxiety and suspense ? "

" Oh, be quiet, Laura," answered Lucy ; " matters may not be as bad as you think ; and in a few days you will be calmer, too."

At this moment a servant announced tea, and in a few minutes more the two sisters walked into the supper-room together. Mr. Brandon saw that Laura appeared agitated, but said nothing, as he knew the cause.

CHAPTER XXXII.

" 'T is an old tale, and often told."

HENRY BRANDON continued in his whimsical resolution of remaining two or three weeks longer in the
city, where between reading " Blackstone," and crotchety
but pleasant disputation with Judge Lorn on every conceivable subject, whenever the Judge was at sufficient leisure, the time was passing rapidly away.

The Saturday following after his sending the book to
Laura, Campbell informed him that he intended that day
visiting the country, and asked him if he would accompany
him.   Brandon told him that his appointed time for visiting the prairies had not yet come ; but would thank him to
take a note for him, asking him if he would deliver it according to direction — *in person.*

" Oh, certainly ; I comprehend," said he, laughing, " and
shall play confidential messenger with the most approved
caution."

Leaving the office, he promised to return as he left town.
Brandon merely wrote a short note on a card, and enclos-
ing it, waited for the return of Campbell.

Early in the afternoon he came by, and Brandon, handing him the note, asked him to speak to his mother and
Violet at church the next day ; and if the girls should go
there to dine, to go with them.

" Yes ; thank you.   I shall certainly speak to Mrs.
Brandon and your sister, and probably will dine there."

As Campbell rode off, Brandon followed him with his
eyes as long as he remained in view, and could but sigh for
the difference in their feelings and their prospects.

Campbell had already seen Mr. Robert Brandon, and

asked permission to address his daughter, to which the latter had given his consent, with only the proviso, that his personal influence must not be expected; but that any course his daughter might see proper to adopt, would meet his approbation.

This was all that Campbell desired, as he had already had some conversation with Lucy in regard to the subject, and felt assured that it would all go as he wished. Having seen more of the girls since the return of Henry Brandon, than before, and caught much of his ease of manner, he had not only secured the affections of Lucy, but become quite a favorite with Henry Brandon and with Laura.

Reaching "Starlight" before sunset, he was met at the gate by a servant, who conducted him to the house; and was there met by Mr. Brandon himself, who welcomed him cordially. It was not long before the young ladies made their appearance, who also seemed much pleased at his visit. Mr. Brandon did not remain with them a great while, which gave Campbell a good opportunity to hand Laura the note from Henry, as if but just to have remembered it. Laura, judging from its size and appearance that it contained nothing of moment, with apparent carelessness opened it in his presence.

"Not a very long communication, Miss Brandon," said Campbell, as he saw her twirling the card in her fingers. "He might even have trusted me with that much, verbally."

"Yes; it would not have burdened your memory very greatly."

"Perhaps its point supplies its deficiency in quantity. You would scarcely risk the reading of it."

"Oh, yes; there is but little to risk; he says I must write to him by you, and that we must all dine with Violet to-morrow."

"Curt, indeed; I think you had better return it to the

young gentleman by me, as its own best answer," at the same time reaching out his hand as if to receive it.

"Oh, no," said she, blushing, and rising at the same time. "I will just leave you *two* alone, that you may pave the way to the preparation of longer ones," and laughing, moved to leave the room.

"Why, Laura, you certainly do not intend to leave Mr. Campbell and me in this great room to ourselves, and at this strange weird time. Twilight and midnight are the favorite hours of the mystic world, and we may both get terribly frightened."

"I would be pleased to have you remain, Miss Laura, but you need not fear for the danger. I will engage to defend us both against all comers and goers from the unseen world."

"Yes; I shall risk you at all events."

Lucy was quite half in earnest when she said they would get frightened; at least, it was certainly true of herself, she having reason to believe that Campbell intended formally addressing her, on the first suitable occasion, which Laura's absence would now furnish — indeed, it appearing to be an invitation for him to do so. Lucy saw and felt this, and instantly rose as if to object to her sister leaving; but Laura saw that it was perhaps the desire of Campbell that she should, and, still laughing, left the room, saying that she would be absent but a short while. Lucy now resumed her chair, which Campbell also did, after drawing his own nearer to hers. For a few seconds, he appeared about as awkward, as she seemed confused. Both felt that the time had very unexpectedly come, when their relations were to be permanently changed, and both trembled with excitement.

Lucy, however, first had the courage to break silence, by humorously asking him if he had begun to feel a little frightened.

"Yes, miss, a little agitated."

"Why, sir, do you see or hear anything to alarm you?"

"I more fear that I shall, than that I now do hear something to frighten me; and I certainly do see something that a little agitates me, even while it charms me, and would give anything in my power for only one half-hour of Henry Brandon's ease of speech, that I might describe it."

"He certainly excels in that; and as I am his kinswoman, I may have some of his same facility, and assist you, if it is of difficult utterance."

This last remark Lucy had unguardedly made, and quickly seeing the use to be made of it, suddenly rose, as if a little frightened, and said:

"There! Mr. Campbell; did you not hear some strange sound?" but had not executed her ruse, before Campbell rose, and, catching her hand, asked that he might be her defender. Lucy now saw that she was detected in the device, and both laughed, as Campbell reseated her, he saying: "But now I claim the proffered offer of assistance to my speech, as recompense for my protection."

"Proceed, Mr. Campbell," said she, with an effort at appearing indifferent; "I may assist you at the crisis of your need."

Campbell seeing at once that she was really more agitated than himself, did not feel repulsed by the reply, and only said in answer: "That is all that I can ask, Miss Lucy."

"'Tis this rose you saw, or see, Mr. Campbell — mayhap a mere conceit," said she, going back on the conversation, and scarce knowing what she *did* say.

"It may have been, or be," he said, as he playfully took her hand; "but whatever the beautiful thing may be, will you permit me to claim an interest in its loveliness?"

Looking sweetly in his face, she smilingly replied:

19

"If I have the right which you imply, it would be un-generous to refuse, after so pretty a petition."

She had not more than spoken the words, before he raised her hand to his lips.

Tea was announced, and they walked out pleasantly and happily together. Laura met them with a smile as they entered, feeling perhaps quite as happy as themselves, having been writing to Henry Brandon; and the mere fact of having been giving expression to her feelings, im-parted the highest glow to her beautiful face, and a bril-liant animation to her conversation.

CHAPTER XXXIII.

"With a smile on her lip, and a tear in her eye."

THE next morning, the family of Mr. Brandon left for church, at the usual hour. When they reached there, a large part of the congregation had already arrived, and it was not long before all had met and services were begun. Mr. Jerome preached one of his very best sermons, so much so, as to occasion it to be remarked. It was manly, replete with Christian truth, and free from that complexion and taint which has, for so many years, degraded the pulpit of this country into little else than a mere vulgar hustings, from the teachings of which congregations have gone to their homes with the fury of devils burning in their hearts; and in which fact is to be traced one of the directest causes of the late unholy war. When women go beyond the domes-tic circle, and ministers beyond the Bible, to exert their in-fluence, society ever suffers; and when these get to be reli-gion, women should go barren, and churches to ashes.

After the services were over — as was usual in the olden time, when the white population was comparatively small, and that, too, almost individually separated by large plantations — the congregation lingered for some time while exchanging salutations and other amenities peculiar to the social relations of planter life.

As they were about separating, each asked the other home to dine. Violet succeeded, however, in spite of other refusals, in getting her peculiar circle of young friends to accompany her.

The days were now getting short, and not much formality was observed. Dinner was found to be ready, on reaching Mrs. Brandon's, and not very long in being ended. It was no sooner over, than all the company met, in a free and easy manner, in the parlor, and for the next hour or so enjoyed themselves with great zest. As the conversation crossed and re-crossed from one to the other, Laura Brandon remarked to Mr. Jerome, that it was profanely rumored that probable contingencies would shortly render the presence of *two parsons* necessary to the performance of parish duties, and asked if he had heard anything of such reports.

"I can't say, Miss Laura," said Mr. Jerome, "that I have; but from what I saw one of the young ladies of the congregation do to-day, I should think that *one* parson is hardly sufficient to hold their attention. I think I saw one of my fairest parishioners draw a watch upon my sermon, as if in great impatience at its length."

"Ah! *I* plead guilty to that, Parson; but it was far from a feeling of impatience that made me do it. I heard you to-day with unusual interest. It was an idea — a recollection, if you please — that came over me, and I *did* look at the hour."

"Was it the right one?"

"Yes, sir; just about," said Laura, blushing, supposing from the question that Mr. Jerome had somehow guessed at the point; "but after that, I did you all possible honor in the stricter attention."

Standing near Violet at the time, she held the card from Henry, concealed in her hand, that the latter might read it, in which he had asked her to remember him at 12 o'clock, and he would do the same by her. Violet comprehended the whole matter at a glance, but said nothing.

The company were now in the act of leave-taking, when Laura playfully insisted on Mr. Jerome telling her whether there was any truth in the report of the two parsons being necessary in the parish.

"I am afraid not, unless you in some wise contemplate introducing another, of which, indeed, there is some little said by those I know of."

"Come, Parson; you say that in a bad spirit."

"No, not by any means; for there have been some very pretty speculations in regard to yourself, and a certain dashing young genius, who has lately reappeared among us; and who I regret not meeting with to-day, as I had some very fine messages for him from old Mr. Thaxton, and I must not omit to tell you too, what a friend he is of yours. He thinks Henry Brandon the finest genius who has appeared here for years, and Laura Brandon the finest girl in the whole country."

"Yes; old Mr. Thaxton is a great friend of mine, I know, and so am I of his — really have quite an admiration for the old man. But never mind that just now. I want your confidence this evening, Parson. Now, just tell me in your most artless manner, whether etymological instructions to Miss Sally, in regard to the famous word βαπτιζω are having any good results."

"Ah! the time is too short now to enter upon that subject. Let me reserve the answer for some day when we have more leisure — when, too, you may be better prepared to throw some fresh light upon the 'law matrimonial,' in which I suppose, you have quite an able instructor, and of which I am anxious to learn something."

"Why, Parson, you are positively growing malignant."

While Laura was talking with Mr. Jerome, she was watching a favorable opportunity to hand to Mr. Campbell the letter which she had written to Henry Brandon, and seeing it at this moment, she asked Mr. Jerome to excuse her. Without being observed she handed it to him, and saying only a word stepped back to the side of Mr. Jerome. They soon separated after this, and were on their different ways home.

So soon as Campbell reached the city, he sent Laura's letter to Brandon's room. The latter spent the remainder of the evening in reading and re-reading it. It ran as follows: which, though reposed to our care, we hope, at this late day, is no violation of confidence to give to the reader.

"STARLIGHT, *8th December.*

"A *contraband* letter came into my possession some days since, from my dear cousin Henry Brandon, which, it is needless to assure him, is held as the dearest treasure I possess. Its various evidences of true affection, its humor, and its gay-heartedness, found either their response or appreciation, in the bosom of his *own* affectionate Laura.

"When I first read it, I could but give way to a flood of nervous tears; but recovering then, I have felt calmer and happier every time I have read it since, which if I continue to do, as often for the next few days as I have for the past few, the power of numerals will be quite severely taxed in their enumeration. This will appear extravagant, but is nigher the truth than might be supposed; but let me beg you, my gay chevalier, not to let it make you vain —only let it encourage you to write me more such, and oftener.

"The few foregoing lines were all that I had written when I was called to tea; since then, after remaining a short while in the parlor, I have returned to my *task* of *love*, asking Mr. Campbell and Lucy to excuse me, which they

19 *

appeared to do *very willingly*.   But now that I have sat
down to this pleasing duty, I scarce know how to resume;
and certainly cannot see how I shall ever stop — quite a
dilemma to fall into, as the more I think, the still further
am I led to think — rather likening my situation to that
of the famous inexhaustion of the widow's cruse.

"Out of such abundance, you will very naturally think
that I might have written before — and so, indeed, I might
have, and greatly wished to; and you are therefore entitled
to an explanation.   First, then, I did not suppose that you
would so persistently carry out your resolution of remaining so long away from us, and somehow continued to look
for you riding up every evening.

"This was the reasoning of my *affection*.   The next and
only other, was the reasoning of my *caution*.   I really saw
no opportunity likely to arise, which could be intrusted
with so important a missive — there was no 'Earl of War-
wick' at my command, and I have almost feared to in-
trust it to a less responsible envoy.

"Mr. Campbell's return to-morrow, particularly as it is
by your request, is the *very first* chance that has presented
itself, and as you see, I am embracing it.   I have, too, quite
an assurance of his suitability, from the particular manner
of his handing your last note to *me* — doing it as if a
matter of no unusual moment, when no one was present
except Lucy and myself; and then, as though he had just
remembered it.   I have for a good while been much disposed to like him; but now, am even ready to declare myself his friend, and hope you will find it agreeable to cultivate a nearer acquaintance with him, particularly as he
is very likely to become a member of our family at no distant day; and will possess a certain sort of influence with
mother, which *we* can probably make available to *us*.   He
is aware of the many advantages of mind which you have
over him, and *you* can therefore *afford* to make advances.
He, too, is a stranger, while you are at home on your
'native heath.'

"'Such a diplomatist,' say you.   Yes; but my intentions
are not to take advantage of any one, but to do all the
good I can.

"This much in regard to *ourselves*.   With regard to
yourself, it is proper for you to receive the friendship of

such men, if you desire success and promotion, either as a professional or public character. By the necessary operations of society, all the *honors* of life are confined within certain particular limits; and an effort to obtain them outside of these circles or coteries is of doubtful experiment, or at least places an aspirant in the aggressive, which, to say the least of it, must be very unpleasant to one who possesses social and generous impulses. What a politician I would have made! *Nous verrons.*

"You said, in your letter by father — the 'Last of the Barons' — that it was your first *love-letter.* I think you are mistaken. You have merely got your position reversed. It was your *last;* as I always *felt* that every one you ever wrote me was a genuine love-letter, and met response, too, in my own heart; elsewise, why should it now belong so entirely to my *wild* young cousin? I must be right.

"The only difference I can see between this and all previous others is, that in this you are my *openly avowed* 'sweetheart,' as you call it, while always before, the same fact was disclosed, but under different disguises; but they were all the same to a woman's penetration, and to a woman's heart.

"You see that I am quite resolved to believe that you were always, as you are this day, *my own* Henry Brandon; and yet I will confess to you that an *avowed* profession of your feelings — one that I could see, ay, and feel too — brought a *new* and an unknown joy to my heart. Oh, cousin! I can never tell the dreamy happiness, the sweet ecstasy, the brilliant hope, that came as angels come, and colored the future of my life with the softness of the sky's own blue, when. I held your letter before me, *telling* me that you *loved* me! The innocent fancy of childhood, and the beautiful vision that had ever floated along the path of my girlhood's wild and shy romance, came gushing over me in a flood of light, and love, and truth. But I fear you grow weary of this lightly told history of a heart you have appeared to win so easily; yet I hope not; nor yet must you think it an unmaiden thing to tell so plainly the *life* secret of my woman's soul. But I know I wrong you when I use such words, even with Love's sweet privilege, as the very spirit that hovers over my being, ever tells me that *you* are *my own,* even as *I was ever yours.* Though

I scarce did know how our hopes, our fortunes, and all
the shadows of our lives were to commingle into one, yet
every year brought its own bright imaginings, with not one
doubt to darken their glowing freshness. But still, with
all this unrippled smoothness in my feelings' flow, and all
my present blissful gladness, there is some vague and aching fear of the future, some uncertain woe, which I scarce
can trace back to its bitter source. Yet, never mind ; it
may be but a baseless apprehension, and I will hope it is.

"Lucy has already returned from the parlor, asleep, and
dreaming of the bright future, it may be, while I am still
writing of the bright past. From the first-mentioned fact
you may know it is growing quite late, and I am warned
to stop, elsewise Mr. Campbell might find some inconve-
nience in carrying such a package. And now may the
angels guard you! *My* spirit is ever with you.

"Yours, affectionately,   LAURA BRANDON.

"P. S.—I have kept this letter open until since dinner
was over, just to tell you that precisely at 12 o'clock, to-
day, in accordance with your *boyish* request, I thought
of you, when your image was on my heart as palpably as
ever your form was present to my eye. Yours, L. B."

As we have already said, Henry read and re-read this
letter, re-opened, re-read, and speculated as to the future,
until a late hour, and, falling into a gentle sleep as he sat
in his arm-chair with his gown around him, dreamed of his
lovely cousin.

CHAPTER XXXIV.

"It were all one,
That I should love a bright, particular star,
And think to wed it, he is so above me."

THE time had at length arrived which young Brandon
had capriciously set apart for his visit to the country.
Having, too, completed the first reading of his Blackstone,
he felt at full liberty to take all the recreation he desired.

Judge Lorn evidently disliked to give him up, even for so short a time, and said to him that he had better remain but a few days, as the law differed from most other studies, and a student would soon lose the whole system of reasoning and induction, by disuse.

Henry admitted that it was doubtless so, but told him that there were two events which would necessarily intervene before his return — the Christmas holidays, and his sister's wedding — the latter being appointed to take place early in January. He very fortunately had these excuses; but even had they not existed, all the Blackstones ever published, would not have restrained him from the enjoyment which he promised himself within the next few weeks. "Sam Brandon"—who had been with him—was accordingly ordered to take to the country such matters of apparel as would be necessary for a month's sojourn, and, the next day after that, Henry himself followed.

Life soon assumed all the old heyday of pleasure, even as if there had never been a book published; and much of his time was passed with his cousins, who never failed to meet him with pleasure, while Mrs. Brandon was forced into the same appearance of welcome. He was made to feel, however, that there was really but little pleasure felt by her in his visits. This, however, he cared little for, as he had learned not to expect it, and knew that she had no *direct* cause to receive him in any other wise than respectfully.

His mother and Violet had begun to be troubled about his attentions to Laura, feeling satisfied that it would produce a rupture between the families, as soon as he should attempt a change in the relations between himself and Laura, with the certainty, too, of failure on his part.

Mrs. Brandon finally resolved to have some serious conversation with him in regard to it, if it was possible to do so; and on the first opportunity which presented itself she began by suggesting once more, that, in consequence of the approaching marriage of Violet, some changes would be necessary to be made in their private affairs, and asked him if he had thought of the matter.

"No, not a great deal, mother. I have just thought that they would go along as most affairs of the sort do go."

His tone of voice was a little irritable, which induced her to say, in reply:

"I know the matter is not a very delightful one to you, my son; yet we cannot always have our own choosing in the course of events. Some things force themselves upon our attention; and while not pleasing, perhaps, are exactly such as the pleasantnesses of life hinge upon, and therefore we *must* attend to the one, in order to secure the other. Every sweet has its bitter; but every bitter has its own recommendations."

"Well, mother, that is a comforting sort of philosophy. I am therefore at your service, for the discussion of any *little* subject that you may propose. What view do you wish that I should take of this very serious subject?"

He had not more than spoken these words, when Violet entered the room, to whom he turned and said:

"Sister, these nuptial enterprises seem to be quite serious concerns, in these latter days. It is but a short time since when something connected with a certain one, forced the fact upon my attention that I was approaching that rubicon of manhood, which twains midway the masculine part of life, ycleped *vingt-et-un*, when, forsooth, it rises before me again, in a more formidable shape. Now, can't you and Hunter, with mother for judge-advocate, arrange the whole affair, and release me of all connection with it?"

"I can't say, brother. Perhaps I might assist, if I were aware of its nature."

"Oh, I thought, as a matter of course, that the suggestion was made at your instance, and assure you that I am wholly unprepared to enlighten you in the premises. What is the character of the disquisition, mother, which I am invited to participate in?"

"It was with regard to what arrangement you wished in reference to the division of the estate."

"Ah, ha! Well, as I have always done very well without a division, suppose we still remain *united*."

"That would be very agreeable; but it must, at least, have a nominal head, which your uncle has been for many years; but he cannot do so much longer."

"Well, if I must speak, let me get up some evidence. Violet, to whom do you intend clinging for the future— to mother, or to Thomas Hunter?"

"I must try to cling to both, brother," said she, blushing, as she turned her mischievous face toward him. "I cannot leave mother, and ought not to leave Mr. Hunter. What do you advise?"

"Just exactly as you say—cling to both. That relieves me."

"But do you not intend remaining with us?"

"Oh, yes, for a few days, probably. But then I might partially lose my senses, and conclude to unite my fortunes with those of some sweet, unsuspecting girl; and then, you know, we should be compelled to separate."

"Not necessarily. We could continue to live together then as well as now—particularly if it was Miss Gray."

"Yes—Miss Gray; but suppose it should be our pretty cousin Laura?"

Mrs. Brandon now again joined the conversation, and said to him: "My son, let me beg you not to think of Laura in that way. She is one of the sweetest girls I ever knew, and with her cultivated mind, her generous character, her industry, and her beauty, would make a becoming wife for the best gentleman in the land; but I tell you in all sincerity she will never marry you against her mother's consent, and *that* you will *never* get; and you will only bring unhappiness to her now peaceful and pleasant life, by putting that question to the test. She admires you I know; I had almost said *loves* you, and has done so from a girl; but as yet, it has only been as toward a gay, dashing cousin, and let it remain at that."

"Mother, you are making a very solemn affair out of it: you really frighten me. Can't a young gentleman love a pretty cousin just a 'wee bit,' without making all the world miserable?"

"You should not attempt to turn it off so lightly, as perhaps I know more than you think for."

"Ah! what is that?"

"If you will answer me a direct question, I will tell you."

"I may if I can."

"Then, have you not written Laura on that subject within the last month?"

"Oh, mother; that is what *we lawyers* call a leading question, therefore must not permit you to ask it. But why do you put it?"

"She showed Violet a note, which you would not have written had it not been preceded by another of a different character; and then I saw her hand Mr. Campbell a letter, which I supposed was for you. Is this so?"

"It is."

"Have you the letter with you?"

"I have."

"Will you show it to me?"

"That would never do, mother."

"Of course, I do not wish to read a letter to you which was intended to be private, but I know that you would not hesitate, were it a mere letter of friendship."

"Brother," said Violet, laughing, and evidently for the purpose of changing the conversation; "let me ask you to visit Miss Gray; she is a beautiful girl, and I think you would be pleased with her."

"Yes; and I rather thought, too, the young lady was pleased with me — and she rather appears to be such an one as a gentleman might afford to *flirt* with, for a season at least. But then, my dear sister, you appear to proceed on the amorial hypothesis that your brother is frantic on the subject of matrimony, whereas I am extremely indifferent; and moreover, do not admire this idea of roving over the country in quest of a sweetheart, as if looking for a horse. I wish the young lady who may have the *good fortune* to receive my attentions, to *happen* as it were, in my way."

"Well, your first meeting was certainly fortuitous — just of the very description you speak of."

"Yes, so it was; and I have heard that you wished her for one of your bridemaids."

"I had thought of asking her; but she has gone to Memphis on a visit to some relations, and will not be back before spring."

"Ha! ha! so there was a most beautiful failure in your scheme."

"No, no scheme at all."

"Just my luck then — see how the fates are spinning out my thread. I am forced to fall in love with Laura, from the pure necessities of the case; but who have you to fill her place on that blissful occasion?"

Violet then told him all her arrangements, and answered his question directly, by telling him that a Miss Jenny Morris, an orphan niece of Judge Hunter, on a visit to him from South Carolina, would be one of her attendants, "and really one of the prettiest girls I ever saw."

"Indeed; and what is the style of her surpassing beauty?"

"Medium height, faultless figure, graceful, elegant in her

20

carriage, brilliant but soft black eyes, hair black—black as a raven—fresh complexion, with just enough of the olive tinge to give it perfect beauty; pearly teeth, without which no woman can be pretty."

"I agree with you, nor even *decent*—go on."

"The prettiest mouth, and the reddest, sweetest lips—"

"All very good—go on."

"Highly educated, a beautiful performer on the harp and guitar, and one of the finest singers you ever listened to."

"*Very* fine!—proceed."

"Well, altogether, she is just the girl to secure a full share of your august admiration; and according to your own ideas, has fallen accidentally in your way—no hunting up done on either side, every thing perfectly *natural*, and you are to wait with her."

"*Very* fine—perfectly enchanting; but why did you not say at once, sister, sent expressly by the gods to meet me on this hymeneal occasion. The *contre-temps* would then have been sublime—leaving nothing for me to do, but to go through the short and vulgar preliminary of obtaining a—*license*, in consideration of the payment of three dollars. But why, all this while, have you not had Laura as one of your lady-waiters? This looks like a conspiracy against me, sister."

"Oh! no, brother; you know my feelings too well to think that. No, she positively declined."

"For what reason, Violet?"

"I cannot say, as she positively refuses to give any. I accused her, in pleasantry, of some sort of superstition; because I was younger than she."

"I merely said what I did in jest—of course did not think it. But it is strange why she refused. But 'all's well that ends well.' So I shall wait with Miss—what did you say?"

"Jenny Morris."

"A very pretty name. Pity that she should change it, even for the noble one of Brandon. She has high authority, though, for believing that a rose will smell as sweet by any other name; and therefore I, the imperial Henry Brandon, may stoop to pluck this gentle flower, and wear it on my royal bosom without injury to its fragrance," speaking in a tone of mixed levity and irony, which he intended to be noticed by his mother and sister; and Violet observing it in an instant, said:

"I was only jesting when I suggested Jenny Morris to your attention; and yet, from what I have seen of her, and heard of her, I believe she would be an eligible match for any gentleman who did not desire fortune."

"You are quite enthusiastic, Violet, in the praises of your new friends. First Miss Gray, and next Miss Morris. But you spoil your picture of the latter, in the last touch of your brush. *No fortune*, at this advanced age of the world! That condition is particularly unfortunate. But do you think there would be any *objections* in *that* quarter?"

"None, of course; for what objection could there be to *you*, in any quarter, but in that one of which we have spoken; and you know the source of that. Now, sir, does my complimentary explanation appease your ire?"

"Most effectually; and I now feel all the inspiration of the Jenny — who? — proposition. Yes, Jenny Morris shall be my motto for — I can't say how long. Beautiful, accomplished, fine family; but — *no fortune!* Alas! Oh, cruel fate! say I, as I am a fortune-hunter. But then she has the especial recommendation of having no towering papa, or lynx-eyed mamma, to supervise her inclinations. Very agreeable facts generally, but have a particular beauty to me about this time."

"Yes, and —"

"Enough, Violet. You will overwhelm me, if you add

another recommendation.   You would force me to go directly in search of this HEBE.   But what shall I say to sweet Laura Brandon when she sees that I have made myself a Romeo to another Juliet ? "

" You need say nothing to Laura, for she will see your right to do so, knowing that she will never marry you, nor any one, against her mother's wishes ; and in your case already knows that she will never get it.   But remember, brother, that both you and Laura have no better friend than I, in any cause."

Henry Brandon saw the purpose of Violet, and while he could not but feel bitterly in regard to it, he affected to treat the whole matter lightly.   Let us wait and see the end.

" Ah ! that is the true ring, sister ; and, win or lose, you place me under the same obligation, and in return for it I now offer you my services in any capacity relative to your entertainment, from running on small errands, to the icing of cake ; " and he left the room with a bitter laugh.

CHAPTER XXXV.

"I hold the world but as the world, Gratiano ;
A stage, where ev'ry man must play a part,
And mine a sad one."

YOUNG Brandon, feeling out of humor, without scarcely knowing why, remained at home for several days, only varying the monotony by an occasional partridge hunt, with "*Sam Brandon*" for his companion. Wearying with this sort of mixed sullenness and trouble, he resolved on a visit to Hunter, who had, indeed, been over to Mrs. Brandon's the evening before, but he had failed to meet him, from being absent on one of his hunting excursions.

Ordering *Sam* to have the horses, he had no sooner finished his breakfast, than he rode off, telling his mother and sister not to be *uneasy*, as he was *not* going to see *Laura*, but intended spending the day with Hunter.

"My son," said Mrs. Brandon, "I fear that you have felt hurt with me, for a day or two past; but —"

Henry Brandon rather laughed, and told her not to finish the sentence, and left the house without waiting for her to conclude her remarks.

The day was cold and clear, but beautiful for the middle of December. The wind was still, and the warm, yellow sunshine rested softly on the bosom of the brown sward, as if soothing it for the crisp frost of the morning, and was now resolved on melting away its memory. As he rode quietly along, the peculiar winter softness of the scene gave cast to his own reflections, and he wondered why the unseen hand that guides and rules the seasons could so forget the destinies of human life, and all the hopes, the loves, the anxieties, and the sorrows of the heart, as to permit events to transpire so irregularly, and so rudely to sweep its tender chords. The laws, thought he, which govern the changes of nature, work with a certain positive regularity — one season legitimately succeeds another, and we know what and when to expect it. Spring, with its glowing beauty, and buoyant youth, comes, with its mysterious germinations, and lays the foundations of the year; then comes the glorious, splendid Summer, commanding all the singular and unknown energies of the earth, and with certainty drives Nature on to full fruition. Next, is the lovely, quiet Autumn, to rest this Nature, as it were, from its heaving toils; and while the sighing west wind mourns, in vesper cadences, the Summer's fadings hand over to the hearty, hale old Frost King the full account of its stewardship. "And now," said he, "here he is in all the majesty of his reign, honored by the groaning abundance of the year; and

20 *

this bright, balmy day is some grand gala-time in his boreal court. Yes," continued he, in his low soliloquy, " all is regular, smooth, and right in this kingdom of the earth and sky ; but not thus in human life. There all, everything is uncertain, dark, and unreliable ; nothing is to be depended on — no, devil the bit — rather, everything appears to work by *contraries*. Now, why can't I claim the hand of Laura Brandon? Her heart is mine — and, by my faith, 't is a puny sort of acknowledgment ; but mine is hers — and yet all the consolation I get for this, is in that babbling nonsense of old Shakspeare, that the course of 'true love never did run smooth.' Now, does his having said it, and every other fool repeating it, make it any the better for me? No; it 's just what I dislike, the more I think of it. I wish the old ass had had no dream on that midsummer night, but had slept with the soundness of the seven sleepers — or at least dreamed something else. But, never mind; it will be right against the twentieth century.

"Come, let's ride up," said he, addressing *Sam* for the first time; and both started their horses at a rapid gait, but had not gone far before they met Dr. Wilton.

Henry and the Doctor seemed mutually pleased with the accidental meeting, and in a running manner talked over the neighborhood gossip.

Brandon supposing, as a matter of course, that he was out on professional calls, presently asked who was sick.

"No one, particularly," he rather stammeringly replied; "I am from Judge Hunter's this morning."

"Anything the matter there?" he innocently asked.

"Oh, no," he answered, laughingly; "I merely passed the evening with him; or with the young ladies, you will say."

"Ah, I beg pardon. But that was quite as pleasant as practising, and mayhap more profitable, too."

"More pleasant, I grant you. As to the profit, deponent saith not."

"I learn, Doctor, that the stars are all right in that quarter of the hymeneal heavens, and I congratulate you on being under their influence."

"I am obliged to you, indeed. And now permit me to congratulate *you*, as there are some pleasant rumors afloat in which you have an interest."

"Well, I shall not be so bashful as to disclaim having an idea of what the rumors are; but as *I* hear them, they are not very flattering to my vanity or prospects."

"Then you must let me sympathize with you," said he jocosely. "But yours is not the current statement. By the way, you have a very warm friend, and a great admirer over at our house, Mr. Brandon; and if all the world were as he is, you would certainly have fair skies and smooth sailing; but he is much disposed to grumble at your never coming over to see him."

"Yes, you allude to Mr. Thaxton; and I am really ashamed of never having gone to see him."

"I also met another very warm admirer of yours yesterday, and he asked me to deliver you a message if I saw you which I had scarcely thought of since. Do you remember Jack Gaulding?"

"Oh, very well," replied Henry Brandon, laughing; "one of my old boyhood friends, down in the hills."

"Yes—well, I met him yesterday in company with several others, armed to the teeth, all of whom appeared to know you, and knew that you had returned; but had not met with you, and expressed a great desire to see you once more before they were all *killed*, or were compelled to leave the country."

"Yes; but why do they say 'killed,' or compelled to leave the country?"

"I believe they have all been associated with Miller in his outlawry, and I suppose they think one or the other result will follow."

"Ah! yes—well, did they designate any particular day or occasion?"

"Yes, next Saturday week, at Manese's grocery; when there will be a '*gander*-pulling' during the day, and a *ball* at night."

The Doctor pretended to hesitate as he delivered the message; but there was an evident twinkle in his eye as he did so, which Brandon discovering, replied:

"Good, my lord; I shall take one chance, cost what it will. I may not win a great deal, but I shall certainly not lose much. It is about the last flicker of the old hill-country life, I should judge, and I must see it. Would you like to go, Doctor? It will be worth more than ten nonsensical, formal, court receptions—it will be human nature nude. Will you go? It may lose you some few old patrons up here, but it will gain you twenty there."

"Oh, damn the expense on a spree, as the two Yankees said when they divided the glass of hard cider. Yes, I will go; but we need make no blowing horn of it."

"Certainly not. Then, let us meet at St. Mary's Church next Saturday morning week, at eight o'clock. The Parson will think you out practising, and mother and Violet will scarcely question me." After some other general conversation, the two wild Southerners parted to meet again at the appointed time.

After going some hundred yards, Brandon turned in his saddle, and called out:

"Doctor, how do you think Miss H. will like it?"

"I can't really say; but the tender passion must lower its crest, when a frolic is on the wing—but how do you think Miss B. will take it?"

"Ah! that matter is about lost anyway. 'Gone glimmering through the dream of things that were,'" and with the last words dashed on.

It was now but a few minutes' ride to Hunter's residence,

and reaching there, without ceremony he entered the house; and found his old friend and classmate comfortably seated before a good fire in his library, diving deep into the mysteries of the celebrated Resolutions of '98–'99.

"Ah — the top of the morning to you — extremely comfortable," said Brandon as he entered very unexpectedly.

"Why, good morning, Henry," said, he rising. "You surprised me — just from home?"

"Yes; grew weary of looking at the 'woman-kind,' and thought to come over and tax your time. What pamphlet is that which seems to have so absorbed you?"

"The Virginia and Kentucky Resolutions. I happened to pick it up after breakfast, and becoming interested, had not laid it down. It contains the notes upon them, of Professor —"

"Have you a mind to join the State Rights party?"

"No; yet the doctrine has some very plausible reasons in its behalf, to say the least."

"Pshaw! the devil! fiddlesticks, man — Utopian, absurd — nothing short of the immaculacy of angels could carry out the idea. No people on earth before ours ever tried to live under *two* governments at once; and taken in connection with human nature as it is, the doctrine is bound to lead to collision and destruction of what we are pleased to call our republican government, but that would be no *damned* bad idea. If we admit these resolutions to be the true text of the Constitution, we had better have given over the whole thing to Jefferson, and let him run the machine, for no one else ever caught the idea. They are the embodyment of his visionary nonsensicalities — partly derived from Locke, partly from the revolutionary French writers, and twisted into their present shape by his own idiosyncratic mind."

"Why, Henry, you must have swallowed a paper of tacks. You don't appear to think much of our great constitutional apostle, nor of republics either. You must have been in close confab with your uncle Robert."

"Uncle Robert! Your grandmother's goose! I expect he is a very clever man, but he has but a poor share of independence, and therefore not a man for me to copy after in anything."

" Hah! — what's the matter now, Henry?"

"Oh, nothing; but speaking of old Jefferson and republics — I am happy to say that I have not the least infatuation in those directions, Mr. Robert Brandon pro or con; but Jefferson really puts off the tricks and quirks of intellect for intellect itself. And as to republics, I should have thought that that damned Puritan effort, with Cromwell in the lead, and the woful experiment of France, would have satisfied all the world of the absurdity of the idea of men being capable of governing themselves; but we have got the old shoe revamped, and think to wear it, and while our country is a forest, and men do not live nearer than in cock-crow of each other, it may work very well; but just wait till they step on one another's heels, and then will come the *explosion*. We could live under *any* form of government just now — the worst despotism could not hurt us, with our territory and resources; but just wait till we come in sight of each other, and interests begin to clash — if you want your eyes to feast on ruin. There will not be a vestige of this thing left in twenty-five years, and in fifty years we will not be able to locate the idea of an American Republic, any more than we can locate the site of Troy or the garden of Eden; and old Jefferson, Washington, Adams & Co. will be as great myths as Priam, Hector, and Achilles, or Adam; and we will be farther from *freedom* than if we had never attempted the foolish but dangerous experiment. It will, indeed, then require the very worst form of a despotism to get us back to even a *decent* standard of conduct and feeling. No, men are but little more fit for self-government than the brute creation; the Almighty never intended the idea to pass even into the appearance of a system, further than as a sort of penance or crucible, through which they should pass for purification from some great pestilential contamination. If there was nothing else to disprove the idea of men being capable of self-government, the mere fact of such as Clay and Webster being held in subordinate places to such as Van Buren, Polk, 'et id omne,' is a complete demonstration. Just look at all the various causes that work the defeat of such men, and you will see your idea is perfectly untenable — not reconcilable to the first legitimate purpose of government."

"Well, Sir Satirist, what style would please you?"

"Just that which every sensible man knows is the *only* one under which men can or will live in peace, and that to which every civilized people have returned to, whatever may have been their departures from it — a *constitutional monarchy*, or any other sort of monarchy, in preference to the turbulent anarchy of a republic. All governments based upon the idea of man's capacity for self-government — from Adam in Eden down to the American people — have and will prove terrible failures — first a republic, then democracy, then anarchy, then despotism, and last a monarchy, is the short history of all governments and people."

"Henry, you are wild this morning. Is your digestion good? are your bilious secretions all right?"

"Never better; but I may be a little jaundiced this morning, as I have reason to fear that some of my small matters are not working smoothly. If I had a little despotic power — rather think I could bring them all right."

"Ah, my boy! I fear you are approaching a premature senility. I have never seen you unable before to control your affairs as you wished."

"Something of the sort, perhaps; but I have truly fallen into an evil place this time, I fear. One that I cannot get my hand on—it eludes me."

"What has happened so disastrous to the fortunes of Æneas?"

"Just a new leaf I have turned over in the 'Ars Ama-toria,' which I doubt my capacity to translate."

"Stop your enigmas and tell me your trouble."

Henry then told him the probable state of affairs between himself and Laura, when Hunter advised him to the course which he thought best for the present. But to the suggestion of calling on Laura the next day, and getting her consent to let him speak to her father in regard to the affair, Brandon laughed, and said:

"Tom, to-morrow is *Friday*, man; an ominous day to begin an important work."

"Pshaw! my good fellow, put Friday in your pocket, and go along about your work. There is no man in as bad luck as he that puts off till to-morrow."

"Well, I will do as you say; but I have no idea that any good will come of it—it's gone—gone to the devil!—past praying for. Some things I know so well, as never to trouble myself about the wherefore—fate!"

"Faint heart never won fair woman."

"No, nor any sort ever won a conceited old one."

"Conceit in weakest bodies works strongest, Shakspeare informs us, and as he knows every thing, I suppose he told the truth."

The conversation now gradually ran into other channels, and the day was spent in such ways as young men under such circumstances usually dispose of them. The weather growing colder, Henry left rather early after dinner on that account. They had not ridden far, when "Sam Brandon" rode up to his side, and in a sort of confidential tone, said:

"Mass Henry, what's all this hully-be-lu they is gittin' up 'bout you and Miss Laura?"

"Hully-be-lu, Sam? what do you mean by that?—is there any such thing going on?"

"Why, yes, sir, they is making a big to do, I hears; but its all 'nigger news,' and maybe it ain't so."

"What have you heard?"

"I hears Miss Laura stays in her room, and ole Miss Catherine is mad as she can be with everybody, and you in particular. Mass Robert he says nothin', but keeps out in the plantation."

"That *is* a hully-be-lu, as you call it, and we must go over and see about it; and what I can't find out, you must."

"I will that; for the niggers all knows, and I hear they is mity mad about it. Miss Laura, you see, is the favorite of 'em all. But anyhow, if old Miss Catherine went to makin' too much fuss, I would go to see some other young lady. S'pose you go to see ole Mass Gray's daughter, she is a *mity* fine-lookin' young lady—rich till thar ain't no end to it, and she was rale struck with you; I sede it—niggers knows them sort of things; and thar's a beautiful one at Judge Hunter's, not long come thar, and is going to wait on Miss Violet."

"Yes—well, I will see about this other first, Sam."

"Oh, yes, of cose; but I would'n' stan' 'em raisin' a rackit over my head; an' you know they alw'ys did say that every thing had to go as Miss Catherine said—the old devil can't turn her head when it once gits sot."

As "Sam Brandon" ended these wise suggestions, Henry rather impatiently struck off in a swift gallop, saying to himself, "The devil must be in my luck, even Sam must take part and recommend—Miss Gray. Very well, we shall see."

21

CHAPTER XXXVI.

" The good are better made by ill,
    As odors crushed are sweeter still."

THE following morning, in accordance with the suggestion of Hunter, Henry Brandon went over to see
Laura, for the purpose of learning the actual condition of
things, and if possible to make some more reliable arrangement of their relationship.

Reaching there, he was met by his aunt, who appeared
more gracious than usual, or at least than he expected ;
and he at once began to think that his fears were either
unfounded, or that she had carried her point.   Assuming
his customary gayety of manner, he soon asked for his
uncle and the girls.

Mr. Brandon came to the parlor, as soon as he heard
that Henry was there, though at the very time in the act
of riding out.   Everything appeared as natural and easy
as usual, and conversation was going glibly along on general matters, when Lucy entered the room unaccompanied
by her sister.   "Ah! something in that," said Henry to
himself; but choosing not to notice it, rose and met Lucy
with his ever-merry face and salutation.

"Where is the Lady Laura this morning?" he at length
ventured to ask.

"She will be here directly," Lucy replied.

At this moment Mr. Brandon took occasion to leave
the room, asking Henry to excuse him for an hour or so,
but asking him also to remain till his return, as he wished
to see him.

Mrs. Brandon had already left the room, but as if from
no unusual cause.; Henry, finding himself alone with Lucy,
had just begun to inform her of what he had heard, when

Laura entered. She met him pleasantly, but with so evidently a subdued manner as at once to expose the suffering of some mental conflict now past. He endeavored to rattle along in his usual vein, but had manifestly wearied in the effort, when he recovered and said:

"Girls, we have all certainly been to a 'Methodist meetin''—we are as serious as if we had been on the mourner's seat, or preparing our ascension robes in honor of Miller's prophecy. I mean this more for you than for myself—but even *I* feel some sort of embarrassment, which, you know, is not often the case; I therefore propose a little music by way of thaw to this rigidity. Come, Lucy, you hold a very nice relationship to one we know; suppose you sing a *love-song* — in character."

"No, cousin, I am not in that mood this morning; I am thinking of *briefs*, declarations, and professional matters generally," said Lucy, rather affecting to be cheerful.

"Oh, I had thought you had gone higher in your case, and was now ready for *trial*. I really wish to hear you both sing, as I fear some great evil has befallen your voices. Come, Laura, suppose, then, you try yours first."

Laura responded with a faint smile, but made no motion as if to rise. Henry, observing her rather listless look, rose himself and said, "Come, cousin, sing, play, or talk, or I shall leave in twenty seconds — I am growing frantic."

"You promised father to remain until his return," said Lucy.

"So I did, but I did n't promise to let his girls freeze me to death during his absence. Business is about the last thing I ever intend to respond to; your trades-people attend to business. At all events, I can meet him in one of the temperate latitudes and attend to what he wants — *this* is a *frigid* zone. But come, my fair kinswoman," said he, as he rose and took Laura by the hand, "allow me to *support* you to the piano; and I beseech you to let one more ray of genial warmth and happiness gladden your sad face. Come, sing a song of joy and love, and I will even join you."

Laura rose at this, and, walking to the piano, asked him what she should sing for him.

"Yes — I am obliged; well, there is a sweet old song that just occurs to me — and I have n't heard it for years — beginning with these beautiful words —

> "'If a body meet a body
> Comin' through the rye,
> And a body kiss a body,
> Need a body cry?'"

Lucy had purposely left the room as Laura rose to go to the piano, and when Henry had finished the words, he gallantly leaned over, and kissed her colorless cheek. She made no resistance, but neither spoke nor smiled, and immediately began to sing, in a low voice, that really beautiful old love-song of "Go, forget me," and, though perhaps she did not know it, sang a *destiny*. She had sung but a few lines, when her voice became so tremulous as to compel her to stop. Henry Brandon now laid his arm gently around her neck, and said:

"Laura, dear Laura, what is it that so greatly troubles you?"

For a few moments neither spoke; but she, seeming to recover, gently displaced his arm, and rising from her seat, said to him, in a soft, low voice:

"Cousin, can you forgive my woman's lips for having spoken what my woman's courage is too weak to execute?" Then taking his hand, she said, "I once told you that my heart was yours, and partially promised you my hand, and still so much is this the truth, that neither will ever be another's."

"Oh, Laura! Laura! this is too bad — too bad; tell

me why these strange words, and why this singular course?"

"Do not pain me, cousin, by asking that question; you know the cause."

She then proceeded to inform him that she had dropped his last letter to her, while walking in the garden, from her bosom, that it had been picked up by a servant, who knew not to whom it belonged, and taken to her mother, who, at once recognizing the handwriting, sent for her and rather demanded to know the nature of it.

"I thought it as favorable an opportunity as I should ever have," she continued, "and told her of the whole affair — from girlhood till now."

"What did she say?" he asked, eagerly, with his heart almost choking his utterance.

"She spoke of you appreciatingly in many things, but dwelt upon your *wildness*, your youth, and, above all, on our being *cousins*, which, she said, she never could become reconciled to, and could never feel to you as she should to my — husband — as to a natural member of her family."

"Did you consent to these objections?" in a voice illy concealing his contempt.

"No, not one moment, and you wrong me by asking such a question."

"What feeling, then, made you yield?"

"Cousin, you know that *we* are but *two*, that we have been reared immediately under our mother's eye; her wishes have ever been our law, and a law which we delighted to obey. On her part, our pleasure and happiness have ever been the leading objects of her life; therefore I *can* not — know not, how to go counter to her wishes, and even have conscientious scruples on that point. To become your *wife* under such circumstances, would be to receive me as in some sort with a *perjured heart*, and no blessing could follow such acknowledged filial disobedience. I have there-

21 *

fore thought it would be best for *your* happiness, at least, and possibly for my own, that we — dissolve — the promise we are under to each other, and *try* and *forget it.*"

" Laura, my dear·Laura," said he, greatly excited and seizing both her hands in his, "are your heart-strings made of steel that you can sweep them so rudely, or expect to hush their deep throbbings by such rough handling; and to crush, too, your first affection as you say this is, and as I know it to be to a mere *idea* — a conscientious scruple as you call it? This is superstition, not reverence; fear, not love. I, too, have a high reverence for filial obedience, but still I think the obligation mutual. Obedience should not be exacted at an entire sacrifice of feeling — particularly, when demanded at the suggestion — I must say it — of *wil-fulness* and *prejudice.* When all the facts are well known to the younger parties, control presently passes from the parent's hand. Nature more clearly points out the way than reason."

" Oh! cousin, speak no unkind word of my mother : she does not deserve it — indeed she does not."

"Nor do you deserve to be held in this strange position. I do appreciate all of her high and kind qualities; but still I think her pushing her authority to an unwarranted limit. At best, she can but wither up your feelings, she cannot direct them, or control them."

"She has exercised no undue *authority,* cousin. She has only expressed her opinions, her feelings, and her wishes."

" I grant you; but then she knows such expression is equal to authority with you, or she would endeavor to do more. If this is not so, Laura, then you alone are responsi-ble for your course, and as you do not desire your mother's consent, I cannot ask yours; but just take it for granted, that you have heretofore mistaken your own feelings, and let us in all truth dissolve the *promise forever!*"

These words sounded, indeed, much like a last farewell, as he released her hands; which falling motionless to her side, she stood before him with an ashen paleness on her cheek, and, without even the utterance of a sigh, sank down to her chair. With a mixed look of vacancy and wild despair she gazed him in the face, with that expression of helpless reproach which only a soft eye and a breaking heart ever assume.

Brandon, seeing the strange effects of his words, quickly drew to her side, and pressed his cheek to hers as he again took her hand in his. Seeming to revive, she said:

"Oh! cousin, cousin! what must I do! what can I do?"

The truth was, that trained up as she had been, obedience to her mother was not only a law unto her life but a part of her religion; and she had promised her, after a severe conflict between obedience and affection, that she would break up the engagement which existed between herself and Henry Brandon. But she had done so, not without a lingering hope that she might still occupy some relation to him, through which a future arrangement could be effected. She had not realized the full force of the promise to her mother; and above all, did not know the full extent of her affection for Henry Brandon, until she saw the tie between them about to *sever*. This she was not prepared for — could never be.

Henry Brandon looked deep down into her clear, innocent eye, and saw nothing there but girlhood's maiden love, as she asked him the question in the soft tones of sweet appeal. In an instant, all the fiery energy of his heart rose to his lips and, in low but earnest language, said:

"Laura, I scarcely know what to tell you; but this I feel, that I cannot quietly yield up the longest hope of my life, nor can I now shut out from my soul the gentle star that has ever floated in the far-off heaven, and by its silver light guided the wayward walk of boy and man in the

paths of peace and safety, joy and love; only say once
more that your heart is mine, and no earthly thing or word
shall throw a shadow on the sunlight of my life."

At these impassioned words of Henry, a joyous brightness came back to her eye, and the delicate blush of maiden
feeling again bloomed upon her youthful face; and rising
from her seat, with an animation that told of a partially
regained confidence and happiness, which but a few minutes before had appeared fled, she asserted with a spirit she
had not previously shown —

"Cousin, by all the chaste laws of woman's love, and by
all that is sacred in a woman's truth and virtue, my heart
is only yours — no other has ever made a passing impress
there. The spraying stream of childhood, and that where
the brook and river meet of girl and womanhood, have
never, on their glittering currents, borne any other bark
than that which promised to bear me on the great ocean
of life, with Henry Brandon at my side; and when in my
sleeping dreams or waking visions that bark passes beyond
my sight, life becomes one great sea of madness, darkness,
and despair." Then placing her hand softly upon his arm,
in all the confidence of boundless affection, she continued :
"But with that in view, a picture floats before me, in which
the waves are all calm, the earth all bright, and the skies
all blue. In *these* moments, the probable storms of life,
and all vicissitude, are shorn of their strength, and robbed
of their terrors. Now, forgive me, cousin, for thus expressing to you the deep and glowing emotions of my heart-
life — they have ever clustered around your name, and you
are entitled to know them."

This demonstration of feeling from Laura, under the
particular circumstances, seemed to give his heart a joy it
had never known before; and smiling with the thought of
possessing the undivided love of so noble, so pure, and so
grand a girl, a thousand generous and manly resolves

rushed to his heart. Laura again broke the silence, which he seemed powerless to do, by saying: "And now you know me, cousin, and whatever I have appeared or may appear in future, I yet have ever been what I say I am to-day; and what I am to-day, I will ever be! Remember that! and now, I will prefer you not meeting father or mother to-day; you nor I can effect anything now; prospects may brighten of themselves. I will now excuse you and let you go, which they will think quite natural," at the same time extending him her hand, with an effort to smile at the innocent ruse she was practising. Henry Brandon laughed a low joyous laugh, as he caught the unsuspecting girl in his arms and kissing her now ruby lips, tripped lightly from the house, and mounting his horse rode swiftly away.

All right now thought the gay and happy Henry Brandon. But who yet hath ever cast the horoscope of Love? We shall see whether he did or not.

CHAPTER XXXVII.

" Let me have men about me that are fat,
    Sleek-headed men, and such as sleep o' nights."

AS Henry Brandon wildly galloped his horse over the gently rolling prairie, his bosom throbbed with all the tumultuous emotions which the scenes he had that morning passed through, were well calculated to inspire. Hope, doubt, and fear, alternately held supremacy. He could not see why his suit with Laura should fail, yet could not realize that it would succeed. The charm had been broken, and he feared the consequences. He, however, tried to comfort himself with his usual careless sort of philosophy, and said to himself, "I'll trust to fortune, and take the chances as they rise; and well I may — I can do nothing more, ha! ha! ha!" Then turning to Sam, he said:

"Well, how did matters look to-day, Sam?"

"Right hot, I tell you, Mass Henry, accordin' to Sally's 'count of it."

"You don't think there is much chance for master or man with mistress or maid, there?"

"I don't know as I zactly understans you, sir; but they ain't much chance, if that's what you mean — things ain't goin' right, but Sally says Miss Laura is hard to give up, and Miss Lucy stans right up to her; but Miss Catherine is strong agin you."

"How about Uncle Robert?"

"She says he don't say a word for you, nor agin you, and won't listen to the talk; but Sally says you will win if you holds on — if you will play right smart."

"Yes; but *smart* does n't do much good in such cases, 't is all *luck*, Sam!"

"You is zactly right 'bout that — for what is to be will be, and I don't care what anybody does."

"That's so, Sam."

"Mass Henry, Miss Laura is one of the nicest young ladies they is; but I wouldn' let nobody make sich a fuss 'bout me, as Miss Catherine is makin' about you. *I* says, go somewhar else — just as good fish in the sea, as was ever cotch out."

"Yes; I expect it will turn out that way at last; but let's ride faster, *Sam*, and get home to dinner."

Henry Brandon passed several days at home, after his customary fashion, hunting, riding over the neighborhood, and several times visiting his cousins. Mrs. Brandon was under the impression that the engagement between Laura and him was finally broken up, and was therefore rather disposed to receive him after her old fashion; but kept, as she thought, very close watch, and not unfrequently alluded to the bad results of marriages entered into without proper consideration. By the advice and request of Laura, he showed no temper in regard to what had happened, and thus threw her completely off the track.

The evening before the appointed time for going to the *gander-pulling* had at length arrived, and Henry gave full directions to Sam about being ready to go with him, by the time breakfast was over with.

"Yes, sir; I'll have everything right; but, Mass Henry, what is a *gander-pullin'?* I has never hearn of sich a thing."

"Well, I can't exactly explain it to you —just wait, you will see it; but don't you speak of it among the servants. I don't wish it to get out where I am going, or where we have been when we return."

"No, s-i-r; this chap would lose his ole woolly head 'fore he'd tell anything whar you is concerned —I say tell."

The following morning Mrs. Brandon saw *Sam* bringing out the horses, and inquired of her son where he was going, that he should leave so early.

"I thought that I would ride down to the *Hills* to-day, as I have nothing to do. I have some curiosity to see how my old haunts look after four years' absence."

"Ah! such places and visits will do well enough for a boy, probably, but not for a grown man, my son; such jaunts are looked on as *frolics*, and the world will not permit *men* to *frolic*, with impunity, and if you wish to succeed by its assistance, you must regard its prejudices — if you choose so to call its opinions."

"Mother, I regard *your* opinion more than any one's on earth, and you know that I have never had any purpose in visiting those people beyond a mere desire of innocent amusement; and as to what is called the *world*, let me assure you that I do not value its opinion three jack-straws. I *intend* never to do a wrong, but *will* do just as I please, and am perfectly willing for the world to do the same. If the world can do without me, I am vain enough to think I can do without the world; and this thing called public opinion is but little else than an expression of the conceit, ignorance, and prejudice of the common multitude, and is really the source of nine-tenths of the troubles of life. I had rather know, in my old age, that I had, even for one day only, defied the opinion of all the sublime and solemn fools of society, than to be the recipient of any *honors* they can confer."

"I must have touched you on some tender spot, my son," said his mother, smiling, "as you appear to have had your homily all prepared — so I will say no more; but let me ask you not to remain there to-night."

"No, madam; not if I can well get back; but I *may* stay, as you know those people used to make quite a *pet* of me, and if I am still as popular, I may remain."

"Yes, your *popularity* got you a very wild name — one that will cling to you forever."

"Well, mother, I expect I deserve it, and I must consent to abide by it."

"I know you will have your way, Henry; but there are other eyes on you than mine, who will not judge you so leniently."

"To whom do you allude, mother? — my *dear* aunt?"

"My remark is a general one; you may make a particular application of it, if you will."

"I will just then make that application of it, and tell you that I imagine myself just as badly damaged there as I can ever be."

At these words he walked out of the house, and, in a few moments more, was on his horse. When he reached the appointed place of meeting, he found Dr. Wilton already there. Exchanging salutations, they immediately galloped off, and reached Manese's about 11 o'clock. Miller was already there, accompanied by quite a number of his immediate comrades, and was expecting Henry Brandon. As the latter rode up, Miller met him, expressing great pleasure at seeing him.

Henry Brandon, as we have said, had known nearly every one that was present, in his younger days; and the old acquaintance was now renewed by each one coming and shaking hands, and passing a few pleasant words with him. Seeing that Henry had pretty well gone the rounds, Miller, in a loud voice intended for all to hear, said:

"Come into the grocery now, boys, and take a 'smile' at my expense;" and then saying, in rather an under-tone, "come, Henry, let's you and I take something *thin* together for the sake of 'auld lang syne.'"

"I will take a 'wee dhrap' with *you*, Miller, on that score, but I have never yet learned to drink."

"Nor had I, Henry, until just before that dreadful difficulty; but since then I am as regular to my grog as a pig to his tracks, and I am free to say, that had it not been for whiskey, there would never have been anything of it. Drunkenness is *the big* curse of the world; it's all *habit*, and the *damnedest*, meanest, lowest, worst of all habits, and if God will help me, I shall forever quit it after to-day."

"How are you intending to proceed, Miller, to get out of this difficulty?"

"I scarcely know — but I am now getting up money to leave with, and to assist these poor boys, whom I unfortunately have involved in it, with me; but they appear to care less for it than I do, which is some consolation to me; and if I am not disturbed for the next ten days, I will be able to get them off. I dislike leaving in this manner on account of my old mother; but for the killing of Hall, I rejoice at it, and only wish he had a hundred lives, that I

22

might take every one of them, for at the moment I shot him, he was cutting my old father with a bowie-knife."

"Where do you expect to go to, Miller?"

"Oh, to Texas, or Arkansas, where all the outlaws go, and then get my fool's brains shot out in less than a month by some desperado, I expect."

"How many of your friends will go with you?"

"Only some two or three, as the others have as *yet* done nothing that the law can get hold of."

At this moment, a tall, fine-looking fellow — being no other than Jack Gaulding, who had sent him the invitation — stepped up, and said, "Henry, you have just got back with a great college edecashun; but I'm afeard the damned sheriff will run us boys all outen the country 'fore we can give you a lift."

"No, no, I hope not, on your own account, Jack, to say nothing of mine."

"But there is danger of it, certain as you live."

"Not so durn much, Jack, as mout be supposed. Thar's some of the old blue hens' chicks will stay to the last day in the mornin', and see the triflin' devils out," said fighting Bob Mosely.

"That's my hand, Fighting Bob," said Wire-grass John Holmes; "thar's nuthin' kin make me leave 'ceptin' its *wimin*, and they must be *over forty*."

"That's so," responded some six or seven who were standing round, with a hearty laugh.

"Yes, you is true to wimin an' your friends," said Lazy Farl Bowen. "By my mother's suck, you talk to my notion."

"I am greatly obleged to you, Lazy Farl," answered Wire-grass; "but you are too durned slow to git outen the way of either man or woman — but no insult, Farl."

"But *here's* one that ain't afraid to go or stay," said a small but well-made chap, with a flashing blue eye and very red hair. "I am the little red cock that crows for day at the old widder Higgins's house; and lets no dung-hill walk his walk, or tote his hens — no s-i-r-ee, he don't."

"Oh! you are jokin' now — the biggest sort," said Yaller Bill Skipper.

"A-jokin'! the hell, I never jokes on sich subjicks when wimin is in vogue."

"What wimin are you talkin' about?"

"Darned ef I know; but look a-here, Yaller Bill, do you wish to pass any insinuations? ef a row is what you want, old fell', just shuck your dry goods, and you can git it at the shortest notice."

The crowd immediately gathered round, for the purpose of seeing the fight, but leaving a sufficient hollow circle for the combatants, when DICK WINN from the outside of the crowd called out, asking in his well-known manner:

"What in the hell are you wild-cats at, in there — you, you red-headed cuss. I say, if I hear another word out of your dirty little fly-trap, I'll come in there, and cut round the skin of your neck, and unjint your head. I will, damn me, and fire burn me."

This had the effect of drawing off all attention from the proposed combatants to Dick Winn, with a roar of laugh-ter, which, in a rough-and-tumble fight such as we used to have, amounted to breaking it up.

"Well, Uncle Dick, as that ar' you, that makes those re-marks, you can say it, as you is a privileged char-ec-ter; but no one else can say the same, I'll *be* durned."

"Well, that's good enough — all settled; and now, men," said he in a loud voice, "no fights will be expected till the *gander-pulling* is over, and you had better keep your cour-age for the sheriff, who I expect will be here to-day, any-how; but anyways, after the *pulling* is over with, we shall expect to have, at least, twenty first-class fights, and several eyes lying about loose on the ground, and as many ears and noses; and rather than fall short of the number, I'll agree to mall the dog-water out of five or six of you myself—do you understand the programme now?—dang it! And now, every fellow have his horse ready for the ride against his name is called." He then cried out to the crowd, and informed them that Henry Brandon, Miller, and himself had been appointed judges.

Miller immediately declined, and asked Dr. Wilton to act in his place, as he wished to ride, or would be expected to do so, as he had got up the sport. The Doctor accepting, Dick Winn called them together and instructed them in their duties. Dick himself, and the Doctor, were to judge the goose stakes, and Henry Brandon was to act at the starting-point.

Twenty riders had already entered their names at a dollar a-piece. These were soon stripped for the ride, and stood ready to hear their names called, which Henry Brandon was to do after drawing them from a hat.

"Gander-pulling" was one of the many muscular pastimes practised in the days of chivalry on festive occasions, and was long traditional in the South as one of the sports of their Norman ancestry; and as one of the thousands of small evidences of the *difference* in—race, between the Northern and Southern people.

Whether this account be correct or not, it is yet historical. And while the Northern people were severe in their laws against the kissing of young girls by their lovers, whipping cider-barrels for working on Sunday, burning old women for witches, and inventing facial and thumb screws for the torture of freshly imported African slaves, and groaning under the whinings of some brutal "gospeller," the Southern people were having their deer-drives, their fox-chases, cock-fights, *gander-pullings*, balls, dances, and *duels*.

More latterly, while their temples rang with prayers for

the oppressed negroes, and indulging in self-laudations for their surpassing virtue and intelligence, their whole land teemed with bastardy, child-murder, free-loveism, Mormonism, model artists, Black-Crook exhibitions, brothels, and assignation, and in every other manner of crime that even makes hell itself blush in modest shame. On the other hand, let the truth be told. Even after every degradation and wrong, which the North, in the truculent exercise of power has inflicted, the Southern people themselves began a course of harassment and persecution, almost unparalleled in the history of any *decent* people. It seemed to be the wish of a few men to deprive all others of their homes and the last vestige of property, in liquidation of debts created under an entirely different state of affairs, and which there was subsequently, and now, no possible chance of meeting; and this we consider quite as criminal as anything the North had ever been guilty of, and far more unfeeling.

To all of this there was an exceptional class on either side, and upon this exceptional class will devolve the future peace and welfare of this continent — not government.

To revert to "*gander-pulling*," there is to say, that it continued to be one of the popular sports of the South among the humble classes until within the last half-century. Since then it has measurably passed *out* of practice.

This was the only one the writer ever witnessed, and the scene of it was at a little country grog-shop on the public highway leading from ——, on a level stretch of the road, about four hundred yards in length. And as, perhaps, many of my readers have never seen anything of the kind, it may not be uninteresting to learn something of the arrangement. About two hundred yards from the starting-point were two posts set into the ground deep enough to secure steadiness, and leaving them about fourteen feet above-ground and twenty feet apart. From the tops of these two posts was

22 *

stretched a very strong rope, and from the middle of this the gander hung suspended by the feet, the head and neck having most of the feathers removed, and then well greased. This completed the arrangement so far as the gander was to play a part. Men were then placed all along at short intervals, with good whips in their hands, from the starting-point to the goose-poles. Judges then took positions at the poles at either end. The rider was then started at the upper poles, at the words "Are you ready?—go!" It now became the business of every whipper to strike the horse as he passed, in order to keep him at the top of his speed, and as the rider rode under the gander, for him to make an effort to catch the head. Between the well-greased condition of the head and the fowl dodging when caught at, it was difficult either to get or to keep hold of it. The duty of the judges at the poles was to decide on foul whipping or any other unusual circumstance; whipping being considered foul if done anywhere but on the rear parts of the horse.

At two o'clock precisely, on this occasion, the sport began.

"All ready—down here!" sung out Dick Winn. "Draw your rider, Brandon—dang me!"

Dick Winn, though associating with the class of men we here find him with, was very far their superior, both in intelligence and position, and was truly a representative man in many respects as regards Southern character. He was an enthusiastic politician, and as well known as any private citizen of the country; with education he would have been equal to most civil positions, and was even so almost without it. His opinions were forcible, fearless, and highly respected; his observation was shrewd, and his language, always quaint, was either caustic and direct, or rambling and humorous, as occasion called for. His knowledge of character was intuitively correct. His industry and energy gave him command of very considerable means, and his home presented all the advantages of great ease and abundance, and was often the scene of convivial entertainment for his friends. He loved his *fun*, as he called it, and would go into any place that promised to furnish it: having that almost perfect fearlessness essential to the enjoyment of a *frolic*, he never failed to secure it, regardless of all consequences. His face was manly and handsome, his person strong, and his temper, though bold and defiant, was placable and generous. While he could be serious, earnest, and severe, he was yet generally in a pleasing mood, and had a pleasant word for all. These qualities made him a fast friend to others, and others to him, and gave him the position of a leader in his neighborhood, whenever a leader was wanted.

"Here's my gander spilin' for a mate! Send on your goose, Brandon, dang it!" he again cried out, as the latter was placing the names in a hat.

Jack Gaulding's was the first drawn, and when called for, came riding up on his horse "*bareback*," his bridle wrapped securely round his wrist, with one hand free wherewith to catch at the gander's head.

"Here I am on *terry firmy*, and ready for the row," said Jack, as he took position.

"Are you ready?" cried out Henry Brandon.

"Ready!"

"Go!"

At the word the first whipper struck his horse, and away he flew, each whipper striking him as he passed. It was but a few seconds before Jack was under the gander, but missed the prize.

"All right—a fair ride! but here swings my gander, live and kicking—no, fluttering. Send on another of your *Rossum heels*, Henry; I'm on expenses, dang it!"

"Pedlar Jim" was next called for, and rode through with no better success.

And thus through all the entries. The whole sport was

now to begin again, and was repeated several times before any one had secured the prize — with various accidents to both horses and riders, which indeed seemed to furnish a large part of the entertainment.

In this manner the evening had passed nearly away, when a large portion of the company left for their own homes, leaving only those who were going to the *Ball*.

CHAPTER XXXVIII.

"Here are we met, three merry boys,
　Three merry boys I trow are we."

TWILIGHT had not more than set in, when the young people from all the neighborhood began arriving for the ball, and by the time it was starlight the house was crowded. A fiddle, tambourine, and triangle were soon in full blast, and the cry sung out of "Git your pardners!" by no less a person than Dick Winn, whom old Manese had requested to act as general manager. "Dr. Wilton and Henry Brandon from the prairies have first choice, gentlemen — by reason of hospitality; and then you fellows from the hills take second." This last regulation was of Dick's own conceiving, and announced in his own peculiar manner, but assented to without an opposing voice.

Henry now introduced Dr. Wilton to May Walters, the sister of Nanny, whom Henry Brandon had already engaged as his partner.

Nanny and May Walters were twin sisters, and were nearly the same age with Henry Brandon. They were old acquaintances of his, having known them before he left for college, and this was the first time he had met them since his return, and still found them to be the same pictures of rustic beauty.

All classes of society have their "belles," and Nanny and May Walters were the belles of the circle in which they moved — holding that enviable position in virtue of their beauty, intelligence, and industry.

They were tall, graceful, and well developed in their figures, and were light but rich brunettes in complexion; their eyes were dark, lustrous, and instinct with life and joyousness; their full suit of dark, glossy hair most superbly matched their eyes and complexion — which being dressed loosely, gave it all the advantage which nature had evidently bestowed — but being fastened securely, gave it all the tidiness of thorough attention and dress.

As we have said, these two girls had been great favorites with Henry Brandon, in the dashing wild days of his boyhood; and they had prepared themselves with great care, with the expectation of meeting him at the dance, knowing that he had been invited, and supposing that he would of course be there, if not greatly *changed* in his character. They were dressed in the highest style of those fashions which are peculiar to that *class* of girls, and kept up year after year, with but little reference to the changes in the fashionable and higher circles of society; and in most respects far more graceful and flowing, than those which frequently, not only embarrass the movements, but ridiculously disfigure the forms of young girls in the more distinguished coteries. Among the former, the æsthetics of dress is based upon its adaptability to the human form — nature is their only guide — as they have little or no access to those circumstances which engender morbidity; and too frequently, not only vitiate taste in this, but in far greater matters.

A large "set" was now out on the floor. The dance was an old-fashioned Scotch reel, and as Henry and Nanny led off, Dick Winn, who as we have said was master of the ceremonies, spoke out loud enough for every one to hear:

"Come down to it manly, Henry Brandon; you are among your friends, and dancing on your same old puncheon, with the nicest gal, too, in this neck of woods. Ain't he, Nanny?"

Henry answered for both, by replying that Nanny was floating on the wings of the wind, and that he was doing his handsomest.

"All right — go a-head! after your own fashion; but cut and come again! remember that hind-foot foremost is the figure — ain't it, Nanny?"

Henry found time to get back and cross to Nanny, for the purpose of having some little talk with her, which he began by saying: "Nanny, I had never expected to dance with you again as a single girl; but here you are, as pretty and fresh as ever, and I dancing with you too; but tell me how it is that as pretty a girl as you has never married. Can't capture any of these wild boys?"

The color seemed to leave Nanny's cheek for a moment, as she said, "They are *too* wild. You can't keep one after you catch him."

"Well, there is some mystery about it, which I shall inquire into. When I came here to-night, I almost expected to have your oldest daughter for a partner; but here you are, prettier and brighter than ever, and single still."

"Why, sir, I am not as old as you are — have you brought a son old enough for me, or for such a daughter to dance with? And if you must know, maybe I will tell you, why I did not get married before this."

"Yes, tell me."

"Well, it was just because I wanted to see you once more, dance with you once more, and talk with you: after this I am ready. Do you know any clear, sensible, industrious young fellow, that would be likely to fall in love with as pretty a girl as I?"

"Many a one. I take all such chances myself."

"Yes, I believe you do; but if I tell you a little secret, will you ever tell it? very few ever even suspected it."

"No, not unless you give me permission."

"Well — now remember, I have never told any one but May and mother. I *have* been engaged to Robert Miller there, for over a year; but he has got to be so wild, and got into such trouble, that I had to break it up. I have got afraid of him."

"Really afraid of him?"

"Yes, really afraid of him. Now, would you marry a *woman* that you were really afraid of?"

"No."

"Well, I can't marry a man that I am afraid of. He has frightened every bit of love I ever had for him away from me. I don't love him, and I'm sorry for it."

"I am sorry Bob has got into such habits, but he says he intends to quit them after this."

"Yes — I know; but still I am afraid of him. I can't risk him. But never mind, that is all over with. I don't love him. Now, I want to know why you did not speak to me last fall, up at Gregory's Spring, when your uncle spoke there. I went there almost entirely just to see you, and you passed right close by me, and did not speak. I never felt so mortified in all my life, and I have been mad with you a little bit ever since."

"On my honor I never saw you; were you really there, Nanny?"

"I was, indeed; I wanted to hear Mr. Brandon speak, because you know we are all Whigs down here — just as everybody else did; and then I had heard you had come back, and just thought I would be so glad to see you, too, and to see if *you* were so handsome and pleasant as you used to be; but, oh! how you cut me. I tried to forgive you though; for you had two such beautiful young girls with you, that I knew poor Nanny Walters had no business even looking that way."

"Poor Nanny Walters, indeed! You are one of the prettiest girls I ever saw, and you know I think so; and if I had seen you, I should have left a queen to speak to you, and I reckon would have done just what I am going to do now," and as he said this, bent down and kissed the rosy lips of the lovely country girl.

It was done so suddenly that there was no time for resistance on her part, even if she would have made any; as it was, however, she only slapped him coquettishly on the face, but blushed deeply when she discovered that Robert Miller, her old beau, had seen it. Henry Brandon had not intended to be seen, and thought from the intentness with which the dancers were engaged that he would not; but poor Miller had scarcely taken his eyes off of her from the time he entered the house, and with any one else might have made it the cause of some words; as it was, he only said: "Ah! Henry, at your old tricks."

"Yes, Bob; and now that I have set you the example, it is your own fault if you do not follow it."

"I'll do it, Henry, if I die for it."

At the time, he was dancing with little Betty Lane, a pretty little blue-eyed lass of eighteen summers, who, when her attention was directed to it, caught a glimpse of Henry Brandon as he kissed Nanny Walters; and was enjoying the confusion of Nanny, when Miller walked round, and without her even suspecting his purpose, found herself in the same category.

"Come, gentlemen; I bar all sich amusements, unless they become gineral," said Jack Gaulding, who had some little claim in regard to Betty Lane.

"Oh!" said Betty, "Mr. Miller, I had no idea that anybody would do such a thing but Mr. Brandon."

"Oh! you didn't, hey!" said Dick Winn, in a great

laugh. "My turn next, dang it!" and kissed Samanthy Roberts.

The dance now became so confused, that Dick gave orders for them all to seat their partners until the excitement was over, and kiss them if they could, just to get *even*. The "set" was soon broken up in a sort of half romp, the young beaux laughing heartily at the girls, for taking to the new fashion so easily.

"Ah! Mr. Brandon, the young men have all been so well-behaved for a long time; but now, you have spoiled it all."

"Yes; and not three of you have been married since I was here, and I am going to put you all in motion."

"Are you going to set the example in that, too?"

"Yes, if I can;" and for the first time that night or day, the sweet face of Laura Brandon appeared before him. "What would *she* say," thought he to himself, "if she could only have seen me to-day, and to-night. But I can't help it — right or wrong, I'll trust to luck;" and before he had scarcely finished the thoughts, he dashed along with Nanny Walters in the dance which had again been organized.

"I thought that was your idea, when I saw you with those pretty girls last fall, and I will let them know how you behave yourself when you get down here, if you disturb me again — indeed I will."

"You will," said he, in a sort of momentary distraction.

"Yes, I will."

"Why, what do I misbehave in, Nanny?"

"Well, you tell us how pretty we are, and how you admire us, and turn all of our heads by flattering us."

"And by *kissing* you all."

"Yes," added she, "and by kissing us too, whenever you catch a chance."

"That would make me more popular, Nanny, and you

23

had better not let that get out if you ever wish to see me again as a single man, for some girl would marry me in less than a month — *vi et armis, nolens volens.*"

" *Vi et*, what ?" asked she, laughing.

"Just as I kissed you to-night—and just as I will do again."

"Yes, and I will tell how you talk about them, too!"

"Yes, and I will tell how you let me kiss you twice in one evening!" And, while unobserved by any others, quickly placed his arm around her neck, and gave her another kiss.

"Oh, Mr. Brandon! I have a great notion to leave here, and go straight home to mother."

"I would follow you if you did, and contradict every word you spoke."

"Would you dare dispute my word?" said she, laughing.

"Indeed, I would!"

"I believe you would. Going to college, I am afraid, has ruined you; but in earnest, now, you must not do that again; I would not mind your impudence at home, but these people will speak of it."

"Oh! no one saw me, then."

"No, but they might have. I will not get mad about that if you will behave yourself for the rest of the evening."

"Very good, provided you will dance every other set with me during the evening."

"Yes, I will agree to that, too; but I am afraid it will make my old friend Robert Miller very jealous — you know men are mighty jealous things."

"Ah, ha! you have not given Bob up, then?"

"Yes, he is nothing to me, more than you are, but then — you know — I hate to hurt him."

"Yes. Well, I will do the best I can; but don't you look *too* pretty at me."

"No."

The evening now passed gayly along with every one, until a late hour, with the exception of our friend Dick Winn, who had his pleasure spoiled by a very unexpected incident — the nature of which we will relate in another chapter.

CHAPTER XXXIX.

"Kings may be blest, but Tam was glorious,
O'er all the ills of life victorious."

THERE was at this time, and had been for several weeks, a distant female relative on a visit to old Manese, who rejoiced in the name of Miss Amelia Simpkins.

Miss Amelia was not wanting in good looks, but was hard of hearing, and had passed those years whereat girls are considered young. At her own proper home she was in circumstances sufficient unto her support, but having unfortunately passed the years of girlhood without the incident of matrimony intervening, she had left home *really* as an adventurer in that great cause, but ostensibly as a *teacher,* and had learned the happy art of living principally by visiting. Miss Amelia had been jokingly informed by some girls who had found out the leading object of her life, that our old friend Dick Winn was a well-to-do old bachelor, who lived but a mile or two distant, and that he had expressed a desire to become acquainted with her. After this information had been given her, she had made many unsuccessful efforts to get an introduction to him, but had failed — every girl finding some excuse for not gratifying her; but she, like all old girls who have not clearly crossed the matrimonial Rubicon, had cultivated her nuptial hopes up to a quicker sensibility, as the time for their gratification seemed passing away, and they had now reached a sharp climax in regard to Mr. Richard Winn, the supposed well-to-do old bachelor.

Dick's happy face had, indeed, quite naturally led her to believe that he *was* a bachelor, and she allowed her matrimonial designs to become enlisted in his behalf. At the particular time seeing him sitting apart from every one, and not engaged in the dance, she could restrain these feelings no longer, but stepping up to him said:

"Mr. Winn, I believe."

"You are right, madam, Winn is my name."

"My name, sir, is Amelia Simpkins. I see, Mr. Winn, that you have not succeeded in getting a partner; will you excuse the boldness of offering myself, sir?"

Dick knowing nothing of who she was, and while thinking it a very unusual method of getting into a dance, gallantry forbade his refusing to accept — and not being aware of the defect in her hearing, replied in his usual tone and manner:

"Ah, yes, Miss Amelia Simpkins; but you are mistaken about the partner. I will, however — yes, madam, I will dance — dang it, yes."

A general titter went round as Dick came up with his partner to join the set, when he saw at once that he had been victimized in some manner, but allowed it to worry him no further than to cause him to ejaculate some three or four times, as if soliloquizing — "dang it."

The dance at length ended, when Dick joyfully led her to a chair, which she politely declined, expressing a preference for walking around the room.

Dick now found himself the object of all observation, and the subject of the suppressed conversation of every one. He yet bore his sufferings manfully by the assistance of an occasional ejaculation of his favorite *dang it.*

"You are not married, I believe, Mr. Winn?"

"You miss it most damnably, madam; I am very considerably into that business."

"I supposed not. You have not the *serious* face which married gentlemen usually wear;" saying this with a faint smile of facetiousness.

"The devil you say, madam. Does a married man have to look serious forever, madam? dang it! But perhaps I look so happy because my old wife is not here. Damn it! I have got dang nigh a dozen chaps of one sort and another at my house, madam."

"So I suppose; single persons generally love children."

"Well, I can't say as to that, but I have wellnigh a dozen, I say, of my own that I can remember. Dang it! not single a great deal, that I can see."

"Yes, I have always loved children, though I have none of my own. The maternal feeling always reigns paramount in a woman's breast."

"Perhaps so, madam; but dang it, you don't appear to understand me."

"Yes! I was struck with your appearance from the first moment I saw you. People are often drawn to each other from a certain sort of affinity, even when they have never met before."

"So I would suppose; but as I never dive very deep into such matters, can't say. Damn me! What in the hell did she mean?"

"Yes, sir. I feel flattered by your remarks."

"Oh, not so, madam! Damn it! I have made no particular remarks."

"Certainly, sir; I shall be glad to hear you in whatever you have to say."

"The very hell you will! I think, madam, we don't hear each other. Will you have a seat? Dang it!"

Dick had now discovered that Miss Amelia was hard of hearing, and, rushing to a seat, rather compelled her to take

23 *

it, and with equal precipitation rushed into the crowd, who had now got into convulsions of laughter, having overheard some portions of the conversation. Dick joined in the laugh, and was very anxious to find out which girl it was, who had "*sicked*" Miss Amelia upon him, as he said.

Calling Henry Brandon to him, he said:

"Good-by, Henry, I must leave you, or be married to another wife in thirty minutes, and off for the Mormons by morning. Ha! ha! ha! I will—dang it!"

At this moment Dick seeing his new admirer rise from the seat in which he had placed her, and appearing to come somewhat towards him, dashed out of the house, saying as he went: "No, not any. Dang it!" and was followed by quite a number who knew the joke, with roars of laughter.

After remaining in one of the out-houses for about half an hour, he ventured back to the dancing-room, and seeing Henry Brandon, proposed to find the kitchen, and if possible, to get something to eat—and a *drink*.

"Why, Winn, I went there with you once to-night, when you got something, and supper will be ready directly."

"I say supper. Dang it! It's nearly midnight now, and I've not heard a word of supper."

In this time not seeing Miss Amelia Simpkins, he had the boldness to enter the house; but Miss Amelia's eyes were already on the watch for him, and as he said: "I say, got something—three eggs—and one of them not the best," Miss Amelia caught a glimpse of him, and moved directly towards him, when Dick again rushed out, saying as he left the house: "Hell and pistareens! Three eggs, and one of them not good, to say the least, is not enough for any well man! Dang it!—with a new sweetheart! Damn me!"

The night was thus passed off with that joyous hilarity peculiar to the humbler classes of the South, which must be seen to be appreciated, when the alarm was given that the house was surrounded by armed men.

The truth was, that the sheriff, having heard that Manese was that day to give a *gander-pulling* and a ball, and that Miller was to be there, had come with a company of men, and had so stationed them that he could easily, as he thought, take Miller after the dance was over — while getting their horses. The plan might have succeeded had it not been discovered.

Miller and his friends quickly gathered their arms, and left the house in a body. They had not succeeded in reaching their horses, however, before they were hailed, and commanded to stop, to which they replied by a volley from their pistols in the direction of the voices. The firing was returned, and followed up from each side by repeated discharges. This being rather more than either party had expected, both retreated. Miller's men were soon mounted, and as they left, Miller, himself, cried out: "Farewell, friends! farewell, Henry Brandon! farewell, Nanny!" and after that night was never known to be in the State.

After the firing had begun, the whole company left the house in the greatest confusion. The girls, being terribly frightened, and screaming for protection, seized on the first man who fell in their way. Dr. Wilton and Henry Brandon were, at the time, dancing with May and Nanny Walters. In an instant, the girls seized them by the arm, and begged to be taken home, and just as they left the door, a flying shot passed through the coat sleeve of Henry Brandon, slightly wounding him. He then called for "Sam" to come up with the horses. The latter answered some distance off, and told him to "come to me, Mass Henry, the hosses wount go a step dat way."

"Can't you come up a little, man?" asked Henry, in a loud, impatient voice.

"No, sir. De hosses, I say, wount budge a feet dat way."

"You are a lying coward, sir; I know they will."

"No, sir; I swar dey wount move dat way—an you ought to know it, Mass Henry."

Brandon saw that it was impossible to get him to come up, and said to the Doctor that they would have to go there.

With the two terror-stricken girls still holding on to them, they went in search of "Sam" and the horses, and found him very securely situated between and behind a clump of large oaks about a hundred yards distant, whose shade made it perfectly dark. After wrapping up the girls in a pair of blankets which "Sam" had brought for his own accommodation, they succeeded in getting mounted by the assistance of "Sam," who now made himself very useful, and were not long in reaching old Mrs. Walters' residence. The old lady was still sitting up waiting for her daughters, by a large fire. The story was soon told, when the good old woman had them a cup of hot coffee, and something to eat. The girls had now recovered from their fright, and seemed well pleased with the adventure — particularly since they had secured two such handsome protectors.

"Doctor," said Henry Brandon, "did you see what became of Dick Winn?"

"No; but just as we left the house I saw him going in."

"Ah! you need not be troubled about Mr. Winn, he will take care of himself," said old Mrs. Walters. "This is not the first scrape he was ever in, and came out of safe."

"No, I know not; but I should like to have seen Miss Simpkins meet him, about the time they were all rushing out of the house."

"She did appear to be flying about there, as if she was crazy, and I expect was really looking for him," answered May Walters; "but then I can't laugh, for I was as badly frightened as she was."

Henry now suggested that it was getting quite late, and

they had all better go to bed. Nanny then showed him a room, and as he left, bid them all good-by, as he would leave very early in the morning.

In the meanwhile "Sam" had succeeded in rousing a negro boy, and getting him to assist in putting away the horses, had got back to the kitchen, when, as some compensation to the old cook for his supper, he was giving a most wonderful and exaggerated account of the affair, and the particular part he had played in it. He had already finished his meal, and was ready for his nap, when he capped the climax of his story, by saying: "And I 'specks dar is twenty men lyin' about dead in dem woods dis minit."

"De law!"

"Yes; but dis nigger ain't one of 'em."

"I wonder."

"No; he ain't dat," and dropped off to sleep.

When Henry pulled off his coat, Dr. Wilton looked at the wound on his arm, and putting a piece of sticking plaster upon it, pronounced it slight, saying it would get well by first intention.

"By first or second, it stings like the devil."

Dick Winn had indeed entered the house, just after the Doctor and Henry Brandon had left it with the Walters girls, and found that every member of the family as well as the company had left, save the veritable Miss Amelia Simpkins, who had failed to secure a protector, and seemed in great terror. The moment Winn stepped inside the door, she flew to his arms and asked his protection.

"Well, yes, dang it; Miss Simpkins, or whatever your name is, I will certainly protect you; but damn me, madam, if I know what to do with you."

Without appearing to hear him, but giving a very apt answer, she said:

"Oh! my dear Mr. Winn, do carry me to your own peaceful home, away from this dreadful place."

"Yes, dang dreadful place; but, Bustamente and the devil! my home might not be so peaceful, if I take you there! No, not much — damn me!"

But being unable to make her comprehend him, she still clung to him.

"Very well — dang it! I must do something with you, so come on — damn me!"

With these words he took her to where his horse was tied, and getting her up behind him, left in the direction of his own home at half speed. About a mile and half from there, lived one of the young girls whom he had suspected of getting him into the scrape; and as he came up to the gate, saw a bright light in one of the rooms, and giving her to understand that this was his home, assisted her down, and motioned her to the house. No sooner did he see her safe at the door, than he said: "Now, dang you, Miss Smarty! suppose you take her for a while. Come, 'Soaptail,'" speaking to his horse, "let us get away from this 'dreadful place,' as our new sweetheart would say," and rode off at full speed. After getting far enough to be out of danger, he drew the horse up, and began soliloquizing. "Ain't this hell? — *gander-pulling, ball, bad eggs,* Miss ELMINA SIMPKINS — dang — shot at — bursted up generally! but damn me, Miss — who? — Jinkins! the devil and gourd fiddles!" and at the thought of Miss Simpkins started "Soaptail" at full speed again, and reached home just as day peeped from the east.

We will now bid farewell to our old friend Dick Winn, knowing that he will make fair weather, as to his whereabouts and doings, even if by telling many truly improbable stories.

CHAPTER XL.

"He is from the South, sir."

VERY early next morning "Sam Brandon" had the horses ready at old Mrs. Walters' gate, and only waited for his young master and the Doctor, who were not long in getting ready. As they rode along, the various incidents of the previous day and night were talked and laughed over, and no regrets were expressed at the manner of their conclusion.

Brandon at length said, that he cared for nothing that happened, but getting shot at the "damned place," as he did not know how to get round telling his mother and Violet, and very soon it would be the general neighborhood talk.

"No," said the Doctor; "that has got us into a close place, and I imagine about the best way to do is to 'own up,' and laugh over it."

"Yes; I could manage it all very well, if it were not for my very dignified uncle, and very correct aunt, Mrs. Robert Brandon. They will talk over it as seriously as if I had sinned against the Holy Ghost, in addition to all human morality."

"Well, Brandon, I see your next trouble, and should like to help you out of it, but *my* assistance would only help to sink you deeper," said the Doctor, laughing.

"Yes; you will have your hands full to take care of yourself. But I feel very well paid, let the matter go as it will. The social aspect which the whole thing presented, very correctly indicates the substratum of Southern character, and sustains it equally in the lower and higher circles. Beside many lighter attributes, there is a feeling and a habit of personal resentment among Southern people, which is not seen at the North. An insult here is dealt with at the moment, and by the parties to it, which has the effect of adding to the courtesy of intercourse, by forcing every one to a sense of personal responsibility. This gives dignity and bearing to the individual. The *law* is never called in to uphold a man's honor, the walking-stick or the bullet settles the trouble. There is no such thing as laying the foundation for a fortune on the *damages* given for defamation of character. Wounded honor — from the highest to the lowest — dies in its own defence, kills the offender, or gets satisfaction. This is a proud heritage to the son, and he walks through life with a lofty consciousness of one who has inherited an untarnished crest, and so intends to transmit it. Now, these fellows that were about to fight yesterday," said Henry, had no heart-burnings, no regrets, no mortifications, for the insulting reflections that each conceived, the other thought, the other wished to pass, because they were the occasion of the other exhibiting his fearlessness. This, at once, half destroyed the difficulty, while the other half was perfectly subject to control; and in ten minutes, men, who had been willing to cut each others' throats, were as good friends as ever. Just the opposite to this is the case at the North; there, the law and jury-box settles everything — the great umpire in every difficulty. This breeds contention and cowardice, and makes them a nation, if I may so speak, of *scandalizers*. To call a man a 'damned scoundrel' at the South, is to get your brains shot out — at the North it is worth a thousand dollars. The slander of a wife or daughter *buys* a *farm*, and therefore is rather desired than not. But damn it! this cold wind makes my arm sting. Let's ride faster, and get out of it."

They then mended their gait to a brisk gallop, and were not long in reaching St. Mary's Church, their point of separation, and promising to meet again very soon, the two young friends bid "good morning."

Henry had not gone a great way, before "Sam Brandon," who had had no opportunity of speaking to his young master before, in regard to the affairs of the previous day, said :

"And that was your *gander-pullin'*, Mass Henry ?"

"Yes ; how did you like it ?"

"Mighty well ; but that shootin' like to a bin a bad scrape."

"Yes ; and you played coward too, Sam."

"No, sir ; I got out the way, 'cause the hosses wouldn' stan', and then I had no pistil, nor didn' see nobody to shoot, if I did, an you got away yo'self, Mass Henry."

"So I did, Sam ; but don't you tell anything about it, and besides, one of those flying shots hit me."

"Dar now! I was feared you would get hit ; but you didn' git hurt much, did you, Mass Henry ?"

"Oh, no ; just scratched on the arm."

"I 'm glad of that ; and as for my tellin' anything 'bout your scrapes — no, sir ; nary time. I never tells *our* secrets."

They soon reached home, where Sam got a subaltern to take his horses, while he went directly to Henry's room, and soon had a fine fire ; and when breakfast was announced, Henry went to the dining-room, looking as fresh and gay as though nothing unusual had happened.

24

CHAPTER XLI.

"Well, thou wilt be horribly chid to-morrow. . . . If thou love me, practise an answer."

THE greetings of his mother and sister were particularly pleasant, as they met Henry in the breakfast-room, for the reason that his presence was unexpected. In the course of conversation, Mrs. Brandon remarked to her son, that as he was sufficiently near to reach home so early, he might have given them the pleasure of his company the over-night.

"Yes, madam, I could have done so; but it was so very cold that I deferred it till this morning."

"Where did you stay, brother?" asked Violet.

"At my old friend, Mrs. Walters'."

"And have you come from there this morning?" she asked with surprise.

"I certainly have; why, is it so great a feat as to cause astonishment?"

"Yes, indeed, both. I should consider myself entitled to immortal honors. You must have come with the swiftness of a winged Mercury, and so cold too."

"Yes it was very cold, and we did ride fast."

"Your old friends could not have made you welcome, or you certainly would not have left at so unreasonable an hour."

"Yes, I received a very warm welcome; that class of people always welcome their friends. 'T is your wealthy people who know how to meet you coldly, and while affecting hospitality, virtually ask you to leave."

"Was it the mother of the pretty twin sisters that you used to talk so glowingly of, when you were a boy?"

"Yes; the same."

" Are the girls single yet, and as pretty?"

" Yes ; both."

" We are to suppose, then, that they were the attraction?"

" No ; not so much the attraction as the cause."

" Explain your distinction."

" I will, some Monday morning—this is Sunday."

" Very good ; well, did you wind up with a dance?"

"Oh ! quite a frolic."

" Had they expected you?"

" I believe they had."

" Well, I will ask no more questions, but this one, as I see you begin to think me too inquisitive. Did any one go with you from this neighborhood?"

" Why? do you *suspect Hunter?*"

" No, no."

" Dr. Wilton was with me, sister."

" Then, I suppose you initiated him into the Elysian merriments of ' Hill life?' Well, I am glad you enjoyed yourself, and glad you are back ; but you would have enjoyed the day at the church with us yesterday. Nearly all the ladies of the neighborhood were there assisting us to decorate it for Christmas Day, and several gentlemen. Uncle Robert among the number of the latter, and *cousin Laura* with him, of course."

" Was Lucy there also?"

"Oh, yes ; I only mention cousin Laura, as you appear to think so much of her."

" I am sorry then I could not be at both places, but will go with you to-day, if you will ask me."

"Oh ! we will take the greatest pleasure in having you ride with us ; and now that you have half proposed it, I shall insist upon it."

At the usual hour, Essex had the carriage at the door, and Henry, indeed, rode with them to church. A part of the congregation were already there when Mrs. Brandon's

carriage drove up, and were standing about in groups enjoying the warm winter sun. In one of these was Laura
Brandon, looking as glowingly beautiful, happy, and animated, Henry thought, as he had ever seen her. As Mrs.
Brandon's carriage drove up, Laura immediately came
meeting them, not thinking of course that any one was in
it but her aunt and Violet ; but when the door was opened,
and Henry made a motion to get out, she stepped back in
surprise, but, with a merry laugh, instantly said :

"Cousin, you took me so by surprise that I did not at
the instant recognize you. Come, you appear to be awkward, let me assist you," and pleasantly offered him her
hand.

Henry accepted the proffered assistance, but gave her
his left hand, and thanked her humorously for her assistance.

"You gave me the wrong hand, sir, or I should have
waited on you more gracefully."

"Oh! it is good enough for him, Laura ; he did not deserve
even that, for he was away all day yesterday, and only returned this morning."

"Ah! where have you been rambling, young gentleman?"

"Come, Violet ; you should not tell tales out of school.
I will tell you some other day, Laura."

"Were you at that show, or frolic, or whatever it was,
down below, yesterday? — were you, cousin?"

"Yes, I was at one yesterday, Laura ; but hush: you two
girls, and mother, are ever on the watch after my comings
and goings. I am all safe — what more do you want? and
equally prepared with the best of you to make the most
pious responses," and then said quickly to Laura, as if to
change the conversation : "I came to church chiefly to-day,
Laura, to criticise your Christmas embellishment, as Violet
and you were the principal artists."

Laura had already seemed to lose the brightness of her

face, after Henry telling her that he had been to a frolic down in the *Hills*; but the congregation beginning to enter the church, she made no reply. She had heard her father speak of the *gander-pulling* to be at Manese's, as the only one he had ever heard of in the State, and express his disapprobation of such sports; saying further, that Miller had got it up, and it was rumored that the sheriff would be there for the purpose of apprehending him. She therefore quickly saw that her cousin would be likely to reap a full share of severe censure, as soon as it became known to her mother that he had participated in it.

After the services in church were over, and the congregation were passing out, she sought the opportunity to get near him, and said to him that she had listened with but indifferent interest to Mr. Jerome that day, from the fact that *he* had been uppermost in her thoughts all the while.

"You compliment me highly, Laura, by such a distinguished preference; what special attribute of mine so engaged your reflections?"

"I am in no mood for jesting, cousin. I am really troubled. Will you let me ask if you were at that *gander-pulling* sport, yesterday? You know it will make no difference with me."

"Then, why do you wish to know, Laura?"

"You can very well imagine without putting me to the pain of saying."

He hesitated for a moment, but thought it best to tell her positively that he was.

Laura, for a few moments, appeared to lose all consciousness of where she was; and, as Henry Brandon thought, was on the point of giving away to her feelings, when he said quickly: "Come, Laura, let's go out, and I will tell you all about it."

As they stepped out of the door, they were met by Sally

24 *

Morton, who was, as usual, full of life and wit, and congratulated them on looking so handsome and so happy; and in reply to some remark of Henry Brandon, said that the parish could furnish several couples, if the parties could get their consent.

"Yes," again said Henry; "but your qualification is a very serious one. Consent is not only difficult to obtain, but more difficult to retain; so Mr. Jerome and I concluded not long since, in a confidential exchange of ideas — had he never spoken to you on that difficult question, Miss Sally?"

"No, sir; not as distinctly, at least, as he and you appear to have discussed it."

"Perhaps, and I hope it has ceased to be so difficult of solution as it then was; so far as it applies to him at least."

"I was not aware of his having had any difficulty of the kind, Mr. *Barrister*."

"None, at least, that an officiating priest could not remove — rather a better state of affairs than he seemed to hope for at that time."

"My dear young friend, I see that you aspire to wit as well as learning."

"No, no; only to truth."

Mr. Jerome, overhearing a portion of the repartee, approached them, and asked if they were getting up the preliminaries to a hostile meeting.

"No," replied Brandon; "I was only making a sort of defence of your interests, to which Miss Morton appeared to take some exception; but had you not come up, I cannot answer for the extreme to which she might have gone, and I thank you for your timely presence."

"And you, sir, in the true spirit of decaying chivalry, endeavored to urge me on — fie upon you! Quarrel with a woman!"

"Well," replied he, laughing; "I must cry *peccavi*, but

then some one must quarrel with you girls, or there would be no living on the continent with you, and considering the popular favor running in behalf of your sex, I rather think it showed high moral courage on my part to dare the collision."

"You are ambitious, then, of that distinction?"

"Yes; I *ambition* that, as I once heard a Yankee Governor express himself."

"A vaulting ambition."

"So it may be; but for a long while I have thought that I should like to get into a serious difficulty with a woman, just to see if I had nerve enough to go through with it."

"Jocky of Norfolk, be not too bold! You may get into one sooner than you think, and then you would give a kingdom for a horse to fly the field with, but not to fight upon. I pray you therefore, young knight, not to court your fate too soon."

"Come, come," said Mr. Jerome, "desist, or I shall be compelled to read the 'Riot Act.'"

"I accept your mediation, Mr. Jerome. I already see that the contest would be an unequal one; and now, Miss Sally, I withdraw my provoking banter, provided you withdraw your semi-threat and prophecy."

"Very well, I accept, with this injunction to you : beware of entrance to a quarrel — particularly with a woman, for I tell you in all truth that few men ever made a woman beware, or survived unhurt, the contest; it is one of those victories, even when won, that ruins the victor."

The congregation were now beginning to leave, and Laura, who had not even spoken during the conversation between Henry Brandon and Miss Morton, now asked Henry, in a subdued sort of tone, if he would be at church on Christmas Day?

"Yes, I expect to, of course; particularly if *you* request it."

"Yes; I would be glad to see you."

"Any especial reason, Laura?"

"Yes — no. Well, perhaps so; I may have something to say to you *then* — not now though."

"Christmas does not come until Thursday, and you are all to meet here on Wednesday again; suppose I meet you here?"

"Very well, Wednesday."

"Well, suppose," said he, laughing, "I ride over to-morrow evening?"

"Oh, you know that I will always be glad to see you. Come when you may," attempting a smile, as she said this.

"Ah, Laura! I am afraid you are too timid, either for your own happiness or mine."

They had now reached the carriage, where her mother was waiting for her; who, of course, saw their confidential tone and manner, with no great pleasantness.

CHAPTER XLII.

"The strong base and building of my love
Is as the very centre of the earth."

ACCORDING to the appointment, half jestingly made the day before at church, Henry Brandon rode over to see Laura on the following evening.

He was fearful that the excuse which his aunt now had, in his participation in the affair at old Manese's, would be sufficient to bring his intercourse with Laura to a final crisis; and that prurient desire which most people have for finding out their troubles in advance, induced him to be punctual to his engagement.

He had observed the expression of her face when he had walked up to the carriage with Laura on the day before, and knew that it boded no good to his hopes; and when (as he knew she would) she should hear of his visit to old Manese's, he had every reason to believe that she would concentrate all the energy of her opposition, and bring it to bear against him in such a manner as to make it impossible for him to longer visit at her house. Although the incident was trifling in its character, as Laura had said to him, it was yet a sufficient spark to kindle into flame the intense opposition to his marriage into her family, which she had felt for several weeks, and had given unmistakable evidence of. From this very fact, that Laura had spoken of it as an unimportant matter, and yet seemed so deeply affected by it, he was convinced that she had already passed through a severe ordeal with her mother — much more so, than she had revealed to him.

These, and other such reflections, had disturbed him all the morning, and no sooner had he concluded his dinner than he was on his horse, and galloping over to Mr. Robert Brandon's.

Mrs. Brandon had that morning had a long private interview with her daughter, and for the first time in her life, Laura had shown her some temper.

"You refuse to tell me then, Laura, whether you have engaged yourself to Henry Brandon or not," said Mrs. Brandon to her daughter, after they had been talking some time.

"Yes, madam, I hope you will allow me the privilege of keeping silence; it is the first time in my life I have ever asked such a leniency of you."

"I certainly should, my daughter, if I did not know and feel, that by that single secret you were about to destroy your own happiness, and the peace of your own family, as well as Henry's; it is a most unsuitable match for you both, view it from what point you will; and I shall never give my consent to it."

"I have not told you, mother, that I was engaged to him,

but I am almost prepared to tell you that I will never marry against your wishes, if positively expressed. *Love*, so far as I know anything of it, is — with me at least — a sentiment; and if any man should sufficiently become the object of it, as to make me willing to marry him, I still will love him, even if our marriage was frustrated. Marrying is only a desire to increase my domestic and social happiness — certainly not destroy it — which I would do if I should intrpduce discord between myself, husband, and parents."

"Then you are certainly guilty of a great wrong to Henry Brandon, by encouraging his attentions."

"By that I suppose you mean that no circumstances can mitigate your opposition to him — not even affection on my part?"

"I mean that under no circumstances can I ever receive him into my family as the husband of my daughter?"

"If you express such open disregard of my *feelings*, how do you expect me to respect — nothing more than *your prejudices?*"

"They are *not* prejudices; they are *feelings* and opinions, and regard yourself more than they affect me. I have lived for you, my daughter, and I would die for you, but I could never forgive your marriage with Henry Brandon."

"It is but fair, mother, to suppose that I have inherited strong feelings from yourself. Then, again, suppose these feelings *should* drive me on to marrying cousin Henry — even as yours drive you on to opposing it — should I expect to be driven from your heart and your home?"

"I place before you no such alternatives, nor do I desire you to establish them; yet you can do as you please — you have heard what I have had to say."

"Yes, mother, you certainly do make alternatives, and the very severest that a mother can make to a daughter."

"There we differ."

"I have never wilfully disobeyed you, mother, nor will I now, however cruel your exactions; but it does appear to me that you might have some regard for the feelings of such a daughter as I have ever tried to be."

"I think you mistake your feelings, Laura," said Mrs. Brandon, in rather more soothing tones. "When did your feelings become so interested in Henry Brandon?"

"If you will know the life-long secret of my heart, and the only one I ever kept from you, I must tell you — from my *earliest girlhood*."

"Is it possible, my daughter, that you so long kept this from me?"

"I have, and from every living creature but himself; and no other will I ever marry; and no persuasion, no threat, can induce me to move from these positions; and if I was as any other girl I know — even as Lucy — with such feelings I would marry him, if you drove me, penny-less, from your door forever, and with him alone meet every sorrow, and breast every storm, as they rose upon the troubled sea of life, and, clinging only to him, as he would cling to me, laugh at every frown of mortal eye, and scorn every hate of mortal heart. Now, mother, you know the secret and the force of my woman's bosom. Do as you will, but let me beg you to consider well your action."

"I came for no *scenes*, Laura — I merely wished to have a serious talk with you in regard to a matter which I think of the highest importance to us all."

"No, mother, you mistake your position: it concerns no living being but myself; and my being is so involved in it, that no human thought, nor human deed, can separate them. With me it is everything — it is *all*. With you, at most, 't is but a *part*."

"I say, Laura, I did not come to witness a *scene;* and you are certainly *acting*, my daughter." She said this with the vain effort at a smile; but it was the smile of helpless desperation, and therefore entitled to sympathy; as perhaps there is nothing tenderer than the feeling of a parent to a child; and there can be nothing more unfortunate than a difference between them. To yield up a child, then, under any circumstances, against the will — or a daughter to the love, and care, and arms of one in whom the completest confidence is not felt — is certainly the severest ordeal through which a parent's heart can pass. There was this much to be said in behalf of Mrs. Brandon, in her opposition to the marriage of her daughter with her cousin.

"Mother," answered Laura, "you too deeply wrong me, by the use of such words, when you apply them to one whose happiness trembles upon your decision. It is *my* heart that has received the wound, not yours. I have done nothing to wound you; and yet you insult its agonies by scoffing at its aching, bursting throbs, in speaking of them as ACTING. Neither have I enacted any scene. I have told you, in the only words that could express it, the deep secret of my heart, and you yourself did persecute me into revealing it."

"This interview is becoming too unpleasant to be longer carried on. I only wished to advise you, for your own happiness, as well as that of Henry Brandon, that if you did not intend to marry him, it was but proper for you to refuse his attentions."

"Your words, mother, are colder to my heart than icicles."

"Then you refuse to tell me whether you have re-engaged yourself to your cousin, or *not?*"

"Yes, madam, you must permit me to refuse. I have told you all that I now feel willing to tell; and as to refusing the attentions of cousin Henry, that must be as my feelings dictate when we meet."

Mrs. Brandon now rose and left her daughter's room, and no sooner had she done so, than Laura fell upon her lounge in convulsions of tears, only saying: "And must I give him up? Must I let this poor heart break and die?"

Lucy returned to the room very quickly, after hearing her mother leave it, and by degrees soothed her sister to quietness.

What the feeling was, she perhaps scarcely knew herself, but when she met her mother at the dinner-table, she never appeared more beautiful, more cheerful, or happier, and was still so when Henry Brandon came in the evening.

CHAPTER XLIII.

"But love can hope where reason would despair."

FOR a winter day, the evening was calm, bright, and lovely, and imparted something of its own beauty to Henry Brandon's heart. In spite of the anxieties which had disturbed it in the morning, he felt a strange happiness come over him while galloping along over the prairies to "Starlight." He had dressed himself with scrupulous elegance, and never looked more handsome. His coat buttoned in front, with his arm resting in the breast of it, only gave him the grace of an unpremeditated act, as he came walking from the gate to the house. He was met at the door by a servant, and immediately shown to the drawing-room.

Lucy and Laura entered in a few moments, both appearing delighted to see him, and were very soon followed by Mr. Robert Brandon and his lady. Henry ran to meet them, with his lame arm still resting in the breast of his coat. Lucy had observed this before, but had said nothing about it until now, when she said, with a pleasant laugh:

25

"Cousin, I really admire it very much; but then you are certainly *attitudinizing* for our pleasure this evening. Did you learn that new figure at your friend Manese's?"

"I certainly did, Lucy," he replied, very pleasantly.

"May I ask who your instructor was?" said Laura.

"Yes; but you place me somewhat in the predicament of Hotspur, when he told Glendower that he, too, could call up spirits from the vasty deep, but was in some doubt as to their coming. I know *how* it was done, but can scarcely say *who* did it."

"You speak in riddles, when the occasion requires plain words, cousin."

"Then, if I must, I will tell a tale which will harrow up your souls—are you prepared for it?"

"As well, perhaps, as we will ever be."

"I received a flying shot from a gun of the sheriff's party, the other night, at Manese's, when the attempt was made to apprehend my old friend Miller."

This announcement was even more than Laura had expected, while Mrs. Brandon affected the greatest surprise at young gentlemen attending such sports and places. Henry only laughed, saying that he was much entertained by the whole thing, and certainly was heartily welcomed by the people down there, which was more than he feared was his case nearer home.

"You do not say seriously, that you were shot there, Henry?" said Mrs. Brandon.

"I certainly do, madam."

"What do you think will be said about the accomplished and highly educated Henry Brandon being at such a place?"

"I really have not concerned myself about that feature of the affair."

"Do you say that you are indifferent to public opinion, Henry?" asked his uncle.

"Yes, sir, about that, as I really don't see any good to come to me from either private or public estimation. I rather think the signs favorable to my being compelled to make my own way through the world, regardless of the stupidity of both; at all events, I stand in that position at present."

"You are not likely to win any great favor by playing such cards."

"No; nor with any other in this portion of the great moral vineyard, as I see matters."

"You do not think of leaving us, do you?" said Mrs. Brandon, her eyes ill-concealing her pleasure in the probability of getting an affirmative answer.

"I contemplate it as among the probabilities of the future."

"Not of the *present*, then?" asked Laura.

"No, cousin; not so long as the young maidens smile upon my stay."

"Would it not be better to select only one, cousin, and let her smile upon you for life?"

"I have entertained such illusive hopes, but find myself about to give up the strife unto that beatitude."

"I am afraid, Henry, your getting *wounded* has done nothing for the softness of your feelings. We will leave you to the girls and the piano, perhaps they will soothe you. Come, Catherine, let us leave them," said Mr. Brandon.

Mr. Brandon had come in with his wife, fearing that she might say something unpleasant to Henry, and now suggested her leaving the drawing-room with him, as an additional safeguard; thinking that matters would take their course, if even left to themselves.

They had not been left long to themselves before Lucy rose to leave also; but saying:

"I am glad, cousin Henry, that you had the independence to speak of that foolish Manese affair as you did, as I do not think that silence would have done you any good. I have never known mother to take so decided a stand about anything as she has in regard to — you and Laura — and cannot see into it; and though she has often in her life checked me, I have never known her to even cross Laura, and I think if Laura will be firm, and say but little, that she will eventually give way; but to be candid, I ask you not to be too much encouraged. I have done,. and will do all I can for you both," then left the room, Henry saying to her as she left: " Glorious for you, Lucy."

Laura alternately blushed and changed her color, during the time that her sister was speaking.

Henry now turned to her and half laughingly said:

" All alone, Laura, now tell me my fate."

" I have passed through a scene this morning, cousin, that has almost taken my senses; I scarcely believe I could bear the shock of such another without — but never mind."

" What was the nature of it, Laura?"

" Oh! I can scarcely tell you;" but proceeded to relate as nigh as she could the nature of the interview between herself and her mother.

" The whole force of her inquiries was in regard to a re-engagement, not as to your feelings?"

" Both, probably; but mainly with reference to that."

" What did you say to her?"

" Oh! more than I can ever say to my mother again, cousin."

" I am sorry, Laura, that I have brought this trouble on you; but did you tell her?"

" No, I refused; and she was very bitter in regard to my course. Now, can you advise me what course to pursue? You know my feelings toward you, and you know the circumstances. With your man's heart, tell — mine is a woman's."

"You must tell her, then; and if not sufficient to bear the pressure of her opposition, break it up. *If you are,* you can depend on me under all situations. This is as explicit as I can be."

"And leave me, cousin?" she asked, with the last tinge of color leaving her cheek.

"No; not leave you, Laura, unless you command it."

"That I can never do."

"Do you mean then to go against their consent?"

"These are the only two alternatives, I know; but how — oh! how am I to choose?"

Henry now discovered that she was slightly disposed to wildness of thought, and saw at once that it was better not to bring matters to a conclusion, and suggested that she let them remain as they were for the present. This she seemed willing to do, and became more calm. He then told her that it would only increase her troubles for him to come there again under the present circumstances, and for a while at least, only to meet each other on neutral ground. This she also thought advisable; but asked him, with a modest smile, to make the occasions himself, as it would be out of her power to do so.

She then sang him a plaintive little song, on a low key, but with a more quiet expression than she had had that day. Henry seeing that her feelings had resumed a natural channel, proposed to leave, telling her that he would meet her on Christmas Day, as he believed that Violet was to have all of her young friends with her then, for the last time before being married.

Rising from the piano, in response to Henry's "good-by," she quoted Byron's words:

> "Farewell!
> For in that word — that fatal word — howe'er
> We promise — hope — believe — there breathes despair."

25*

"No, no; not yet Laura," said he, smiling, and, drawing the almost hopeless girl to his bosom, and kissing away the tear that dropped upon her blanching cheek, left the house, never again to enter it.

Christmas week, that festal time, under the old *régime*, for white and black, had now come and gone.   During the time, however, Henry Brandon had met Laura on many pleasant occasions, and was himself the gayest of the gay; but she was evidently giving way.

CHAPTER XLIV.

" Good night, good night! parting is such sweet sorrow,
    That I shall say good night till it be morrow."

ACTIVE preparations were now being made for Violet's wedding, and during the time, Laura and Lucy were frequently at Mrs. Brandon's; but the former seemed to enter with but small zest into the animated arrangements, and was evidently living under a pressure too great both for her spirits and her strength. Henry, however, saw proper to allude to the unpleasant circumstances but seldom, as he was well satisfied that no favorable change in affairs was going on.

At length the wedding night was at hand, and the occasion was a bright and happy one for every one; even Laura seemed to forget her sadness, and entered with something of her former animation into the joy and gayety of the evening.

Henry Brandon paid her marked attention, and danced with her several times, which appeared to give her great pleasure, and was as often with her at the piano, when she sang for him with all her former joyousness and sweetness; and yet behind all there was a rooted sorrow, of which but very few in that gay assemblage dreamed, that loaned its bright but unearthly light to her beauty, and to the elegance and elasticity of her conversation — for while the one was universally remarked, the other was the charm of every group. Henry Brandon saw this and knew it, and the fact sank deep into his heart, yet knew no soothing word, no healing remedy — it was the cold, bright light of the evening star before sinking down below the horizon of eternity. They were the last happy hours she ever knew on earth!

Some few days after this, her mother sought an occasion to say to her, incidentally to some other general opinions, that she should be cautious in receiving the attentions of Henry Brandon, as it would certainly lead him to entertain hopes which she had promised not to gratify.

Laura simply replied, that as she had surrendered the dearest hope of her life, she wished never to have the subject again alluded to.

It was but a few days after this, that she wrote the following note to Henry Brandon:

"STARLIGHT, *Wednesday Night.*

"MY DEAR COUSIN: — The purport of this note will not, I know, surprise you, though you may not expect it; nor many days since, did I ever expect to write such. But causes have existed, and do still exist, which render it just and proper that I ask you to relieve us both of our anomalous sort of engagement. The nature of those causes you already know too well, to demand of me the pain of repetition.

"I might tell you of what my feelings are still towards you, but it would not be right; it would be as an effort to bind the living to the dead. I will, therefore, only ask you, generously to *forgive* all the parties to this wretched drama, and if you can, to *forget* one, who, as a tender, clinging vine, had flung its soft tendrils out upon your name, your character, and your manly virtues, but broke when the first storm came, from their own weakness and tenuity, and now lies helpless at your feet. The morning rose gives no promise of its early fading, yet when twilight comes, its hues are gone, its fragrance shed; 'tis thus with me. In the morning of my life I little thought to wither all so soon, but the evening has already come, and my life-leaves faded; nor can the sweet night-dews of even *your* affection revive their early morning tints. In after years —'t is all that I dare to ask — will you still remember me as some strange, and bright, and joyous thing that floated along your youthful path, but early paled its light away, and left no trace behind of having ever been? And now—

> "'Farewell! a word which hath been, and must be,
> A sound that makes us linger, yet FAREWELL!'"

> " In heart, ever yours,
> " LAURA BRANDON."

Although the purport of this note, as Laura said, was not a great surprise, yet when he read it, he sat stupefied, and nearly paralyzed, and could find no power at his command suitable for a reply.

In this time Hunter had already become perfectly domesticated at Mrs. Brandon's, and Henry made haste to make all preparations for returning immediately to the law-office of Judge Lorn. A few days more found him at his old quarters in the city. Books were his only refuge; society presented no charms, and for many months he had never studied in his college days with half the same assiduity; never visiting in the city, and but seldom even visiting his mother.

Early in the following spring, after the marriage of Violet, Lucy Brandon was married to Mr. Campbell, with a wedding entertainment quite equalling in extent, sumptuousness, and gayety, that of Hunter and Violet. Henry was asked to attend it, by an ordinary invitation from Mr. and Mrs. Brandon, and by an especial note from Lucy, but declined to attend.

Lucy immediately removed to the city, but Henry never visited her, though repeatedly insisted on to do so, both by Mr. Campbell, and by messages from Lucy, but once for all declined, saying to Mr. Campbell that he loved Lucy almost as his sister, yet the associations in connection with her were too painful to him, but would go some time or other without invitation, when he felt that it would be pleasant to him to see her. Laura never visited the city, and visited but little in the country; they, therefore, never met.

His uncle he frequently saw, but always avoided him — as either wanting in sincerity, or the *proper manliness* to *control his wife*, either of which, to one of Henry Brandon's character, was sufficient cause of alienation.

Growing weary both of books, and the sort of isolation which his feelings had led him into, he determined on a stroll, as he called it, and selected the *West* as the theatre of his wanderings, with no defined purpose, beyond the mere passing off of his time; and in the latter part of the autumn, made all arrangements for carrying out his design, Hunter agreeing to take charge of his planting interest. He had already completed his other preparations for leaving, with the ubiquitous "Sam Brandon," as he always spoke of him, as his only friend — the latter protesting most seriously against being left behind.

Feeling, however, that he could not leave without either seeing or letting Laura know of his intention, he wrote her a few lines, informing her of the fact, and as an excuse for doing so, returned her the many notes, letters, and little favors which he had received from her through many years — among them the ring that she had given him and had never asked for, and the little bunch of faded flowers which she had given him on the eve of his leaving for college.

The note and package were sent by "Sam," who was told to wait and see if there would be a reply, and ran as follows:

"BUCKHORNS, 2d *November.*

"MY DEAR LAURA:—It is with deep and sincere regret that circumstances render it proper, perhaps, to send the package which accompanies this note. It contains some letters and other small favors sent and conferred, when the present was all joy, and the future all hope, both of which have ceased to exist, so far as WE are concerned.

"It is my design to leave the State in a few days, without appointing a time of return; and while I cannot get my consent to destroy these small mementos of the happy past, it will be better not to have them with me, connected as they are with events that must ever bring their own peculiar sorrows.

"The ring you have never asked for, and till now, I could never get my consent to return; but as it was given to represent a *never-ending* attachment, it is only right that I return it, now that the promise has been virtually broken. The notes and letters explain themselves; they are yours now—not mine. The little bunch of flowers you probably have forgotten, but may recall themselves to your memory, and even in their withered condition and faded colors, are the best emblems of our youthful feelings; and ay, too often, when no eyes were upon me but those of heaven, have I pressed them to my heart and lips, and thought of her who gave them.

"I sometimes think that I would like still to know you LOVED me—still to know I had a place in the heart of the fair young girl who stood before me in her lovely innocence, her maiden truth and gentle beauty, and promised to be *mine;* but then I fly from the knowledge of so sad a truth, as one which has embittered my life. The wither of age and the blight of grief rest upon all things, and I fly from them as from a curse and a woe. Home, friends, and the *love* of early boyhood are as nothing to me now, and I leave them, perhaps, forever.

"Yours, very truly,   HENRY BRANDON."

On reaching STARLIGHT, "Sam," as he had been directed, called for Laura's waiting-maid, and placed the package in her hands, saying to her that he would wait for a reply.

The girl carried it directly to her young mistress, who was in her own room; and having already become a partial invalid, was reclining on her couch, and listlessly engaged in turning over the pages of "Childe Harold."

Nervously opening the note, and reading and re-reading it, time and again, she at length laid it aside with a sigh, and opened the package. As her eye fell upon the ring and withered flowers, she could no longer restrain her feelings, but, with a look of wild despair, laughed a low, hysteric laugh, and fell back upon her couch.

The very throbbing of her breaking heart soon nerved her to consciousness and to thought, and asking the girl to place the writing-table near her, wrote the following note in reply:

"STARLIGHT, 2d *November.*

"MY DEAR COUSIN:—A note from you, with a package, has just been handed to me. The note I read with that deep interest which you *must know* anything from you will ever secure. The package contained some evidences and mementos of the relation that (you say) did once exist between us; but which I, in my wildness, perhaps, almost had dared to hope did still exist; and I make haste to respond to my heart's deep emotion.

"The note, when I first saw it, brought a bewildering joy, such as my heart had long been a stranger to, and — shall I confess it? — there was the secret confidence of a moment that it would tell me *something* to restore my lost hope and forgotten happiness; but, oh! its words! its words! I deserve, yet do not all deserve them. I have brought sorrow to you, but a broken heart to myself—and still have not the courage to meet the causes. What your grief has been, I can well imagine. Mine has been even more than that, and I have suffered more than I thought a human heart could bear. Nor *have* I borne it; yet, as I do, I bear in silence.

"It has been some months since I saw you, or even received the attention of a note; and while this, which came this morning, was so different from any I had ever before received from you — so bitter and so sad, and — shall I tell it to you? — the very way-notes of my path to the grave — it yet brought a gladness to my spirit that *death* alone will give me a brighter, clearer title to. 'What was that,' you ask, 'that brought this bliss?' Only a reference to the fact that *you once did love me*, and a reference, too, to the fact that Laura Brandon did *once* love you — ay, and still doth love, and will ever love *you.*

"There is no living thing that my poor timid heart would thus expose its beatings to but *yourself;* but with *you* I feel that perfect confidence that knows no wrong, and feels no fear; and it will ever breathe its fragrance and its truth about a name that has twined itself about my life forever, and will not, cannot cease to be, until my pulses cease to count my troubles and my days.

"This might seem to some to be the excited language of a frenzied madness. To *you* I know it will not, but only the trickling drops of a bleeding heart falling into their own dying bosom.

"To think aught else, would only be to wrong one whose tenure upon the things of time and sense is already loosed. Even now, while I write, existence seems to have lost its substance and its joy, and I stand on time's farthest shore, with my spirit fluttering for a flight into the still, mystic realms we know not of. Why it lingers there, I cannot tell, unless to plume its wing with yet another sorrow.

"You say your design is to leave the State. Oh, why did you tell me this? Why not have left me to find it out as I would — to fate? And yet I would have known it — since I think I have the right, in virtue of the past, to meet you *once* more in life; after that, we may never meet again.

"To-morrow, then, I ask you to meet me, at three o'clock, under the old oak-tree at the 'cross-paths.'

"As ever, yours most truly and affectionately,
                              "LAURA BRANDON."

CHAPTER XLV.

"Early, bright, transient, chaste as morning dew,
    She sparkled, was exhaled, and went to heaven."

THE servant-girl had been sitting near, during the time that Laura had been writing, engaged with her needle, and when she had concluded her excited and hastily written note, she handed it to her, telling her to give it to no one but "Sam Brandon." The girl, sympathizing deeply with her young mistress, almost flew to "SAM," and told him to lose no time in delivering it. "SAM," thinking that the success of the whole matter depended upon despatch, left the gate at almost full speed.

The " cross-paths " to which Laura alluded was a spot well known to both Henry and herself, one of them being the path which led from Mr. Robert Brandon's to the old school-house, where the two young people had spent so many blissful hours in their early days; the other was the "herd-boy's" path, that led out into the adjoining prairies; and the two crossed each other, at acute angles, on the outer edge of a small but rich forest-wood, some three or four hundred yards from Mr. Brandon's house. At the immediate crossing stood an old oak, remarkable for its size and symmetry. Directly beyond, lay spread out a broad and beautiful prairie, as a bright sea of gold, with a shore-tinge of autumn green. The evening was still, and calm, and beautiful. The long, yellow rays of coming winter glanced through the old oak's top, and bathed the prairie beyond with a flood of soft, yellow light, while the gentlest breath of air only trembled the purpling leaf, as if to welcome to a court of sadness the lovely girl whom it expected there.

At the appointed hour Laura was there, her waiting-

26

maid having attended her to a point in sight, and was to remain there until she returned. She had already been under the tree for some minutes, awaiting the arrival of Henry Brandon ; he, however, came up by rather an unusual direction, and seeing her there at some distance off, had lighted from his horse and came walking up, and was near her without her discovering his approach.

Laura was not looking for him from that direction, but stood intently looking for him from another. She had not heard from him, but certainly knew he would be there.

She was dressed in a rich flowing black silk, with snow-white collar and cuffs ; and having taken off her bonnet, stood, rather swinging it by the strings and veil, as she gently leaned against the body of the tree. Henry paused in his advance just before reaching her, and was struck with her changed appearance, yet thought he had never seen a more lovely picture ; her dark, glossy hair hung loosely but elegantly at the sides of her face; her complexion was almost transparently clear — seeming to have lost all the grossness of earth — with only the softest hectic flush upon her cheek, adding to her almost heavenly beauty. As she stood under the wide branches of the old monarch of the woods, that stood immediately at the crossing, she looked more like a Dryad, wrought out in the highest sculpture of Grecian art, or some chaste statue of love and beauty, from an angel's hand, than any real, living thing of earth.

Henry making a slight noise to attract her attention, she turned with some surprise, but instantly stepped to meet him, and offered him her hand, which he accepted very affectionately, but without being able to speak.

Laura was the first to break silence, by saying :

"Cousin, I am only too happy to see you once more ; but fear you will think the request to meet me here a *singular* one, at least."

"No, Laura," he replied ; "you have yet to do your first

exceptional act, though some for which I may have cause to reproach you."

"Your words bring me a strange happiness, cousin, even if a barren one, in spite of your reproof. I had not hoped so much, and feared more."

"No; in regard to anything you have ever done, my only feeling is *regret*."

"If 'regret' is all you have felt, I can assure you that your sufferings are not as mine have been."

"Yours, Laura, were self-inflicted, from which you could have escaped at any moment; mine were different, imposed upon me."

"You do me injustice, cousin; there has been, and is, less escape for me than for yourself — for instance, even now, you declare your intention to leave the scenes of these great heart-troubles; and mixing with, and becoming a part of the great outside world, will of course, to some extent, forget those you leave behind. With me the situation is the reverse. *I* cannot go; but must remain, and every day, every hour, be brought in association with persons, places, and a thousand little nameless events, relating both to you, and the *love* which we so long have borne to each other," then hesitating for a moment, continued, "and which *I shall ever bear to you.*"

Taking her by the hand as she uttered these words, he said: "Laura! Laura! this is really too much to bear, and appears to me to be either trifling or insanity — more than that affection of which you speak. What possible manner of feeling is that which can crush itself and another too? It is only *that* which has ever cast a shadow upon the clear blue sky, which floats upon its bosom — your name and love, only that I do assure you."

At these remarks, Laura's eyes brightened with an almost celestial light, and she asked in reply:

"Oh, cousin! cousin! after all that I have said to you,

and after all that I have endured and am still enduring, can you find it in your breast to doubt me?"

"No, I cannot; nor do I doubt you in anything; but I must confess that I do not comprehend this feeling of extreme obedience, with which you have blighted your own happiness as well as mine. Does your mother know the true condition of your heart, and still oppose you?"

"No, she does not; cannot — never can — nor do you. Neither of you can conceive the power of a human heart to crush itself to a sense of duty and *family happiness*. She does not comprehend that I can sacrifice myself to an obedience of parental authority. Nor can you, that I can still be true to a feeling, but never gratify it. Yet I have done — am doing both."

"Laura, you have allowed some sort of religious abstraction to carry you beyond the bounds of human reason, into the mystic realms of infatuation. Rationally, either aunt's prejudices should be disregarded, or you should discard all preference and feeling for me. You know her, you know me, you know yourself, and in justice to all should take a different stand."

"You do not mean that I should forget you?" she replied; looking a little startled, and shrinking back.

"No, I do not; nor is there any demand on earth that I could meet, which I would not meet, to remove all obstacles to our mutual happiness. After that, I would take the cause in my own keeping; and as I am willing to do this, so should you be."

"Do you mean to imply some special act on my part?" she asked eagerly, supposing he had some proposition to make.

"To any other girl I ever knew, I might reply: to *you* I cannot; but this I may say, that could I have known only one year since, what the present would be, all of this sorrow could have been avoided: as I did not, it is too late to yield to regrets; and I can further say, that should you persist in your present course, I cannot see the end — the future grows darker as I go, and in a few days I will leave the causes to themselves forever! and yet I can see no refuge from the fate that awaits us — darkness and despair for you, and over me there rests a cloud that threatens a never-ceasing sorrow. We must either endeavor to retrace our steps, or go *forward*. Do you understand me?"

"Perhaps I do not; but, oh! cousin! speak not thus — oh! speak it not — do not all crush this aching heart, before its life is gone — only say what I can do — a poor, weak girl can do, to shield you from this grief; and I will throw my peace, my happiness, ay! if need be, my life, my very soul, into the scale to weigh against it!"

"Spoken like a true woman, as you are, Laura." Then taking her by the hand, said: "And now, after all that I have said, and am willing to perform, there is but the one course for us to pursue — adopt that, and these murky skies will clear away that now overcast our hopes;" and then in tones which showed he felt all the responsibility of the position which he was about to ask her to assume, he continued: "Only promise me, Laura, that *against* all the *world* you will be my WIFE."

At this proposition the color left her cheek; and rising before him with a gentle but resolute majesty, to her full height, with her soft eye beaming steadily but affectionately upon him, she replied with a low but distinct utterance:

"Could I have *ever* availed myself of such a proposition, it is *now* too late — my life is only suspended by a thread."

"Yet you are as dear to me, Laura, as you ever were in the most joyous hours of bloom and health; ay! even dearer for your weakness."

"Thank you, cousin, you only increase my obligations to you; but let me say once for all, as we may never meet again, that if it can be so, my love for you is more than

26 *

mortal, yet a mortal power has controlled it.   My mother did not yield when she might, *now* 't is needless, and I have long since ceased to ask it; therefore, remember what I tell you — for I know and feel it, and say it calmly too, that the evening of my life draws nigh — the sun is already sinking to its setting hour, and throws its long dreamy shadows on this wasting form; yet my undying love is yours, and while on earth only can be yours! intenser and purer too, in its hopeless, helpless despair, than in its roseate flush of joy, and strength, and hope; and this I further tell you, that wander whither you will, and do as you may, I yet do know your princely mind and royal heart, and will forever know them; and shoot as wildly, madly, as you dare, across the course of other men, and the world's despotic power, you will not! cannot! shall not FALL!   On earth I still will follow you; in heaven even, with the angels there, I still will be your light, your love, your guardian, and your star of destiny!   Dearer to me than all else beside, in this sad world, yet I can never be your wife on EARTH!   I release you — FAREWELL!"
Fainting, she fell lifeless in his arms.   They never met again.

THE INTERLUDE.

"'T was but for a moment, and yet in that time
  She crowded th' impressions of many an hour:
Her eye had a glow, like the sun of her clime,
  Which waked every feeling at once into flower!"

IT will be remembered that Laura Brandon had fainted, and fallen into the arms of Henry Brandon, as she told him that she could never be his wife. Her waiting-maid came up in an instant, and by gentle manipulations she was restored to consciousness. Supporting her on either side, they returned with her to the house; not a word was spoken by either, but when they reached the gate, Laura merely remarked, in tones scarcely above a whisper, that she could walk alone. Henry then kissed her livid lips, and bid her FAREWELL — forever!

Laura was assisted immediately to her own chamber by her maid, and that evening, not going down to tea, simply sent word that she would not be present.

She was taken with a fever, and continued to be confined from it for several weeks, but never breathed it that she had had an interview with her cousin Henry.

Eventually recovering from the attack, she yet never regained her strength, or became what she had been, but gradually grew weaker, until she sank into being a confirmed invalid, seldom leaving her room, and only then in some short ride for recreation. This lasted for nearly two years, when, without even having let the name of Henry Brandon escape her lips, she sank to a peaceful rest.

She had long known that her life was ebbing away; and as a beautiful star of early morning, whose soft beams fade away into the greater light of day, so this gentle girl, who had ever been a joy, a sweet happiness, and a light to herself and to others, faded from the bright scenes of human life, into the grander, but more mild effulgence of eternity. Her love for Henry Brandon, as she said herself, had been almost more than mortal; and mortal sense and feeling was not a fit tribunal before which could be arraigned its delicate, spiritual emotion. Love, to her, was an apotheosis of the object to which her heart had given its whole devotion ; a shrinking tenderness and sacredness of adoration, which, once blighted, revives no more on earth, and only reappears beyond the shores of time, as part of heaven itself.

To an exquisite social organization, she added as exquisite a delicacy of intellect — and the two commingling, as it were, with an almost spiritual beauty of person, made such a being as is rarely met with in the walks of human life; and her way from earth to heaven glowed with the constant light of love, and truth, and virtue. Her death was a lovely picture of her life — drawn in most delicate lines, and tinted with the softest brush; calm, peaceful, fearless, and resigned, yet glowing, and hopeful, and lovely.

Her last words were to Lucy, who, with her mother, was at her bedside; making an effort, she reached out her hand, and with eyes beaming with a steady, but a soft, unearthly brightness, she said, in low but well-articulated words: "Lucy — Cousin Henry Brandon — Let us meet again — Farewell," and closed her invalid life, with a BROKEN HEART.

Henry Brandon, in accordance with the purpose which he had formed previous to his last meeting with Laura, and which he had then announced to her, left the State only a few days after, rather intending to make the tour of Europe. But meeting with some old college friends at New Orleans, who were preparing for a hunting excursion to the extreme West, he was persuaded to change his purpose, and to accompany them. After spending several weeks in the prairies of Texas, he returned to Little Rock, and made that place his headquarters, from which he radiated on many a roving, and to be confessed, idle excursion in the country round about.

Little Rock at this time presented many attractive features, for which it neither then nor since has had credit abroad. It had long been one of the principal frontier military posts of the Government, and officers of different grades, with their families, had made the place their temporary home; these, together with young officers without families, and with the citizens of the place, made society there remarkable, both for its elegant abandon and cultivation. At the time we speak of, it possessed all the charms of a gay little capital, and a bright little society to itself. Men of genius and education were there engaged in civic pursuits and professions, whose families and themselves would have contributed to the refinement of social life in any part of the world, and would have ornamented life in any of its coteries. The young men and young girls who had grown up there, all gave to its society a freshness, zest, and friendship, seldom to be found, and peculiarly acceptable to Henry Brandon at that particular time. He had taken rooms at the then fashionable hotel, "The Anthony House," and with the society we have spoken of, he passed much of his time, as an apparently gay idler, and felt, even as the place itself was, shut off from all the unpleasant events of his own home. To the citizens, in the course of a three-years quasi residence, he became a popular and an almost necessary feature of their social intercourse.

"Sam Brandon," who was with him as *body-servant*, was quite as popular in his own sphere as his master, and was really the servant of every one who wished his attentions.

To the rude people of the *more* frontier settlements, among whom he made frequent expeditions for hunting and for purposes of amusement, Henry was familiarly and pleasantly known. His agreeable manners, richness of dress, and affluent habits made him an object of interest, and they welcomed his presence with unreserved hospitality to their homes and families.

War was declared against Mexico only a few months after fixing his residence at LITTLE ROCK, when he joined the regiment of Governor Yell, and was chosen a lieutenant of one of the companies. At *Buena Vista* he was wounded, but a few minutes before the fall of Colonel Yell, and was near him at the time. As soon as he sufficiently recovered to travel, he returned to *Little Rock*, somewhat in advance of his regiment, but before the troops of General Taylor were ordered round to *Vera Cruz.* Here again he soon entered upon his same kind of aimless life, with occasional trips abroad, but never to Alabama, whither his mother and sister were ever insisting upon his returning. He had heard all the circumstances of Laura's death, and so far from inducing him to return, it only made him more determined to remain away. Such had still been his affection for her, and his regret for her death.

He had now been absent from home over three years, when an apparent accident — as it really was — changed the whole tenor of his life and feelings, and carried him back to his native State.

On one of such excursions as we have described his taking, occasionally, with only *Sam Brandon* for company, he was at Memphis, and, walking along one of its main streets, not of business, but of private residences, there came meeting him a young girl, richly dressed, tall, and graceful in her walk, but with the face partially concealed by her veil. He passed her, without further remark than the simple facts called for, when SAM BRANDON, who was with him, stepped quickly to his side, and said: "Mass Henry, that young lady we met was ole Mass Gray's daughter back in Alabama. I saw her face good, sir."

Henry turned immediately, and thought he did indeed

recognize her figure and walk, though measurably concealed by her wrappings. At the hazard of appearing rude, he retraced his steps, with a view, if possible, to get the sight of her face; and even before he overtook her, he was satisfied of the identity, and confident that, if he could get the slightest glimpse of her face, he would recognize her, if indeed it should prove as he now supposed, her features being well fixed upon his memory, from association with the amusing events of the happy and joyous day of their first acquaintance. Coming up with her, he *did* get a passing glimpse of her features, and at once recognized her. Hesitating at the apparent rudeness for a moment, he as quickly recovered, and addressed her:

"Will Miss Gray permit an old acquaintance of some years back to recognize her?" said he, smiling as he spoke.

She was a little startled at the suddenness of the salutation, but recognizing him in an instant, she replied, while looking him pleasantly but steadily in the face:

"Why, certainly, Mr. Brandon, and confess, sir, to as great pleasure as astonishment in meeting you;" and rather confusedly continued: "Where are you — where — "

Brandon, seeing her mixed confusion and surprise, said:

"I see your perplexity, and your wish to know why I am here, Miss. I can only answer that, since we last met, I have gradually degenerated into the character of a mere *idle* rambler, and have no business here nor elsewhere. I therefore cannot answer you as to the *why* of being here, unless you will excuse me for saying that it is in obedience to some *destiny* which I am not prepared to interpret; and my stay," he very pleasantly added, "may regulate itself by your own, if you will permit it. You must pardon me for saying this, as you are the only person I have met from home since I left there. I have not seen the first familiar face from there before, and I scarcely know how I can leave you."

"Thank you, sir; I will not think of rejecting so agreeable a proposition; and I shall expect you, too, as you have renewed our acquaintance, to tell me all the whys and wherefores of your singular, self-imposed exile."

"I am obliged to you, Miss, for your interest, and for that pleasant privilege, as I look upon it as such, and will take all pains to give you the details and incidents of my life for the last three or four years, as far as I can remember them. I scarcely think, however, I can crowd the rehearsal into any limited period of time."

"Oh, sir, my curiosity is now excited, and I will endeavor to arrange for all your stories, even if it should require a 'thousand and one nights,' as I have no doubt but they will be quite as entertaining as those of the Arabian princess."

"That, indeed, is a larger liberality than I had looked for, and the source of a peculiar pleasure which I had not expected to meet with, when I came here — that of your society; one, too, which I shall be tempted to protract, even beyond the generous bounds you have already assigned to me."

"I see, Mr. Brandon, you have not forgotten your early felicity in compliment, even if you have, as I have learned, been sojourning for several years in the wilds of the West."

"No, no; I hope never to forget it; indeed, I cannot, so long as nature will continue to furnish *such brilliant* subjects. But let me thank you for having known, even indefinitely, of my whereabouts, and for recognizing me this morning."

"You do yourself injustice, sir, if you suppose that a few years would erase your name from a young lady's memory. You should at least demand a lifetime."

"My fears ran counter to my hopes, Miss Gray; and your implied assurances to the contrary, however facetiously expressed, are most gracious to my feelings, associated as those memories are with one of the pleasantest days of my life, one which I neither have nor can forget; and it is that to which I am indebted for recognizing you this morning. Your features have ever been singularly impressed on my memory."

Evidently pleased, she replied:

"Mr. Brandon, your manner and style of expression bring back more vividly to my mind the pleasing incidents of that day than I even at first remembered either you or them."

Brandon was now walking slowly at her side, in the direction which she was going at the time he met her, and supposing that he might probably be interfering with her purposes, asked if he could be allowed to accompany her further.

"Oh, certainly. I have only been making a morning call upon a young friend of mine, and am now returning to the 'Gayoso House,' where I stop when in the city."

"Indeed! I am happy to know that we stop at the same place, and am sorry that I had not met you before. I will accompany you thither, if pleasant to you. May I . ask who is with you from Alabama?"

"My mother and father. My mother has a sister near the city, and they visit each other alternate years. This is my mother's year to make the visit."

"Yes, I remember that you were absent on a visit here when my sister was married. She was quite disappointed in not having you there. You will excuse me for telling you away off here, and at this distance of time since, but she was quite resolved that we should all at least become better acquainted, if nothing more. Young girls, you know, *will* bother themselves about such matters."

"Well, I have to regret her kind intentions, as I, perhaps, have been the loser," she replied, laughingly. "Our acquaintance certainly began very merrily."

27

"And so auspiciously, I hope—at least appearing so much so, that *I*, it is, who must be considered to have lost," he rejoined, laughingly.

"Let us divide, then, the loss."

"Very well, and *unite* in paying the losses up," he replied, again laughing at the quickness of his conceit.

"Ah, sir," said she, smiling, and enjoying his little quirk as much as himself, "I see you still retain your capacity of subtle conversational manœuvring."

"I was only fearful that it was too *plain*. You must allow me another trial at this subtlety of which you speak."

"I shall not promise you. I discover, Mr. Brandon, you have not lost any of your gallant gayety, either. You certainly have not been, as reported, rambling on the frontiers."

"I shall not tell you my story yet, but will reserve it for one of the 'thousand and one' audiences which you have promised me; but in regard to my gayety, I think you are right — that is constitutional; as there have happened some sad events, since we met, well calculated to make me feel anything but gay, whenever I pause to think."

At once recollecting the sad story of Laura Brandon, and of course supposing that his remark referred to that, she replied:

"Yes, I remember Miss Laura Brandon was with us that day; and I will never forget the joy of her face, and the impression it made upon me. I can even now recall, with perfect distinctness, the calm sweetness of her expression, the exquisite beauty of her conversation, and the gentle playfulness of her manners. And strange it is, too, as I never met with her again."

"She was all that you say, with a thousand other nameless virtues, that passed unobserved except to those who knew her."

They had now reached the ladies' entrance to the "Gayoso," and Brandon hesitated for a moment, as if not knowing whether to ask her to the parlor or not, when she asked:

"Will you not walk up to the parlor, Mr. Brandon?"

"With pleasure, Miss, if you have the leisure?"

He accordingly accompanied her there, where the conversation was continued.

"Will you now permit me, Miss Gray, to display the same interest in your life for the last few years, which you evinced in mine, so far as to ask its incidents?"

"Oh, yes; as far, at least, as giving you the head-notes, which are very few, while the details would be endless. You know a man's and a woman's life are very different: one is all leading-points, while the other is all minutiæ — small details. When shall we begin our mutual stories?"

"Immediately, my impatience says; but let me first ask how long your stay will be in the city?"

"Only a few days longer, at this time. I am here with some cousins — a young gentleman and a young girl — on a mere pleasure-trip, more for the purpose of attending the THEATRE, than for any other purpose that I can describe; and after some little further enjoyment in that direction, we will leave for the country."

"The Theatre! has Mr. Gray relaxed in his Methodism to that extent?"

"No; I cannot say that he has very greatly relaxed; but does not positively object, as he knows that I generally find some means of getting my way. I tell him, too, that I will probably adopt his views of such things, when I get to be a *full* Methodist."

"You have never then risen to the austere dignity of a 'full fellowship' — only a protracted case of probation — at liberty to fall whenever occasion may call for it?"

"A pretty fair description; and did you not exact a half

promise of me, as we parted at Gregory's Spring, to become 'a church woman,' as you expressed it — do you remember?"

. "Yes, very well," said he, smiling; "but then I did not think you would observe it so well. I feel quite complimented."

"Oh! I shall not acknowledge that it was to compliment you; but it is really so, that I have never progressed with my Methodism from that day, and I have sometimes, indeed, blamed you *for* it. You see now, I probably have thought of you and your mischievous expressions and conversation, when you had all forgotten your half-proselyted Episcopalian."

"No, no; I have never forgotten you; but our paths diverged so widely, that I had not the opportunity to cultivate the good seed I had sown. There are few young persons I have thought of so often, and so pleasantly."

"You will at least give me credit for keeping my promise more nighly than you did yours. Do you remember that you promised to come over to our 'meeting-house,' as you called our church, and had me looking for you with the greatest anxiety, only to be disappointed?"

"Yes, I will give you the credit you ask; and as to my promise, it only has a heavily accumulated interest, all of which, it now occurs to me, I will pay to the uttermost demand, before the moons of another year shall come and go. What says Miss Gray to taking that promise?"

"Ah! so far from refusing, I shall even make the demand that you *do* most honestly comply — particularly as I have a very handsome young lady-cousin going home with me to spend the summer; and I promise that your visits will not only be received in payment of the old demand, but with great pleasure by us both on new account. I must make you acquainted with her."

"I am obliged to you; and shall not only take great

pleasure in visiting *both* the cousins in Alabama, but if they permit me, will take an interest in their amusements here — what says *this* cousin to that?"

"I shall not refuse that either, Mr. Brandon; if from no other feeling than that of vanity. The attentions of an Alabamian, so distinguished in appearance, and so distinguished, too, for his aristocratic eccentricity, are not to be slighted." Paying him these compliments half jokingly, she continued: "And I am more than half disposed to go further, and even *claim* you for the time I remain here, as a matter of *State* pride."

With a dashing, bantering sort of gallantry, Brandon gayly replied:

"You may extend your demand, Miss Gray, to your stay in *any* State."

With an affected coquetry, she replied:

"I am obliged to you, Mr. Brandon; but think I can only consent to the acceptance of a part of your generous offer, and confine the pleasure to my stay in this city."

"Ah! perhaps I am to understand your qualified acceptance, as a rejection of my kind and entire proposition."

"Oh, no; by no means. I assure you, only a desire of giving you room to go no further than you wish. No, sir; I cannot release you," she answered, with a merry laugh.

"That is a very satisfactory solution. I then may extend my own terms, even to attending you back to Alabama?"

"All badinage aside, that would be very delightful, if for nothing else, than in the idea of restoring the prodigal son to his mother and friends."

"Prodigal son! indeed; can't I force you to some other acknowledgment?"

"No, not just now; I may at some future day."

The first *gong* now rang, and Brandon rose to let her leave the parlor; but asking if he might have the pleasure

27 *

of meeting her there again, for the purpose of attending her to the dining-room.

"With pleasure, sir," she replied; and withdrew to make preparations for dinner.

. . . .

At this late day it will not be required of me to give further details of the intercourse between Henry Brandon and Miss Gray; suffice it, that they were married in the following spring. Her father gave them a plantation, almost centrally situated between Brandon's own old home, (where Hunter now resided,) himself, and Dr. Wilton, and surrounded by many other very excellent neighbors and gentlemen.

Brandon devoted himself to planting, which he prosecuted with great success for many years, living in great elegance, and dispensing a most generous hospitality. Between his plantation, books, and friends, his life was passing along in perfect smoothness, until the question of secession was raised, which he plainly saw was to result in the defeat of every point which it was intended to protect; and then for the first time entered the political arena, as candidate for the State Convention, which was to decide this question. He bitterly opposed it; but was unable to stem the current which now strongly set in, from the affirmative side.

Hunter had continued to reside on his plantation, and at the time of secession was very wealthy. He always continued to be a close student, and took much interest in public affairs, and had been repeatedly elected to the Legislature, either as representative or senator. He, also, had most earnestly opposed secession; but, unlike Brandon, he never became reconciled to the measure — while the former immediately entered the army, and remained in it until after the battle of Gettysburg.

Mr. Campbell had become one of the leading men of the

State. Though not a brilliant man, he had yet risen to a very fine position, both as a lawyer and politician; and had thoroughly identified himself with the measure of secession, and went immediately into the army on the first call for troops.

When the State of Alabama seceded, she was in the very highest condition of agricultural prosperity; her people were happy and contented; her homes gave every indication of elegance, abundance, and order; her labor was ample, well organized, well provided and cared for, and peaceful, and satisfied.

Let the contrast explain the nature of secession, while it presents the true character of Republican government.

PART II.

CHAPTER I.

"To be, or not to be? that is the question:
Whether 't is nobler in the mind, to suffer
The slings and arrows of outrageous fortune,
Or to take arms against a sea of troubles."

THE author need not be told that he violates all the established rules of author-craft, in allowing nearly — years to elapse between the beginning and end of the story, which he has promised to relate. He is perfectly aware that his work is not *secundum artem*, that is, according to the laws of the CRITICS, yet he has no fears, deprecating no censure, nor courting any favor — growing bolder even as he goes.

"Bravo!" quoth the critics; "now, boaster, let's have fewer words and more performance toward this defiant violation of our power and laws — let's see thee try the strength of the bulwarks and battlements that protect the sacred art of book-writing."

"And bravo for thee!" quoths the author; "and now that our blades are drawn, and the scabbards thrown away, there's nothing to do but come to time, and at it. Let the strong help themselves, and God help the weak."

Then go forth, my book, neither fearing, nor caring.

A novel! — and what's a novel? but the ideal representation of human life, as the author believes it to have been, or to be. The type of some one human life or more, and nothing but a prurient itching for small details would demand a consecutive narrative, where there is nothing to relate. Therefore, good reader, it is my design to leap over

320

all intermediate events in the lives of our old friends, in Part First of our story, and come at once to the concluding scenes.

. . . .

The present fallen condition of the South, from its once proud eminence, so far from being a source of shame to her people, is her highest title to immortal fame; and clothing itself in all the noblest adornments of chivalry, she scornfully rebukes the truculence of the conqueror, even in her powerless but fearless sorrow.

In her lineage, her character, her intellect, her institutions, and her wealth, she stood boldly before the world, the bright cynosure of its envious gaze; and from it never fell, till her shield was pierced by a shaft from every nation of the earth, and now lies like a " warrior taking his rest," shrouded with a spear from every armory of the world.

Her grand old life in the past, the phases which foreshadowed her overthrow, her subsequent chivalry, vicissitude, and misfortune, are all the property of the historian, and not of the novelist, and are already traced by the styles of time on the illuminated pages of eternity; while the mingling light of a dazzling glory, and a tenderer grief will ever be brightly reflected from the jewelled diadem which her gallantry has placed upon her brow.

The intervening years between that period at which we left off our story, and that at which we see proper to resume it, were passed by our former acquaintances, much after the usual fashion of Southern life, making such allowances for the accidents of human existence, as may be supposed to occur in that length of time.

Great prosperity, and perfect peace in its social, domestic, and political history, marked their course, and yet there were causes at work which, though they did not appear on the surface, were destined to destroy all of this at no distant period. A pseudo-moral party, marching under the colors of emancipation, bearing along every symbol of earnest philauthropy before it, with a frenzy only equalled by the early crusades — came to the *rescue !* of the African slave, from the *cruel grasp* of him, who alone had civilized him. Organizing under the constructions and influence of that fanatical, fatal, but senseless sciolism of an " irrepressible conflict," in American organization and interests; and pretending at the same time, to be the only true representative of Northern sentiment and feeling — it gradually acquired the position of holding the balance of power between the two leading national parties in the Northern States, and subsequently controlled them both.

This party was, of course, of an exclusive Northern paternity. But while this was going on at the Northern end of the Republic, there existed another party at the Southern end, rather more compact, but with none of the insignia of fanaticism to commend it to the ignorant multitude, and consequently had grown but slowly.

This latter party stood boldly against all assumed powers, or affirmative authority of any kind, on the part of the General Government, and boasted of having in its ranks many of the greatest intellects of the South. The Northern party were the followers of Hamilton, and represented the centripetal forces of the Government, while the Southern, were the advocates of Mr. Jefferson's doctrines, and represented the centrifugal forces of the States, and arrogated a representation of Southern feeling and opinion; and though it had for many years stood almost still in its growth, was suddenly stimulated to full size by the fall of the Whig party, under Mr. Clay, and now indeed did embrace all of a large majority of the Southern people within its influence and control.

In this manner the two old national parties — Whig and Democrat — became absorbed by the two sectional ones that had grown up, and which, for the first time, fairly met in the Presidential canvass of eighteen hundred and sixty.

The Northern, led by Lincoln, bore inscribed on its banners every wild, fanatical measure which had ever been hinted at, with a view to enlisting the sympathies of the vast and ignorant hordes of the North in the intended crusade upon the South.

The Southern, led by Breckinridge, came to the contest, not only armed with every doctrine of the "State Rights" party, but with the very fire of hell burning in their bosoms for the *wrongs* which the Northern people had, for a few years, endeavored to inflict upon them.

Probably it is but fair to say that the leaders of each lashed their followers into the highest possible rage, by every possible extravagance of representation as to the fiendish purposes of the other. They met in the canvass of 1860, and Mr. Lincoln carried the election overwhelmingly. By this result the South now plainly saw her immense inferiority of numbers, and should have been cautioned as to her course; but she was not, and went on even more defiantly to that fatal climax of modern error, SECESSION.

Against this course, the united *conservative* voice of the South protested, with all the earnestness it *dared* to exhibit in the face of the maddened multitude, even until hushed by the roar of the cannon, and the carnage of the battlefield, and is not responsible for the ruin of her people and the devastation of her homes.

CHAPTER II.

"With grave
Aspect he rose, and in his rising seemed
A pillar of State."

SO soon as it was definitely ascertained that Lincoln was elected, Governor Moore, in accordance with the previous legislation, looking to the success of the *Black-Repub-*

lican party, called a Convention of the State, to consider the necessity of withdrawing from the Union.

Colonel Haywood was still a citizen of the State, and having long held a prominent position in its public affairs, and having been a leading spirit in the advocacy of the right of a State to secede, had been nominated as one of the candidates for the Convention, and was borne into it most triumphantly, on the swollen current that flowed in that direction.

Henry Brandon, who for several years had been leading the life of a wealthy planter, resolved on canvassing his county for the same position, as an independent candidate; and though he proclaimed himself opposed to the alternative, or remedy of secession, was elected by a most flattering majority — attributable, however, to his personal popularity, and not to the popularity of his opinions.

The appointed time for the assembling of the Convention had come, and a full membership was present. In addition to these, a large, wealthy, and fashionable company, composed of both sexes, had met at the capital, with a view to enjoying the gayety and spirit of the extraordinary occasion. Madness, confidence, and a reckless hilarity ruled the hour, and reigned paramount in all ranks of society, particularly among those who were of the original State-Rights school, looking upon themselves as movers in the *great cause* of Southern rights.

There was, nevertheless, a large number of members, who were bitterly opposed to Secession, yet seemed to have no power over the current that was sweeping against them, and said but little. Had they, or could they have made more effort, the State would never have perpetrated that stupendous folly.

The talent of the Secession party was fully represented, that of the Conservative, not so much so, as many of the best men of the State had felt disinclined to exposing themselves to popular opprobrium, and had refused to be candidates. Indeed, it required nothing but the highest order of moral courage to oppose the maddened course of Southern feeling.

Several days after the Convention met, Colonel Haywood introduced a set of resolutions bearing upon the occasion, requesting that they be brought up the next day on a second reading.

It was, of course, expected that he would support them in an elaborated speech. At the appointed hour on the succeeding day, every lobby of the chamber, and all the galleries were filled to overflowing. Up to this time there had been some difficulty found in getting the proposition of Secession through, on anything like a *unanimous* vote, and the resolutions of Colonel Haywood were framed with a view to meeting this hesitation: his speech was consequently looked forward to, with deep interest.

Rising and calling up his resolutions, with an air of confidence and authority denoting the *acknowledged leader*, it was not long before he was at the full height of his argument, his mind working with the speed and power of an electric battery. In both personal and moral courage, there was nothing mortal to surpass him. He feared nothing, and courted any responsibility, and yet was wanting in many of those minor qualities, so essential to successful oratory, which flow from kind and gentle emotions. He was by nature a revolutionary agitator and leader, but not a conspirator, nor possessed of the insinuating eloquence of a conspirator, and nature had endowed him with all necessary qualities, by setting no bounds to his ambition, or limits to his daring. The meeting of this Convention was the culminating period of his life, and his addressing it on this occasion, the culminating hour of that period. His mind flashed, flamed, and corruscated in all the jewelled affluence which the occasion, to him, presented. Those

28

who thought with him became even more confirmed, while the doubtful came over, and the obstinate trembled. The final vote on his resolutions, some two or three days subsequently, was the proudest achievement of his life, which soon died away to sorrow and to darkness, never to rekindle again its noble fire.

It had been the expectation of his friends that he would be the ruling spirit of the great movement, but for some over-cautious reason, *another* was selected to direct its destinies.

It is not too late or too soon, to hazard the opinion of his more superior excellence for the position, and had he been selected to *drive* the fortunes of the South along, on the thundering, crashing track of *revolution*, as it really was, instead of the more cautious but equally tenacious Davis, to *lead* them in the open ways of an acknowledged constitutional government, the END would at least have been different. His address upon this occasion was truthful in its assertions, chivalric in its tone, and picturesque in its representations, yet it was an exaggerated drawing of our past wrongs and future destiny, and, certainly, a very great error in statesmanship. It was bold and masterly in its spirit and execution, adroit, plausible, and inflammatory in construction and arrangement, and exactly suited to hurry the Convention on to the point which he so much desired. When Colonel Haywood concluded, the Convention adjourned; Mr. Brandon having previously signified that he would reply to him on the following day.

Again the capitol was crowded with an audience, who were anxious to hear an argument against the course which now appeared to be inevitable, and from a man, too, almost entirely unknown to the political coteries of the State.

He rose as calmly as if only before an audience of children, and proceeded in a cool and methodical manner to a scathing rebuke of the course which the Convention was on the verge of adopting, of the prejudices and fallacies of

Colonel Haywood, and of the illegitimacy and fearful consequences of Secession.

He was listened to with the profoundest attention, and
his points evidently had the most serious influence; so much
so, that it was thought proper to defer any final action for
several days.

These were the two leading efforts before the Convention:
the remainder were pieces of patchwork and lobbying, and
through the machinery of the latter the question was finally
carried by a small majority.

The proposition was then made, to make the vote unanimous; to which nearly all of the delegates consented.
Brandon refused, saying that it was but a mere fiction, therefore too ridiculous for consideration; that it was nothing
short of *revolution*, let what would be said about its consti-
tutionality, and while he opposed it, both in principle and
in practice, he yet would go as far as he that dared go
farthest: that his opposition was not a desertion of, however he might differ with his people.

CHAPTER III.

"Ay, I knew her well;
She was my friend in early youth."

THOUGH there were numbers of both members of the
Convention and citizens, who felt all the inherent
gloom of the condition, yet, as a general thing, a joy and
a glow of chivalric excitement rested on the bosom of
society, which well expressed the gayety and the daring
of Southern character.

On the day that the ordinance of Secession was finally
passed, there were but few men bearing a respectable rela-

tion to society, who would have dared to express disapprobation of the measure. *Treason* was too good a name for opposition, and would have been treated as such by the first man who heard it uttered.

Expressive of this feeling, a *ball* was given on the night of the adjournment of the Convention, by the military companies of the city, to which the members were particularly invited, and perhaps there has never been a finer display of Southern intelligence, chivalry, beauty, and abandon, than was represented there that night. There was, too, everything in the surroundings to entrance the senses, and to lead the hesitating out into the deep current of popular feeling and hilarity. Altogether, the occasion was a carnival scene of gallantry, wit, wealth, beauty, and joyousness, which it will ever be difficult to excel, and certainly not likely to be even equalled under the present coarse, vulgar, and tyrannical governmental regime.

The prevailing feeling appeared to be that of escaping from further association with a people, who for years had respected neither the laws of amenity, decency, or humanity, in their relations to them ; and that, henceforth, they were to be a people to themselves ; homogeneous in blood, feeling, sentiment, interests, and pursuits.

Happy ! but fatal delusion ! Could that gay assemblage of men and women have sufficiently penetrated the future to see the terrible calamities of a four-years' civil war, and the miserable degradations to which the conqueror would subject them at its close, a chill feeling would have crept through their warm veins, and warned them to an adjournment of these mocking festivities.

Brandon was present; for while he had opposed the measure which these festivities were in honor of, with all the earnestness and eloquence of a mind that clearly foresaw the disastrous failure which must inevitably follow it, he yet did not see proper to divide off from his people, nor was he even disposed to lose the pleasure of so gay an hour, for a mere difference of opinion, and therefore entered, with his natural zest of such enjoyments, into the reckless but elegant hilarity of the evening.

The splendid military band had already played several of its spirited pieces, among others, two that afterward became so famously *national* in the South — "Dixie" and the "Bonnie Blue Flag" — and sets were now forming for the dance.

It would be unjust to say that this music had not imparted to Brandon's feelings all the glow which it was calculated to inspire, and did inspire in others; and as he stood off rather to himself, enjoying its combined sweetness, its wildaway grandeur, and the gay scenes before him, his eye fell upon his old college friend, Randolph Ray, who had just entered the hall, with Mrs. Ray upon his arm.

Mr. Ray had been, for more than three years, a United States Senator from Alabama, but being a prominent advocate of secession, he had remained at home during this winter, for the purpose of urging the adoption of that course, and had been present during the session of the Convention, with a view to assisting in placing the question beyond uncertainty. Working with his whole energy, and using his entire influence, he now felt all the gratification of success.

Brandon had met with him repeatedly during the time the Convention had been in session, for the first time, however, since they had separated at college; having renewed their old intimacy, they had had many arguments in regard to the course which it was proposed that the State should adopt, neither, however, had been able to influence the other, but had always ended their debates in the friendliest spirit. Brandon had very often been in company with Mrs. Ray. whom he found to be quite as formidable an adversary to *his* views as her husband was, possessing, as she

28 *

did, a very high order of intellect, and a clear understanding of political affairs; with a face distinguished for the softness of its beauty, and manners of the most fascinating character, she had even superior advantages for playing the rôle of Madame de Staël.   He had never met with her, however, outside of the small quasi-political circles that always revolve around such places, nor had he yet called upon her, as he had several times intended to do, and had been really desirous of doing, on account of his own wife, who had been an early friend of Mrs. Ray, but of which fact the latter was ignorant.

Standing, as we have said, rather to himself, as he saw them enter the room, Brandon immediately approached them.   The pleasure of meeting was mutual, and very soon an animated conversation was going on between them; in the course of which Ray remarked, that he was pleasantly surprised to see him present at the Secession festival.

"Ah, my good fellow," replied Brandon, "you measure my grain by your meal-tub.   I never allow my political opinions to invade my social pleasures — and to give an instance of my sincerity, have come to ask Mrs. Ray to be my partner in the dance."   Then turning to her, he said, "Madam, these beautiful airs, and the gayety of the scenes about me, if not the occasion, have re-inspired me with the passion of my young days.   Will you confer this desired pleasure?"

"I must accept your invitation, Mr. Brandon, both as a pleasure and as a distinguished compliment; but, sir, you must look upon the acceptance, as I do upon the invitation, after I tell you that, something at the suggestion of age, but more," she added, smilingly, "at the suggestion of Mr. Ray, I have declined to dance upon any occasion during the whole winter."

"I revoke, Henrietta, both the suggestion of age and my

own, and even command you to dance with my once very gay, but now very solemn friend," replied Mr. Ray to his wife.

"I am obliged to you, Ray, for your opportune revocals, and also for your grim comments upon myself." Then turning to Mrs. Ray, said, "But I claim, madam, the benefit of both."

They then walked out on the floor, and in a few moments more they were floating on the full tide of music, to the light measures of the fantastic art.

While dancing, Brandon said to her, that he had not advanced any *particular* claim to her hand, as his partner, but that he really had both, a particular and a double one. "One of which is, that you are the wife of my old college friend ; and the other is — one of which you are not aware — but in virtue of one and the other, I shall in future claim more intimate terms of acquaintance."

"But, Mr. Brandon, let me assure you that a very important one, and only personal to yourself, has not been considered — is there still another ?"

"There is, madam."

"Pray, tell it to me. I already grow impatient to be informed."

"Yes ; well, I shall have to begin the story with all the romantic circumlocution of a novel, as the facts and the characters possess a rare fragrance of sentimentality and interest."

"Ah, well, sir, to the story."

"I would, but we have to dance."

"Very well."

Having again returned to their places, she again asked for the story.

"Now, Mr. Brandon, begin."

"I suppose I must, though it appears to grow in length and difficulty as I approach it."

"Let me insist that you immediately begin it, Mr. Brandon, after some fashion. Your dallying sentimentality is even more provoking than your primitive politics, excuse me."

"Certainly, but I must indeed be very provoking then, since I see the interest which is taken, of late, by your sex, in 'progressive American' affairs."

"Very good, I will stand the repartee, provided I get you to the story — don't stop," she said, as they again entered the dance, "we can do both ; at least, you can relate, and I can listen."

"Just so, but that is a slight reversal of the course of things : men are the listeners now-a-days, and women the talkers."

"Somewhat as you say, but we will discuss that point at another time — the story now."

"As you say ; then in the spring of 18—, but no matter when, suffice it, that on a winter's day, not a century since, I had the good fortune to meet a young girl, with whom I have since passed many blissful years, and who, to-night, is at my country home, with a little brood around her, that doth call her mother. This earthly angel of my heart hath often told me, in our long winter-evening talks, of the friends and pleasures of her joyous youth, and often hath she dwelt, with a brightened eye, and a pleasing memory, on the name of one, who since then hath soared so high as to have forgot, mayhap, a friend, whose wing hath been never spread, nor glittered in the bright skies of popular applause. The name was indeed a pretty one, and if I remember right, 't was HENRIETTA TERRENCE."

"Mr. Brandon," she exclaimed, stepping slightly back and clasping her hands in expectation, "do tell me the maiden name of Mrs. Brandon !"

"Mary Gray."

"Mary Gray ? Mary Gray !"

" Ay, Mary Gray."

" Oh, sir, she was the bosom friend of my school-girl days; and you certainly have even more than a double claim upon me. And Mary Gray is Mrs. Brandon ? How is she, and where is she ? "

"She is well, or was a few days since, and as I told you, at our country home to-night, with a happy little brood of children at her feet. How do you like the beginning of my story ? "

" Oh, most handsomely told; and I am satisfied, too, that what Mr. Ray has very often said, since meeting you here, is even more than true, since I know that Mary Gray would never have chosen a husband from the common herd, or one that she did not know could not only reflect honor on himself, but upon her too."

" Indeed ! What flattering tale hath Ray indulged his fancy in, respecting one so unpretending as I have been ? "

" Why, just as you say, unpretending and unaspiring, you had never done yourself justice, nor been done justice to, else you would long since have been in public life."

" I am obliged to him, indeed, for his flattering opinion; and perhaps 't is both — perhaps neither. I have no taste for public life, nor any appreciation of public honors ; and outside of what I considered a *private duty*, I should never have come to this Convention. You must not think that what I am going to say has any personal reference or application, but I really have a cool contempt for *any* office which the American people can bestow — take the least possible inter-est in *party* questions — seldom attend an election ; and when I see the very exceptional means resorted to for the purpose of obtaining positions, and the style of men who almost universally secure them, my contempt amounts to a loathing, both of the offices and the officers. The only wonder is that this evil day has not come upon us before. Political life, by degrees, has assumed all the mean stringency of a low order of Free-Masonry, by which all petty aspirants are enabled to secure public positions in their turn, and by some sort of black-balling system, to exclude all men of a better style of mind than themselves."

"I presume there is much truth in what you say; and I very often hear Mr. Ray speak of the disgusting means necessary to success. But, then, men of intellect should never abandon the field, else why was intellect given? and what would soon become of society, if inferior men are permitted to control it?"

"Yes, that is the correct position; but *disgust* is a very strong feeling or sentiment, and very often paralyzes effort. But we have to dance again."

They soon returned to their places, when Mrs. Ray resumed by saying:

"Well, let me insist, for Mary Gray's sake, at least, that for the future you do not allow such feelings to influence you; and now that you have begun, never permit yourself to tire, while you *feel* that you are right. Now, sir, how pleasant it would have been to us both, for Mary to have been in Washington with me! It would have been our old 'PATAPSCO' life over again — perpetual youth. You have let your old comrade in letters lead you, in conferring honors on his wife, at least."

She said this with a playful badinage, which induced Brandon to reply:

"Ah! Ray has just got his *grist* in first, and I fear, from present appearances, the good fellow will get it ground out sooner than he expects it."

"Come, Mr. Brandon, I see your allusion, but shall not talk politics with you. You have yourself suggested a more pleasing subject — your wife, and my friend."

The dance was now ended, and Brandon led her to a seat, taking one by her side. They were enjoying a familiar and social talk, when Ray came up, with Mrs. Sheldon on his arm, with whom *he* had also been dancing.

Mrs. Sheldon was the wife of a member of Congress from Alabama, and was held to be one of the most attractive females who visited the great American Capital. Brandon had known her for several years, but had not met her during the evening, before this. The meeting was very agreeable to them both, and they were not long in getting into a pleasant conversation.

"Brandon," said Mr. Ray, "I saw by the way in which Henrietta and yourself began the evening, that it was to be a sort of an epitomized mutual-admiration society. I therefore set immediately out in search of some one to supply her place; and you see what success I met with. For the first time in five years I went through all the giddy mazes of a dance with Mrs. Sheldon, who took pity on my forlorn appearance, and has, moreover, promised to patronize me for the entire evening, if the engagement between yourself and Henrietta is to last so long."

"Yes, Mr. Ray, but only with the consent of Mrs. Ray," said Mrs. Sheldon, pleasantly.

"Certainly, Mrs. Sheldon, I very cheerfully resign all claim to the gay young gentleman for the evening, as I have a double labor of love and duty to perform in the case of Mr. Brandon, the first, in requiring him to tell me about his wife, who is an old friend of mine, and next, in having him explain to me why he is so far in the rear of the present excitement, Southern opinion, and feeling, rather."

Mrs. Sheldon now joining more familiarly in the conversation, remarked, in support of the last remark of Mrs. Ray:

"Yes, Mr. Brandon, we all hold you amenable to the charge of pure perverseness, as the clear and brilliant effort you made in the Convention certainly forbids us bringing any other."

"Were my years less advanced, ladies, my gallantry would persuade me to yield to this pleasing pressure, but as age is but a synonym for obstinacy and obduracy, I find myself compelled to remain in my present position."

"Intellect," replied Mrs. Ray, "is not individual property, but public, and the world has a right to command its services; and we, as part of the world, inform you that we cannot do without yours — what does Mary say to you in regard to this matter?"

"Oh, she pretends to be quite out of patience, and quite as ready as any of her sex, to fire the Ephesian dome, if she could only imagine Greeley, or Seward, or Lincoln, on the top of it."

"I am satisfied she is with us, if her spirit has not lost its youthful ring, and I am only astonished that she has not controlled you more than she has."

"Yes, I have rather taunted some of my friends, with being directed by their *wives* in this matter: it looks very like female work."

"Ah, you do your own sex injustice, Mr. Brandon," said Mrs. Sheldon; "as up to the time of this Mr. Lincoln's election, my husband was seriously opposed to the then proposed measure of redress, and would not even discuss it with any one, looking upon it as a pure political heresy, and would not believe that the Northern people were so lost to all sense of justice as to elect a man holding such opinions. But his success has led him to believe that the North must design crushing us, and that secession is a matter of necessity, not a political consideration, nor one of state-craft, and I think the inference correct, from the fact, that Mr. Lincoln has never been associated with either of the great national parties of the country as a leader, nor with anything except that of 'Abolition.' Entirely without education, and without reputation beyond that of a common jester, he must have been selected to carry out this terrible purpose alone. Nor is it singular that such a man should have been selected for this work, as it is oftener so than otherwise, that coarse jesters conceal the most brutal character."

"In behalf of the State, I thank you, Mrs. Sheldon. It needs Mr. Brandon's services, and must have them," said Mr. Ray.

"Come, Ray, it is I that require help, and not these ladies, and I protest against your assisting them. • Moreover, I have already offered such service, as this thing you call 'peaceable secession' will certainly render it necessary — but, Mrs. Sheldon, will you allow me to."

Before he could conclude his remarks, the band had filled the hall with the deep voluptuous swell of one of its finest pieces, and next proceeded by request to repeat that strange wild air, half-martial, and half-plaintive, "Dixie;" which by some means had already become famous as a sort of Southern slogan, and possessing, as it did, the peculiar power of rousing passion, sentiment, and that feeling of romantic resentment, which an oppressed people might be supposed to entertain, had its full share of responsibility. for the excitement of the day.

The entire company, as if by one consent, hushed their voices into attentive silence, as the band flung out its rapturous notes.

CHAPTER IV.

"We must be free or die, who speak the tongue
That Shakespeare spake."

BRANDON was the first to break the silence when the music hushed, and said to Mrs. Ray, with a laugh, that the band ought to be prosecuted for encouraging

29

seditious impulses, and being accessory to treason. "Just such music as that encourages you all to assume the position of great sufferers, and willing martyrs."

"Why, Brandon," said Ray, "I fear you are becoming really barbaric in your tastes. You speak of that beautifully wild and tender air with the coldness of one who has no generous emotions."

"Yes," said Mrs. Sheldon; "and affects to be unmoved; but I think the very fact of his attempted disparagement shows that he felt its influence."

"Oh! you mistake, madam; I do profess to be very greatly influenced. I believe all Southern people to be more sensible to the influence of music than others. Indeed, that 'language of the soul' only reaches perfection in Southern lands, and therefore has a greater influence there than elsewhere. The only sweet-singing birds belong to the tropics; the sweetest human voices are all but universally from Southern countries, and we may remark too, that there is far more softness in the *natural* sounds of Southern climes. The soft whispers of the Southern breeze are proverbially acknowledged, and the murmer of the sea on the Southern coasts is well known for its sighing beauty; and yet, Southern latitudes are as peculiar for the grandeur of their thunder-storms, and, pardon me, for the *temper* of its people, too."

"You are correct, Brandon," replied Mr. Ray. "Northern latitudes furnish but little to the romantic, the sentimental, or the musical world— indeed, furnish but little to life in any way, but its rudenesses, its prejudices, and its endurances —and wrapping their people in some sort of wild fanaticism, they themselves mistake it for spirituality, stern virtue, and great moral courage."

"You must allow me to agree with you also, Mr. Brandon," said Mrs. Sheldon; "but then, I am a little astonished at your endorsement of anything Southern, to the prejudice of either Northern people or countries."

"It is not the first time, madam, that I have been misunderstood, nor will it be the last, I imagine," replied Brandon, a little sharply, and added — "my opinions are exactly the reverse; and that, in regard to secession, does not refer to the people, nor the country, from which this State has now withdrawn as a political integer. I view the movement from an entirely different stand-point, and look upon it as an effort to establish a sort of political isotherm, and not as a social movement; and as such, a violation of all the natural laws of governmental science; and should look upon it in the same light, even if the Northern people were ten times more disagreeable than they are, and their country lay around the North Pole itself. I know too, that the Southern people are the very least fitted to become revolutionists: their social organization, their imperial and chivalric notions, unfit them for the rude scenes of protracted civil war; they naturally love all the pomp and circumstance of strong, well-organized government. This secessional movement cannot, therefore, be viewed too sorrowfully — as fatal to their prosperity, their happiness, their distinctiveness, and their individuality."

The music and the occasion had by this time suffused every face with an incandescence of ecstasy and delight, and every heart seemed to yearn for the clash of arms.

The "CAUSE" appeared forgotten in the prospect of a display of Southern chivalry. Young girls now promised to buckle on the swords and spears of their young lovers; and young lovers sealed their vows of truth and faith with the promise of honor or death. This feeling was all aglow when the master of ceremonies called out "get your partners." And there gallantly walked out on the floor those with bright and happy faces and brave hearts, basking in the geniality of the hour, and the sweet and blushing approval of their lady-loves, who never came to claim the guerdon of their love and chivalry ; but, before the summer had come and gone, lay stiff and stark in the cold embraces of the battle-field.

Brandon now asked Mrs. Ray and Mrs. Sheldon, if they had any engagements for the set.

"No ; we have not," replied both of the ladies at once ; "and I," added Mrs. Ray, "as I have said to you, dance but seldom, and only did so to-night in special compliment to Mr. Brandon."

"I am yours to command, madam," he replied with a smile ; "and Mr. Brandon is obliged to Mrs. Ray for so distinguished a mark of favor, and will remember it as such."

"And I," said Mrs. Sheldon, "only danced in compliment to Mr. Ray."

"There, Brandon," said Mr. Ray, "only contemplate the great obligation we are under — such a weight could not be easily borne, were not the *substance* so *spiritual.*"

"And the spirituality so substantial in its own support," replied Mrs. Sheldon, who was growing a little *embonpoint.* "But, Mr. Ray, you are appearing in a new character — long as I have known you, I do not recollect to have seen you aspire to the giddy height of so gallant a speech."

"Ah, you have only known him, madam," said Brandon, "since he has been in that arena which calls for stratagem, treason, and spoils ; had you known him, as I have, in the days of his youth and innocence, you would have heard many such, and better."

"Tell me, Brandon," replied Ray, interrupting him, "how it is that I find you and myself to have so completely changed positions. At college you were always on the top-wave of excitement, while I was out in some quiet eddy ; now, I am riding on the dashing, foaming billow, and you have floated off into the still waters. Why is it ? "

"Simply for the reason that I soonest exhausted that

element which to a greater or less extent enters into every man's character — a certain sort of sympathy with anything novel, exciting, and adventurous — corrected in some persons by age, modified in others by experience, and yet in others again, runs riot to the very *funeral.*

"Then," said Mrs. Ray, smiling, "you think my husband, and they who agree with him, as but just entering upon the actual experience of life, and the present movement but an evidence of the want of it."

"Expressed most admirably, *madame.* I am most truly indebted to you for the happy question, giving, as you did, its very best answer."

"Well, Brandon, you know the wherefores of our action, and it is not worth while to repeat them. But if we had no other cause for our course, that infamous affair of old BROWN at Harper's Ferry would justify us, endorsed, as it was, by the party now in power. While I well know the dangers that threaten us in the undertaking, I yet had rather suffer in the attempt to quit such a Union, than to be degraded in it; I prefer an honorable death to a despicable life, or a cowardly peace. If we can only secure peace at the price of our honor, better to be exterminated — and the sooner the better. We can make a proud history, if we cannot secure our rights."

"Yes; that is all very commendable, but you must remember that all of us have n't the same amount of *nerve,* wherewith to meet this *exterminating* process," said Brandon, laughing.

"Ah, secession will furnish you that gratis," replied Ray, laughing in return.

"But seriously, Ray, those are all very noble sentiments, and are such as all men should cherish. You must remember, however, that the laws which rule in state-craft, are quite different from those that rule in private life. The dusty old adages of 'Honesty being the best policy,'

' Cheating never thrives,' and so forth, scarcely hold good, even in private life, and must not be interpreted *too literally* in public affairs."

"You don't pretend to say that political science is a system of dishonesty, do you, Brandon?"

"I will not use your words, but I am almost willing to use your meaning. *Nature* is only truly honest. Society is a modification of nature, and what we call law. Civil law is the offspring of society, and made by those who are *interested* in the subject. Ergo, ex parte — ergo, selfish — ergo, not very honest."

"You are radical — agrarian, Brandon."

"No; far from it. Not so much as you are. I am even an extremer advocate for society, but am willing to admit its real character, and as it is expected to be when *men* undertake to control the laws of nature, and have carried that deviation into a *system*. The exception is then made the rule, and the rule *necessarily* dishonest. Society is an invention of intellect and capital, and wars upon natural justice, and the higher society advances, the more corrupt its agencies become."

"I can't argue against such positions as you advance, Brandon."

"No, I suppose not. You wish me to admit the rights of natural *law*, under the sanctions of *society*. But let us look on, and discuss these matters some other time."

CHAPTER V.

" Prithee, friend,
Canst tell me who that lady is?"

EVERY possible place in the room was now filled with sets of dancers. The old mingled with the young, and all seemed equally borne upon the gladsome and sparkling current of the hour; while young hearts glanced with love and joy, old hearts caught the infection, and were living over again the roseate hours of youth.

Mr. Ray had been called off by some gentlemen, and had left Brandon in company with the two ladies.

In the set dancing nearest to them, was a couple whose remarkable appearance and youthfulness — the young girl for her beauty, and the youth for his gallant bearing and handsome face — attracted the attention of Mrs. Ray, who almost in a tone of exclamation asked Brandon who they could possibly be.

" The young girl," replied Brandon, " is a niece of mine, Alice Hunter, about fifteen, and the youth is a second cousin of hers, McKenzie Campbell, and only a few months older. The girl is indeed beautiful, and as intellectual and spirited as she is beautiful. The youth is quite remarkable, both for his mind and his manliness; both of them are boarding in the city, attending school. He is already prepared to enter college, but his father has not wished to send him from home while so young. He has been a member of one of the military companies for some time, and quite a pet with the members, which is the reason of his being in military dress. He is a son of Colonel Campbell, who, I believe, is one of *your great men.*"

" Certainly, I know Colonel Campbell ; and he *is* a great man, anywhere."

" Yes, perhaps so ; but the girl is a daughter of Thomas Hunter, the State senator from this district, and my sister's husband."

" Ah, I know him very well, and had missed him. Where is he, that he has not been here ? "

" He does not approve this course, and has remained at home, as I tell him, 'sulking;' but he says, '*gloomy.*'"

" I regret to learn that he looks so despondingly to the future. Say to him that I was disappointed in not meeting him."

"I will; but changing the subject, can you tell me who that very handsome girl is, with the long, curling, brown hair, there dancing with that eccentric, but brilliant genius, young Stafford?"

The young girl who had thus attracted his attention was probably not over twenty years old, and her appearance was of that peculiar character which universally fastens the eye of the casual observer, and gives eminence in the social circle, indicating a temperament which at once expresses energy, spirit, gentleness, cheerfulness, and always accompanied by a high order of intellect. She was full height, lithe in her figure, but not delicate, and rounded at every point, with all the perfection of the most exquisite art. Her head and face were models of Nature's own sculpture. Her forehead was high and square, but not *too* high, nor *too* square. Her eyes were deep-brown, lustrous, and soft. Her hair was full, glossy, and a deep, pure auburn, with a complexion that corresponded to these, both in cast, tinge, and richness. At the moment of Brandon's asking this question, she was dancing with Mr. Stafford, a young gentleman of handsome fortune, gay, eccentric, highly educated, and well known in all the fashionable coteries of the State, and, like nearly all young men of that style, had floated off in the current of Secession. He was now present at the capital, as others were, for enjoyment, and was the acknowledged admirer of Margaret Sedley.

"Yes," replied Mrs. Ray, "she is a near relation of Mr. Ray, a Virginian, an orphan, and a girl of some fortune. She has been with us for two years, and came here in company with us. She is highly accomplished, and one of the most brilliant girls I have ever met. I will introduce her to you when the dance is over with. I think you will admire her. She is already a great admirer of yours. Hearing your reply to Colonel Haywood, she was quite carried away with it, and said it was the only speech she ever heard that she really did admire. I think, though, she said that to tease her uncle — as much as to say that she had never admired any of *his*. I take occasion to tell you this, so that you may be prepared to admire her" — making the last remark with a smile — "and to foil any prejudice you may have against her political opinions."

"I appreciate the compliment of her good opinion. She is certainly one of the *handsomest* girls I have seen, and, from her face, must have a high order of intellect. As to her political opinions, they are but the result of the general direction of affairs, for which no one, particularly, is responsible, and but few can resist. In her case, it would be difficult to resist the influence of her distinguished association."

"Thank you."

"I believe, Mr. Brandon," said Mrs. Sheldon, who had, during this time, been conversing with some ladies sitting by her, but had again turned to Brandon and Mrs. Ray, "from what I gathered of your reply to Mrs. Ray, that you think women rather reflect than originate opinions."

"I certainly think as you say, as a *general truth ;* but in this special matter of Secession, leaving out the *exact leaders* of it, I think your sex well up to popular opinion, if not in *advance*. There is an equity about it, which is the base of your opinions; but what is of very nigh as great importance, it has a certain dash of chivalry about it, and defiance, too, with a distant view of the clash of sabres, and the silver bit of the war-horse, as he proudly bears into the fight the plumed cavalier, which captivates the female heart, even while it is the source of the tenderest grief."

"Your compliment is rather an equivocal one, Mr. Brandon."

"I did not design my words to assume the form of compliment, but of a *fact*."

The conversation now took a wider range, in which the right of State secession, the moral, social, and economical features of slavery, the particular and general effects of its destruction upon society, were freely but summarily reviewed; and last, the question of a difference of race between the Northern and Southern people, as evidenced by each of them in their relationship to the different questions of the day.

The dance had again ended, and the dancers were marching round the great hall in a grand promenade.

Brandon, seeing Margaret Sedley approaching them, leaning on the arm of young Stafford, suddenly brought the conversation to a close. Begging pardon of Mrs. Sheldon for his abruptness, he turned to Mrs. Ray, and reminded her of the promised introduction.

CHAPTER VI.

"This is the very coinage of your brain."

WHEN nearly opposite, by a look from Mrs. Ray, Miss Sedley and Mr. Stafford left the promenade, and came to her. Brandon had frequently met with the gay young gentleman, and had some acquaintance with him, and as they met in the presence of Mrs. Ray, spoke very cordially.

"Mr. Stafford," said Mrs. Ray, "I fear Margaret is making a monopoly of your society, this evening, and depriving you of much variety, at least."

"By no means, madam. I rather fear the charge might be brought by her."

"Don't be disturbed on scores so slight, Mr. Stafford, I

am taking matters very calmly; we will at least let honors go easy," replied Miss Sedley.

Mrs. Ray now asked Mr. Brandon to let her introduce him to Miss Sedley, and as she did so, immediately turned to Mr. Stafford, saying: "Come, sir; I have something for your private ear: I will therefore relieve you of Margaret for a few minutes, and accept your company myself for this promenade."

"With a pleasure, madam, which nothing can exceed that I dare to tell."

"Ah! sir, most artistically worded, but accepted."

"Mrs. Sheldon, I leave you in undisputed possession of Mr. Ray."

"Mr. Brandon, will you accept charge of Miss Sedley in trust for Mr. Stafford, to be returned on call, as the merchants say? Now, sir," addressing Mr. Stafford, "allons."

These changes were made so quickly, and so handsomely, and so pleasantly, that all of the parties but herself were bewildered and perfectly in her power, and took their places without further thought.

Mrs. Ray immediately took occasion to say to Mr. Stafford that she had taken quite a liberty with him, "But, sir, I had a good woman's reason for it, which I will explain not to-night, but, as the first act of conciliation, I have taken you myself. Now, sir, are you satisfied?"

"Could I, if I would, madam, refuse to follow any path lighted by the bright genius of Alabama's fairest daughter."

"Indeed! I thank you most truly, and think too, that you should thank me for the change I have made, as it has certainly added even to the usual brilliancy of your fancy; or have you thrown out similar scintillations before the admiring gaze of Margaret?"

"I can't say that I have: the present is rather the more inspiring occasion."

"You improve, Mr. Stafford. Shall I inform Miss Sedley of your brilliant corruscations?"

"Oh! for heaven's sake, no," said he, with a laugh.

"Then, as the condition of my silence, I impose upon you the obligation of keeping up the strain : you have now spoiled me, and I must have more of the same delicate nourishment."

"You should never need it, madam, if my mind could only equal my heart."

"Very handsomely said, Mr. Stafford."

"And were I a *Chaldean*," he again responded, "I should be at a loss to decide which star to worship: the brilliancy of either so dazzles my sight."

"Come, Mr. Stafford, no *sky*-scraping with an old lady, nor will I permit you to take your eye off of the bright particular star, that already attracts your mortal gaze and worship ; and let me, in sober earnest, explain to you why I made these changes: which, in few words, was to *show off* Margaret Sedley to the husband of my old friend Mary Gray — and himself, Mr. Ray says, a man of the first order of mind. Now, sir, I thought you would take as great pleasure in that thing as myself."

The promenade was continued for some time, during which Mrs. Ray, aware of the liberty she had taken, made it a point to entertain young Stafford ; and elaborating all the passing subjects of the evening with the highest conversational art, it is needless to say that she so far succeeded as to give the liberty she had taken all the features of an elegant favor.

In the meanwhile, Brandon had glided into a pleasing conversation with Miss Sedley, when the latter, in reply to a remark of his concerning Mrs. Ray, said :

"Aunt will have her way in such matters, and we have all learned to give way when we discover her intentions."

"There is no apology due to me, Miss Sedley, particularly as she promised me much pleasure in your company."

"Ah, I fear she has contracted too heavily for me; I was satisfied of some design on her part, in regard to me."

"No, no; not more than you will be able to comply with. You have two sureties that you will not fail: one is, that she knew exactly what to promise, and the other is, that I shall only demand the most natural and easy performances; for instance, an occasional smile from your happy face, or a merry glance now and then from your bright young eyes. These will meet the full measure of my demands, but to increase my admiration, you can add whatever else you wish."

"I shall give you, sir, the full benefit of both, and consider that I have made most excellent use of them. But really, Mr. Brandon, I should feel some apprehension before you, after hearing your brilliant reply to Colonel Haywood, if I did not in some sort look upon you as a *family* friend, if not one of my own. Uncle has done but little else than sound your praises for three days past."

"I am more fortunate than I had a right to expect, and in my heart thank Ray for the flattering complaisance; and you must allow me, Miss Sedley, to dispel whatever there is of apprehension in your feelings, by assuring you that while with an old friend of Ray — it is only optional with yourself to say whether or not — you shall be with one of your own," and then with his old gallantry of manner, continued: "I already envy Mr. Stafford his youth and genius, as I should then aspire to be esteemed even more than friend."

"Your gallantry conceals your years, and your genius stands for itself, Mr. Brandon; you therefore have an even start with Mr. Stafford, at these two points, at least."

"You banter me then, young lady, to enter the lists with your admirers?"

"Oh! no," she laughingly replied; "I did not mean so much: for with all my vanity, I cannot expect to be remembered beyond this evening. Not altogether *mal-apropos*, Mr. Brandon — let me tell you that my uncle never passes a day without giving us a chapter of laudation on yourself, and never ceases to be surprised in regard to your course on the question of Secession. At college, he says, you were the wildest, gayest, most reckless, and most *talented* member of your class, or that he ever knew; but that he now finds you quite the reverse of all this, except your talents. In the last particular, he gives you great credit still, and says, you came near defeating the question."

"Yes; I am obliged to him for his good opinion; and he has expressed to me his surprise at the apparent change, and at what he calls my 'caution.' I have replied to him, that my dissent was more than ordinary caution — it was *thought;* and I have expressed the same surprise at him, too. I now find him calmly riding on the wild waves of popular clamor, and I fear will assist in wrecking the fortunes of us all. At college, he was quite as noted for his prudence, as I was for the reverse."

"Yes; I do not think his present course the suggestion of his real character; but, having been in association with the Northern politicians, fathomed their character, and discovered their purposes, he has grown to think it both humiliating and dangerous to remain longer in unison with them; and since that cowardly attempt at massacre by old Brown, he appears to have no control over his temper, and holds the Northern people equally guilty — as they endorsed it."

"He has had no greater apprehension than I have, nor any greater disgust, for the character which the North is developing; for, indeed, they seem to be relapsing to their witch-burning, Blue-law period; and he has doubtless had his temper more disturbed than mine has been: for that very reason I claim to be the calmer judge of the real nature, import, and result of this measure. They could possibly do no more than *provoke* us, while we held the advantage of being in the Union. We could retaliate, and in that instance, we did do it most terribly. There is no people on the earth more vulnerable, from a social, political, and even an intellectual point, than the Northern people, and who defend themselves so poorly. They are not cowardly, but have no lofty, noble sentiments, nor that natural appreciation of chivalry, to know how and where to resent, or when and where to attack. They are not so mean, as small and conceited; they are fanatics, and think themselves Christians; wranglers, and think themselves philosophers; they are muddled in their ratiocinations, and think themselves metaphysical."

"Could anything good ever grow out of such relationships, or such retaliations as you speak of?"

"Yes; causes would in time have worked out their effects in a natural manner—we would have *fallen* apart in less than twenty years. Remedies would have grown out of the very errors that we complain of, and, then, the South would have been in the ascendant. Passion must not take the place of reason. Statesmanship deals with the head, not with the heart; at least, only as the heart is reflected through the head."

"You think, then, that we have had provocation sufficient; but that public policy should have dictated some other course?"

"Yes; secession is the poisoned chalice, which they have long desired us to swallow from. The Northern people know and so do we, if we did not give way to temper, that the Government cannot be broken up at this time, and in that way; but they hate us for wishing it, simply because, the wish is a broad-world-wide reflection upon them. They wish us to attempt it, however, in order to get satisfaction for the disgust and contempt which we have long felt and shown for them. They know the vast resources of the

Government, which if left in their hands will make it easy to crush us. They would then fasten the most obnoxious laws upon us, and, above all, humiliate us through the negro. The Northern people — I speak of them as a class, not as individuals — are just of that character which can only be elevated in proportion to our humiliation; and when they get the power, as they now will, they will push measures in that direction to the furthest extreme."

"Yes; your remarks in the Convention were made from that stand-point, and made a very serious impression," said the handsome girl, as she turned her lovely face full upon him.

"I have now," continued Brandon, "but one hope for the South, and that is, that after the destruction of slavery, it will turn its attention to *manufacturing*. She has every possible advantage of the North, in climate, timber, water-power, minerals, and the production of all the raw materials; these facts will be developed after a time, and change the entire track of wealth and commerce in this country. But violence throws nature off the track; natural causes work their natural ends, better and more speedily than we can force them. The present moment will throw us back many, many years, both in wealth, power, and improvement."

Brandon seeing Mrs. Ray take a seat, proposed to Miss Sedley that he now return her to Mr. Stafford.

CHAPTER VII.

"A skirmish of wit between them."

WHEN Brandon returned to Mrs. Ray, he apologized to Stafford, by saying that he not only apologized, but owed him a *double* apology, first for depriving him of his beautiful friend, and next, for using the occasion in an effort to proselyte her.

"I will not say, Mr. Brandon, that you owe me an apology for the first act, but cannot say so much for the second, as North Alabama is but poorly represented here in *patriotism*, at best. It would be an indifferent report to make of Miss Sedley, as she is looked upon as one of the brightest stars that float upon our rather dubious skies."

"I am truly obliged to North Alabama, Mr. Stafford, for placing me in so proud a galaxy, for I really did not seek the honor, and wear it a little awkwardly, I fear," she replied.

"Ah, Miss Sedley, I fear you are about to yield your noble position. Mr. Brandon must, indeed, have exerted great influence in the short time he was with you."

"Your remarks require a double answer, Mr. Stafford. In the first place, I have but few of the prerequisites for even a female politician; I am not persistent enough in my opinions; I cannot maintain them for the sake of popularity, when I fear myself in the wrong. Nor am I sufficiently ambitious of notoriety — as notoriety is all that a woman can acquire in that field. I already think that arrangements should be made to send me back. I am getting anxious to leave this whirl of excitement, and return to retirement, from sheer unfitness for any other position. This confession is quite mortifying, but I believe correct."

She had alternately turned from one to the other of the two gentlemen, while playfully making these remarks, with her eyes sparkling with mischief, and a smile playing about her mouth, and evidently enjoyed the effect that her words had upon Stafford, which cannot be appreciated by those who do not know the anxiety which was felt to secure female favor during the first days of the Confederacy.

Brandon saw that she was talking more to tantalize Stafford, than with any real seriousness, and therefore paid but little attention to her words, while he was struck with her uncommon beauty, and said to her:

30 *

"If there is such beauty in your regrets, Miss Sedley, what the effect would be of more generous feelings, and really correct opinions, is a high question of both morals and art. It occurs to me that even I would be tempted to regret the early frost on my locks, were it not there is one at my humble home, who breathes around me the atmosphere of love and beauty."

"Most gallantly spoken, Mr. Brandon, but the qualification destroys the force. That must be modified if you expect to charm me."

"Come, come," said Mrs. Ray, "I shall not permit even platonics, in the absence of my friend Mary Gray."

"Do you speak of Mrs. Brandon, aunt?"

"Yes; an old friend, of whom you have often heard me speak."

"Certainly, I have, but I had not connected the two."

"Yes, she is Mrs. Brandon."

"Then, for such considerations, I must decline further designs upon you, Mr. Brandon," affecting surprise at the information she had just received, and adding, "Oh, Mr. Brandon, what cruel work you might have been guilty of! I should far sooner have taken you for a gay Lothario, than inchoate patriarch."

"I beg pardon for the unintentional deception, Miss Sedley; and now permit me to restore you one who may more nearly approach the character of a Lothario than myself. Mr. Stafford, will you let me have the pleasure of returning your half-lost treasure."

Pretending to some hesitation, this gentleman replied:

"I suppose I *must;* but the lustre of the diamond is a good deal soiled, by her own confession. Miss Sedley, will you return to your allegiance, and to my care; for — if you will permit me to make a very tender quotation, 'I know that I love thee, whatever thou art.'"

"Ah! Mr. Stafford, had you not better reserve your

tender confessions for a more private occasion? Is this your first, or your last?" said Mrs. Ray.

"My first, madam, of course; the last, I shall take your advice in, and reserve for a 'more private occasion.'"

"I am equally delighted, Mr. Stafford, with your sympathy, your poetry, and your confessions; and give you the evidence of my sincerity in accepting your offer to receive me. But, Mr. Brandon, I had scarcely thought that you would display so ready and so ingenious a facility in giving me up."

"You mistake me, fair lady. After hearing the confessions of Mr. Stafford, and seeing the evident pleasure they afforded you, it is I who have the right to complain; and you must further allow me to indicate the extent of my indignation, by asking him to exchange places with me," at the same time rising, and offering Mr. Stafford his seat. This exchange brought him to the side of Mrs. Sheldon, who was conversing with Ray.

"Ah! Mr. Brandon," said Miss Sedley, "that is insult to injury — 'Ossa upon Pelion' — and leaves no room for conciliation."

"I will leave the whole matter to Mr. Stafford, and if he thinks any *amende* due to you, I will immediately return to your side."

"No, no," said Stafford, laughing; "I do not think the matter requires the least explanation of the kind — suppose you let the affair rest at what it is at, ' *quiescat in pace.*' A general amnesty is the best method of restoring peace."

This change, placing Brandon by the side of Mrs. Sheldon, the latter asked in an undertone, how he was pleased with the North Alabama belle.

"Very much. She is really very beautiful, and I should think, a very superior girl."

"Yes; she is all that you say; and you will be delighted with her, should you become more familiarly acquainted with her. She is very finely educated, modest and gentle, and yet very spirited, and entirely free from affectation. I was with her at Washington last winter, when she attracted the admiration of every one who met with her. It is said, and I presume truly, that she is engaged to Mr. Stafford, who is himself a young man of fine mind, education, and fortune; but has the reputation of being *wild*, and I think she holds him under probation."

"Yes; I discovered something of the kind. But your mentioning Washington, reminds me to ask how the Southern ladies will feel at giving up the glittering attractions of Washington, for the rude scenes and life of a revolutionary capital."

"To speak sincerely, Mr. Brandon, I have not the glowing anticipations which are generally entertained by our friends. Mr. Sheldon, too, is far from being clear of apprehension for the future. This course does not meet his approval, yet he says, the South has had to bear with so many different kinds of indignity, that he holds it *excusable* for almost any course she may adopt. But to reply to your question directly, I am perfectly willing to give up the gayeties of Washington, and never go there again. A few years since, society there was of a very high order, and the winters were very gay and attractive, but it has changed very greatly. For several years past, the North has been sending a certain sort of fashionable society there, without vitality or nature in it, and to a Southerner very disagreeable, and difficult to describe —*jejune, parvenue*, possessors of sudden wealth, with no higher lineage than descending from some successful inventor of stoves or mowing-machines, or at the best, from some passenger on the Mayflower. In England, they would be styled *cockneyish*. I do not condemn the South for her temper, yet I cannot endorse the wisdom of her course; but I am a Southerner, and whatever the South does, right or wrong, I shall sustain in all the ways that a woman can."

"We are not far apart, either in feeling or opinion; but for the life of me, I can see no possible chance of success, which is the criterion of right in the political world. The physical inequalities are too numerous and too great; and as to *principle*, there is no such precept in the whole roll of state-craft, as the right of one integral portion of a government to withdraw from the remainder at pleasure. The idea is at variance with the spirit and organic law of all government, STABILITY, and the duty and right of *self-protection*.

"We are told that there will be no war. This is a mistake, and however successful the South may be in the *battles* of the first period, it will be unsuccessful in the *war*, from simple exhaustion; even victories will ruin her, while the persistent power of an established government can easily bear up under protracted disaster."

CHAPTER VIII.

"Now call we our high court of Parliament;
And let us choose such limbs of noble counsel,
That the great body of our State may go
In equal rank with the best-governed Nation."

EARLY in the Spring of 1861, thirteen of the States known as the Slave States, had, in some sort, seceded from the *Union*, and formed THE SOUTHERN CONFEDERACY, of which Richmond soon became the capital.

It was now plain to *both Governments* that they had drifted into war — contrary to the expectation of either. Fort Sumter had already fallen into the hands of the Confederates, after enduring a most terrible siege, and the whole South was all ablaze with martial excitement.

Mr. Buchanan was averse to war, and evidently hoped for a reconciliation. A *peace* convention of prominent citizens from both sections had met at Washington with a view to arranging the difficulty, in the last days of his administration and by his advice; but the North, arrogant under the triumphant success of Lincoln, made as arrogant demands, while the South, growing every moment more chafed, was in no condition to accept unjust propositions. The North, falling back upon her superior numbers, and the strength of the position she would gain by the naked secession of the South, grew every hour more imperious, while the South, at every such evidence, grew firmer in her hate, and confidently fell back upon her historic chivalry. It was the NORMAN face to face with the SAXON, but with history and the facts reversed. The moral elements were the same; a thousand years had not affected them, but the occasion was changed and new. *Present results*, so far from modifying these Norman and Saxon differences, have only intensified them. Let the future make its own record.

But as we have said, Fort Sumter had fallen, and the South blazed with impatience for the unequal struggle. It was the martial heart of the South moved to its deepest depths. The note of defiance rung through the land, and her people gathered together at the sound, with souls that felt no fear, and an enthusiasm that courted the fray. This excitement was outside of all party feeling. Even those who had bitterly opposed secession, and were still opposed to it in opinion, now rushed wildly to arms. The wrongs and insults which they had long borne with, now seemed uppermost in their minds, and who or by what means the contest had been precipitated, were matters of secondary consideration. Had those who had been in the political lead of the people, been themselves actuated by less *partisan feeling*, and had met the out-gush of this popular enthusiasm on the part of the people, in the same generous spirit, the "Bonnie Blue Flag" would this day, whether for weal or woe, have proudly floated over the loveliest land, and the proudest, noblest race of men and women, too, who walk the earth, and who even in their fallen condition, grace the records of the world with all the magnificence of chivalry, and the loveliest pictures of heroism.

But old political prejudices, favoritism, speculation, and beyond all, the abstractions of constitutional law, crept in, and marred the force, which even the simple cause itself possessed. Arguments always cool ardor, and check the impulses of the heart, and Richmond early became the gladiatory field for second and third-rate contestants, on points which should never have arisen. The occasion was *revolutionary;* revolutions are despotisms, and it is their duty to compel *all* men to bow to them. Power should not be divided, and Mr. Davis was divided between thousands. God knows how many. Anywhere in Europe the thing would have succeeded, where the people had not been *pestered* by *democracy* and discussion. It was *democracy* that defeated the South — a social condition foreign to her whole nature, but which had gradually slipt upon her shoulders, without her knowing when, why, or how; her natural aristocracy of character would have led her to success.

On this occasion the South evinced her true character. The masses wanted leaders, and when they obtained them, drove them on before. Any man of the least influence, either in intelligence, character, or wealth, could, and did, raise either his company, regiment, or battalion. To these facts Brandon was no exception, but immediately raised a company in his neighborhood, and reported to head-quarters. In the formation of a regiment from single companies, who had similarly reported, he was unanimously elected Colonel.

Colonel Campbell, now a prominent man in a near part

of the State, passed through the same process, but went on to higher positions, until reaching a Brigadiership, and in this relation to the army, went to the seat of war. Stafford, in North Alabama, had also been promoted to a Colonelcy, and while in Virginia, had his regiment transferred to General Campbell's brigade.

General Campbell's son, McKenzie Campbell, who had so attracted the attention of Mrs. Ray in the ball-room, by his father's permission, had remained in his company, and been chosen third lieutenant, and was now in Brandon's regiment.

.   .   .   .

About or near midsummer of that year, the Federal Government began moving heavy forces on Richmond, the REBEL capital; which rendered it necessary for the Confederacy to evacuate Norfolk, and come to its support; and having already advanced beyond, met with Lincoln's army on the famous field of Manassas. And there, the CAVALIER met the PURITAN! and made one other glorious record of the *differences* between the *two people*. What that record is, the world already knows!—will forever know! Hate cannot alter history, nor despotism obliterate deeds. There it is! proudly tracing its own story on the old walls of time, and indelible as eternity! Try your blade again, Puritan, and refute the record if ye can!

Campbell's brigade, and Brandon's regiment particularly, had attracted attention during the whole day, by its repeated engagements, persistent gallantry, and heavy losses.

Young McKenzie Campbell had commanded, boy as he was, his company during the latter part of this terrible day, by the fall of all his superior officers; and now felt all the pride of a young soldier, who had won his sword by victory.

About the time the last act of the dreadful drama had transpired, General Campbell rode up to his youthful son on the field, and said:

"You have acted nobly to-day, my boy."

"That's enough, father," replied the merry but powder-burnt young officer, interrupting him. "Next to my sweet-heart's smile, I appreciate yours, sir."

"Ah! you will never be serious, you young dog."

"No, sir; not while I have so much to be proud of, and to rejoice over."

"Then, take care of yourself, my son," and dashing a tear from his eye, rode on.

When night had set in, and the Southern army had returned from pursuing the fleeing Federal forces; and the hundreds of amateur spectators who had come to witness the victory of their army, (who, however *pious?* had no objection to the shedding of blood, provided it was not their own, and further provided, it flowed from Southern hearts,) lay sleeping around their little camp-lights with their half-eaten rations at their side, young Campbell was sitting there alone, writing an account of the affair to Alice Hunter.

"BATTLE-FIELD OF MANASSAS, *July* 3d, 1861.

"MY SWEET COUSIN:—And who has a better right to say sweet cousin than I, who have this day won my *knightly spurs?* so cousin Henry Brandon says, and he is a judge. Well, sweet cousin—I'll say it again, because I am away from you, and not afraid to say it—I have sat down, with a piece of broken gun-carriage for my table, and sundry such articles for my light, to write you some account of my *first* battle, which I promised to do if I should survive it, which you used teasingly to tell me I would never fight. But I have fought it, won it, and not been killed, and now feel almost inclined to write as Cæsar did to the Roman Senate, ' *Veni, vidi, vici!*' and if I were writing to any one but a girl, I believe I should be tempted—anyway, to rival his pomposity. Either to girl or senate, I shall be tempted to do so, if I shall ever again come off so fortunately.

"Just for the present, however, I will not assume such vast proportions, and content myself by merely giving you some few incidents of this terrific day, in which I acted up

to all my duty so far as I was able. You must not expect
so full an account, as you would doubtless like to see, or I
would like to give, as I am very greatly fatigued, and not
over the excitement even yet. But I hope to meet you
before long, and, after kissing your rosy cheek, will fight my
battle over again.

"But let me begin this wild, dreadful story, before sleep
asserts its authority. For several days we had seen that the
Federals intended fighting us, with an army very superior
to ours both in numbers and appointments; but as we believed that we could whip two for one, at the very least, felt
no alarm.

"This morning, some time after day, a pretty heavy
firing began on their side about half a mile to our left,
which was soon returned from ours. The firing rapidly
extended, and in less than an hour our regiment was into
it; and your humble servant found himself, for the first
time since being in the army, under heavy fire. It seemed
to me that every man in the Yankee army was firing at me
individually, which, you may imagine, made me feel a little
curious; balls and cannon-shot flew almost as thick as
hail. I got accustomed to it after a while, but oh! cousin,
I could not describe to you my feelings for the last ten
minutes before actually going into the engagement, if I
had every word in all the languages of the world. The
sun had risen beautifully, and was as calm and glowing as
if all unconscious of the suffering which men were about
to inflict on each other. Not a word was spoken by the
men, and in their eyes there seemed to be no capacity of
sight for external objects. Their vision, if it may be called
such, appeared to be coldly turned within, or abstractedly
dwelling on those who were far away, never probably to be
seen again with mortal sight. Such vacancy of expression
I never saw men wear before, and, oh! that I could never
see it again.

"The first cannon fired in our front was an electric shock,
and brought us up to a full realization of our condition.
For a very few moments, the apprehension was terrible;
indeed, I was no less really frightened than every one else,
but this soon passed away, and the work of death began in
earnest. After this there was no fear, no anxiety, no more
care for self; these were all forgotten in the awful scenes

around us. Very soon the strife raged mortally; the dead lying around us, and the wounded falling and groaning in the agonies of death, while the living, with teeth clenched, and with the rage of fiends, moved, fired, and loaded in silence. We frequently changed, and were compelled to change position during the day, and it was only during such times that we had any respite.

"These scenes lasted for many hours, with all the phases of an inferior army fighting one vastly its superior in strength. We felt this inequality very often during the day, and at times it appeared that we would be overwhelmed in spite of ourselves. Our army would appear to have done all that men could do — waver, reel, and fall back — yet their spirit never abated, and with every giving back, there came a revival of the desperate resolution, to be victorious or to die. Observing this, I felt that it was impossible for mortal power to conquer us, short of extermination.

"These shifting fortunes continued through the entire day — rather until about four o'clock, when, without any appearance of extraordinary cause, the Federals were seen to give way, and but a short time elapsed before a *panic* ensued. The victory was ours! Crushing, overwhelming, complete! A more perfect *rout* could not be imagined, assuming all the features of personal cowardice. Flying thus from men only half their number, as if from the very wrath to come, must ever be a most humiliating memory. But what is one person's sorrow, is another's joy, I've heard, and *my* heart swelled with all the varying emotions of joy and pride, and even exultation, at the sight of the troops of a people, who, for years, had sought to insult and injure us, and at length had invaded our country with a view to destroying our property, and our homes, made to degrade themselves by their own miserable poltroonery; for certainly, had they had the hearts of men in their mean, boasting breasts, they could have exterminated us, if they could not conquer us; and even now, while our men have had a hearty laugh, and are quietly sleeping on the battle-field, these miserable creatures are still fleeing from them with the fright of hares.

"It is reported, to-night, that some of our forces, among other prisoners, captured a little copper-cent sort of Con- gressman, who had come to witness the Puritan *victory*.

If so, I hope General Beauregard will refuse to treat him
as a prisoner of war, but order a corporal to whip him and
turn him loose, as a thing utterly unworthy to be guarded
by a Southern soldier.   But it is all over with, and I am
unhurt, so I shall not get in a bad temper with Puritan
amateurs.

"What strange things turn up in this little world of
ours sometimes!   Just, if you please, think of a country
lad from the far-away South, sitting, at midnight, on a
battle-field, with no human sound to break the silence that
reigns around him, except the soft, slow step of the sentinel on his lonely round, writing some account of the awful
scenes of an awful day, by the dim light of a summer camp-
fire, to his fair young cousin at her distant home, who he
hopes is this moment quietly sleeping, and sweetly dreaming of him who has thought and *seen* her lovely face ten
thousand times during the terrible day that has passed.
That was a long speech, but I had to make it.   So here
goes, my pretty cousin, for something else.   Ah, yes! I had
nigh forgot to tell you of quite a romantic — so I may call
it — incident of this morning.   You know the beautiful gold
locket you gave me containing your picture? which, of
course, I wear next my heart.   Well, it saved my life to-day,
and after this fashion.   Now every word I shall tell you
is just as true as that we have this day fought the battle
of Manassas.   No imagination, no fiction, no story about
it — for what else had your sweet little picture to do, but
to save my life?   It could not fight.   But let me tell my
story.   About eleven o'clock I was struck by a spent ball,
I suppose, which prostrated me, and for a moment, took
my breath, and, as an Irishman would say, for a few
seconds *thought* I was *dead*, but discovering that my eyes
were open, and my lungs breathing, concluded to rise, and
did so to my perfect satisfaction; but still supposing myself
badly wounded, thought to play surgeon; and on examination found no damage had been done, except that your
locket had been battered in.   The whole thing flashed upon
me in an instant, and I went on as if nothing had happened.
The whole affair did not go through one minute, I don't
suppose, but it looked to me like two years; but need I tell
you that I pressed the little guardian angel to my lips, and
thanked it for its presence on the battle-field? and need I

tell you too, that it is now open before me as I write, with its lovely face looking as laughingly in mine, as you did the day that you hung it around my neck?

"But, heigho! it is nearly morning, and I am too tired to write more, even to my little sweetheart away down in Dixie; so I shall close, and lie down where I am, to dream of Alice, home, and mother. I had already, before beginning this to you, written a few lines to Colonel Brandon's wife by his request, and also a short letter to mother; but this is intended for you to read to them all, except in such parts as — you know what I mean — and now, good night!

"Yours affectionately,

"McK. CAMPBELL."

CHAPTER IX.

"But sorrow returned with the dawning of morn,
And the voice in my dreaming melted sadly away."

THE electric wires flung the intelligence of this great victory, almost as soon as it had transpired, from one end of the Confederacy to the other, yet it was many days before the details of it became known. Young Campbell's letter was the first received at ——, containing anything like particulars, from one who had actually participated in it; and Hunter's house was thronged for several days by friends, neighbors, and citizens, to hear some real confirmation and details of the affair. The curiosity seemed so great, that Alice, under the direction of her father, prepared it for the press, only leaving out such parts as we have seen were intended to be private.

The young officer was so generally known, and the spirit with which he dashed his letter was so accordant with the feelings of a large part of the people, that the letter soon

31 *

passed into the columns of every newspaper in the State, each one making its own laudatory comments.

It was now believed by all that peace would follow, some thinking that it would result in a reconstruction of the Union, while the larger portion were *satisfied* that a *recognition* of the Confederacy would necessarily result from so overwhelming a victory. All desired *peace*, and all rejoiced in the triumph of Southern arms.

A day or two after young Campbell had written, Colonel Brandon seized a stray occasion to write to his wife. The letter was a mere running one; but we subjoin it, for the purpose of showing the feelings of Southern people at this time, even among those who had opposed secession.

"MANASSAS, 5th *July*, '61.

"MY DEAR WIFE: — I have not written to you as early as I desired, and as I would have done under any possible circumstances, had I not known that intelligence of *our* safety had reached you through McK. Campbell. Until now I have had no suitable opportunity to write to you; but finding from my almost unremitting duties, that I am not likely to get a better, seize upon such as I have.

" Well, my dear Mary, after every effort on my part to check the current of secession, I have just come out of a most terrible battle, resulting from it — against my opinions, my own people, and my own Government; but confess to all the pride of a soldier, in the great victory we have won, not without a hope, however, that it may lead to peace, as both the Government and the Northern people must now see that we are not to be insulted, slandered, and wronged, without properly resenting it; but when the battle was going on I lost sight of all such considerations, and only thought of *victory*. The desire of success superseded all other feelings. I never once thought of Colonel Haywood; men and causes dwindled into their proper insignificance, before the terrible solemnity of battle-scenes.

"I am now fairly launched into it, and though I still, and shall ever condemn the policy of it, I shall remain in it so long as it lasts, and continues to be *sectional* in its character and purposes. It certainly appears to be a war of *envious fanaticism*, waged against *temper;* and as I am no fanatic, and as the temper belongs to my own people, I shall certainly maintain it in their interest, and every impulse of my heart forbids my doing less than a man's work — I will not say *duty*. I might possibly think, and even act differently, if the Government of the United States could divest itself of the odium of moving in obedience to a purely sectional prejudice, and a wish on the part of the North to *crush* us; but their refusal at the Peace Conference, though informally held, to accede to, or to propose any concession, indicates beyond doubt, that the Northern people *desired* the South to *secede* — knowing that the power which would thus be left in their hands, would make them as ten to one in the contest.

"I still, as I have said, condemn the policy of the war, and look upon the arguments in behalf of Secession as simply *absurd*, and am still as hopeless of ultimate success. As a thing of *reason*, I have no approval of my own, or the course of the South; yet, from a social point of view, I could never forgive myself for taking part against my own people.

"But to revert to the *battle:* I will say that after a day of terrible fighting against large odds of every character, victory went overwhelming by in our favor. Fright, panic, rout, flight, and an utter desertion of every material thing with which a great army goes on the battle-field, does not approach the picture which the Federal forces presented, as they turned toward Washington.

"One of the, to me, pleasing but singular facts in this affair is, that our army is largely composed of 'Old Whigs,' and men who opposed secession, yet this did not appear to affect them, and the battle was fought outside of all political feeling. It was a collision between men who essentially differ, both in mental, moral, social, and ethnological elements.

"If the Confederate Congress could only appreciate the differences between the two people, which this battle has developed, and then, too, remember that governments only wage protracted war successfully, somewhat in the proportion which they approach a *despotism*, and hush up all this senseless wrangling on *constitutional* points, and send every *capable man* into the army, and ay, go themselves, too, there might be some prospect of success; without this, I fear there is but little — and I am *not* a *croaker*, but a *soldier*. The *one man* power is the only kind which can win such prizes as are now up on the hazard. But there is little hope of this. The future, therefore, is gloomy enough to those who look beyond the ephemeral brightness of the *present.*

"But I did not set out to write a political letter to my absent, anxious, and loving wife, but rather to write to her cheerfully and hopefully, as I certainly feel, for my late escape from injury. You can tell those who feel an interest, or have young friends with me, that the regiment, through the whole day, behaved with the most unwavering gallantry, as much so, apparently, as if each man thought the issue of the battle depended on himself; and all that is to be regretted, is its severe losses.

"I was frequently at the side of McKenzie Campbell, during the day, and youth as he is, he behaved with all the coolness and daring of a veteran, and all the gallantry of a Southern gentleman's son. If this war will do no other good it will develop Southern character, and the chivalry of the Southern heart, and let the outside world know that we are more than the bloated, effete "slave drivers" which Northern pulpits, Northern politicians, and Northern writers, have slanderously represented us to be.

"McKenzie went over to the quarters of General Campbell, the morning following the battle, and a soldier who accompanied him told me that he never saw a more affecting meeting. Campbell, he said, cried like a child, as he hugged the brave boy to his bosom. He may well be proud of him, as I will venture that neither army had such another in its ranks. Tell Alice that I tease him about writing to her before he did to his mother; he, however, denies it, acknowledging, though, that he did write Alice the *longest* letter.

"Tell her, too, that she may boast to all the young damsels of her young hero cousin, and that he makes quite as good a soldier as he did a student, and that is saying a great deal. As I just remember it, you must excuse me for making a romantic allusion in connection with him.

"About the middle of the afternoon, on the day of the fight, I passed near him, only a short time before his captain had been wounded, and taken from the field. McKenzie was then in command of what was left of his company, and at the moment I saw him, was under a very severe fire, but he stood as calmly, and looked as pleasing as if enjoying some pastime. I thought I had never seen so fine a picture of a young soldier, and could but pause for a moment to look at his handsome face and figure, bringing back to memory the lovely face of Laura Brandon, as we saw her more than twenty years ago, at Gregory's Spring, and for a second, the poor broken-hearted girl of a later day nestled again in my bosom. Strange memory to pass through the mind of an officer on the battle-field, you will think. So it was; but constantly through that day of blood and havoc, there came back to my mind sweet memories that had long lain silent or been forgot. Strange, too, none but the pleasant ones came up. You and my children were ever in my presence. Every pleasant event, from the time we first met, up to the reception of your last letter; and in the ten thousand times that your dear face appeared to me, never once did it wear anything but the same soft beauty, and the same gentle expression, which I never saw it without; and by the time the day was over with, and now, you were more the *lady-love* of my heart than ever before. I can afford to tell you this, now that we are separated; but rather think it would sound very boyish if with you — distance and danger make it all right.

"The night after the battle we slept upon the field in great disorder, but perhaps more quietly, from great fatigue, and from a feeling of security from interruption by the enemy. *They* were having rather a restless time of it, but their wild unrest was our repose.

"The summer moon shed its clear silver light upon the tragic field, and the pale stars looked sadly down, as angels' eyes from heaven, upon the dead, the dying, the sleeping soldiers, and mystic scene —and never had I a happier rest or brighter dreams. My spirit floated off to my Southern home, and dwelt in the blissful realms of peace and love — where my children, with their mother, were as palpably before me as ever in actual life.

"You must excuse this rambling sort of letter, my dear wife, as the circumstances do not allow of me writing more connectedly; but I shall try to improve upon it, in a few days. Write to me often, as your letters are the greatest happiness and the only comfort I have on earth. Give my love to all the children, and tell them I will kiss them when I come; and you, dear absent wife, have, as always, the un-divided love of your affectionate husband,

"HENRY BRANDON."

"P. S. — 'Sam Brandon' sends kind love to his family, and his respects to you and the children. He is the same faithful old servant that he ever was. I could scarcely keep him off the battle-field: he was repeatedly during the day on his horse looking out for me, in perfect range of the enemy's fire; he seems fearless, and swears harder than ever. He has a fresh subject in the Yankees, and does it full justice. Yours, H. B."

In reply to this letter, she immediately wrote the follow-ing, which we give, as indicative of the feelings of Southern wives, their employments, and their efforts to sustain their home affairs:

"*July* 12*th*, '61.

"A letter bearing date 5th July, has just been handed to me, from My Dear Husband, informing me over his own name of his safety. My first impulse was to sit down and reply to it; but for some time I was so overcome by my feelings as to render it impossible to perform that task of love, duty, and thankfulness. I have at length, however, become sufficiently composed to do so.

"I had already heard of the battle, and your escape, my dear husband, through the letter of McK. Campbell; but my anxiety refused to be quieted, until I should receive the same intelligence in your own writing. That I now have before me; and on this beautiful Sunday morning, with the children around me, I feel that 'Our Father in heaven' had reserved this happiness for me to this blessed morning, that I might be more mindful of His goodness and His mercy, in still sparing you to me.

"Oh! my dear husband, as right, as facts have developed within the last few months, the South have been in begin-ning this war, and resisting the current which threatened her happiness, her welfare, and her particular civilization, yet I confess, in my sorrow, and my bitterness of life, that I am almost unable to stand up under the various endurances it calls for. When I hear that a battle is to be fought, in which it is probable you will be engaged, I really have no control over my mind; and though I still strive to perform the duties which now devolve upon me, I yet am too sick at heart, to go through with them as I should, and am only *driven* to hold up, just to sustain the children, who, at times. are nearly as much disposed to yield to despondency as myself, and appear to live in a nameless kind of anticipation of trouble.

"For some time past, our home has looked as gloomy as though some dreadful doom impended it. Nothing has appeared to escape it; a sort of listening, lingering, sighing stillness pervades everything around, both in nature and human life — the negroes are as much affected as ourselves. But let me change the subject, and endeavor at least to say something of actual home matters.

"I am informed by the negroes, that the plantation affairs are going on very smoothly, and the prospect for a good crop was never better. Whether so or not, they deserve it, as I have never known them to behave so well and so industriously, and take the greatest pleasure in bringing me pleasant reports, thinking, I suppose, that matters of the kind will cheer me; but, oh! how mistaken the poor creatures are. I, however, am none the less obliged to them, and particularly as they evince so much feeling for *you:* for the last hour, since the word got out that I had heard from you, the house has been literally thronged with them, expressing their joy for your safety.

"I, like most all Southern women, favored secession; but now confess that I did not comprehend its real character and results. I only looked to the *causes*, from a social point, not from a political — from which I very naturally viewed with indignation the course of the Northern politicians, in regard to our private affairs; but with a still deeper indignation, the pharisaical presumption of the Northern *women*, in their insulting assumption of superior virtue, morality, excellence, and intelligence, over those of the South, and this feeling I have never yet been able to overcome. That wretched slander upon the South, 'Uncle Tom's Cabin,' seems to have fastened it upon me; and I will forever think that the social condition of my sex must be bad indeed, when even its literary taste can only be gratified by a meretricious slander, perpetrated by one of their number upon their own sex, in another part of the same country. But even with these just causes of resentment, I should never have contributed my mite to the present condition of affairs, could I only have foreseen the *results*. In some atonement, I would now be perfectly willing to let that wretched people have matters their own way — in philanthropy, morality, and literature, if by it, peace could be restored to our wild, distracted, maddened South, or even bring my husband back to his home, his children, and his wife.

"My heart aches by night and by day, as I think that anything I may have said and done, did by that much contribute to our present separation. Oh! my husband, it is impossible for me to describe the bitter anguish, and the heart-breaking solicitude that I bear up under — a pressure is upon my very soul — and all the refuge I have, is with a bleeding, stricken heart, to bow in prayer for you, for my children, and for peace. But I have promised to write more cheerfully if I could, and I will.

"The weather has been very hot for several weeks, but yesterday there was a fine refreshing rain, and to-day the air is cool, and nature appears all fresh and young again, and how happy I could be if you were only with us! Every breeze seems softly to breathe me the name that is dearest to me on earth; but, alas! he that bears it, is far, too far away.

"I know that you will do your duty nobly, as a gentleman and a soldier, yet I can derive no pleasure from *that* thought. Your honor is your *danger*, and *that* I cannot contemplate with the least resignation whatever, however mortifying it would be to me, for you not to meet it properly.

"Surrounded as I am, by these gloomy shadows and fearful solicitudes, you may judge that I have but few moments unclouded by sorrow. In this perplexity and anguish of spirit, after caressing our dear, innocent, grief-stricken children, I turn back upon the past, as my next source of happiness; when our first meeting at Gregoric's Spring comes vividly back to my memory, with all the merry, joyous scenes of that day, and linger upon that sort of prescience which I even then had, that you would some time or other hold a different relation to me, from what

you then did. I next think of the many intervening years
in which we never met; and still, how in all that time
your name would so often come up before me, without any
apparent association — how perfectly I remembered your
face, and how instantly I knew you when we accidentally
met in the streets of Memphis. And, oh! then, the many
happy, too happy years we since have spent in our planta-
tion-home.

"Until the clouds of this wretched war darkened the sky
of our home-joys, everything, and everybody, was happy
and contented — ourselves, our children, our friends, our
negroes, and the stranger that entered our gates; yes, these,
all of these, had a joy and a gladness to beam in their eye.
Oh! that Heaven, in some kind manner, would spare me
the sight of the contrary in the coming time.

"I would now ask you, my dear husband, to take care
of yourself, but that I know you cannot do. I still can
pray though, that some good angel may set a light in the
skies, which shall guide you through all the terrible dangers
of battle, and some day lead you back to the bosom of
your sorrowing family.

"Alice Hunter was over to see me yesterday, and though
her father is so opposed to the war, *she* is quite enthusiastic
and jubilant, and very proud of the reputation which her
young *sweetheart cousin*, as she calls him, has appeared to
win; and almost admits there is some *little* promise between
them — looking at, and speaking of the future most glowingly. Poor girl! I almost fear there is some bitter drop in
the bottom of the cup which she little dreams of, and from
which she is drinking the ambrosial draught, only known
to youth and to innocence.

"The relations and friends, such as are at home, are all
well and very kind to us; and nearly all of them very hopeful now of our 'independence,' very resolute in their cause,
and appear astonished that I too am not so.

"I do not suppose there will be any military movement
on foot very soon. I shall, therefore, look for you every
day until I see you. The children send so many messages,
that my letter, long as it is, would not have contained them;
but they are all full of love: they have done nothing but
talk of you for the last month, and seem ever to be won-
dering 'Where is father now?'

32

"Tell 'Sam Brandon,' his wife and children are all well, and send him all kinds of messages and love, as do all the negroes, and our own children.

"Our hearts all yearn to see you again, which we now hope will be before a great while; until then, my dear husband, you have the prayers and love of your devoted wife,   MARY BRANDON."

CHAPTER X.

"Thoughts are but dreams till their effects be tried."

THE letter of Mrs. Brandon was but a simple expression of the feelings which too many heart-stricken wives suffered from, at some period of the war, and many through it all. It was not, however, representative of the general sentiment of the sex, which was even more inflamed, and more proscriptive than that of the men. We will not give the philosophy of this fact, but leave it in the condition of a mere assertion which cannot be denied.

On the part of those who had advocated Secession, we mean on the part of the opposite sex, there was an almost undivided belief that war would not, nay, could not follow. It was really *believed* by that particular school of politicians, who had been educated in, advocated, and had at length inaugurated the doctrine, that the States had a constitutional right to withdraw from the Union when it might be thought judicious to do so, without responsibility to any superior power whatever; and as a correlative part of the doctrine, that those which remained as the original government dared not overleap these constitutional rights of the seceders. The singular and anomalous position was here presented, of one part wilfully throwing off the obligations of the Constitution, yet expecting the other to

be controlled by them. This singular obliquity was the
sure guarantee of war, when least expected, and the least
prepared for. Had it not been for this theoretical position,
there would, indeed, have been no war. Whereas, the
practical application of the doctrine did unknowingly drift
the South into its terrible current, and her own destruction.

It must, however, be admitted that the character of the
debates on the Constitution very significantly pointed to
this right on the part of the States, and much of the language used in expressing its meaning is susceptible of construction favorable to the idea of extreme State sovereignty;
and though it had never been tested, it yet had never been
lost sight of. It perhaps would never have been tested, if
the Northern people had not perpetrated so many indig-
nities upon the South — which gave out high and false
social aspects of Southern life and character — and finally
begun a systematic attack upon their *personal rights,* in the
matter of their slave property. These latter facts at length
determined the South to put the right of separation to a
practical test. Southern extremists thus secured all the
advantages they had long desired over the conservative elements; and we know the results.

This point in the science of government is so plain and
so palpable, that it is difficult to believe that well-informed
men could have so far lost sight of it; and can only be excused on the score of *temper,* which, itself, had foundation in
deep-seated ethnological causes, which had shown themselves
before on various occasions, though not so fully illustrated.
The war of 1812, the United States bank, the tariff, slavery,
and other questions, had, in the previous history of the Government, developed organic antagonisms between the people
of the South and North; and the country had never been
wanting in ambitious men on either side, who had inflamed
them to the utmost; but it was reserved to the fatal year
of 1860, to bring culmination and collision. The election

of Lincoln was nothing of itself, (even as he was nothing of himself,) as the rights of the South were *safe*, so long as she remained in the Union; but it was the evidence of things unseen, and a sign of the bitter extreme to which prejudice on the one part, and temper on the other, had been wrought up. Slavery was but the *ostensible* cause of the collision — the *quasi* cause of war. The "irrepressible conflict" was not really between slave and free labor, but between the NORMAN of the *South*, and the SAXON of the *North, nor* can the *difference ever* be *reconciled*, except under a MONARCHICAL government.

The Northern people, however, made the mistake of supposing that slavery was the cause of the war, and almost to the very last period of it, the South was informed that she could retain her slaves, provided she would return to her allegiance; but the scorn with which the proposition was rejected, at once gave evidence that the sources of the war were far deeper than that called for; and this the Government of the United States might have seen, yet it went on to the perpetration of a most malignant folly, and the unmilitary expedient of setting them free — a lasting shame upon its sense of justice, upon its chivalry, and its statesmanship. Whether slavery was right or not, aristocratic or not, valuable or not, it was still the *property* of the South, acquired under constitutional guarantees; and while it was not actively engaged in the war, its wilful destruction was only a private injury and a national wrong, in which the innocent suffered equally with the guilty. Their dwelling-houses had as well been burned, because they sheltered them. If it had been the *cause* of the war, and it certainly was such *ostensibly*, the very apprehension of its destruction was a perfect justification of the South in defending herself against the trespass. If it was not the cause of the war, the act was indefensible, and the South should now be paid for her property, equally with the bondholders of the North. If it *was* the cause of the war, the South was right for defending herself, and should still be paid for its destruction. The law of rebellion applies to persons, not to property. Even in its simplest form, any other position, let the custom of governments have been what it may, cannot be sustained either in spirit or in practice.

The Government professed to be defending itself — granted; but governments also are instituted for the protection of individuals in *all* their *rights,* and not for the destruction of those rights. The reasons in favor of these positions are too manifest, and the results of a contrary course too plainly unjust, to require much argument in their defence, and nothing but the mobocratic and fanatical spirit of the Government will continue them to be rejected.

The war had now been going on for over two years, and Southern arms had been victorious on every important battle-field, since it had begun. The seven-days fighting around Richmond had already taken place, and had left the rebel capital without the apprehension of any early danger, and all aglow with the expectation of recognition on the part of the United States. The fighting had been terrible indeed, in which prodigies of valor had been shown on either side, and was a fair test of the military character of the two people. It was not the inferiority of the one which had lost the campaign, but the superiority of the other that had won it. And yet, the Northern army was overthrown with every feature of ignominious defeat, and Southern independence most surely calculated on. But it did not come!

Mr. Ray had been elected as one of the Senators from Alabama, and had taken permanent rooms in Richmond, Miss Sedley still remaining with them. Colonel Stafford had been a regular visitor there, with the understanding of being married at the ending of the war.

32 *

Colonel Stafford had been in the army since the beginning of the hostilities, and had participated in several of its severest engagements without injury, until the charge on Malvern Hill, during the fight around Richmond. In that desperate affair, however, he had received a most terrible wound in the shoulder, and was taken from the battle-field directly to the residence of Mr. Ray. After a long confinement, and the best attention, he had sufficiently recovered to return to his own home, in North Alabama.

Many weeks expiring after this celebrated campaign, without any appearances of "recognition" on the part of the United States, the Confederate Government at length, with some confidence of success, determined on an *invasion* of the enemy's country, not with any other view than hastening an acknowledgment of its independence. So soon as that policy was determined on, the War Department began making all necessary preparations for carrying it out.

Colonel Stafford learning that this enterprise was in contemplation, and having measurably regained his strength, determined on returning to his regiment. In writing to Miss Sedley, he spoke of the current intelligence in North Alabama to that effect, and merely mentioned that he thought his strength sufficient to return to the army, and that she might expect the *pleasure* of his presence in a couple of weeks at furthest. Immediately replying to him, she urged him to remain, as she was satisfied from his condition when he left, and from the length of time he had been gone, that his strength was not sufficient to bear him up under the excitement and fatigue of such a campaign.

We subjoin the letter, as somewhat illustrative of the feeling of that period:

"RICHMOND, 25th August, 1862.

"DEAR COLONEL STAFFORD: — Your last letter, informing me of your intended early return to the army, was handed to me not over half an hour since, and I seize this immediate moment to reply to you, in order that no mail may escape me, urging you to remain in Alabama. On reading your letter, I communicated your purpose to uncle Ray, who happened to be in his room at the time, and to aunt, both of whom unite with me in urging you to remain away, as we are all satisfied that your physical condition cannot be such as to justify your joining your regiment so early. So, sir, with this accumulated authority, my request rises well up to the dignity of a command from your superiors, and you are too well-trained a soldier to disobey it. Rather than you should suffer with your men, which I know is part of your feeling, I will, myself, go to them, and represent your condition, and if the which shall not satisfy them, I will propose to play Joan d'Arc, and lead them into the next battle in your stead. But in addition to the arguments I have already used — and in all seriousness, too — I *know* of quite a number of men both about Huntsville and Richmond, strong and healthy in person, who were very strenuous advocates of Secession, and still profess to a very high order of patriotism, who yet have never raised an arm in this war. Let some of such noble-souled gentlemen take your place for the next campaign; give them a *chance* to woo, if they cannot win, the favors of Mars; let them ventilate their quiet souls with the fumes of sulphur and saltpetre. I know they are willing, and only *want* an *opportunity* to prove it. Yes, I am serious in this very proposition, but I am even more serious when I say that such men deserve the lasting scorn of every *woman*, even in the South. They are even worse than cowards, no matter what their plea for remaining out of the army; who, while they watch for, and nose out every 'bomb-proof' position for their own mean persons, yet use all their efforts to drive others into it, and whether we succeed or fail, I hope they will be held in everlasting scorn. So much for these *Buckinghams*.

"Mr. Davis and his friends so highly estimate the effects of the late Confederate victories, that they look with much confidence for peace and recognition, and as a sort of additional *persuasive*, have indeed resolved upon a move into the enemy's country. The army, therefore, will soon be under marching orders. I very sincerely hope his expectations will have some better foundation than those he has heretofore expressed; having, allow me to say it, every private consideration for thus hoping, in addition to public considerations. Such as are personal, I will give you, provided you promise not to think me transcending the narrowest limits of female delicacy.

"First, then, all my brightest and best hopes in life, so far from connecting themselves with the scenes of which I now compose an unwilling part, concentrate upon a future that locates itself far away in "Dixie," surrounded by the quiet pleasures of a retired home of my own, with a certain rebel officer I know of, for its master. This, sir knight, is the salient sketch and pleasing outline of the plan with which I very often, of late, refresh and soothe my anxious heart. Does it please you? If so, your remaining where you are, is the prominent figure in the picture.

"Since the defeat of the Federals, Richmond has exceeded itself in gayety, reckless dissipation, and as I learn, corruption of every kind. All of which, I presume, naturally proceeds from that peculiar society which invariably gathers about a revolutionary metropolis. But somehow, I cannot but argue badly for the social condition of the South, in event of success, on account of it, as it is very far from representing that devoted and elevated patriotism with which we first set out, without which I have always feared we could not succeed, or even ought to succeed. An improper appreciation and use of success, would be worse for us than defeat. Those who have done the very least in this war, by which I mean those who have lived in the most perfect ease, luxury even, and cowardly safety, are now the loudest in the use of the pronoun we, and appropriate the chief honor of our success up to this time. I am still as devoted to the Confederate cause as ever; but confess myself very often feeling great disgust for its assumed leaderships, and almost feel willing to see it fail just to crush out these miserable people; and sigh for escape and for a refuge from them in the society of one whose fate seems wrapt up with my own, and whose place in my heart none other ever has or can fill. But I grow lack-a-daisical.

"Uncle, in common with others, thinks we shall soon have propositions of peace, and I think rather prides himself upon the idea of being senator for the long term, from the great cotton State of Alabama. Aunt, too, looks forward with much apparent pleasure to the future, which, indeed, seems quite flattering to her now. I can see but little, however, to compensate her for the perfect absence of domesticity, which I know she dearly loves, and adorns in so lovely a manner; but she is acting a part for the sake of her husband, and certainly performs it very handsomely. To please *me*, though, it is all too hollow, too unreal; and if *she* should, from any cause, fail in her ambitious purposes, there will be nothing to fall back upon.

"Maugre all this, you must tell the people at home, that the people *here* are very exultant over our condition and successes, and jubilant over the prospect of an early peace; and not to relax in their efforts to assist the Government, as failure now would be a reflection upon their courage forever, beside bringing upon themselves such a despotism, as no Christian people have ever endured — that the North is mortified beyond measure, and will visit their shame upon us to the fullest extent, if it should ever be in their power to do so. Yes, keep their hopes and courage up now. We have nothing to hope for outside of success.

"Indeed, the North has just found out that it will not only require all their own military strength proper, but all they can hire from abroad, to overcome the poor, unarmed, hungry, naked South; and in addition to calling for 100,000 more men, are swelling their plethoric ranks with such of our deluded negroes as they capture or can induce to go to them.

"Yes, they feel with a burning shame that had the South possessed one-half their resources, in either men or munitions of war, her banners would now be floating from every hill-top in their frozen, barren land.

"Deeply as I deplore this desolating war, I yet feel willing to see every man a cripple, and every woman and child working in the field to support them, in preference to submitting to a people who appear so lost to every generous emotion toward us.

"This may sound unfeminine, but better be that than degraded, as we all shall be if the Confederacy should prove a failure. I am now satisfied that the Northern people have traditional, as well as personal causes of hate toward us, and personal shame to avenge; and judge so from their insults to the people, and their actual thieving and robbing wherever they have gained possession in the South.

"I wish you to tell them for me, if that will do any good, that right or wrong this is no time to inquire — our best and only hope is to conquer, or to die — to go to the bitter end, let it be as bitter as it may. But between ourselves, I fear there are too many already lost to all such emotion; and the accusation, too, lies mainly at the door of those who precipitated us into war. Richmond is full, and I hear it is the same in other places, of able-bodied men, young and old, holding some execrable 'bomb-proof,' the which, together with the terrible speculation in the currency, and in the hard-extreme-necessities of the country, will greatly endanger our prospects, if peace does not soon follow our late successes. I fear the *fighting* element of the country has been fully brought out and very much exhausted. Conscripts, and *safety-seekers*, never will carry this revolution on to success, and our *same* army cannot long sustain such drafts, as these terrible battles make upon it.

"I have now written you a long political letter, which I did not intend, but not without its social features, I hope; but as subjects of this kind are all that I ever hear discussed, my mind naturally runs upon them, and you will have to pardon me. When we meet we will talk of something else — shan't we? Until then, be it long or short, you may rest assured that I remain affectionately your own

"MARGARET SEDLEY."

"P. S. — I enjoin you to remain in Alabama, until you hear from me again.   M. S."

CHAPTER XI.

"And homeless near a thousand homes I stood,
And near a thousand tables pined and wanted food."

THIS letter reached Alabama just as Colonel Stafford was slowly recovering from a relapse which precluded all idea of his immediate return to the army; he was, therefore, compelled to remain in Alabama, much against his inclination, and replied to Miss Sedley, as follows:

"ROSE HILL, ALA., *September 5th*, 1862.

"MY DEAR MARGARET:—The fates were in your favor, and I obey your commands on compulsion. A slight relapse, just before receiving your letter, has rendered it impossible for me to carry out the design of returning to my regiment, and think I now have a very clear idea of the trouble which rose up before the *great* soul of *Falstaff*, when he protested to Prince Hal against the idea of 'compulsion;' whether I have or not, I know that I am still in Alabama, very much against my inclination, in a sort of quasi obedience to your commands — on compulsion — on my own once very completely regulated, abundant, and beautiful plantation, but now, devastated, ruined, and almost deserted. The appearance of everything about my once pleasant home makes the desire to return to the army almost uncontrollable, whether sick or well, and there to remain until I am either dead, or the miserable creatures, calling themselves *soldiers*, who have desecrated my country and my home, shall be driven back to their own or fill felons' graves. You can possibly form no idea of the ruin which the wretches committed on this defenceless country for the short time they held it. The entire valley of the 'Tennessee' reminds me of descriptions given of the deserts, the plains, and the ruins along the Jordan, more than of that lovely country, once so noted for its refined society, its beautiful homes, and its luxuriant fields. The very ring and song of desolation trembles over the extended landscape that lies along either side of this noble river. For miles, scarce a living thing is to be seen, more than now and then an old decrepit negro, or lame horse, who was unable to leave on the exodus of this *gallant* house-robbing, horse-thieving, old-men-hanging, house-burning army of old Lincoln's! In too many, ah, too many places, nothing stands to mark the homes of your friends, but thin, tall, and lonely-looking chimney stems, which I hope may long be permitted to stand as monuments to the chivalry of the Christian Puritan, that other days may have some palpable record of his assumed enlightenment and pious philanthropy.

"From the persons left behind, some of both colors, I learn the utter destitution to which nearly all of our friends have been wantonly reduced, most of whom managed to make their way to such parts of the State still held by the Confederates; and now that our army is again in occupancy of the country, many of our best old citizens have nothing to return to, or to return with.

"I believe the feeling occasioned by such sights, and by such information, was the cause of my relapse, and I now grow so nervous writing of them, that I can scarce hold my pen to write legibly. If the thousands upon thousands of able-bodied men, both young and old, who still hang about their homes on one pretence or another, and, as you say, holding 'bomb-proofs,' would only come to the valley of the Tennessee, they would, if they had the hearts of men in their bosoms, throw aside such despicable employments, and rush to the army.

"I am informed that the Federals who held possession here, were a most godless crew, drawn from their own large cities, and from Europe, with a large sprinkling of our own base-blooded people, and negroes, and the depredations and horrible deeds they committed were just such as this commingled hell-broth of a gathering called for. My own dwelling has been burned — many of the out-houses, most of my fences; and nearly all of the provisions were taken, such only being left as were secured by the more faithful negroes; and most of the negroes themselves left with the army on its retreat.

"Such, my dear Margaret, is the basis of the Arcadian picture, which you hinted at in your letter. I have tried to grow sentimental over it, but my temper gets the better of me, and in place of any beautiful lines of poetry coming to my aid, the old nursery doggerel of 'Humphrey with his flail and Dorothy Draggletail' ever haunts my memory. How do you like the picture and the prospect?

"I cannot, in my present state of health, return to the army, but no persuasion, no consideration can keep me longer than the first hour that I am able to travel. I love life, perhaps, as well as any young man, but I school myself into loving honor, justice, and the land of my birth even more, and I hope I am willing to give every drop of blood in my body to defend them. What has been shed in that way, is welcome to have spilt, and I only regret that I have not a thousand times as much to shed in the same cause. If my arm were only stronger, the desolation of my home should soon be avenged on some one; but I will bide my time — me or mine will yet have revenge.

"I was a secessionist before the war. First, because I disliked living with the Yankee people : they are a people who have but little elevated self-respect, and, therefore, but little respect for others. Again, I was one from education ; yet, on what would have been a proper assurance of good faith at the 'Peace Conference,' I should have been willing to return to the Union, offensive as the thing was to me. But now, after the ravages, robberies, desecrations, and meannesses which they have been guilty of since the war began, I would rather perish by the rope, starvation, or disease, every hour in the day, than go back with them; and if left to ME, I would raise the *black flag* in twenty-four hours, if I were sure of falling the first victim, before I would live an hour in allegiance to a flag which has only proven itself the badge of my dishonor and ruin.

"What I say is in no spirit of boasting, but with the feeling of a man whose home has been outraged by a ruthless band of cowards, under the pretence of carrying on *war*. After what I have seen, I am prepared for the worst, and don't fear it. There is nothing they will not do, if they can do it; and I only wish I had a thousand lives to give my country against such hypocritical miscreants — the last would go as freely as the first.

"I shall leave here at the earliest possible moment, in sheer justice to myself, as HATE is becoming the absorbing feeling of my heart, and while the paroxysm is on me, even *love* loses all its soft allurements, and beauty all its blan-

33

dishments; but don't get frightened. I never fail to *recover* so soon as the name of my own dear 'MAG' comes to my memory; the present then loses all its pressure in the happy visions of the future.

"I would tell you of the condition of many of your young friends, but it is too wretched to relate. Any house that was left unburnt in the valley, has been entered by lawless men, professing to be soldiers, and rifled of everything possessing the least value. In many, too many instances, the very last provisions were taken, leaving the helpless, undefended families in utter want. Every species of stock was driven off, and every vehicle capable of rolling on its wheels, and nearly all of the servants were taken away, after being made to treat their former owners with every possible indignity. You may now have some idea of the situation. Suffice it, that one of the finest landscapes of the South, for grandeur, beauty, freshness and fertility, now presents but the haggard desolation peculiar to the plains of woe!

"Amid the universal gloom that surrounds me, and reigns throughout this portion of the valley, there comes nothing to relieve my sorrow, but the memory of your own bright eyes, the loveliness of your own sweet face, and the joyousness of your own merry laugh. When, either in dreams or in waking hours, these come back to me, I forget my grief for all outward things, and live over again the happy hours of the past. Now, isn't that speech equivalent to many of the pretty ones you made to me? But I have written as much as my strength will allow.

"Write often; your letters revive me. Thanking you for your last long and pleasant letter, I remain,

"Yours affectionately,

"CARTER STAFFORD."

We have given the foregoing letter of Colonel Stafford to Miss Sedley, that our distant readers may have some idea of the devastations of the Federal army wherever they could obtain a foothold in the South. This conduct, however, was used by Confederate leaders, as a strong argument in favor of keeping up the war. This style of reasoning exerted but a sickly sort of influence in that direction, while the people in those districts continued to grow more despondent, yet the network and meshes of a *de facto* government forced them to go on, knowingly, to their own destruction. Feeling all the force of these facts, they still look upon the *last act* of destroying their property without compensation and without cause, and many of the previous acts of the Government, as particularly unjust. They were helpless, and if the Government was not able to come to their assistance, it should not have punished them for its own delinquency, by the destruction of their property, and other political degradations, that have been heaped upon them, for that which they had no power to avoid. The *conscript law* was evidence of their condition and their feelings.

CHAPTER XII.

"Great thoughts, great feelings came to them
Like instincts, unawares."

THE war had continued to be prosecuted with its original unrelenting bitterness and obstinacy, and the Southern army had returned from its fruitless campaign into Maryland, having, for the first time since the commencement of hostilities, lost some of its victorious prestige. Previous to this, the United States Government had trembled to its deepest foundations from the terrible blows it had received; but the attempt to penetrate the enemy's country, at once exposed the *munitial* weakness of the South, and restored the drooping energies of the Federal Government.

This double effect of the battle of Sharpsburg was the beginning of those reverses which, in little over a year longer, ended in the fall of Southern arms, but left their glory and their chivalry the highest inscribed on the monument of military fame, where the Southern "Slave-driver" now stands recorded, in letters of gold, as the Paladin of the modern world. Silence, ye slanderers! Avaunt, ye cowards!

Many truthful apologies were offered for the failure of the Maryland campaign, and the Confederate Congress, which had met again, felt no falling off in its enthusiastic hopes, prophecies, and assurances of success. Mr. Davis, too, had announced in his message that it was the *third* and *last* year of the war, and exhorted the people to go on to their early independence. The Confederate capital was once again illumined by the shimmering lights of a doomed, but a fearless, reckless, and voluptuous gayety.

Enthusiastic but mistaken politicians, fashionable women, speculators, blockade-runners, contractors, professional gamblers, and army officers, were all present, dashing about in the swift confusions, the wild and blood-stained glamour of the rebel metropolis — restless, excited, and panting after that which they knew not of, nor could define.

The politicians were ever plotting, scheming, and speaking, and seemed in daily expectation of some wonderful event. The speculators, blockade-runners, and contractors were looking to gains ; but seemed consternated that the fabulous returns of to-day resulted in nothing to-morrow. They themselves were turning the wheel of fortune, but could not keep pace with its speed and changes — the higher the ascent, the swifter and harder the fall — and to the very last hour, did not realize the cause, the *unreality.*

The fashionable women — we name not their purposes, had none perhaps — were moths, flying around the garish lights that were now burning to their sockets. The army officers, ay, they knew their business: they were on their ways to and fro, from fields of blood.

On an evening in the early spring of 1863, the doors of the Presidential mansion were thrown open for reception, and there met on that occasion the representative men and women of the Confederacy — the political *élite* of this new political movement. Mr. Davis, whatever may have been his attractiveness in younger days, was now on the list of valetudinarians, and of course, not very engaging either in manners, conversation, or person. So much has *health* to do with amenity, and *strength* to do with impression. He yet went through the formality of receiving his friends with rather an uncommon pleasantness, as he moved with dignity through the vast throng; and in return, received the usual, if not the enthusiastic adulations of the multitude, to the chief of what was chosen to be considered the head of a successful revolution, and, in this instance, known to have been borne along by a war, unequalled for its inequality, bitterness, bloodshed, and extent, in the history of revolutions; and waged with a fierce, wild chivalry, which only the stories of mediæval romance can equal, in the lights and shades of gallantry and carnage. His Cabinet were present too, smiling in the pleasing satisfaction of being chief advisers in the proud work of placing the South on this *high tide* of national greatness.

Army officers of every grade were also there, who very justly eclipsed the heroes of peace and "bomb-proofs" in attention from those who, in some of the walks of life, control the reputations of men — the WOMEN.

Prominent among the latter were our old friends, Colonel Brandon, General Campbell, and Colonel Stafford, who, with others of military distinction were the observed of the evening.

Colonel Brandon had never been a warm admirer of Mr. Davis, and this was his first presence in the Presidential mansion. While walking leisurely about and observing the company, he accidentally met with Miss Sedley, leaning on the arm of Colonel Stafford. He had not seen her before during the evening, nor indeed, for several weeks previous to this, and the meeting was mutually agreeable.

33 *

Congratulating him on his first appearance at a Presidential reception, she immediately asked him to let her have the honor of personally introducing him, as he had always promised her she should do, if she ever obtained his consent, to be made acquainted with Mr. Davis. His previous refusal to have personal presentation was well known to his friends, and none of them had approached him on the matter, when Miss Sedley proposed it.

The opportunity was a favorable one, and from his presence that evening she supposed he had overcome what he called his reluctance, whether founded on prejudice or not, and, therefore, she repeated the request, to which Brandon jocularly replied:

"I appreciate the pleasure of having been introduced to Miss Sedley, some two years and more since, far higher than I should the distinction of being introduced to Mr. Davis, even by so fair an interlocutor as Miss Sedley herself is."

"Oh! Colonel Brandon; you certainly have all the elements for making a most successful courtier, and the wonder is that you do not avail yourself of them. Neither the reputation which you have gained of being a man of brilliant intellect, nor that of being a distinguished soldier, appears in the least to have soothed your *secession asperity*, or modified your views."

"No, lady; you are right; the constant exposure of this sacred person of mine to the danger of secession battlefields are but poor persuasives in that direction."

"You should not lay the charge of exposure to danger at the door of secession, since it is voluntary on your part."

"Yes; you are partially right; but then I cannot separate myself from my own people, or plead exemption from their fortunes, because of the mistakes of our *leaders;* every instinct of my heart requires me to go with them. Yet I cannot look upon these prominent officials as kindly perhaps as I should."

"Let me beg you, Colonel, as a young lady who admires you very much, not to indulge in such idiosyncrasies of opinion. You differ from all your best friends, who are desirous of *promoting* you, if you would only place yourself or let them place you in the line of promotion. Why, sir, when this war is ended, our Government will be the courted one of the earth; and nothing is more certain than your securing a foreign mission, which you know would be quite agreeable, and nothing more than you deserve."

"Ah! if I valued such a position, my only chance for obtaining it, lies in the *betrayal* of the Confederacy."

"Why do you say that, Colonel?"

"Simply, because the Confederacy has the only ministers abroad she will ever have."

"Are you not afraid, sir, to make such sweeping remarks?" said she, laughingly.

"Why should I fear, Miss Sedley; can I fear such men as I see around me to-night? What proportion of fighting men is here? one in ten, ay, one in fifty — and this fact is spreading all over the South. If Mr. Davis could only appreciate these facts, he would see his case to be a hopeless one, and at once begin negotiations for a re-entrance to the Union."

"I fear you are about to yield up that favorite idea of yours, with which you once so delighted me. The superiority of the Southern to the Puritan, the Norman to the Saxon."

"No; so far from giving it up, I am more confirmed in it than ever. The few cannot overcome the many, let what advantages exist on the part of the few that may. The true Southern blood, I mean the Norman, whether you find it in the rich or the great, the poor or the humble, is the best in the world; better now in this country than in England. It has improved by transportation, the circumstances of the country, and the influence upon it of African slavery;

yet it has some of the very worst, I had almost said meanest
elements that enter into human constitution, which, when
not controlled by education or other moral influence, cul-
minates in very bad character; but altogether, the Southern
people have more of that combination of qualities which
bears up under any and all pressure, than any people of
the world; but mind you again, all of the Southern people
are not Norman.   There are many; yes, a very large per
cent. now of a nondescript, mongrel cast, whose persons,
character, and opinions cannot be traced to any one race,
blood, intellect, or nationality — don't know who or what
they are; and these are more to be watched and avoided
than any people I know.   This class of Southerners are
dangerous without being brave, unfeeling and unsym-
pathetic without especial ill-will, grasping without being
stingy — with no particular character of emotion, no
standard of conduct, good or bad; nor any well-ordered
purposes; negative as to honor and honesty, and always
acting according to circumstances."

"Colonel Brandon," replied Miss Sedley, "I apprehend
that laggardism in certain quarters has somewhat embittered you.   How can you tell this class?"

"You used the right word — laggardism.   A true Southron may be an idler, either from habit or from circumstances; but never a coward, a skulker, or a laggard, and
by one or the other, you can safely class this fellow."

"By that rule there is many a mongrel among us."

"Yes; enough to have assisted greatly in bringing on the
war, and certainly enough to make it fail."

"And you still think the South will fail, Colonel Brandon?"

"I certainly do."

"Then why do you expose your life?"

"For several reasons; and first, because I did not have
the moral courage to resist doing so after I had opposed it.

I did not wish the charge of fear to be brought against me ; but last, I desired that the South should make history at least, as I knew she could never succeed in accomplishing her purposes ; and required every man's strength."

"Are these the reasons for which you expose your life?"

"Yes ; the leading ones at least, and I feel this moment that I am wrong, and will suffer for it."

"In what way, Colonel Brandon?"

"With my life."

"Oh! Colonel Brandon ; you make me shudder by the coolness of your speculations."

"So I may ; but they are such as I feel."

Colonel Stafford had left Miss Sedley in company with Colonel Brandon, very soon after they met, and they had had the foregoing conversation, while walking slowly together through the room. Just as he uttered the last words, they passed near Mr. Davis, who immediately recognizing her, stepped in front, and spoke in a very cordial manner, as he had always professed a high admiration for her. She replied to his pleasant salutation, and immediately introduced Colonel Brandon.

CHAPTER XIII.

"Lofty and proud, to them that loved him not;
But to those men that sought him, sweet as summer."

I AM glad to meet you, Colonel Brandon," said Mr. Davis, in reply to the introduction of Miss Sedley, at the same time shaking him cordially by the hand ; " your *services*, your reputation, and your friends have made your name very familiar to me, and I have often desired to meet with you."

"I am obliged to you, sir, and also to my friends, for the polite mention which has secured such distinguished recognition, and permit me to be as justly complimentary to yourself — I, too, have heard very favorably and approvingly of Mr. Davis, from his friends."

"Thank you, Colonel," said Mr. Davis, in a more animated manner than usual, with the color rising to his pallid features, as if scarcely comprehending the words of Colonel Brandon; "I have always endeavored to be worthy of the kind consideration and approval of my friends."

"Gentlemen," said Miss Sedley, who was on familiar terms with them both, "pardon me for introducing a card-playing technicality as illustrative of your language — 'honors are easy' between you in the way of compliment; you must, therefore, allow me to add my contribution to the courtesies of the evening, by saying that I have never known a mutuality of congratulations so worthily made."

Both gentlemen immediately bowed to her, and Mr. Davis replied, "Unless you had been one of the parties, Miss Margaret."

"Ah, Mr. Davis, this is not the first obligation you have placed me under; yet I am always happy to see your mind relieve itself from the pressure of *Federal affairs*, and stray away into its natural realm of *poetry* — bagatelle."

"Yes, Mr. Lincoln may be a very clever man, but he is a good deal like Banquo's ghost — he often comes to my mind without bidding, and yet he is graceful enough to vanish before the presence of beauty. Does my answer suit your meaning?"

"Most assuredly," she replied, laughing heartily. "Colonel Brandon, had you any idea that the CHIEF REBEL of the earth could so unbend his bow as to enter the lists of compliment with a country girl?"

"The strongest bow should be unstrung when not in use, Miss Margaret, and Mr. Davis could certainly have no more pleasing and proper occasion to do so, than when meeting with yourself."

The conversation had gradually changed to more serious subjects, when Colonel Brandon said:

"Will you permit me to ask a question of you, Mr. Davis, which, as it may appear rather bold, you may reserve an answer, if you think it an improper one to reply to?"

"Certainly, Colonel Brandon; a soldier of such gallantry has a right to ask what question he pleases."

"I am obliged to you, sir; but it has been asserted, by those, of course, who were not friendly to your cause, that even before the election of Lincoln, the Southern LEADERS had resolved on, and arranged all the details of a separate government; is there any truth in it?"

"None whatever, to my knowledge. The whole thing was improvised at the meeting of the first Provisional Congress, at Montgomery, and I entertained great hopes, up to that time, that the Congress of the United States would offer some conciliatory proposition — which it ought to have done, and was well able to do."

"Would you, then, be willing to return to that Government, if proper reparations and guarantees were assured to you?"

"No; not now. They were refused to us, and we have declared to the world that we are a *free* and *independent* Government, and have, in some sort, been recognized as such; and by the unsurpassed gallantry of our army, have measurably secured the position. To return would, therefore, be to compromise our character, and the chivalry of our soldiers."

"Do you think the doctrine of 'State Rights,' as understood in this country, Mr. Davis, a legitimate principle in the science of government?"

"No, I do not; I think it a pure *Americanism*, growing

out of our confederated system, and therefore, only legitimate by circumstances; but it was the only safety of the South, while in confederation with the stronger States of the North."

"Yes, I am aware of the arguments given in defence of the doctrine, and my reason for asking, was to learn whether you did not think it a dangerous one to introduce into the New Government."

"Yes, I certainly do; it leaves too wide a field for arbitrary action in the States."

"I have heard you say the same thing, Colonel Brandon," said Miss Sedley, "and am pleased to see two gentlemen agree, who the world thinks so wide apart."

"You perhaps have heard, Mr. Davis — that, at least, is the allusion of Miss Sedley — that I opposed Secession, and am yet of opinion, that we will fail to establish a separate Government."

"Yes, sir, I have heard of your views, and fully recognize your right to express them; but would suggest the *policy* of not expressing them *too* publicly, or your own men might desert you."

"Not the least danger of that, sir; but let me ask you again, and pardon me for detaining you."

"Certainly; I feel great pleasure in conversing with you, Colonel Brandon," said Mr. Davis, interrupting him.

"Was the precise purpose, in withdrawing from the Union, that of perpetuating Slavery ?"

"No; it was not mine, at least; as I knew slavery to be stronger in the Union than *out*. I believe, however, that some did believe it would be strengthened, and from them the idea obtained prevalence. *My* course had its foundation in what I saw to be organic difference between the Northern and Southern people — their perfect incompatibility, and the difference in their interests. No; the South no longer required negro labor to the extent — the manner, at least, in which she was using it. Let slavery have been what it may to us in the past, it is now acting as a blight upon the higher destinies of the South, in perfectly neutralizing its capital. We require no more of such development as that style of labor brings about. Mind you, I only speak of slavery, as at present sustained and employed, from an economical point of view, (so far as the negro himself is concerned, he is better off as a slave in the South, than he has ever been elsewhere, or can be as a *free* man. His labor, too, as at present organized, is essential to the *present* prosperity of the South, and to the prevention of a financial collapse;) but I allude to his *title by purchase*, and the single direction of agriculture in which his labor is held. *Purchased* labor is necessarily the dearest that can be used, and you yourself know the operations — it is to make cotton to buy negroes, and buy negroes to make cotton. The cotton thus depreciates, and the labor, which produces it, appreciates in even greater ratio. We must see the eventual result of this — it is already partially developed."

"Yes; I have long looked at the subject from the same point; but have you ever speculated as to any practical method of getting out of this never-ending but narrowing circle?"

"I have; but the popular mind is not prepared to receive any propositions tending in that direction, and this fact is largely attributable to the Northern abolitionism, with which the mind of the whole North has become infected, and which the South is not disposed to bear with."

"Does your plan contemplate the negro becoming a full citizen? — a suffragan? — a freeman?"

"By no means; we do not need him as a citizen; we could make no possible use of his feeble intellect. Suffrage naturally and properly accompanies and flows from intelligence and wealth — where there is neither, it should never

34

be bestowed, and always becomes otherwise a fruitful source
of trouble.   Demagogues who wish to secure place and
power, would immediately make use of him.   No Government can escape civil commotions, when suffrage is universal — its constant effort is to attack capital.   The less
suffrage there is in a country up to a certain point, the
freer, the happier, and the more peaceful the people, and
the stronger the Government."

"I am happy to agree with you in these questions.   But
will you give me your opinion as to the ultimate fortune or
end of the negro, in event of his qualified emancipation,
which I infer you have reference to?"

"I shall have to answer that question by throwing the
whole responsibility on a *special Providence;* his final
exodus is in the hands of the Almighty, by whose special
economy he is here, and for special purposes.   These purposes are in process of final accomplishment, which we can
now begin to see; and we may very properly suppose that
he will pass back to his own native land by the same hand,
pari passu.   From a human point of observation, the order
of nature and progress of society will suggest the proper
method of departure.   Many would soon die, many remain
among us for a great number of years, and many would
pass back to the tropics, in the service of some great
Evangelical economy.   These latitudes of ours have been
assigned to the Caucasian races, by the great Creator, even
as *every* race has been assigned to its proper latitude, and we
must suppose that He knew His own work better than we.
The negro in this latitude is completely abnormal, even
while he has improved and prospered; but this result has
only followed, because there was a *special economy* in it,
and because of his protection by the white man: for whose
temporary benefit he was placed here, so far as we can
absolutely know.   The withdrawal of this care of the white
man will very soon have the effect of perfectly placing

this land in the hands of the white man, and restoring the black man to his. The negro has no natural rights in these latitudes: his mission here was labor, and his reward was civilization; he has performed the one, and is receiving the other. As a trained laborer and civilized man, destiny points him back to the tropics."

Several minutes had been consumed by this conversation, a much longer time than Mr. Davis usually consumed with any persons outside of business; but in this instance he had done so with a marked interest. As he made his last remarks, Colonel Stafford returned to the side of Miss Sedley, when the President bowed partially, and, thanking Colonel Brandon for the very pleasant interview, passed along.

CHAPTER XIV.

"Taciturnity is wise, if men are fools; but foolish, if they are wise."

COLONEL BRANDON, you have been the occasion of the most entertaining half-hour that I have spent for many days," said Margaret Sedley, as Mr. Davis walked off. "I was astonished at his letting you draw him out as you did."

"And you both have been the observed of all observers," said Colonel Stafford.

"Yes; the President very highly distinguished us."

"I don't know," replied Colonel Brandon, laughing; "I think the distinction was at least mutual."

"Oh, Colonel Brandon! I had begun to form high hopes of making you quite a courtier, but here you are falling back upon your individuality — your political cynicism. You made great improvement, Colonel, as the interview

lasted. At first you made me feel *chilly;* did you not feel
a little so ?' ''

"No, miss; if I never have greater cause for chilliness
than from any expression of private opinions to Mr. Davis,
I shall not only always be in a very genial mood, but return home from this war uninjured. Even had I not been
in the army, I should not fear either to ask him questions,
or to express opinions, unless I should foolishly do so, to
damage the public cause he represents. He is said to be a
most excellent gentleman in private life, and much loved
by his friends and neighbors for his honorable and generous bearing."

"Is it really so, Colonel Brandon, that you have never
before been introduced to Mr. Davis?" asked Colonel
Stafford.

"Certainly so; and it was a high piece of *finesse* on the
part of Miss Sedley, that I was, this evening. I did not
desire or expect it. I met with him frequently in Mexico,
but I was then a very young man, and he has, of course,
forgotten me; since then I have never met with him until
to-night. He is unsurpassed for gallantry, and was badly
wounded at BUENA VISTA."

"Did n't you meet with him while the Confederate Capital was at Montgomery?"

"No. I should have called on him probably, but men of
my style of opinion were not very favorably looked upon,
at that time, *at Court.* I, therefore, did not see proper to
compromise myself: I could not have changed him, nor he
me."

"You could have called on him without being expected
to proselyte, or to be proselyted."

"Yes; but I did not feel greatly pleased with, and chose
not to see him."

"You appeared to agree very well, this evening, Colonel. Who has changed?" said Miss Sedley, quizzically.

"Oh, certainly; men who profess to be gentlemen, and men of sense, can't entirely disagree; but I *was* surprised to hear him express himself so freely, liberally, and so philosophically. Yet, I don't feel willing to forgive him for Secession; *he* could have stopped it, and ought to have done it. He knew better."

"And yet, Colonel Brandon, Mr. Davis only presides over it, while you are fighting the only Government you recognize, for it."

"Yes, but you know my reasons — if they can be dignified as such. If I had my way, there should not be another gun fired. It *can* be settled, and should be; one side is as wrong as the other. The time had not come for separation, and it cannot be done; it may at some future time, and I expect it will, even into more than two separate governments."

"What would be your plan, Colonel, for stopping the war?"

"Negotiation. Have the Confederate Congress to appoint Commissioners to meet others from the United States. The South can lose nothing by negotiation. The soiled helmets and battered shields of the Federal army are eternal records of Southern chivalry. Propositions of peace, so far from degrading, would only elevate us. Now, I am no political *sentimentalist*, and feel nothing of this tomfoolery called patriotism. I will love any flag that can protect me, and hate any that *cannot;* and I like that of the United States far less than I did, simply because it could not come, and has never yet been able to come, to my relief. It yet has more power than that of the Confederacy, and that is the ground of my preference: for every other, I prefer the one I am at present under; this *must* fail — I therefore, have but little love for it."

A short pause ensuing in the conversation, Colonel Stafford remarked that he was a little surprised at seeing Mr.

Davis depart from his reputed austerity so far as to enter upon so familiar and easy a conversation, as that with Colonel Brandon and Miss Sedley.

"He was in courtesy obliged to, after seeking it with us; but, Miss Margaret, I am indebted to you for whatever of distinction there is in his unusual course, as you were evidently the first attraction."

"Ah, you do yourself injustice, Colonel Brandon, for certainly, the glow-worm brightness of a weak girl could not have been so attractive as the dashing deeds and dazzling insignia of Mars. No, sir, the honor, whatever it is, belongs to the gallantry of the soldier — I may possibly have been the pretext."

"Well, Miss Margaret; to your part, be it as humble as it may, I owe the effect of being disabused of some misapprehension, or prejudice, in regard to Mr. Davis, which may possibly be of benefit to one or the other of us at a future day. The destiny of some persons is to be — and a lovely one it is — that of developing good in others. Passive as it may appear to be, the capacity or gift, is a rare one, and of the highest value. Shakspeare had the idea of it in his mind, when he makes poor old Jack Falstaff say, that he was the cause of wit in others."

"Thank you, Colonel, for your implied compliment: to be an agency of good would bring me great pleasure; but as I cannot realize it, shall for the present plume myself upon your assertion, and enjoy the satisfaction of having even been the passive source of a better understanding between two such distinguished persons."

At this moment, Mr. and Mrs. Ray came up to them, when the former said:

"Well, Brandon; I believe every one in the room this evening was attracted to the meeting and long conversation between yourself and the President, and we are all now to look for peace with great confidence, on the score of the promise that there shall be universal amnesty, when the lion lies down with the lamb."

"Ah! has that remote promise come up for realization? But who the lion and who the lamb?"

"That subject presented some difficulty of solution," said Mr. Ray; "but I believe every one gave you the advantage of position, and let Mr. *Davis* be the *lamb*."

"Yes," said Brandon, with a laugh, "quite the advantage. It appears to be known then, that we have differed."

"Certainly; you are known to be opposed to the Confederacy, yet fight for it, while you quarrel, with all the peerless gallantry of a knight in the days of chivalry," added Mrs. Ray.

"Thank you, madam; and I am obliged, too, to my friends for this flattering opinion. I really do believe we are nearer a peace than is generally apprehended; but whether in the shape that either Mr. Davis or myself would desire, is another question."

"Has n't the long interview between you and the President quieted your fears on that head, Brandon?" asked Mr. Ray.

"Not at all; his *confidence* has rather increased them; but we were not endeavoring to convince each other of error; and in many things came quite nigh agreeing — in feeling, if not in opinion. If the *Congressional pressure* upon him was less than it is, a rather more sensible course than has of late been pursued, might be hoped for. So much for a people sending weak men to make laws. In our instance, it would be better to let the *conscript officer* have the whole Congress. Indeed, a Confederate Congress is — but never mind. With a Congress, the Confederacy will fall, and everything we have be swept from us. Without it, it *may* stand. We want neither Congress nor Constitution, but a *despotism* — ONE MAN, men and munitions — these are all that any civil war requires."

"You can't help your sarcasm, Brandon; but we shall have to allow it to you, as you hold the strong position of the evening. We cannot attack you while under executive protection," said Mr. Ray, good-naturedly.

"I beg pardon, Ray; as I assure you I had no personal allusion whatever," replied Brandon, laughing.

It had now grown quite late, and the company had begun to leave. Colonel Brandon and Colonel Stafford seeing the President near, walked up and bid him good evening. Mr. Davis thanked Brandon for his presence that evening, and assured him that it would always be a pleasure to meet him, whenever the duties of either would allow it, and turning to Colonel Stafford, said:

"Betwixt you and I, Colonel Stafford, there is already no ceremony."

The two officers then returned to the ladies, and bidding them good evening, left for their quarters.

Not a great while after this, the President "trod" alone the "mansion halls deserted." Many had been there that evening with gay hearts and high hopes, who never met there again. The bright lamps of the levee proved to be "the dead lights" of life to them.

CHAPTER XV.

"High-stomached are they both, and full of ire;
In rage, deaf as the Sea, hasty as Fire."

IN July, 1863, according to the policy which was then popular at the Confederate capital, of invading the "enemy's country," General Lee, *en route* for Washington, was encamped near Gettysburg, Pennsylvania, having halted his forces at the immediate point, until he should receive reliable information of the position and strength of the Federal army from General Stuart, the distinguished and favorite cavalry officer of the army of Virginia. In this instance he failed of his usual success in coming up to time, which proved the loss of the campaign to the Southern army.

General Lee, in waiting, gave the Federal General time to occupy the almost impregnable heights and mountain ranges of the region in his front, with an army vastly superior in numbers, equipments, and munitions. There were routes by which General Lee could have avoided the battle at that point, and drawn the enemy from his position, and, considering the animus of his men, have made a successful march on Washington; but he did not — such is FATE. This is supposition; but as we are not discussing the military aspects of campaigns, we have merely borrowed the assertion, from what has since been said to be the fact; suffice it, General Lee moved up to the enemy, and fought the battle of Gettysburg.

It is said by those who participated in the leading battles of the army of Virginia, that the battle of Gettysburg was fought under tenfold greater disadvantages than any one of the great pitched battles of the war, and with more distinguished heroism on the part of both men and officers.

The inequalities of position and numbers were as great as the enemy could desire, to secure a most overwhelming defeat of the Confederate army; all of which did result in a most disastrous mortuary list of officers, as well as men, on the Southern side — and loss of the battle. It was here that the Confederacy received its first fatal blow. The grand old army of Virginia, here lost its brilliant prestige of victory, and though it afterward fought some of the most terrible battles of the war, with the same undaunted chivalry as of old, its strength was too far gone to even hold a victory which it had won. Yet there were but few, or none, of our leading men, whose penetration or prejudice allowed them to see this palpable, glaring fact.   As a consequence, the South was driven along to the extremest point of vital action ; and on the day of her final fall, and even when degradation came, it was rather a *relief* than a *shock* —she had already done all it was in mortal power to do.

There was a rude but sombre romance in the rocky cliffs and mountains around Gettysburg, that made it an appropriate place for the echoing thunders, and terrible carnage of war — for the solemn death-knell of a great revolution, the fall of a gallant army, and the ruin of a brave and injured people.

The last day of the battle has been spoken of as the great artillery duel of the war, in which men were not so much thrown on each other in individual strife, where passions become excited to the point of fierce brutality ; but of a magnificent contest of arms, carried on with great guns, by regiments, brigades, cohorts, and divisions, at that distance apart, which forbade all personal anger. Outside the desperate charges made to dislodge the enemy, men and officers stood to their places and their pieces, and mutually sent into the ranks of each other, missiles of death by the myriad, and received them too, as quietly as at a council of peace ; and met death as calmly as men going simply to rest.

As an officer or private fell, either wounded or in death, he was immediately carried back, and his place in a moment supplied, while the event itself scarce attracted a word, a sigh, or even a glance from his comrades.

The night which followed the last disastrous day, was in full character with the scenes over which it hovered. Alternate clouds, and showers, and moonlight, variegated its progressing hours. The Confederate forces had fallen back, and the gray old rocks were left again to their repose, and to the gloomy grandeur of their countless ages. There was no change in them! no sorrow, no sympathy, no tears, and yet no joy!—all was as it had ever been, sombre, serene, insensate, and *eternal!*

But there was an offering there, suitable for those great, old high-priests of nature to bring to the gods; and the fitness of it appeased all past and coming centuries. The altars now will burn forever with quenchless fires, lighted up by the human life, and fed by the libations from human hearts! On their sacrificial ledges lay the heroes of a far-off Southern land, taking a *soldier's* rest, on these mountains of the North. The wounds had ceased their bleeding, life's swelling, gushing passions had passed away, and left the manly forms in their calm repose and peacefulness, once more, the images of their God.

On the craggy heights, Yankees as they were, many a noble form with hero hearts, now in their throbbings hushed, lay stiff and stark in death's last, cold embrace — worthier, too, of a better fate than that they found, in trying to degrade their Southern brothers.

Throughout the day there appeared periodic lulls, in the great resounding thunders of artillery, as the rumbling echoes floated off on the sweeping winds and died away to silence. The very spirits of the old mountains seemed to demand these respites from the reeking fumes of human havoc, to enjoy the hoarse answering shouts of their distant caverns and their chasms. But ever and anon, they rose again to higher diapasons of death and woe, as if the very giants of the universe were at war against each other, and hurling great continents from their base. These undulations marked the lulling and the rage of battle — now sinking to the repose of peace, then rising again to the rush and the roar of the unbridled tempest, and the vibrations of the earthquake. In such moments as the last, men like leaves in autumn fell — fell to rise no more!

Just before the nightfall of this awful day, there came

the sounds of a remarked rise in this storm of death, from the Federal breastworks, which bore upon the Confederate lines in that part of the field which was occupied by the regiment of Colonel Brandon, when, almost at the same moment, that gallant officer, and his no less gallant young lieutenant, Campbell, fell mortally wounded.

Thus, on the wild mountains of Gettysburg, without an instant of pain, the rather eccentric and chivalric Henry Brandon closed his mixed life of joyousness, love, grief, bitterness, regret, and happiness; and there, too, the gay and handsome young soldier, Lieutenant McK., as he was familiarly and lovingly called by his men and comrades, closed his eyes upon the bright picture of love and hope, the diagram of which his joyous heart had drawn, to be filled at a future day by the beautiful girl who claimed his homage in the distant South.   They were both immediately carried to the rear, but in the hurry of changing position and falling back, they were left on the field; and thus, they who had been nurtured in the lap of ease and wealth, with every ill closely watched and provided for, were now silent and alone, with no watchers near, but the dying and the dead! Side by side, where their comrades had left them, two gallant soldiers lay — with their softly, half-closed eyes still lingering, as it were, in changeless vision, toward their Southern home!

Sorrowing nature had seemed to pay the tribute of its grief to heroic worth, in spangling their parted, fallen locks with the jewelled tear-drops of the morning mists, and they, reflecting back to heaven the glancing moon's pale, cold ray, as she now and then peered from the passing midnight cloud, reported there, two noble soldiers lying upon the field of battle in normal state!   And then, too, the countless stars, glimmering coldly on the skies, told of the weeping angels beyond — of the ruined homes, and the fatherless ones, made in the South that day!

Hold! sexton of the North! Strike your shovel softly now — two brother soldiers lie beneath that turf. Soldiers of the South taking their hero-rest! Ay, handle them gently now! Let them sleep! No slab is needed there! History hath already written their memorial; the wild-rose marks the spot, and angels keep vigils over their silent slumbers!

There was a mother that night, who sat in her lonely Southern home, with her children at her knees, speaking with an aching heart, but with affected cheerfulness, of him who was lying under the cold moonlight of the North, "sleeping the sleep that knows no waking," and was never again to cheer that home with his happy face, and gentle smile.

We will not disturb the sacred grief of that stricken home, by attempting to describe the scenes that ensued upon the reception of this sad intelligence. Sorrow had then, and since, become too familiar to our people to render its details either a novel, or pleasing subject. Poverty, dejection, political degradation, is the lot universal in the South. We may now leave the families of General Campbell, and Colonel Brandon, to their own individual sorrows.

Other characters with whom we have become familiar in the course of this skeleton-drawing of scenes in Southern life, at the different periods which they are intended to represent, may easily be imagined to have, more or less, partaken of the common lot. But one other there is of whom we must speak, and we have done with our story ; and we do it in justice to a faithful creature who was one of a once faithful race, now — anything else.

It has been seen that Colonel Brandon had been attended in the army by his faithful friend, and body-servant from boyhood, "Sam Brandon." On the last day of the battle, he had been ordered further to the rear, in company with the baggage-train; but learning the fate of his master, on

the return of the regiment that night, he immediately went
in search of the litter-bearers, and engaged them to go
through the lines with him, as they knew the spot at which
he was left. About midnight they found the body of Colonel Brandon, and promised to assist "Sam" in getting it
through; but rage and despair seemed to have taken possession of the faithful negro, and he would consent to
nothing; fearing to remain longer, they left him. "Sam,"
all alone, knelt down by his friend and master, as he lay
in the quiet repose of death, with the waning mountain
moon, and the pale summer-night stars keeping the silent
vigils of his sweet repose, and indulged in the deep, passionate sobbings of heart-stricken grief. "Oh, my poor
master!" said he, "can't you speak one word to your own
old nigger, 'Sam Brandon?' Oh, speak, speak to me, my
dear master, and tell me something to do for you!" Occasionally smoothing back the matted hair from his broad,
full brow, and feeling the marble-like chill of death upon
it, would again burst out in renewed expressions of grief—
"Oh, sir! will you never be warm to this ole hand agin?
Can't I never go wid you — be wid you — nuss you, and
talk to you no mo? Oh, what will cum of your po ole
Sam! What is to cum of my po, good mistis away down
home, an' her little childern, too! Oh, better for every
nigger in the wide worl', be a slave as he orter be, an' for
every mean Yankee in these ole mountains to be dead an'
stinkin, than for my po master to be in this here fix! Oh,
speak! speak to me, Mass Henry! say sumthin! I shill die
right here ef you don't! My po good mistis will say I took
no care ov you; it orter to be yo ole Sam, not you, Mass
Henry!"

Continuing this strain of uncontrolled lamentation till
the very dawn of day, he was espied by a distant retiring
sentinel, who came up to ascertain the cause of the strange
exhibition, and asked him "what he meant." Up to this

moment, "Sam" had not even heard his approach, but with the words reaching his ear, he rose from the side of the dead body, with the quick fierceness of a tiger disturbed in his lair, and, in an instant, drawing his side-knife, grasped the unsuspecting soldier by the throat, and drove it to his heart. "That's what I meant, sir, and take it, and take it agin!" driving the knife deeper and deeper into his body with every word; then hurling him, with only a negro's power, as far as possible from him, said — "go to hell, and tell 'em Colonel Henry Brandon's boy, 'Sam Brandon,' sent you dar!" Then wiping the blade quickly, drove it deep into his own heart, and fell at his master's side, saying, "I am wid you, Mass Henry; what mus' I do for you? I dun him right," and expired.

They were never brought home, and we suppose lie together still; and there they should ever remain, as an evidence on their own soil, of Northern slander against Southern masters. "Sam Brandon" was one of that race, whose many noble, social traits have been more than destroyed by *Puritan philanthropy*; and returned to heathenism, to infamy, to aggression, to treachery, and to a hate of him who alone had cultivated and brought him out from darkness.

CHAPTER XVI.

"What though the field be lost?
All is not lost."

THE entire incidents of the war are too recent not to be familiar to all intelligent readers, and we have only touched upon them to illustrate some of the traits of Southern character; nor in anything we have said, have we aspired to accuracy of detail — we only pretend to have asserted leading facts.

Its real history, both in regard to facts and to the philosophic reasons at its base, will be written at some future day, by a pen with a golden light to illumine its traces, when the world will be better prepared than now to weigh the great equities which it assuredly possessed ; even while the political principle upon which they depended who declared it, may be condemned, as incompatible with those which necessarily underlie all government, *cohesion, indivisibility,* authority !

The martial glory of the army of Virginia culminated at Gettysburg — its power was shadowed by the result; and though it subsequently displayed its accustomed gallantry in several of the most sanguinary battles of the war, yet they were but *sanguinary*, and only pictured martial desperation; its cause was falling, even its victories were not followed by recuperation. It waned, and continued to wane in strength, till the last and saddest scene of all, at Appomattox Court-house, where its glory darkened forever!

Here, a few thousand of that once gallant army, who had waved the "Bonny Blue Flag" in triumph over the countless hosts of the enemy, on many of the most terrific fields of modern warfare; and had sung victoriously the sweet little song commemorative of its honor, now in a state of actual starvation — hushed the song, stacked their arms to the conqueror, and left forever the scenes of their early renown, and their future IMMORTALITY.

General Hood, after the fall of Atlanta, had gathered up the wretched remnants of Johnston's forces, and in the desperation of the time, set out on an invasion of the State of Tennessee; and with these starved and naked troops fought one of the bloodiest battles of the war, at Franklin, winning for himself and men one of the brightest chaplets of martial honor that had yet crowned a Southern soldier's brow, during the whole four years of splendid, tragic folly.

Moving thence upon Nashville, he there *annihilated* his army! Thus ended the career of those whose peerless gallantry in every pitched battle of this bloody, four-years struggle, had won a renown which neither malice, nor time, nor result, can obscure: their deeds, their fame, and their fate, belong to the blazing glories of history, and its faithful muse will preserve them forever! The genius, too, of "Wild Romance" will weave the brightest garlands from their names and knighthood; and Song will send legends of their chivalry adown the current of ages, in the weird rapture of its notes, and the heroic measures of its flowing verse!

CHAPTER XVII.

"They practised falsehood under saintly show,
Deep malice to conceal."

THE spring of 1865 was signalized by the final overthrow of the Confederacy, and by the first of June, the proud, the boastful, the defiant, ay, the victorious South! was wearing, well-set, the galling yoke of *subjugation*, with the PURITAN walking triumphantly through the land, and marking his way by a subversion of all the foundations upon which her society, her civilization, her wealth, and her imperiality, had ever reposed.

Anarchy, chaos, idleness, dissoluteness, and debauchery, followed upon his march; but these were to *him* the sign, evidence, and emblem of his sway and authority, and sweet was his enjoyment: his want of true game and chivalry was to him the impervious shield against the natural shame, of having so long been engaged in the effort to place his foot upon the neck of the hated South. The past was forgotten; it was the present he enjoyed, however he had obtained it.

35 *

Nor yet did the disruption of the whole framework of Southern society, industry, and order, bring mortification for his want of executive statesmanship; his pharisaical conceit was an all-sufficient coat of mail to the oxhidedness of his sentiments and character.

The Pandemonium scenes, as drawn by Milton, were as the prefiguration of those now in the South — at least, so far as a parallel can be drawn between the pictures of an eternal and a temporal hell. It was the full fruitage of the *Harper's Ferry midnight massacre idea*, which, we boldly assert, every *Puritan* who was now trampling on the South, *had endorsed!*

Answer, ye descendants of the pious Pilgrims — ye are in office now, and cannot be afraid — have we charged ye falsely?

The Southern country, which had, in the early days of primeval nature, presented pictures both of grandeur and beauty in its landscapes, and which, through all the changes it had undergone while being subjected to the hand of industry, still presented those of an affluent abundance, comfort, and elegance, beyond any country of the earth, had now wellnigh become a waste wilderness. Large extents of territory, which had once delighted the eye of the traveller, the amateur, or the lordly proprietor, with their combined loveliness of scene and industrial luxuriance, had returned to a state of nature, without any of Nature's beauty. Over the broad fields, so far as the eye could reach, there rested an aspect, wild, weird, and strange. That peculiar hollow ring which nature ever has while uninvaded by man, had again resumed its normal note. The happy laborer's merry song no longer rose upon the evening air. No longer was heard the tuneful whistle, and the long, musical call of the herd-boy, as he wandered in search of his flocks; and no more were the happy young people mixing in those Arcadian scenes of early joy and beauty. All, all had gone — many, alas! too many, never to return! It was as a world deserted; and well did Nature sing its mournful dirge.

Whither have those people gone? Who wrought this terrible change? Answer again, ye brave and pious Puritans! Was it not your preacher, your charlatan, and your statesman — your robber and your soldier, who did it? Yes! Then remember that turrets and domes mantling and adorning palatial halls have fallen before to-day. Retribution is God's own law — none escape it.

But the great STRIFE of modern times no longer flings its banners to the breeze; its wild lightnings have ceased to flash their fires along the bristling ranks of its martial hosts; its loud thunders have gone back to their caverned homes and their sea-girt fortress walls, and PEACE once more waves her white pennons over our Southern homes, and soothes the flaming passions back to rest; and they who long had worn the red sash and the plume, and rode the foaming steed with silver bit, no longer dash their squadrons into the jaws of death; but have shown their true character and manliness, by a perfect willingness to abide the future, which they, to some extent, brought upon themselves. And the people, too, have shown a noble energy in striving against the sweeping tendencies of their circumstances and ruined fortunes. All was lost, save honor — nothing was left but the *soil;* and men and children, born to wealth, and ease, and elevated station, and wholly unaccustomed to the exposures of a severe tropic sun, have gone to its tillage; while the drudgeries of the household have been undertaken by females, young and old, who, by strength, habit, and constitution, were wholly unfitted for their performance. Yet, with all these untoward circumstances, our people will rise again to their normal status — Nature meets us, and points the way. Foreign oppression has already done its worst. With effort, sym-

pathy and regard for each other, we soon may shout, "Sic
itur ad astra!" Men who, for four years, stepped to the
step of the soldier, by the martial roll of the drum and the
shrill music of the fife, while bearing the "Bonny Blue Flag"
on to victory over a hundred battle-fields, and stanched
their bleeding wounds with its riddled remnants, may fall
— have fallen; but will rise again. The iron-heeled horse-
man, who wildly came and trod down the blue-bell on the
hill, and bruised the violet in the valley, could not take
to himself their fragrance, nor their germ: for still the
Southern sun doth gloriously gild the matin sky — still
doth ride along in midday splendor, and still descendeth
to western deep. Spring still doth come; and the blue-
bell still bloometh upon the hill. The violet again will
smile, away down in the sunlit valley; and the young
maidens long will gather them to strew upon the old grass-
green graves, in sweetest memory of their brave young
lovers, while adorning the breasts of the living with their
modest beauty.

THE END.

www.ingramcontent.com/pod-product-compliance
Lightning Source LLC
Chambersburg PA
CBHW030824110726
47900CB00006B/1728